"PARTAKES OF THE MIRACULOUS."
—*Time*

"LOVELY . . . WRITTEN WITH PASSION AND A FEELING FOR THE HUMAN CONDITION."
—*The Houston Post*

"HAUNTING . . . Edna O'Brien writes with the nerve of a tightrope walker . . . prose so lovely it glistens."
—*Cleveland Plain Dealer*

"Has all the O'Brien virtues—complex female characters and lyrical descriptions . . . will satisfy."
—*Library Journal*

(For more stunning reviews, please turn page . . .)

EDNA O'BRIEN is the author of *The Love Object*, *A Scandalous Woman*, *A Rose in the Heart*, *Returning*, *A Fanatic Heart*, and *The Country Girls Trilogy* (the last two available in Plume editions). Her work appears frequently in *The New Yorker.* Irish-born, she currently lives in London.

"A HAUNTING AND DANGEROUS NOVEL . . . O'Brien reminds us of our primal selves, our needy flesh. But she is also the truest keeper of our souls writing today." —*Ms. Magazine*

"Everything you expect the high road in the Irish ballad to be . . . Every breathing inch of it is a good story. The prose . . . fast and quivering . . . images strong and soundproof . . . people alive and vibrant." —*Taxi*

"ELEGANT . . . INTENSE . . . BRILLIANT."
—*The New York Times Book Review*

"A precise and beautiful novel . . . sensual language . . . every sentence is its own experience."
—*Raleigh News and Observer*

"BRILLIANT . . . O'Brien's descriptive powers are at their peak." —*Chicago Tribune*

"EDNA O'BRIEN IS ONE OF THE MOST CAPABLE ANATOMISTS OF LOVE . . . she brings fierce sympathy and a deadly accurate instinct for summoning up murderous love, romantic love, sensuous love, married love, compromised love, mother love . . . she is at her best, though, when she writes about the loss of love." —*Newsday*

"RESONANT WITH INSIGHTS, LUSH WITH DESCRIPTIVE DETAIL."
—*Publishers Weekly*

"The quintessence of O'Brien shines through."
—*The Times Literary Supplement* (London)

"In her maturity [Edna O'Brien] has developed a richness and sensuality in her descriptions, also an intensity in her definitions of feeling, as if a magnifying glass now concentrated a sunray on her characters." —*The Times* (London)

Also by Edna O'Brien

A Fanatic Heart: Selected Stories *(1984)*
Returning *(1982)*
A Rose in the Heart *(1978)*
Mrs. Reinhardt & Other Stories *(1978)*
I Hardly Knew You *(1977)*
Mother Ireland *(1976)*
A Scandalous Woman and Other Stories *(1974)*
Night *(1972)*
Zee & Co. *(1971)*
A Pagan Place *(1971)*
The Love Object and Other Stories *(1968)*
Casualties of Peace *(1966)*
August Is a Wicked Month *(1964)*
Girls in Their Married Bliss *(1963)*
The Lonely Girl *(1962)*
The Country Girls *(1960)*

THE HIGH ROAD

EDNA O'BRIEN

A PLUME BOOK
NEW AMERICAN LIBRARY
A DIVISION OF PENGUIN BOOKS USA INC., NEW YORK
PUBLISHED IN CANADA BY
PENGUIN BOOKS CANADA LIMITED, MARKHAM, ONTARIO

PUBLISHER'S NOTE

This book is a work of fiction. Names, characters, places, and incidents are either the product of the author's imagination or are used fictitiously, and any resemblance to actual persons, living or dead, events, or locales is entirely coincidental.

This is an authorized reprint of a hardcover edition published by Farrar, Straus & Giroux Inc. The hardcover edition was published simultaneously in Canada by Collins Publishers, Toronto.

PLUME TRADEMARK REG. U.S. PAT. OFF. AND FOREIGN COUNTRIES
REGISTERED TRADEMARK—MARCA REGISTRADA
HECHO EN BRATTLEBORO, VT., U.S.A.

SIGNET, SIGNET CLASSIC, MENTOR, ONYX, PLUME, MERIDIAN and NAL BOOKS are published *in the United States* by New American Library, a division of Penguin Books USA Inc., 1633 Broadway, New York, New York 10019, *in Canada* by Penguin Books Canada Limited, 2801 John Street, Markham, Ontario L3R 1B4

LIBRARY OF CONGRESS CATALOGING-IN-PUBLICATION DATA

O'Brien, Edna.
The high road / Edna O'Brien.
p. cm.
Originally published: New York : Farrar Straus Giroux, 1988.
ISBN 0-452-26306-9
I. Title.
PR6065.B7H54 1989 89-9433
823'.914—dc20 CIP

First Plume Printing, October, 1989

1 2 3 4 5 6 7 8 9

PRINTED IN THE UNITED STATES OF AMERICA

To my grandson
Jack Redmond Gebler

God that berreth the crone of thornes
Distru the prud of womens hornes . . .

Curse

Mother, Mother, I am coming
Home to Jesus
And to Thee . . .

Hymn

THE HIGH ROAD

1

It rose, swelled, then burst and dispersed in a great clatter of sound. First it seemed to be a roar inside my head, a remembered roar, a remembered summons, but then through the warrens of sleep it became clear that it was a roar being uttered at that very moment, either in the room or on the landing outside. I thought I heard my name—Anna, Anna—being uttered with malice.

My hand went instinctively toward the bedside table only to find that there was no lamp, nor table where a lamp could be, and then slowly and unnervingly it came to me that I was not at home, that I had come to this place, this new place, and gradually I remembered my walk of the evening before, the strange town, a mountain, and now this intemperate roar while it was still dark. I prayed for it to be at least getting on toward morning, morning that would bring little respites such as bread and tea, morning that sent all crawling things and madmen back to their lairs. It was Easter Sunday, I remembered that.

I reached to the other side of the bed, where I knew the lamp to be, but as I clicked on the slack button no light came. I clicked and clicked, thinking at first that it was the faulty button, but soon it dawned on me that there must have been a power cut. The maid who gave me the key had predicted that, and rats. She had taken me into a shed, pointed to a dark corner behind some wood shavings and bricks, and with her fingers to my throat demonstrated an attack. She had also pointed to where she lived, a few houses away, beyond the bridge, and had said through elaborate gestures that if I was in peril I was to call her. "Celestina, Celestina." She shouted her own name and laughed at her bravura.

I felt for the torch and in the wan light I staggered to the window to call, "Celestina, Celestina." Parting the shutters a fraction, I saw that outside, sitting on the low wall of the bridge, was a man in his shirt sleeves, paring his nails with a carving knife and still shouting. The shout I learned to be a series of "Nah"s that he strung together as he lashed out at life. I did not go onto the balcony but stood between the barely opened shutters, thinking that by standing there I would induce him to go away. I spoke or pretended to speak to an imaginary person in the room, the one I wished was there. He glanced up. He was without coat or jacket and had a scowl on his face. It was a thin face, like the picture of a gaunt mariner on a cigarette packet from long ago, and his hair was a fuzzy white like bog cotton. My reasoning was that he would not break into the house once he saw that I was on guard. In time he got up and sauntered off, waving the knife as if it were a little skittle.

The insect-like hands on the black-faced clock told me the worst, that it was only five; hours before the shops opened, and that maybe, it being Easter Sunday, they might not open at all. In them somehow rested my refuge. I imagined cowering there all day, allowing time to pass, and knew now that I was sadly mistaken in coming. I opened one flap of the brown shutter, the better to see my room. There was a bed with a carved headboard, a kitchen chair, a horseshoe on the whitewashed wall, and a photograph of a girl in a leotard, sitting on a bed, apprehensive before she stood up. Somewhere in her limbs and the recesses of her frightened being she was trying to find the pluck and resolution to get up and dance, to bedazzle an unseen audience.

I recalled the rest of the house as I had seen it when I arrived late the previous evening and had in desperation gone to the hotel to find a room, only to be turned away. There was the big entrance hall, which was a wilderness of rubble and cement, a kitchen with a stone trough for a sink, on the draining board a colony of ants thick and countless as pepper, crawling ceaselessly over an orange rind. In the adjoining room the remains of a fire, as three logs staggered over a pit of cold ashes, like three faltering witches. I threw the few belongings that I had unpacked into one of the canvas bags, turned the horseshoe the way it should be, to intercede for luck, dragged the bags down the stone stairs and over the rubble, unlocked the front door, then from the outside locked it again and put the big warped key in a crevice under a large stone, where Celestina could find it. I was going home.

I waited until it got light and then set out with two of the heavy bags, meaning to bring them a little way, then return for the next two.

> The wren, the wren, the king of all birds
> St. Stephens day was caught in the furze.
> Although he is little, his family's great.
> I pray you good landlady give us a trate.

I heard the verse before I saw the speaker and for an instant I thought it must be the madman.

A sandy-haired man emerged from a path, doubling over with laughter, his bright hair like a vivid crest in the early light. He was tall and gangly and obviously amused by the sight of me carrying one bag, putting it down, then running back to get the next one, talking to myself, pacifying myself, abjuring myself.

"Top o' the morning to you," he said in a pronounced brogue and asked if by any chance he could be of some slight assistance. He waved a sailor's cap, doffed it, and came toward me, introducing himself as David Anthony Ignatius Donne, better known as D'Arcy. He had hard blue eyes, sharp features, and he wore a navy smock which was spattered with various colored paints. Between his teeth he held an amber cigarette holder and was, as he said, in dire need of a weed. As I went to get the next bag, he followed and jauntily hoisted it over his shoulder, then realizing that there were books in it, he said he hoped I was not a word peddler who had come to drink deep from the Pierian spring.

"I can't stay in there . . . It's a builder's yard," I said, quite disgruntled.

"Has Salome worsted you," he said with a twinkle, though he saw no reason for such agitation. Where was my cosmic consciousness!

"I'm going home," I said.

"Ah, a Bethlehemite," he lamented, then went on to laud the providential fact that like himself I was a descendant of the trilobed-foliaged, leprechauned folk, hence on the run from myriad forms of knackers and massacrers.

"Two many swine . . . did not Giraldus Cambrensis find a similar odiousness in the twelfth century . . . never seen so many swine as in Ire-land, anger-land . . . have you thought of that . . . that little association," he said with a sort of glee.

"Is there a taxi in the town?" I asked, a bit curtly.

" 'Tis like this . . . there is and there isn't, he works when he wants to . . . he's newly married . . . poor bugger."

We began to walk together along the dusty road with him spouting snatches of history—"the first conquest by King Jaime of Aragon in 1229; peasant revolt in fifteenth century, great dexterity in slinging; Archduke Louis Salvator responsible for many magnificent palaces, lover of one Catalina Homan, whom he kept imprisoned on a rocky headland, guarded day and night by wolfhounds; another Catalina stigmatist and saint . . . mark the name," he said with casual clairvoyance. "Catalina . . . the Beata whom Satan tempts with sugar."

From behind we heard someone running, and turning, I saw that the madman was trying to catch up with us. Having cadged a cigarette from him, D'Arcy pointed to me and said, "Deutsch, Deutsch . . . Heidi . . . Heidi . . ." pretending I was German. The man gave me a look of such disdain, recognizing me as the woman who had disturbed his matins, his toilette, and he turned away as if repulsed.

"Pay no heed," D'Arcy said and went on to explain that the man had been a nuclear physicist but that the chemicals had got to his brain, hence forcing him to quit, and that now he was a poet of some sort and threatened to read his verses aloud in the village bar, once the season had started.

"Agenbite of Inwit, out of his fucking mind . . ." D'Arcy said, the man still within earshot. D'Arcy paused for a minute to light his cigarette, then fixed it daintily into the holder, while urging me to take a mouthful of my surroundings, my arcadia.

From the reservoir, nearby, there was a croak of frogs and on its surface a green weed that looked to be pulsing with life and electricity. A note on a gateway read, "Toby, we have been three times and have made ourselves lunch." It was signed, "Evangeline."

"That's how it is," D'Arcy said. "We open our doors to caliphs, murderers, and mendicants . . . a leftover trait from the potentate Sheik Bohibe, whom King Jaime routed . . . mixed bloods here . . . great for the hedge pleasure," and he winked and waited, asking himself aloud if I was a full twenty shillings to the pound or not. He took my elbow and literally plonked me on a low wall, not simply to avoid a bit of wet tar that had been randomly smeared on a patch of road, but, as he said, to see the vista in the same sort of light as Wordsworth himself, the poor intense pastoral monk, saw Westminster Bridge. The village looked idyllic, blond drowsing houses clustered together, their tiled roofs shelving one above the other to give the effect of a sprawling fortress. The church, as he said, was the seat of an Iberian moon goddess long before the fishermen—with their transubstantiation gigs—got their clutches on the needy. Terraces dropped from the mountain, terraces that the Moors had built, in perfect serration, with trees and half trees clinging to them tenaciously.

"And they're not going away," he said, with a touch of mischief.

Where would I go? I could not go home, of that I was certain. I thought, in that mindless way as one does, that I would go to a city, but I did not know which one, I would find a room and burrow there like a Steppenwolf, eking out the days, waiting for some kind of redemption.

"Easter morning . . . Resurrexi, et adhuc tecum sum, alleluia," he said as he made rapid crosses in the air with his cigarette holder. Something about him frightened me, it was his mockery, his rasping energy, and the fact that underneath I felt all was seething—amok. As we passed a cavity of a dried stream that was filled with rubbish and punched plastic bottles, he pointed ruefully and said, "In its prime, in its winter prime it is a torrent—torrente."

As we walked on, some shutters were partly opened, or dogs bestirred themselves, and instead of one cock crow there was now a chorus of them, loud, jubilant, proclaiming the Day.

"Hosanna," he said to a woman who peered out, peeved to have her privacy invaded. She was an environmentalist, he said, but like many of that persuasion wanted the sunset and the Milky Way all to herself. The locals and the non-locals did not really mix, they parried, but when it came to the verities they were at loggerheads. He said that many strangers came for an hour and never left, the place putting its effulgent spell on them—bards, pseudo-bards, painters, potters, versifiers, all of whom could be encountered from noon onward.

"Nowhere is moonlight so strong or night so amethyst," he said in a declamatory voice as he listed the merits that nature had wrought: "Capacious and well-sheltered harbors; bays, creeks; earth bulging with fruits, herbs, pulses, and roots; vistas of olive and Aleppo pine; and such a congruence of lunatics and love swains as could not be found in Paris in its heyday, or Barcelona at the present time." I realized only then that he was drunk. He was coming, he confessed, from an all-night séance, where to assist the levitation of "yer man" he had imbibed liberally and also partaken of the hubbly-bubbly, giving inlet to Rimbaud drifts, lilies, those pessaries of ecstasy, violets, the spittle of nymphs.

He winked and said that if I found a little plot of ground I could grow my own narcotic and not be in danger of breaking the law. Then he hiccuped to the serene king and the serene king's lady wife and I could hear his tongue clacking as he supped on his inner emptiness. Feeling the several books of mine through the thin pile of the bag, he said was it Bibles I had brought; had I come to proselytize, and this brought him without any seeming effort to his favorite topic, the denouncement and excommunication of all wandering nerds, pen-peddlers, the squeezed-out Hemingways, who were not worthy to clean that much-misunderstood man's revolver. There was one in particular that I was to beware of, one who visited on all and sundry the dilemma whether his magnum opus should be six hundred pages or the blockbuster thousand. He ranted as he thought on it, his hoary face filling with color, going from red to beetroot, so that he seemed on the brink of a seizure. This sub-Hemingway, one Scottie Jr., hailed from the Midwest of America, and was to be found from noon every day in one of the bars, poised for innocents, particularly female innocents, springing on them, offering a cosmetically induced masculine hand—"Jaysus, he sticks the hairs on"—submitting to have a cognac with them, lamenting that he would be absent for several days, closeted with the Prodigious Muse, and that they would not see him until they saw him; which as it turned out would be that very evening, because these Lolitas had got inside his head; and he was sacrificing the cold pleasure of chiseled words for the warmth and dribbles of a well-heeled dug.

He went on to describe the other artists, many of them eunuched females who painted the sea and the mountains; excrescences, soul-less replicas of nature which they then sold in the land of the Stars and Stripes, flogged them to predatory matrons who yearned for homespun, untortured banality. One in particular got his dander up, claimed the place was no longer primitive enough, and was thinking of going to Nepal, to a remote place free of electricity or plumbing.

"Be warned, they'll invite you for footsie and cocoa," he said.

"What kind of pictures do you paint?" I asked, and he chuckled at the compliment. Turning to me almost with humility, he assured me that he had not yet elevated the bicycle chain or horse manure to the realm of art, or leading-edge art, as it was now popularly called.

"They are not yon customary batik," he said and risked the opinion that they were essentially bold, making a break with the impressionism, post-impressionism and all cliché-ridden wank.

As he went up the last set of steps he strode ahead, both to show how hale he was and to lay claim to territorial rights by shouting at some children who had huddled on the steps, where they were painting Easter eggs.

"Behold the town, in which Moorish, English, and Spanish kings, likewise dukes and archdukes, held sway, dominated by the vista of the chapel, its backside to the town, its windows rayless." Then he most chivalrously greeted a young girl who went by with an Easter cake with marzipan birds perched precariously along its edges. The sight of her induced him to recall the hackneyed poetic dream of the Spanish señorita, the Spanish mantilla, the blood fetish, and most of all . . . the Mirada . . . the long gaze.:

> —that love ne drawe ye not to done this deed
> But lust voluptuous.

Then he darted up a narrow street, in search of an inn, his hands raised in the air to show some sort of militancy.

It being Easter Sunday, the bells were ringing out, rapturous, repetitive; flooding the air with the message that Christ had risen . . . Resurrexi, et adhuc tecum sum, alleluia . . .

Little Holy Communicants in white veils, wearing white kid shoes, hitting each other with their bunches of white flowers, trailed up the hill to Mass; the little boys wore shorts and starched shirts and were the laughingstock of other little boys, obviously the children of visitors, who were not going to Mass but instead were painting on sucked-out eggs. Some they had already painted and were assiduously trying to sell—views of the mountain, the sea, the church steeple, or the big black cannon that stood there like a tarred elephant, a reminder of historic days.

It was getting warmer and the sun gave to everything a luster. D'Arcy was right. I would be mad to leave such a haven; girdled by sea and mountain, the mountain like great vastnesses, gold where the light struck in one place and rust-colored in another. The ribbon of a jet arched over the summit, at first bright and metallic, then fuzzy, and as it disappeared I thought, Goodbye outside world, goodbye all, I need never return, I can settle my accounts here.

I would grow to forget him, the him that I believed had broken my heart, but in my saner moments I recognized as being probably the last to partake with me at that fount of sensuality, and vertigo and earthly love. As with many a thing, we had embarked on it lightly, but it caught fire, escalated, went too far, to the marrow, rekindled hopes, sparked off desires, hurting even as it satiated, creating fresh hungers and fresh fears. Its end dribbled on, an end that consumed my middle years like a terrible wasting sickness, so that I often wished to be quite old, thinking by then it would have faded completely, without a trace. At other moments I wished that it had never happened because the incision was too much. Then again I wished for vengeance, retribution, which I gave vent to only in dreams. At that moment, standing in that world of lambent light, I would have given anything to have my youth back again, for a year, a month, a week, an instant. His letters I had returned. They were in dove-gray flitters, like the pieces of a shredded jigsaw, on his desk maybe, or maybe dumped by a prudent secretary into his wastepaper basket. I would forget him a little each day and of course, in forgetting him, kill that part of myself that for all its pain is the most sacred.

"Hotting up . . . little Druidess . . ." D'Arcy said as he went down the path to an art gallery with a gaudy modern poster on the half of the door that swung open.

I climbed to the top of the town and had my first glimpse of the sea, a patch of blue between two rocks. It was of such blueness that it seemed not to be water but a potion, of magical properties, as if a flock of peacocks had been liquidized and metamorphosed to create this flagrant, saturating blueness. Between the town and the sea were the orchards—trees and foliage giving a softness to the landscape, a sigh, taking the sizzle out of the air, creating a silvery stir as the olive leaves decided to shift upward, then droop again like the wings of a butterfly, lazying. The air was glutted with a smell of orange and lemon blossom, a smell that wafted through, as if gardenias or tuberoses were being pressed, while the oranges themselves were dusk-like, mystic fruits, globes to be worshipped rather than fruits to be eaten.

"They come and grab you, don't they," a woman said, startling me. She was a blond chirpy woman, one whom D'Arcy had sent to regale me. She would have a place for me in a few weeks, an apartment, above her own. It was one of the few houses with a front gate, and a child's new bicycle lay flat on the path leading down to it, its gentian paint flashing in the sun. She had come to the place over ten years ago and never regretted it. Her name was Wanda, she said, adding that it was not her real name but one she had given herself when she moved here. I felt that like me she had come as mendicant, a mendicant from love, from disappointment. Her little boy, Sam, followed with a litter of puppies in his arms and brought them for me to see. They had been born at five that morning and he had delivered them. They were utterly still, adhered together like black-and-white fur-backed gloves in a shop window; silent save for the occasional little mewl that escaped from the thick of the fur.

"We're going to sell them tomorrow, at the market," Wanda said, at which Sam whinged and said, "Not all of them, only one or two."

"We'll see," Wanda said.

"Oh, please," he begged and promised he would look after them and clean up their messes and their dribbles. I knew that he would have his way, he was her idol, blond, round-faced, with the beauty of a child and the perkiness of a little man.

"Please, Wanda," he said. Saying her name clinched it, because he said it like a lover, and like a lover she smiled back, a shy yet coaxing smile, and I had a stab of memory of my own children now grown into manhood, for whom I always wanted to seem happy, even carefree, as if sadness were a disgrace, a sort of blight on one. I remembered a girl telling my son, as they thrashed their way up a public swimming pool in London, that I was not happy, and upon being told this by her, I felt mortified, and later said to my son that she had been mistaken—quite mistaken—and unable to look at me, unable to bear the lie that he knew I was telling him, he stared into a low vase of anemones and asked if they were violets and if they smelled.

"You'll be very happy here," the woman said and added, "You could make a life here if you wanted." The word terrified me. A life! It sounded such a vast thing, interminable.

I had been thinking of days, or months, or maybe half a year, lurching along with my books and my memories, trying to make a fist of things. She said that if ever I wanted coffee or cookies or a chat I could sneak in, as she kept her front door open.

I retraced my steps and through the window of the art gallery I could see a woman on the phone, and soon after, D'Arcy came out repeating the "Resurrexi" refrain, saying I was fixed up for two weeks, at least.

"There is a woman in there now . . . she's a Yank . . . she'll tell you what you have to do and what you have to pay . . ." he said as he summoned some of the children to help me with my bags. He would escort me himself but that he had to catch the bus, as he was celebrating the feast in the city with a Dutchman who owned a nightclub. He said in due course we could meet, either in his town house or up in the hills, where he repaired to commune with nature.

The woman in the gallery greeted me without too much

flourish. She was American and as she said used to being a shoulder to cry on. All sorts of people got stranded, had their money stolen, broke up with their boyfriends, or else fell desperately in love, but always came to her mainly because her gallery was open and because she had a telephone. Along the walls were huge pictures, bold vistas of sea and crag, larded with purple paint that seemed about to crack.

The house she had found me was a little out of the way, up in the hills in fact, like a Red Ridinghood house, but it meant that I would have peace and quiet. I was sharing it with an English lady who was a sort of caretaker, but she was out most of the day as she cleaned other houses and gardens, so I would have no one to interrupt me. As she described it, I felt a pang. I would have preferred to be in the town, close to the bakery with its bread smells, close to the church with its bells, meeting the children in the morning on their way to school, then on their way back from lunch, seeing the lorries coming with the big punnets of fruits and vegetables, standing next to the people in the shops, being part of things, without knowing what they said. She explained to me that the key was in the potting shed, hanging on a nail, inside the door, and that the children would escort me. The name of my house was "Ca'an Pintada—the Painted House.

She selected three of them to be my guides, ignoring the beseeching of all the others. They ran to retrieve my luggage, while I myself picked up my shawl from the roadside. It looked gaudy, assertive, its threads brightened by the sun, each blue, red, and yellow thread distinct from its neighbor.

"Ca'an Pintada . . . Ca'an Pintada."

The word went around the street. People who did not know

me or know of me waved and Wanda ran after me with a torch.

"You'll need this," she said. "You'll need this at night." It was a flat torch and the paint had peeled.

Thanking her, I flicked it on and off for some kind of security. I hated to be leaving the town and as we took to the overgrown path I hated it more. The ground was slithery with pines and there was a smell of scrub and rosemary. As we skeetered along, the children laughed incessantly, bumped into each other, and dropped the bags. There were steps but these were so overgrown with fern and wild asparagus that path and step had merged and at times it was a question of groping through the undergrowth. As we went down into a valley the vegetation was higher and the children disappeared in it. There were paths leading off from our path, some to other secluded houses, some doubling back and connecting with paths that led to the village, and some to still higher terraces that then seemed to straddle their way to meet the road on the opposite side, over which cars already glided and glittered.

The house was surrounded by tall trees, mostly eucalyptus, and the garden was a riot of flowers. Nasturtiums scattered over one bank looked like bits of orange peel, their leaves cool, graceful, and insouciant. Farther down, a bed of marigolds so golden it was as if the sun had lain in them. There were birds and birdbaths and on the terrace itself geraniums in huge terra-cotta pots. The roses had just begun to bloom, some big as cabbages, white roses with a pink ruched edging, others utterly white, unstained, and still others bowing over trellises and arches, arabesques. I thought that later on I would pick a few and put them in my room. A hose wound its way across the terrace and down to the moat of marigolds, but there was no one in sight. I called and waited, then called again, but no answer came. The woman in the art gallery had said that the girl I was sharing with was very retiring and that I might not meet her for days, even weeks. I sensed that there was some difficulty but could not confirm it.

The children gloated over the big tip that I gave them and scampered off, no doubt eager to boast to their friends, to prove that they had made more money doing this than they ever would painting Easter eggs. I was sad to see them go. The place was beautiful but there was a loneliness to it and the house itself did not have the gaiety of the garden. Suddenly the hose was moved by an unseen hand and as it rose and coiled and darted away it was as if a snake had pounced. She was indeed somewhere, but chose not to present herself.

There were two spare bedrooms, one downstairs and one upstairs. I examined both, thinking which would be less isolated, less gloomy. I lay on the bed, listened for a creak or the sound of a cistern, and eventually decided on the upstairs room, opposite the other lodger, whom I knew to be Charlotte. Her door was ajar and I saw music tapes, cardboard boxes, and endless clutter.

My room was simply furnished—a bed, a dressing table, a lamp, and a few hangers on a hexagonal wooden peg, where I was to hang my clothes. Through the open window the trees were pendant in the sunshine, the cypresses dark and gaunt, tapering, like darning needles threaded with rough green wool, and in the flowering oak tree convolvulus wound itself around, giving the effect of teeming butterflies, with a whiteness so pure it reminded me of the little Holy Communicants in their lace and satin.

I hung my clothes on the three available metal hangers, bunching blouses and dresses and cardigans together, realizing that I would probably not wear most of them, that city preoccupations would desert me here, that I would wear the same old thing day after day and for my climbing would have to invest in a pair of espadrilles. The little table was so small that I could not place my books separately, end to end, but had to pile them, one on top of the other, debating as to which should be on top, as if whatever title caught my eye would in itself be significant, even talismanic. In several of them I found postcards, postcards from people I had almost forgotten, and now reading these affectionate tokens, I wondered why I had come, why I had not gone in search of my friends, and flung myself into their lives, their cares.

A year earlier I had gone around America, giving lectures, the same lecture in each city, the summoning up of one's land, battle-haunted, famine-haunted land; woods and glens from where many had come, creeping forth upon their hands, looking like anatomies of death, like ghosts in search of dead carrion—thereby quoting not a Gael but Spenser, the befriender of Elizabeth, the Faerie Queene. I knew even as I said these things, delivered these gleanings of history, that the soul of a race cannot be transmitted any more than the soul of a person, and in trying to bring this past alive, I was both adulterated and adulterating. How could they know what it was to walk roads and byroads where nature was savage; a landscape shot at times with a beauty that was dementing, indigo, fuchsia, but for the most part permeated with an emptiness redolent of the still greater emptiness, giving a sense of having been stranded, left behind by history and by the world at large, a severed limb of a land full of hurt and rage, a rage that enters and transmutes the way the moss and the damp pass into the tombstones.

Afterward there would be a party, a makeshift party, and I

would drink jug wine from a transparent plastic glass, eat a hexagon of cheese with a grape or an olive affixed to it by means of a plastic skewer, and wonder if any connection at all, other than habit, and bland courtesy, existed between these people and myself or these people and themselves.

Once in one of those places, overcome by staggering isolation, I lay face down on the gauze-like pillow slip, kissed it, and looking at the crescent of lipstick I wondered if a kiss on another person's lips or cheeks left its mark forever, its imprint, could be traced for all of time, never to be denied or refuted.

There were two beds in that room, as I remember it, two beds with wicker headboards, and on one, the one where I lay, a hand-printed sign which read, "Hard Bed." Earlier, and before I set out to give my lecture, the woman who kept house called me into her quarters, which were like a jungle, full of thick plants that looped into each other, with little canaries in cages scattered about, piping through the thick, stagnant foliage, and with tears in her eyes she had asked me what life was like in the fast lane.

Another evening in the Midwest I went alone after my lecture, and ate in a revolving room, so that sometimes I saw a singer in a short sequined dress, and at other times saw a bit of water, maybe a lake, then a series of arterial roads, all with cars, which because of being distant had a flicker of magic like the stars, and then again I saw the one main street with the "Black Steer" sign, but no matter how the room revolved I was listening to a young man telling a young woman that he did not think he was going to be able to say it, because he had never said it before, and what he was saying, long before he said it, was that he loved her and wished to marry her.

I thought how the people who had come to my lecture were

going home now, along those arterial roads, in their cars, wearing their cumbersome quilted coats and gloves, thinking maybe or remarking on something I had said, remarking maybe how baffling life is, how things differ between one country and the next, the speech, the expectations, the threads of hope or half hope, and feeling probably lonely or a little bewildered as I was, as I sat in the revolving room looking at the sign of the "Black Steer," or the pocket of water, eating frozen shellfish that next day would confine me to my bed, where through a window I saw the snow swirl down so dizzyingly that I believed myself to be inside a paperweight from which I would never emerge. Lying there, choked with fever, or food poisoning, and believing that I would never get out, I clung to things from my former life as if in them I could find refuge, whereas in fact they were studded with pain. I thought of the day that I had burned my boats with him, how I had degraded myself, disappointed myself in both our eyes. I had cried in front of him, cried because I could feel the oncoming chill, the way one feels winter or indeed any season, cried in broad daylight over thin slices of avocado, and he had said, "Maybe next time I'll be the one that cries," but he did not cry with me, did not even commiserate, and I saw how reduced I had become in his eyes. Gone the days when he saw me as beautiful, queenly, or even formidable. The time had come to throw me off like an old garment, and yet in that snow town, in the Midwest, I believed I lingered within him somewhere, sprouting at times, being brought out into the light like a little urchin, an urchin of his memory, and I believed it afresh in my new room, where I was intending to spend a lot of time, to spend months maybe, to set down my thoughts, to meet myself.

I opened one of my books at random, and read of the three

kinds of knowledge: "The first is sensual; the second is intellectual and is much higher in rank; the third represents that aristocratic agent of the soul which ranks so high it communes with God, face to face as He is. This state has nothing in common with anything else, it is unconscious of yesterday or the day before, and of tomorrow and the day after, for in eternity there is no yesterday nor any tomorrow, but only Now, as it was a thousand years ago and as it will be a thousand years hence and as it will be after death."

Through a sea of tears I heard a step and jumped. I reckoned it was Charlotte. She had a heavy tread, or else it was because of the bare boards of the stairs. I wondered if she was a big girl and I wondered, too, if she would resent me, being used to having the place to herself.

Earlier, I had seen signs of her. I had gone into the kitchen, like a thief, looking at things, at this and that—bean sprouts under a damp cloth that looked like nipples yet were full of beseech. In the refrigerator several cartons of yogurt and some raw fish. The yogurt labels had baby gooseberries hanging from a branch and the raw fish was half wrapped in newspaper. She had laid her place for her supper and there was something a little forlorn about it and familiar—the one plate, the two pieces of cutlery, the used and refolded napkin in its bone ring; a place setting waiting for its solitary rite.

I thought to go and introduce myself but because of the crying and mulling I feared that she might find me depressing and so waited to pluck up the courage, going from the window back to the bed and then to the window again to marshal some strength. From her room there was a sound of music, pop music very loud, and then suddenly, as if under the sway of a command or a whim, the music stopped and I heard her dash out again. She went down the stairs at a frightful speed. I ran to the window and saw her pass beneath. I only saw her back, she was tall and had yellow-blond hair; she was wearing jeans and a red T-shirt. She could have been any age.

At about six, feeling hungry and a lot more buoyant, I decided that I would dress up a bit and go to the town, maybe look into one or two of the bars that D'Arcy had mentioned.

I did not lock the door but left a little note which by its very indecision amused me. "Please do not lock me out" was what it said. I did not sign it, since she must know that I was the only person living there. She had been told by the woman in the gallery, she had even been consulted, which is what the phoning was about. The woman had tried to trace her in one of the many houses where she worked and had eventually found her and it seems she had said okay, so long as we kept to ourselves and ate at different times.

The sun was going down in a great carnival splendor. Gold splashed regions of the sky, while throughout were puffs of cloud, daintily fringed with pink and crimson. The smell of plants and herbs intensified, as if someone had put a match to them, as if they were smoldering, and walking amid the bushes, over the slithery pine needles, I thought how I would make this place my home for a long time. For far too long I had hidden in cities, burrowed. I remembered a shop window that I had once seen in Boston, at harvest time, a travesty of nature, and grotesque at that. The floor was strewn with straw and there was a wire frame in which overwhite eggs were wedged, eggs covered with straw and false dung. The mannequin was modeling a greatcoat and boots but his face had been painted a sickly magenta and in his face more than in the mockeries of nature I saw Armageddon.

Two nightingales let out a range of calls that were urgent and arresting and sounded mechanical and not like notes or calls that sprung from the soft and throbbing throat of a bird. The first star appeared in the dip between two ridges of mountain and I followed it full of sudden, unaccountable optimism.

Where the path came onto the main road there was a Station of the Cross on the gabled wall of a house. That would be my landmark on my way home. It was the fourth Station—"Jesus meets His Afflicted Mother." Flashing on the little torch, I took a closer look at it to recognize it later. The Virgin was in pale blue, as was the other Mary, who had succumbed to an orgy of tears. Both in blue togas, both supplicating. Jesus was impassive, putting a grave face on things, partly no doubt because of the stoicism of his character and partly because the painter must have kept in mind the ten more encounters, including the twelfth, climactic one. I went down the very steep hill, past the art gallery, past the closed bread shop, where two remaining baguettes of white bread looked pleading and not like bread at all. Then on a whim I followed a second hill, following the Stations of the Cross, which I knew would lead me in the end to the church, the seat of the Iberian moon goddess. The figures in the Stations became more and more stooped, with the imminence of the sacrifice. Through an open door a tall and somber man was laying out a collection of shells and talking to himself. His open door meant he was ready to receive. Many doors were open and I thought as the weeks go by I will cross one of them, surely.

In the chapel grounds were the local women. They were older women, with sallow faces, faces of stone; impassive, except that in the eyes there was a message which was hard, outraged, and unforgiving. The years and their hardships had made them look alike, and they all wore black. Some had walking canes, while others limped, and all had gray hair ridiculously rinsed with blue and were primly permed. I felt daunted, yet at the same time I followed them, as if drawn to them in a kind of surrender. They were calling me to their camp, to their way of life, to a repentance and a contrition that I was not ready for, not yet. I stared back at them and in staring I believed that I was defying my own mother, who had pervaded and begrudged every moment of my sleeping and my waking life, persisting even after death. In their eyes, as in hers, were uncharted vortexes of hurt and rage that I believed went back to their own mothers and their mothers' mothers, figures who had usurped their lives from them.

Inside, the chapel had that aura of gloom and theatricality, that uniting of blood and glitter, that I could never resist. Up along the aisles were a series of altars, little altars all decked with statuary and flowers. There were statues of the Virgin, Saint Teresa the Carmelite, Saint John of the Cross, and Christ with a gold-threaded apron around his loins. Mass was soon to be said. On the main altar the candles were ready to be lit, and on the pulpit, a little metal microphone for when the priest would give his sermon. The women had knelt close together, formed a phalanx, and begun to recite the rosary. I sat a little farther back. I did not want to pray and yet I wanted to be there, in some secret recess of my being. I wanted a link with them, a soft look, an exoneration maybe. As they commenced on the litany their voices blended to a uniform murmur, a sort of drone that was subhuman.

Mater purissima,	Mother most pure,
Mater castissima,	Mother most chaste,
Mater inviolata,	Mother inviolate,
Mater intemerata,	Mother undefiled,
Mater amabilis,	Mother most amiable,
Mater admirabilis,	Mother most admirable . . .

Above the tabernacle was one of those Virgins, or perhaps the sum of them, the Immaculata, ascending to the clouds, crushing the serpent rather demurely with her bound plastered feet. Above her was the Sacred Heart, with spikes of gold streaking out from his Heart, skewers of pain and beatitude. Two points of painted flame above him made shadows on the arch, and looked exactly like the bloodied points of two butcher's knives. Now and then, one of the women would look back to see if I was still there or if I had joined in. The looks became more interrogative.

In the end I skulked out and crossed through a gateway into a graveyard, which by comparison was cheerful, glowing with life. The slab stones were flat and friendly, each one engraved with simple childlike lettering, giving the name and the lifespan of each person. On most of them there were flowers or herbs or quaint little souvenirs, things people brought from their own houses and left there—ornaments, mementos, a handwritten poem.

It was growing dark. The sea had relinquished its blues, its greens, and its violets and was now like a great, dark, recumbent wet mother; mother of creatures, animate and half animate, mother of life and death, moon and star, mother of the unknown; indifferent to the wretched pleas or cries of man.

2

In the restaurant that overlooked the mountain I found myself next to a lively group. They seemed like a troupe of traveling players, dressed in exotic clothes and talking rapidly in various languages. Two of them, very young girls, had their faces painted starkly white, like clowns, and their eyelids were a hooded terra-cotta. The younger one suddenly stood up on a chair, unfastened her very short dress, which fell to form black pantaloons with pink-lined pleats. People cheered. Her movements were very delicate, like the movements of a flamingo. She put the palms of her hands forward like an Indian dancer, thanking people for admiring her brief performance. The man at the head of the table was dressed completely in black, a black silk kimono, black silk shirt, and black glasses. Behind his glasses I could feel that he was looking at me, that his eyes were directed on me, and I felt a little self-conscious at being alone. My table had been laid for two and there were two carnations, looking idiotic in a big ceramic vase. I ordered fish and a half bottle of wine. They only had full bottles but the waiter said he would bring the whole bottle and I could drink what I wished, then he would write my name on the label for the next time.

"You come back," he said, and asked where my husband was. I would take a sip and look out at the mountain, which was now a hulk of darkness; the sky above it riven with stars. Then I would jot something in my notebook, simply to give myself something to do. But all the time I was aware of the merry group and aware of the man's eyes, behind his glasses, fixed on me. There was something very still about him, like a soapstone Buddha, and it was clear that he was the center of attention and all were beholden to him. The young girls kept throwing things at him, bits of bread, shreds of the carnations, a feather earring, anything to get his attention. The starkness of their painted faces belied their frivolity. One of them looked down at her ice cream, which was in a coconut shell, then lifted a thin crescent of dark chocolate off it and gave it to him to eat. He in turn gave it to another girl, a quieter girl next to him, who licked it from his hand. She smiled at him. It was an adoring smile, a smile that said, "I would do anything for you . . . I am yours, regardless." An Australian man was amusing them by telling them of his many lives and his many loves. He was thin and wiry, with a hat pushed back on his head, and he had that weather-beaten look of a man who has lived in the bush. His most recent love, his little Rosie, he said, had died a year ago, her little heart gave out. He prayed to her, morning and night. The young girls giggled at this, but he didn't mind, said his little Rosie was in there, and pointed to his chest, which was matted with black hairs. He said it didn't matter whether people were dead or alive so long as they were remembered. So long as one talked to them every day, or prayed to them, because that was food and water to their little souls. Then he told them how in past lives he had been a warrior, a woman, a gigolo, and a black hunter. He had been speared in his belly, in Central Africa.

"Rubbish," one of the young girls said. To prove it, he pulled up his shirt to show a great gash on his bronzed stomach, a long gash with little gashes running out from it, like the vertebrae of a fish. One of the young girls pulled his shirt down and said there was a lady looking, referring to me. The man in black asked if I would like to join them. He introduced everybody very formally, the girls were models, many of the party were from a magazine, in Cologne, the Australian was their makeup artist and he took the photographs. He poured me some wine, said to forget about my own bottle, to drink theirs, to celebrate with them.

The two models and the Australian then started a contest, arguing who knew the most songs from popular musicals. Soon they were singing the hit songs from *Oklahoma*, *West Side Story*, *Porgy and Bess*, *Brigadoon*. Each side sang only the first line of each one in order to be able to jump ahead, and presently the models cheated by humming only the first few bars and immediately going on to another song. They became so excited that they went too fast and we could not even hear what they were singing. The girlfriend of the photographer, whose name was Birgitta, smiled at me from time to time as if to reassure me, as if to say, "You can admire him, you can flirt with him, it's all right." It was only afterward I realized she was deaf, and when he wanted her to know something he spoke to her very clearly and with his face close to hers. Then she would smile, as if he had told her something very special; something that only he and she shared. I felt happy with them, I felt weirdly linked to them and had the daft wish to ask if I could go home with them, to Cologne.

Later the photographer suggested that we all go back to the hotel for champagne. He took out all his money and said it was really no use to him, he yearned to spend it. It was to the hotel on the hill, where I had gone that first night, that we all trooped. There was something very heartening and magical about approaching it, it felt like a homecoming, walking up there with a group of people, talking, singing, nonchalant. The Australian ran on ahead to get us the best chairs in the main salon.

"Just you wait, 'Enry 'Iggins," he said, thumping one of the models as he ran.

We sat on a very long sofa like people in a church and the photographer sat opposite us in a high-backed chair, looking at us benignly. He was very still, yet curious, looking at each of us in turn, to make sure we were happy. His girlfriend asked me if I thought his glasses made him look sinister.

"No," I said.

"Oh, tell him they do," she said. "He'll ruin his eyes, his beautiful eyes."

"His beautiful eyes," he said, mimicking her. But he was not making fun of her. Something tender and playful flowed between them. Suddenly Birgitta jumped up and ran toward one of their suites, which as it happened led off the salon. Another bottle of champagne was brought and I had this nice feeling of being carried along, weightless, thoughtless, like a streamer. Birgitta returned with a T-shirt, a white T-shirt which had one of his photographs on the front. It was black and white, lovers lost in a forest. The woman was taller than the man, wide-shouldered and smoldering, and the man was kissing the nape of her neck, deeply, as if he was drinking from it, drinking life itself from it.

"Put it on," she said. "It will suit you." I felt shy about taking off my own blouse, but the Australian made them all cover their eyes until I had donned the T-shirt, and they all clapped. He then ran down to the suite and came back with a fawn attaché case, which when he opened it had tiers full of bottles with enamel foundation and little round boxes of eye shadow and rouge. He started to paint my face; quickly, assuredly, and even as he was doing it I thought, I shall be someone else, I shall escape being me for this night at least. The girls oohed and aahed and the fashion editor said what a transformation, what a metamorphosis.

"Just you wait, 'Enry 'Iggins," the Australian said as he ogled the photographer to take some snaps of me.

Soon the room was a blaze of strong lights and I was sitting sideways on a straight chair as the photographer clicked away and the girls kept making faces because they wanted me to laugh. They were setting fire to the flimsy papers that were around the macaroons and watching their ascent to the ceiling. A few people came and looked but soon got bored and drifted off again. The photographer told me that I need not smile, said he wanted me to look sad and all I had to do was think of those dirges of my native land. Afterward he wrote down my name and address and said that he would send me a set of photographs but that it would not be until November.

November, I thought with a shudder, a future time that I could not envisage, did not want to. It frightened me.

After the arc lights were quenched, he put his two cameras into a clean yellow chamois and he came and sat next to me. The magazine owner, a very tall, patrician woman, and her young girlfriend, who had not spoken a word, decided to retire, as they were leaving at six in the morning. They gave me their cards and said that if ever I was in their city I was to look them up. One of the young assistants began to carry out boxes and suitcases from the suite. The open suitcases were full of furs, heralds of raw winter. There were red furs, fox furs, some silver, some blue, and still other furs so sleek and dark they brought to mind an army of morning moles crawling over a frosted lawn. The models jumped up and in their own tongue sang a hymn, just like children, before they kissed everyone good night. The Australian said it would be "pissing up a rope" to have a beer but that he would anyhow. I knew that I should get up and go home but something stopped me. It wasn't simply the journey back to my house, which indeed daunted me; it was an unvoiced notion that if I stayed with them, among them, I need never go home. The group was thinning. The Australian chuckled as he filled his breakfast order—cereal, orange juice, two boiled eggs, croissants and pastries; all to be served at five-thirty. He carried his beer with him, gave me a friendly pat, and said, "See you, mate."

The photographer, Birgitta, and myself were the last. She looked at us both, tenderly, mischievously. Then she rose, kissed me good night, took my hand, and placed it in his.

"Be good to her," she said. "Be good to her," and she kissed him sweetly and left. He suggested that we sit in the little salon, where they had the fire.

"Are you sure?" I said.

"I hardly ever sleep," he said.

"Why not?"

"I don't need to, perhaps . . . I am always half asleep," he said as he crossed to the bar and asked the young man to fetch us a bottle of amaretto and two glasses. In the morning, he said, he would tell the cashier how much we had drunk.

The fire still smoldered, and after he had put down the tray, the young barman went and fetched a great long log covered with moss. He did not recognize me as the person who had come in search of a room Easter Saturday and had sat in the imposing dining room, long before the other guests, devouring breadsticks and olives. Had I looked in a mirror, I would probably not have recognized myself either.

"Who is this man who is in hiding?" the photographer asked eventually.

"Oh, someone," I said, trying to sound indifferent.

"Is he dead?"

"No."

"Then it's all right . . . If he's not dead he's in the world . . . and if he's in the world he's thinking of you."

"He's asleep," I said. "He's in England, asleep."

"Then he's dreaming of you," he said quietly, as if it was something he knew, something he was in no doubt of.

"Will your girlfriend be anxious?" I asked.

"It's all right," he said. "Everything is all right." Birgitta loved him, she trusted him. It did not mean he could not love someone else, for an instant, for a fleeting night.

"When I saw you come into the restaurant I wanted to embrace you . . . You kept pulling your blouse up as if you were afraid of being seen . . . or as if you were naked."

"I felt awkward," I said.

"That's nice," he said. "That's very nice."

We would not make love, we would sit and watch over one another like sages.

"I would like to make love to you but it is not necessary," he said.

"I know," I said.

"You don't know," he said. "You think you know . . . you still think it is the most important thing in the world . . . believe me it isn't . . . fucking is very overrated and coming is very overrated, too."

Then he rose and he kissed me, it was a deep kiss and there was something infinitely reassuring about it. At once I felt I had exorcised the forlorn kiss on the pillow.

We sat quite still. The fire made little stirs from time to time. On either wall there were two huge paintings that, as he said, depicted the two aspects of us all, the angelic and the murderous. One showed the backs of women in white djellabas, seated, impassive, gazing out to sea; the other was of a predator, a pig, leaping the abyss, its claws a bright bloodied pink; the crags from which it leaped were a glistening ice-green, jeweled, the same color as those skies under which Peter Brueghel appointed his hounds and his lonely huntsmen. We touched without touching. The touch that we almost made hovered, was outside our hands, outside our limbs, with the antennae of our minds we held one another and I thought that this would be enough forever, this moment of pure life, this stream of abstract love.

3

Next morning I encountered Charlotte. To my surprise, she had not gone out. She was in the kitchen on the rocking chair, which had a little sway to it, a narrow chair with latticed back and a faded print cover. She was staring through the open window and I felt that her sitting there was to do with staking her claim. She had obviously eaten, because the remains of things, a yogurt carton and the gray skin of a fish, remained on the plate. As I entered she turned and gave a sort of smile, but it was not a real smile, more a grimace, and I thought I saw her flinch involuntarily. I assumed it was due to my staying out most of the night. She had a long face, with pale parchment skin and the vestiges of someone who had once been beautiful. Her face looked far older than her body, old and disenchanted.

"I hope I didn't frighten you," I said.

"Nothing frightens me," she said with a slight sneer. Her accent was English but she was trying to disguise it by adding a foreign intonation. The voice or, rather, the distorted voice triggered something off in my memory and I thought of a girl I had known years before, an English debutante called Portia whom I had been in awe of, who was quite a few years older than me and sophisticated, with clusters of men around her, boyfriends, ex-boyfriends, one of those exotic ones who had been to Turkey and Afghanistan long before anyone else and had brought back rugs, cushions, and hangings with which she furnished her flat. She caught me looking at her in this speculative way and all of a sudden she stood up and put a cloth over the beans, which were sprouting. She did it aggressively, as if my seeing them was itself something of an intrusion. More out of awkwardness than need, I picked some oranges from the earthenware bowl, intending to squeeze them.

"I would rather you didn't use the machines . . . I depend on them," she said, and so holding an orange by the sprig and feeling a bit crushed, I slunk down the stairs to the bathroom quarters, thinking could this be Portia with the tantrums and the legendary waist, Portia whose every whim was reported in the gossip columns, how she had had a milk bath or went ice skating in Vienna or had thrown the gold chairs through the window of the Ritz at her coming-out party. Could this be the girl whose decrees made a thing or a person famous or ridiculous. Of a restaurant she would say, "Best pasta in London, nearly as good as Harry's Bar in Venice when Nino is on," then a week later say, "It's the pits," and send the acolytes, who waited on her word, flocking to some other place. For a brief time it was a Chinese restaurant in Whitechapel where people went and brought their own wine. Could this be she, this faded, fidgety, reclusive creature upstairs who was obviously trying to disguise herself by wearing dark glasses, indoors, in the morning? I had lost touch with Portia after her two marriages and had heard that she had joined a commune in Wales, cutting herself off from everyone, including her father. Could this be she? I thought yes and no in the same instant. Portia was not someone I knew well, but I happened to be with her on one of the most important days of her life: on the morning of her first marriage. She was so nervous, and so on heat as she paced the hall of the Registry Office in a cream lace dress, a straw hat a shade darker than her hair, and with a vast bunch of violets, which she sniffed nervously as if they were nose drops. She mocked the other couples who were also waiting to be married.

"Look at them . . . like jellies," she said, and wondered where they got their vulgar habit of kissing, if it was not from television. As she paced she feared, feared that Pirate, her intended, would not come. I did not know her well, but I knew her well enough to see in her eyes and in her expression the look of a hunted animal. Her real bridesmaid, Suki, could not come because she had mumps and I had been called in at the last minute because I was Suki's lodger. I had known Portia slightly but I was never one of her "set." In fact, she was always condescending to me. However, that morning her worries got the better of her and in the taxi she had confided that the cards were stacked against her. His mother, his bloody mother was against it, and he was so vague and so bloodless he probably would not put up a fight. I had met him once in one of those restaurants where Portia held court and insisted on ordering for everyone. At times he believed himself to be Rupert Brooke and at other times Ronald Firbank. His bedroom was done in red silk and he had called it Veronica, after Veronica Lake. He never went to bed, he only went to Veronica.

"Come now, Pirate . . . This won't do . . . this simply will not do," she had said as she sniffed the violets distastefully.

Eventually he came, beautifully turned out, tall and tapering in a pale green suit, so pale it was like the whey of milk, and he had a mauve shirt with frilled cuffs. He had been to Westminster Cathedral in search of that nice Father Something to sprinkle a drop of holy water over him to brace him for this ghastly event. His family were Catholic, and he still believed in what they had taught him at Ampleforth. Moreover, his mother warned him that if he did marry her, his sister, the chinless Camilla, would get everything. His mother thought Portia a nymphomaniac and called her Miss Slut. He did not kiss Portia when he arrived, just asked if she had any fags. A clerk led us into another room, informing us that the Registrar would come through the door in one minute, adding tersely that we had made the proceedings fifteen minutes late and had capsized their morning's arrangements. Pirate suddenly wondered if he could ask a question. I saw Portia freeze; he was going to find a reason to cancel the wedding, a snag.

"Which door does the Registrar come through, that door or that?" he asked, pointing to two doors at either end.

"That one, sir," the clerk said, bending a little, recognizing by the piping voice and the disdain that Pirate was of the upper crust and could make a clerk, or any menial, feel very small indeed simply by the way he asked a question. This very languor was what attracted Portia, drove her mad, and she used to tell the various ruses she had used to get him to bed. When drunk she used to go further and say he was repelled, didn't like her being wet and would order her to the bathroom, to shower and dry herself.

As the married couple stepped from the municipal gloom into a cold June light they were met by a bevy of photographers and journalists. The word had got out. The legendary Miss P. had finally married and would be mistress of a vast estate in Cornwall. Asked where they were going on their honeymoon, Portia said coyly, "To bed." Then, asked where the breakfast would be, Portia said that she never ate breakfast but that chums would drop by, in the evening, and they would all watch television and have sardine sandwiches and champagne, and that they just might, might have a little orgy. She allowed herself to be weaned of the name of the hotel and sent flocks of cameramen flurrying to the one available phone booth, to give the first part of their story while promising a torrid second.

Pirate was livid. He kept saying, "Fuck fuck fuck," knowing now that the photograph would be in the paper the following morning and that consequently his mother would either disinherit him or go off her rocker. In the taxi into which we had tumbled, Portia spoke in a chummy cockney voice to the driver, popped her head sideways so that the straw hat slid off, and said, "Can you do a bunk, Guv . . . can we lose the scribblers . . ." Seeing her so sweet and coaxing with her wedding hat and her wedding ring and a rabble of photographers pursuing her, the driver said to leave it to him. Tearing down the street, he turned into a narrower street, jumped a red light, went farther up, then cunningly took a side road which was a back route to a railway station. We went up a ramp, past postal vans and railway sleepers, then down another ramp and out into a sort of wasteland, where the churned earth disgorged a yellow flowering weed and in one corner an estate agent's sign proclaimed glories to come.

"Who in Christ's name tipped them off?" Pirate kept asking.

"I'm Mrs. Rowlinson now . . . the Hon.," Portia kept saying as she laughed at our ghost ride, said wasn't the landscape festive, divine, just like Jaipur.

"Oh, shut up," Pirate said and asked the driver without the least semblance of manners to give him a cigarette. He broke off the filter part roughly, lit it at that end, and cursed steadily between clenched teeth.

Eventually we were dislodged at Allegra's, a friend's house, for the wedding feast. Allegra had put some sparkling wine and punnets of strawberries on a trestle table out of doors, and even without tasting a sip, Pirate said he had to see someone, wouldn't be long, and he fled, leaving Portia stricken and calling him the biggest shit in the world. Everyone believed he had simply gone to get hashish from Quentin, enough to get him through the remainder of his wedding day so that he could ring his mother up and warn her of the ghastly headlines. The only little anxiety was that he would take an age, that once he and Quentin had lulled themselves into a nice giggly state, they would call on other friends, smoke more, laugh themselves through the vacuous mists, and think what shit, what shit that Pirate had allowed Portia to get her clutches on him. What we never deemed was that Pirate would not come back. Having married her, he felt, insofar as he allowed any feeling to trickle up to the vague repository of his brain, that he had done what she wanted, that he had married her, and that in future Portia could always say, "Oh, that was before Pirate and I got married," or "That was after Pirate and I got married." Portia was too proud to go to Quentin's, the bar in Kensington where it was sure they might be. She waited, downing goblets of the sparkling wine, refusing food, and then flopping down on one of the bunk beds in the nursery, not daring to believe he had done a flit, listening through her drunken half sleep for the sound of a taxi, the creak of a gate, and the arrival of a loping Pirate, who when he was contrite called her Sugarpuss. When she wakened around six, the truth began to dawn on her; she started to undress, tore the wedding dress from her body, tore the rosettes of lace, tore the beautiful satin slip, and tore the cuffs, so that the buttons went askew and the children knelt on the floor to pick up these treasures for their dollies. The flowers she tore as well and people walked on them and pressed them into the ground. Julian, "the Crimper" as he was called, came rushing in with the dire bulletin that in the ladies' lavatory in the bar in Kensington Portia's name was scrawled, followed by an insulting epithet.

"What!" she shrieked.

He demurred. He said that he did not think he could tell her, that it was too hurtful, too crude. He got her to such a pitch of curiosity that she picked up a skewer from the dresser, put it to his temple, and said, "Out with it, snake."

"Portia Whitehead is a lousy fuck," he said abruptly. At first she laughed, the hard rattled laughter of the really wounded. Then she thought to go there and with her bare hands kill Jeffrey, the creep who ran the joint and took phone messages and was the one to give Pirate sal volatile when Pirate passed out. In her lilac knickers scalloped with lace, she ran toward the garden gate, with Allegra running after her, pulling her back, begging her not to go.

"In the lavatory!" Portia screamed as if the venue rather than the tidings was what offended her. Allegra said that they would get nice Rosie to go there later on with a brush and some red floor stain and nice Rosie would blot it all out.

Somehow we managed to contain Portia and the evening passed as these evenings do with drink and people phoning up with conflicting rumors, and someone going for a take-away, and

Portia smoking cigarette after cigarette and putting the ash in the very yellow oozy noodles. At one point she became calm, sentimental, said that all she wanted from Pirate was a baby and that if he gave her a baby she would let him go. Tears welled up in her as she grabbed her satin purse and said she had to find him, that once she found him everything would be all right, they would go to the Connaught, she would take her temperature all through the night so that she would know the best minute to conceive, she would get that baby, squeeze it out of him drop by drop. But even as she looked in her handbag to see if she had the thermometer and as she proceeded to borrow money she was muttering obscene and mostly incoherent libels, to console herself. She went so far as to tell everybody that he had fucked Daddy before he had fucked her. He had done it in the grotto and she had come on them, with their pants down.

Next morning, apart from beholding the photographs of radiant Portia and startled Pirate, we learned that Pirate had done a bunk, had in fact gone to the airport straightaway and had taken a plane to Amsterdam, where no doubt he joined up with friends, including the one who had trepanned himself. Pirate had fled. Portia sat in the child's swing out in the garden, calling him and his mother every name under the sun, swearing how she would screw him for money, every last penny, how she would sell her story to the newspapers and expose the family, who got their filthy lucre from slave labor in the West Indies. There was nothing she would not tell, what happened both between the sheets and in the back rows of the cinema, which was the only place he could get it up.

Within weeks Portia had reentered the fray, back to the various haunts, making little jokes about herself and Pirate being so scatty they had gone on the spur of the moment to the Registry Office, having been on their way to market to buy flowers. The marriage had been a dare and it would have been absolutely ghastly if Pirate had not done the nice thing and hooked it. She talked in mock horror of having to meet her mother-in-law, another Portia as it turned out, and spend freezing nights down in Cornwall with ghastly sherry and dinner like school dinners and those awful stone hot-water jars. People believed her. Not long after, she met Martin, a "country bumpkin" who had come with racing friends to London. She was sitting on the bar stool stringing pearls—Daddy's guilt gift, as she said—fat creamy pearls with a few fat emeralds, and occasionally holding it up for everyone to admire, as if it were a daisy chain. She liked the look of Martin, weathered from all that hunting and hacking in Wiltshire, and she said in her sweet little girl voice, "You can buy me a drink if you like." He bought her champagne, which she drank lots and lots of, then tottered off to the lavatory, put her nail-varnished finger down her throat, and made herself sick, a thing she was adept at doing. Afterward Martin and herself went to the tap room and later on she appeared stark naked except for the pearls and said, "Darlings, I've just got engaged to a very very naughty man." Soon as her divorce from Pirate came through, Portia and Martin were married. It was a splendid wedding, with ten little bridesmaids, orange and myrtle posies, an organist from Hamburg, whom Daddy the sweetie-pie knew, a big reception, and her dotty mother wandering around asking if the caterers would sell her the tablecloths and the baskets of flowers at cost price. In every paper the next day Portia was kissing Martin or about to kiss Martin and announcing to the world that she wanted to start a family straightaway and she would like at least six children but possibly seven. She put all her heart into country life; she wore wellingtons and long sweaters, she rode, she farmed, she gave dinner parties, she awaited her first child, which never came.

Some few years later I heard from Allegra that Martin had been having a fling with a Polish au pair and that Portia had had her deported to Poland and that she and Martin had gone to Barbados to patch things up, which they seemed to do, except that the cow got out of Poland again and Martin began to see her. During or after that time I had seen her once in Kings Road walking a hound, her hair quite askew and her stockings hanging. But by then I was caught up in a maelstrom of my own, indecisive, berserk, and about to lose the custody of my children; I had left home and, according to the tenets, had abandoned them. I had been too frightened to go across and say hello, and anyhow we had lost touch.

Something about the girl Charlotte reminded me of Portia, the haughtiness, the toss of the hair, a jut to her chin, all these being relics of a much more formidable and dazzling creature.

Portia, Charlotte, or whoever she was, had made her territorial rights very plain. The washbasin was full of white things put to soak, and the shower trough had colored things, with bright blue detergent sprinkled over them, beading, like the sugar coating on licorice sweets. I felt threatened. Instead of going back up the stairs and through the kitchen to confront her, I went out by the potting-shed door, along the garden, then through the sitting room and up the second stairs to my bedroom. I tried locking my double doors. Though at first they seemed to lock, the doors themselves began to glide apart, and it was as if an unseen hand were making the metal catch slacken and loose its spring. Slowly it opened. I would have to put suitcases to it at night, I would have to barricade myself in. I waited for her to go but instead I heard her footsteps in the garden outside and soon sprinklers of water sent gauze jets over shrub and tree as she herself knelt by a flower bed, assiduously weeding.

The sun was shining, making dazzling mirrors on the surface of the leaves, and the birds were at their most exultant. Seeing how wholesome it all was, I thought it silly of me and decided that she was just an eccentric woman who resented a newcomer. I would make friends with her. I would pretend that nothing amiss had happened. I went down, made some tea, drank it by the open window, placed my cup and saucer a little apart from hers, and then went back to my room. I could not sleep, even though I had not been to bed. At times I would hear the rumble of an airplane and at other times the sound of the birds, not a chorus, just the occasional single note, then the whoosh of the water sprinklers as they spun around. I stared at what I had written in my journal, reading it like someone in the aftermath of anesthetic.

"Mother. When I last saw her alive she was indisposed. I was with a fancy man, young, had his own reliquiae of despair, but to her he was a fancy man. A touch of the Jesus to him, long hair, licentiously ringleting, pale face that implies: 'You have pierced my hands and feet, you have numbered all my bones.' She was in agony, her body and her scalp crusted with shingles. All the ire, all the fret, and all the longing had culminated in this, this harvest of purplish scabs. She would wait for us, myself and the fancy man, to come back from our little drives, our little jaunts, and put a good face on things and thank me profusely for the presents. I would bring things that smelled nice, eau de cologne or perfume sachets, or scented paper to line the dismally cluttered drawers: ploys to take the whiff of death away. I bought her a little cooker, a Baby Belling. Choice name. I propped it on the bamboo table and she sat up, all the while moaning and groaning. Yes, the nurse had been, she had been washed so they ought to be quiet for a bit, the demons, they were like lice, only of the substance of scabs, big as threepenny bits . . . have a look at them.

"She thrilled to the little gift because it would now mean she could reach out and boil an egg saucepan to make a cup of tea, without waiting, without having to wait for someone to come to her, to tend to her. Unspoken eons of wretchedness and neglect lurked in the matrix of those words, but they were not emphasized, not then, in the flush of gladness. What was emphasized was the joy in the new purchase, how ingenious, how adaptable, how simple; and look, it could be carried under the arm, like a little infant.

" 'A Baby Belling,' she said, and let out a range of sighs that reached far back to her youth and earlier. What unfinished cravings calcify in us.

" 'You're not going to die,' I said. I was leaving next day. I said it two, three times and she believed it because she had to . . ."

4

Charlotte was in the kitchen at lunchtime, making one of her shakes with yogurt, wheat germ, orange juice, and God knows what else. She was quite affable, asked if I found it too hot and if I realized that there was a portable fan in my room. We discussed the weather, the tourists, and so forth. She said that I came exactly at the right time. August was the worst, with people eating and littering the main street. Buoyed up somewhat by this conversation, I decided to venture it.

"You're not any relation of Portia Whitehead's—are you?"

She looked at me coldly and without the slightest show of comprehension, but behind her eyes I saw startle, terror, which in no way I could counter.

"Whitehead," she said as if it were the name of a prize herd or some porcelain, and then she put the liquidizer on full blast so that the liquid bubbled out, and the cat, perched on the windowsill, leapt across to lick it. She hit the cat roughly as if to hit me.

To undo my blunder, I said fairly casually, "She was a debutante . . . I lost touch with her."

"I didn't think they went in for that anymore," she said.

"Not anymore," I said.

"I simply despise that world; it's old-hat," she said, and I could feel the loathing as she sawed on some brown bread that had raisins in it. I knew now that it was Portia and that she knew I knew, and I determined to do everything to rid myself of the secret. The thing was to make light of it and to pretend that I was in some muddle of my own making. She kept moving things, picking them up and plonking them down, simply to give vent to her anger.

"You must think me daft to have mistaken you for someone else," I said.

"It's this place," she said. "Everyone goes a bit loopy."

Then I carried my cup of tea, and went out humming, to give the semblance of goodwill. I would have to leave of course, but the question was whether I should leave at once, abandoning my luggage, or whether I should drag it with me. I had this fear of her, this fear that she would do some harm either to me or to my belongings. I suppose I felt she was a little mad, her isolation had driven her mad, as indeed I feared it would me, if I persisted in it.

Soon after, she went out and called up to say goodbye. I leaned out of the window and watched her go down the track, carrying a rush basket with very long handles, which she trailed behind her. Her hair was like egg yolk in the sun and there was a quickness to her stride. I waited until she was out of sight, and a few moments longer, then reckoning that she would be down on the road, walking past the reservoir, where the frogs croaked and the green weed pulsed, I decided to take a look.

Her room was locked, but as with the lock in my own room, it was slack and all I had to do was exert a bit of pressure for the double doors to sunder. The room was full of her clutter, the cardboard boxes with garments spilling out of them, gray-white stockings filled with things, an Andalusian shawl, tapes of music, and a few paperback books, all with death or murder in the title.

Her bed was low and covered with a sumptuous Eastern hanging with saffron fringing. Above, there was an antique sword in a worn velvet sheath. On the low chest a man's morning hat covered a bowl and I lifted it, thinking maybe that it was more bean sprouts, but no, there, among the combs and sundry pieces of jewelry, was the famous necklace, the fat cream-and-green beads that she had strung together long ago and had flaunted the night she met Martin. I could still see her naked, her waist like a belly dancer's, the pearls reaching almost to her navel. I felt my whole body turn to ice as the past in all its pain, bungle, and aspiration flashed before me—hers, mine, everybody's. I saw our lives like specters, or those pieces of paper that the young girls had burned and sent whirling to the ceiling. They would all be back in Cologne now and I wished that I had braved it and gone with them. It hurt, with a raw hurt, to recall our gadfly days, and yet I did, our days, nights, beaded jackets, shawls, nightclubs where we sat till three and four in the morning and sometimes had our hands read or were given bunches of roses or heather that the gypsies sold; those days when every new love affair brought us, as we thought, to the brink of a sustained happiness. I thought of the day I too had gone a bit mad, slipped from behind this girl with all these hopes to the woman who would count in morsels from that moment onward the pleasures and excitements of her life. I was going away with a man, a doctor. It did not matter how long I was going away for, the thing was, we were going to a secret rendezvous and at the end of it our fates and our futures would be bound together. It happened to be the day of the school fete. I had gone early and saw my children flushed and merry, entering for this race and that, and had arranged for them to be with a friend overnight. I was in my own house waiting for him, sitting down, dressed for travel, well aware of the afternoon passing, but in no way doubting and still possessed of hope as it grew dark and the shrubs outside the window became blurs and the clock chimed hours that were not daylight hours. He was a doctor; he had had an emergency call, a series of calls, a birth maybe; a home delivery; but he would come, otherwise he would have telephoned; his not telephoning meant he was coming; that was for sure.

When my children came back the next day with the au-pair girl, who had also returned from her own little tryst, I noticed the strange look on their faces, the shock, as they saw me there sitting in the chair dressed to go out as I was dressed the day before.

"Is Mama sad?" one child said, without quite knowing what it meant.

"Bitch . . . snake," Portia said as she burst into the room and saw me standing there holding the necklace. She had guessed my intention. She had deceived me into thinking that she had left for the day, when in fact she had doubled back, come up by one of the more hidden terraces, and crept in, unbeknownst to me.

Her eyes were so violent the sockets seemed to be filled with blood. They were no longer the pale blue eyes of a woman, but those of a bull. As she crossed I imagined she was going to strike me. She picked up the scissors, and snapped them open, and then started to cut the necklace. She cut viciously, making quick, hateful jabs, so that the beads with their snouts of white thread went falling all over the floor, the fat cream beads like rosebuds and the green like artificial grapes.

"Oh, Portia . . ." I said.

"I am not Portia . . . mutt," she said as she went on cutting, then she laughed bitterly as she thought how Daddy got his comeuppance at last, his adored boyfriend had hopped it, ripped him of his Fabergé eggs, and now he was in a wheelchair with no one, only his virago Austrian cook, whom he might have to marry in order to keep her. "Come home, Portia, come home and look after me" was his monthly plea. It was terrible to see the bile and the poison pour out of her and equally terrible that I had unleashed it. She crossed the room then, treading on the beads, indifferent to the way they swirled in all directions.

"I won't stay," I said.

"Do anything you like," she said, and she went into a little inner room that adjoined the main room. She slammed the door.

I began to pick up the beads and put them back in the china bowl, all the while rehearsing something to say, something that would make amends. Through the door I could hear her being sick. I went to it and made a last plea. I said could we talk for a few minutes and then I would go. By the way she retched and then the way she forced herself to retch, I knew that she was telling me to get out.

In my room I threw books, sweaters, shoes, everything, pell-mell into the several bags. I feared that she would come and lynch me. I flung the bags out the window, where they made an ungainly thud on the terrace beneath, and then crept down the stairs, conscious of every almighty creak. As I left, the cat stroked and nuzzled my leg as if saying, "Don't go, this is a lonely enough house already," but I left without even turning around, wielding my bags with the prodigal strength that panic produces.

5

In the hotel on the hill I was lucky enough to encounter the waiter who had brought us the log of wood covered in moss. He smiled when he saw me, he had something for me. From behind the reception desk he took a pot of the terra-cotta makeup and several little soft pink buds to apply it with. They had left them for me. He laughed as if he knew some wicked secret of mine, while the receptionist reeled off the prices of the rooms that were vacant. I decided on a small room which, as she said, was really an annex for people with small children.

"How long do you intend to stay?" she asked.

"I don't know," I said, and she looked at me with a certain suspicion.

I shook as I entered the dark room. The shutters were closed, the light came through a narrow slit in fretful shivers. I sat on the white crochet-covered bed and opened one of my bags to take out a toilette bag which I had bought in New York. Even in the dark I could see the ridiculous garish patterns of it. Yes,

I did have them, a bottle of sleeping capsules that I had carried for so long, just in case. It seemed unbelievably absurd that these capsules made in some factory in Switzerland, the grains carefully poured into one half of the capsule, then sealed with the other half, had the potency to permit me to take my life. A mad thought came to me of how they refuse suicides a Christian burial and I felt disappointed that I would not be allowed in the little graveyard behind the church, which I liked so much. Many clashing thoughts came to me, including the memory of my parents who were dead and the terror that I might meet them. I saw my mother's face as she lay inside the lined coffin, smothered somewhat ridiculously by those folds of white satin, like half-beaten egg whites, an unfinished quarrel on her face, a quarrel over her own acres, with one of her own, acres she had striven for. I had felt no pity for her then, or to be precise no surge of pity, the surge that seeps and flows through one and alters one forevermore. My dead father by comparison was serene, with a rose that a nun had put in the crook between thumb and forefinger, a red rose, his waxen skin like singed rice paper, but unangry, all anger gone. Last time I saw him alive I had brought a friend, another woman. "Don't leave me alone with him," I begged of her, because that was what he most wanted, to be alone with me, to say something, anything—a curse, a harangue, a plea. When the time came to leave him he conveyed us through corridor after corridor of this gaunt nursing home, talking to me, trying to shut her out, and in the end, admitting to failure, he led us into a large room, a concert room where they put on the Christmas show, where he had, as he said, astonished all by singing "Danny Boy" in tremolo, and all of a sudden in the empty room he sat in the one chair that was left there by mistake, put his head in his hands, scratched his scalp, and cried out, "I was never meant to be left in a place like this . . . I was never meant to be left in a place like this . . . like this."

If there was an afterworld I would meet them, them and a little sister who had died before me and who I believed had left a lining of sorrow in my mother's womb, which I felt to be my natural habitat. I was not afraid of her, this little sister, perhaps because I did not know her or because she was so young. The pills I laid out on the bed, and then put my hand over each one, to count and recount them. They were like a necklace in themselves, turquoise and scarlet.

Suddenly there was a knock on my door. I thought for one startled minute that it was Portia. It was a young girl carrying a great bowl of flowers. I saw her in the light, because as soon as she entered she turned on the switch, so as not to frighten me. Her hair was thick and shiny, her skin very dark like the skin of an aubergine. She crossed the room and laid the flowers on a little bureau and then she turned and smiled. The flowers seemed like a tree, branching, growing, extending, to fill my mind with something other than death. They were white flowers on green foliage, and the pistils were of spun yellow.

"My name is Catalina," she said.

"Catalina," I said, as if I should know. She would be on the landing outside if I should need her.

"On the landing," I said, guessing her concern.

Oh, yes. She had sewing to do. Visitors destroyed the linen, especially the French, they made ribbons of the sheets. Her English was very clear and precise.

I could not do it, not then, she had by her sudden arrival hauled me back. In the wardrobe I found a big quilt and lay down on the bed, pulling it around me, half thinking that I might sleep forever.

I dreamed of rings. An entire room covered from floor to ceiling with them—throbbing, darting, as if they were lizards; had pulse, had life. Each wall arrayed with gold, silver, platinum; rings such as never existed in any jeweler's window. There were stones too, stones from the seashore and stones with purple seepage in them, others with the glisten of mineral, and still others vaporous, like dew. Some were as big and as smooth as birds' eggs, speckled eggs, and others were tiny and fiery, like sparks. I wanted to touch them, lick them. Likewise the floor was strewn. It sagged and rose and resagged and rerose, imparting a sense of wonder and sway, beauty and risk. In the dream I am obliged to pick my favorite ring, and though tempted by many, by such luster, by such gleam and gleamings, I pick a gray-green stone with half its color drained, a forgotten stone such as might be dredged from the bottom of the sea or the bowels of the earth and left to molder, and as I picked it I thought, even within the dream, that it was a precursor of things to come.

6

Very early next morning young boys were hosing the walls, the several sets of steps, the flower beds, and the big terra-cotta pots that were spilling over with geraniums, bright as grenadine. Those on night duty loped away, with sleep in their eyes, nodding to those who were coming on duty for the day. Soon there was a smell of warm confectionery and coffee from the kitchen, and not long after, these young boys went up the several stone staircases with huge basket trays on which there was coffee, croissants, and a type of bun plaited on top and doubly tempting because of being dusted with fine white sugar. Flower smells, pollen smells, shrub smells, and now food smells made me feel again a nameless thrill as in childhood, a giddiness at the onset of things.

Red and white blossoms spattered the steps, and up by the pool a slight breeze was stirring the cream silk fringing of the white umbrellas. Everything was being prepared for the day, mattresses put on the sun beds, piles of fawn towels laid on a table, coffee percolating, and cakes of every variety being put into refrigerated trays. A sleepy-looking young man squeezed oranges on a metal machine and the halves piled one on top of the other began to resemble Halloween lanterns. Beyond were the orange and lemon orchards, the oranges in clusters, cleaving together, meshed; the lemons with a greater poise, each lemon hanging separately on its stem, and in the air showers of floating blossom, like gauze. A rosemary hedge seemed by its darkness to be resisting the sun and yet webbed by it as if by a glistening cobweb.

The town itself was coming awake, too. A shutter opening here or there, and being fastened back. The cats had already appointed themselves on the tiled roofs. I asked the sleepy-looking waiter if I needed to book a sun bed. He looked perplexed, then shrugged, then said, "If you want, I do." I waited and after some time he walked across, picked up one of the fallen lemons, and placed it on a chair, a guarantee of my reservation. It was time for breakfast and so I made my way back to the main buildings.

She was by a long refectory table arranging flowers. I recognized her as the girl who had come to my room the evening before. Her hair was plaited, a prerogative of work, perhaps; and she had placed the plait over one side of her neck, so that when she moved, it bobbed like a thong. There was something untamed about her, a sort of recklessness as she hauled flowers from a barrow and threw them a distance away, onto the table, as casually as if she were flinging wet fish. She must have felt my presence, because suddenly she turned around and fastened me with a look that was half courteous and half brazen. Then she recognized me and asked if I felt better. Other girls were passing through the courtyard with mops and brooms and buckets, and like her they wore turquoise tracksuits.

Suddenly her name was called from one of the balconies up above. "Catalina . . . Catalina," a young girl said, as she leaned over a balcony, holding bits of raw meat that she winced at.

"Crazy people," Catalina said, and smiled as she tore up the short flight of stairs to confer with her companion.

The flowers, strewn about the table, looked as if they had landed there in some primordial storm. There were roses, red, pink, and white; sweet peas like wet jewels; anemones with black startling centers; and flutes of lilies, pale, waxen, saintly. They all smelled of water, as obviously they had been sprinkled at the market. There was something infinitely sweet and harmless about them and I thought how could anyone not want to remain alive in a world where such tender things exist.

On the balcony she was laughing and frightening her friend by dangling the bits of meat. Later when she came down she described the couple who occupied that suite. The man was portly. She stuck her chest out to indicate his paunch. The girl was thin and blond and slept most of the day. The girl loved cats and at night when they went to the grand restaurants the girl brought home strips of raw meat. They ate very grandly, lobsters which had to be specially ordered, and they drank magnums of champagne. She said it must be nice to be a visitor, but she was not bitter about it, there was an impish gaiety to her as she described their salon, which was full of saucers with bits of old meat and bits of old fish for the various stray cats. Luckily for everyone, they had gone on a tour that day, and the maid was instructed to do a big cleaning.

I ate breakfast on the terrace. I ate ravenously, piled different types of jam onto slivers of bread, enjoyed flavors that I had long since forsaken. It was as if the jams and the honey and the sugared bread preempted a life I was about to start on, instead of one that was more than half over. People sat at other tables or merely stood and looked across the orchards to the town and to the church. At the table next to me there was a German couple, a man and a woman wearing identical seersucker shorts and laced leather shoes. As soon as he finished eating, the man lit a little thin cigar which he did not draw on, he just held it there, his lower lip jutting out to secure it. The woman went on eating with a steady joyless rhythm as he delivered a monologue, which I was glad not to understand.

The mountain was a soft gold, as if gold leaf had been painted over it, and the trees were silken, too, and like feathers. Papers were brought and passed around, waiters and waitresses went back and forth, and the cats, who looked a bit like rats, scurried under the tables to be given the pickings.

Once, I saw her pass with a vase of lilies so tall that her face was overwhelmed by it. She moved them to one side as she might a Chinese mask, and gave out of the corner of her eye a little wink which bordered upon connivance, as if she pitied me somewhat for being among such dull folk. Her eyes were dark like damsons. I had this trickle of happiness, thinking to myself that I knew someone, even as slightly as this, and that at any moment I could stop by her table and admire the flowers. I even thought I would buy a special little notebook to learn a few words, from her, in Spanish.

The hotel guests had appointed themselves around the pool. Some were deep in conversation, others settling and resettling themselves, moving their chairs to get the best of the sun, still others already lying out, prone mahogany figures drinking in the sun's rays. A little boy with red-and-blue water wings was at the shallow end by the steps, calling for his sister, who called back to him in German. His name was Otto. No sooner had she lifted him out than he got in again and was beseeching her to rescue him. The Germans and the English had divided the terrain, the English commandeering the side nearest the bar, while the Germans sat at the far end, near the line of poplar trees.

My own bespoke seat with the silly little lemon was midway and next to a veranda, so that I could pull my chair in under the matted roof if it got too hot, or if the shade from the umbrella was not enough. The people stretched out on the fawn towels were oblivious of each other and of everything except the sun. I passed these nameless creatures, identifiable only as one with beauty spots, another with a mat of hair under the armpits, a hip that curved so gracefully it was like the handle of a salt spoon. On one woman's stomach, birthmarks had formed little blue veins, inroads. Next to her a very thin older Englishwoman was telling a young man, a newcomer, about an evening coat she had at home, an evening coat with silk revers, and how she should have *brought* it, cut a dash. She was prompted to say this because at that moment a woman in a violet coat with a thick lace collar arrived and looked about imperiously. Two waiters helped her with her towels and her various baskets. From one of the baskets jutted the dun canvas backing of a piece of needlepoint. She wore bracelets which tinkled as she pointed in one direction, then another, unable to decide where she would like to sit and obviously irked that so many vantage positions were already taken. The thin Englishwoman shrugged, and said to the young man, "All right for some, isn't it"; and they both watched as the newcomer went down toward the far end, where the Germans lazed. Meanwhile, little Otto kept his sister busy by jumping in and then having to be lifted out. The Englishwoman went on with a story to the young man about her daughter, how they did not really need another child and how, let's face it, two children were enough; and how it made her sick to see how many children some couples had, but that her daughter was a good girl, stubborn mind you, but good, would listen to sense in the end and not have a third child. The daughter was obviously the woman with birthmarks, because every so often she called to her mother, "Oh, do shut up."

"Men! Men!" the mother said peevishly, as if the young man she spoke to was a pigmy.

A little boy of nine or ten slipped by, carrying a toy cruiser and trailing a dog. I could see that the dog was going to be a nuisance. He found a single mat that was not next to anyone, away from the pool, one that had obviously been left there by some absentminded waiter when he was called away.

The fashionable woman was invisible, having withdrawn under two umbrellas and spread her baskets and paraphernalia around her. Suddenly the calm and composure of the place was disturbed by a rude English voice.

A proud father was addressing his little boy as he lifted him up and carried him toward the pool.

"Now say one, two, three, go," he said to the little baby, who whinged and refused to say it.

"O.K., let me hear it again—one, two, three, go."

"Daddy and Baby Michael go toward the pool," he says as he goes down the metal steps, holding the irate baby.

"Cold . . . is the water cold?" he asks loudly.

"Look at the thermometer," a woman's voice says, sharply. It is the imperious woman under the two umbrellas and her voice sizzles with disdain and authority. People laugh. The elderly

Englishwoman laughs so much that she has to take the cigarette from her lips to cough.

The baby screams, but its father is undaunted.

"Kick, kick, kick," the father says, while the baby cries and exclaims that the water is too cold. Little Otto deserts his perch on the ladder and runs about with his red-and-blue bands, waving his arms like a butterfly.

"The water's not cold . . . Daddy doesn't feel it cold . . . warm . . . warm water."

Proud now and masterful since they are the only two people in the pool, the father inveigles the baby to kick.

"Daddy says Baby Michael has got to kick." Baby Michael refuses, says he does not want to, causes such a furor that the dog who had been sleeping or dozing quietly under the boy's chair jumps up and starts to bark furiously. People on all sides declare that things are getting out of hand. The haughty woman is sitting up and in disbelief asking if she is in Blackpool, or Benidorm.

"Take him out," Baby Michael's mother calls.

"Not yet, Mummy. Baby Michael has got to do three kicks . . . like this: one, two, three . . . And then Mummy is going to order him a hot chocolate."

"Or the municipal baths in Tokyo," exclaims the haughty woman.

"Better bring him out, darling," the mother pleads.

"Daddy's going to bring you out and Mummy's going to wrap you up in a towel and order you a hot chocolate," the father says as he hands the baby to its mother, and then, not to be intimidated, he dives into the pool, splashing furiously and churning his way to the opposite end, much to the irritation of people already discomfited. The German couple whom I had seen at breakfast order their first snipe of champagne and others jolted out of their languours are asking for tea, coffee, orange juice, Campari, while the waiters move with the utmost servility, ignoring the barbs that are being exchanged.

The imperious woman in the violet coat is suddenly standing over me and asking me if I find it as Bolshie as she does. She asks, she says, because when passing she could not fail to notice the book on my table. It is the final volume of *Remembrance of Things Past*. Her voice is soft and in addressing me it is as if she is helpless.

"Oh, very déclassé," she says. Her eyelids are covered with silver shadow and her hair, which is also silverish, is strewn with little diamanté things which glitter like dew. A woodland creature. Although no longer young, she is extremely slender, and to emphasize her slenderness or perhaps to give vent to her temper she keeps tightening a snake belt which she is wearing around her waist. She asks if I would mind terribly if she were to take the empty chair next to me. Meanwhile, she flicks her finger and wags the braceleted arm to alert the waiter to the fact that she needs her baskets and her belongings moved. Then she orders a citron pressé, in three languages, Spanish, English, and French, stressing the fact that she does not want sugar. She introduces herself formally but I catch only her first name, which is Iris. As she lies back beneath the umbrella she starts to chuckle, murmuring under her breath, "Their awful bellies, their hideous bikinis, their bags with trade names plastered all over them, and as for Baby Michael, he should be put in the deep freeze."

"Who is that child with braces on his teeth and all that sticking plaster who is allowed to bring a mongrel in?" she asks the waiter as she taps her long, pearled nails on the lid of her lacquered box. He chooses not to understand and within his hearing she calls him a burro, a donkey. She asks me a ream of questions about myself but never once waits or even pretends to wait for an answer to any of them. I am her new friend and she is going to give me lots of tips, the phone numbers of the best restaurants in Rome, Venice, and Paris, secrets. For instance, if in Paris I wanted a late lunch, à deux, and felt like caviar she knew exactly where I should go. The patron, who was of course Russian, Georgian in fact, made these divine blinis and did not use grade A, or even grade B, but still a delicious caviar which tasted just as good. She would write out these addresses for me and by offering to do this she hoped that I realized we were chums.

"When in Rome, do as . . ." she said coquettishly and reeled off her plans for the months ahead . . . Biarritz in August . . . Milano in September . . . New York in the late fall . . . Paris when she felt absolutely homesick or wanted her hair done, although to be fair the chap in Rome was better at cutting, far better . . . a sculptor, absolute master, could make any head of hair a work of "art," knew exactly how it should look. She shook her hair as if on a swivel. It was thick hair and it had been dyed a beautiful ashen silver. The little diamanté ornaments looked like petals now that had fallen from the trees. Suddenly she was laughing, saying how nice to make a friend, that it was Proust who did it, always Proust, and then to her great and astonished delight she was called to the telephone. It was the sleepy waiter who called her and at first she did not know whether it was for me or her. Realizing it was for her, she jumped up and ran like a gazelle, past the other mats, apologizing sweetly, then past the tables, to the phone, which was behind the counter. I had stood up along with her because a habit, or rush of hope, had made me believe the impossible, which is that it was for me, that the man whom I had repudiated, yet hoped for, had traced me. She had her back to us but by the movement of her shoulders I could see her excitement and I guessed that it was a beau and my disappointment sharpened all the more as I slunk in under my umbrella, to give way to a surge of tears.

Sitting there in the sun, bunched up, fetus-wise, I thought that I had thought the worst was over. The worst were the years, the eternity of years that I had solemnly waited for him, believed in his coming, and then put a death to it on the day when I decided to destroy his letters, choosing to drown them, rather than burn them in my grate at home. I had gone to Hyde Park, to the Serpentine, full of false hope, as if by doing this I would exorcise him, believing that the pain would buckle into rage. They were innocuous letters, quite harmless really, but because they had come from him, each word, each gray-black letter was significant, conveying more than words could convey.

It was a wet day, the wet chestnuts in flower were like tassels without any tautness or any spring. The rain may have had something to do with it, the incessant rain and the several canoodling couples, but I broke down at the moment of doing it. I tore the letters in small pieces and dropped them on the water, where they seemed like shreds of colorless confetti. They lay there, tiny scraps and not so tiny, the innuendos and the non-innuendos, words from which I had derived so much hope, so much doubt, so much ecstasy, each letter a little square, like a child's tooth, handwriting portraying the oscillations of his mind that tried to cancel what it was saying and to affirm what it had just denied.

"A drink, maybe Wednesday, if deliverance permits." In that promise or semipromise I had read so much else, his wish to see me, which of course he had to counter with doubt, but I knew that he would do everything to see me because his very doubt was his confirmation and those syllables, those characters traced on grayish-headed paper, contained and always would contain his essence, his secretiveness, and were the precursors of our eerie lovemaking. All of a sudden these fragments were sacred and dear to me, sacred as any scroll; were all I had of him. Why was I throwing them away, these transfusions, these utterances, that would have to see me through, to eternity? At least they did not sink and for that I was thankful. They had coagulated. But the words were washed out, or washed into one another, to lose their meaning. The ducks converged on them, mistaking them for crumbs, but did not try to eat them.

Suddenly and as if an unseen hand were skimming them toward me they drifted back in my direction. Something to do with the ripples of water from the ducks' wings, or the plash of the oars from the excitable punters. I took this to be a sign and knelt and reached in and pawed them out, giving the ducks the idea now that perhaps they were bread, or even crackling. I held them, the damp remains that they were. I saw the buildings that I would forever connect with the moment—the beige dome of Harrods, the obelisk of Big Ben, the fawn wings of the Houses of Parliament, a glass restaurant with peaked corners, laburnum, daisies, peonies drained of their color, and the sighs of couples whose happiness was a dagger in itself.

The awful truth was that, though I wanted to throw them away, I did not sufficiently want to throw them away, and retrieving them was a solace in itself. I put the wet and matted pieces back into my pocket, castigating myself, and headed homeward.

Tall gray tower blocks in which window and concrete seemed as one surrounded me. I headed for the Albert Memorial. No reason for this, simply to walk, to get through the next minute and the one after. The grass was high and soaking from weeks of rain, and the daisies were myriad. Each daisy holding on to its little bit of ground just as I was holding on to the damp, discolored, long-since abnegated words. June, half a year gone, half another year. I saw the people as ghosts, laughing ghosts, talking ghosts, kissing ghosts, linked or not linked, sometimes halting, other times moving in the rain and shrouded in it. I thought perhaps that I would never speak to anyone again or shake their hands or that such an event would be so far hence in the unforeseeable future that I would have lost the ability to do it—the hand would wobble maybe, like a prong, certainly would have lost its swivel, its suavity. The lips, too. The lips that kissed a pillow slip or pieces of blotting paper, to keep in practice, would become blubber. All of a sudden there was a downpour, sealing everyone in, in pairs, with dogs or alone, or however they happened to be, and I thought this is what it will be like on the last day, we will be caught in whatever spot we are standing in and under whatever circumstances, and how dearly I wished that it was the last day, lacking as I did the gumption to go on.

There was wet plywood around the base of the Albert Hall, which meant that renovation was in progress, and the cupids and angels at its perimeters were grimed in soot. I thought that by the time I came close to it and touched it something would have changed within me, that the pain would have abated enough for me to say, "I might go to a concert soon," or "I must see my friends again," but close up to it, no such thing had happened, and so I thought it would happen in the next succeeding moments, in the journey from the park to the roadside, where I would press the button for the pedestrian crossing and wait and watch those lines of cars like vicious buffaloes roar up, to beat the red light, doing everything to ignore the forlorn pedestrian; that as I crossed to the other side deliverance—his very word—would come, except that it didn't. I stood to see if Bach or Mozart was soon to be performed, thinking I might buy a ticket, that my interest in life might reburgeon with those sublime and beautiful chords, an interest that would replace this wasting passion for him. I crossed the road. I read the notice regarding future concerts and walked around the circular fort of the Albert Hall, lamenting its too-red brick, and its lumpenness, yet wanting to embrace it, to be absorbed into its vast inhuman depths; then down dozens and dozens of steps, onto another street, where I set myself the same unlikely forfeit, which was that the pain would grow less, or that even if a fraction of it stayed with me it would not, as it had done in the past, immunize me to all other relations, to all other links with life, to friendships and to such innocuous things as Christmas and midsummer and people's birthdays.

My room was in semidarkness and yet I could see the flowers, feel them as if they were breathing. It was a fresh bunch, so beautiful, so immense that I knelt before it as at an altar. Opening the shutters, I saw they were sweet peas—airy, rampant, glorious; she had included every color: red, deep purple, pale purple, pink, and white. They were in such profusion it was as if they had not been plucked from their high, thin, curving stalks but had grown like that, in a shoal, a wayward profusion. She had added sprigs of myrtle, its pungent smell an echo of the forest, in contrast to the soft airy smell of the flowers.

I hurried out of the room to thank her, buoyed now with some purpose. She was not to be seen. The flowers were piled one on top of the other, great breathing bunches, waiting for her, for her hands to pick them up and separate them, to take the roses and pull them gently apart, the red, and the white, and the yellow roses, and to take the remainder of the sweet peas, which would be bruised if they were left to lie there too long; to put the tall, chaste, waxen lilies into tall, chaste jars. I stood and thought that any moment she would appear. Then, not wanting to draw attention to myself, I moved away, hiding behind some trees, resting my chin on a bit of railing, thinking that if she did come, I would not know what to say, I would revert to that childhood vertigo, that overwhelming of mind and senses, as when one saw the object of one's desire one was lost for words, or said something stupid, something blundering, even something sarcastic. I went in search of her, up various stairways, and down others, all the while meeting her companions in their turquoise tracksuits, with their brooms and their mops and their cleaning stuff. I saw into a large room, where one of the girls sprayed liquid polish wantonly over everything while her companions bounced up and down on the four-poster bed. It was a vast suite which overlooked the mountain and had antique furniture and tapestries on the wall.

Then I retraced my steps, thinking she had been on one staircase while I was searching on another. I asked one of the maids, a very quiet girl, with a faint mustache. She answered so quickly that I did not understand what she said, and so set off on another target. The young waiter behind the bar looked as if he were being disturbed from a waking slumber. The coffee machine was hissing, the brown powder falling onto filters. Whatever he thought I asked him remained a mystery to me, because he simply said, "If I remember to, I will."

Going back to the reception desk, I saw her suddenly. She was in the laundry room with a group of her companions, putting laundry into big white bags. It was clear that she was the leader because they all looked to her, listened to her, and laughed at the joke she was telling them. As she told the story she gesticulated wildly. They stopped laughing, and as she turned and looked at me I found myself mortified. I rallied and asked her if she knew how many days it took for a letter to reach England.

"Soy inglesa," I said, self-consciously, and the others exploded with laughter. She reprimanded them severely, said it was obvious that they had never traveled. She told me that if the letter went Express, it would take four or five days, but that surface mail would take weeks. She explained that one got stamps in one bodega but posted the letter in another, and apologized for the national erraticness, which extended to her boon companions.

Lunch was almost finished but I found myself walking toward the poolside restaurant and sitting down. Some newcomers had appeared, but they were obviously not guests, from the way the waiter plonked the bottle of mineral water on their table. They were eating paella, the mother and father seizing bits of fish and shellfish, while their little daughter spurned it and was licking from a strawberry-and-chocolate ice-cream cone. At times she would lick it and then put it close to her father's lips to taunt him. He begged her to have some of the paella. She was called Fiona and the little boy was called Ernest. Ernest did not want paella either, being very happy with the strawberries. He had heaped a pyramid onto a plate and was now running his spittled finger over each one to proclaim his rights. Fiona protested, so that he was ordered to put some back. His lips were very thin and his nostrils thinner; he looked like a little weasel as he bent down over the strawberries, touching them with his features. Mother and father addressed each other on the subject of the paella, and then on the subject of their children. To the proud father, Fiona was a water nymph, and to the proud mother, little Ernest had the makings of Hercules. She ate ravenously, and as she chewed, she kept her eyes closed, then opened them, to consign the choicest bits of fish first to her plate and then to her eager lips.

"I don't believe it, Madeleine," her husband said; he said it twice.

"You don't believe what?" she asked.

Her husband expressed his extreme astonishment at the fact that she could eat at all, considering that she had such an upset tummy, had been sick on the boat, queasy all the way in the car ride from the city, vomited twice.

"But this is good for me . . . this is bland," she kept saying, while also telling Fiona to put that ice down. Fiona ignored her and held the cone to her father's lips, but as he was about to lick it she wrested it away.

"For goodness' sake . . . you spoil her, Russell," the wife said, and ordered Fiona to eat the strawberries, for her bleeding gums.

"I don't want strawberries," Fiona said, nettled at her mother's tactlessness.

"Then you can go without," the mother said, and pulled the remaining strawberries to herself.

The huff that might have ruined their lunch and impaired the jollity of the vacation was suddenly and surprisingly dispersed by little Ernest. All strife was put aside, all greed ignored, as little Ernest stood up, huffed and puffed, and said, "Daddy . . . Daddy." Daddy was ready, they were all ready, for whatever it was that little Ernest had to say. It heralded great importance because of the way little Ernest huffed and puffed, then rallied.

"Horses like hay, so, Daddy, I think that if horses had a lot of hay, as much 'hay as this' "—he described a width of it in the air with his outstretched arms—"horses would never quarrel and would be very happy." The family were united again. Russell was so overcome that he stood up and announced to the restaurant at large that his son had a great sense of justice and that the world had much to learn from him.

The waiters looked at one another, puzzled, amused, disbelieving.

In the late afternoon as I dozed on my bed, half aware of the hum of life, the random voices in the courtyard below, the maids on the landing outside, there was a knock on my door, a waiter delivering a letter on a tray. It was an invitation, handwritten on the hotel's embossed ivory card. It said:

Iris Beaugrave-Mallory-Heron
Drinks
6:30–7:15

Hers was the very large suite that I had seen that morning, a suite with a sweeping view of the mountains. She met me at the door, in a long blue crepe-de-chine dress and a necklace that was of single thin threads of silver and which lay across her bare throat like catgut. The lamps were lit and there were flowers on the several tables but I was the only guest. She said she had to see me, because I had been such fun, had saved her from the Blackpool Bolshies. She was leaving the following day for her finca, there had been some mix-up about dates, but she simply had to give me a drink and she hoped I liked beer because it was simply the only thing she drank nowadays. Wine, she declared, could no longer be trusted, since it made one so liverish, and she asked in a taunting voice what had happened to Montrachet, to Meursault, even to Chablis, that little upstart, known only because the English and the Americans could get their thick tongues around it, not even good enough for a vinaigrette. Then she laughed at her own asperity and led me across to a table on which there was a silver dish with thin biscuits, cat's-tongues coated in sugar.

"Parfait," she said, tasting one, and derided the local olives as being shriveled, bitter, and boring as their peasants. Why she came, she simply could not understand, particularly as she had read that their bulls were second-rate and their men third-rate. Still, she had her finca and "a friend" was coming from South America and she envisaged a very nice time, thank you very much. Her friend was wonderful, met him by the merest chance, their luggage had got mixed up in Munich and after the initial frisson he asked her to dinner. Roman Catholic of course, and with a very tiresome Catholic wife and a little boy, but they were doing something about that, and life, yes, definitely, life was on an uptrend. She did a little swirl and then told me where to sit and sat opposite me, running her hands through the silver threads of her necklace. She said she had thought of the most wonderful thing for us to do; to make the most of the three-quarters of an hour, she had set an agenda. We would each think, but really think, of the most beautiful building we had ever seen, that we yearned to return to, preferably with a lover. In the dim and artful light of the room she looked far younger; a night creature, startled, like the bark of the pale ash tree, her blue dress so sheer it seemed to melt into her limbs.

She smiled, anticipating my answer. She even conjectured on what it might be—the Taj Mahal maybe, or Campidoglio, or one of those wonderful skyscrapers on Park Avenue, or the Russian Hermitage, or maybe an Indonesian temple. She simply ached to know. I said that, at that moment, the place that sprang to my mind was a cemetery at San Cataldo, which, although a charnel house, had the look of a theater with its curved, coral front and bow windows like peepholes into magic.

"How interesting!" she said, but I knew that she was appalled. A charnel house!

"How interesting—how interesting," she said, allowing a slight flinch to appear around the eyes. Yes, she knew it, of course; so charming, so humble. It was the word "humble" that showed her distaste. Her favorite was a tomb which had recently been excavated in China. The First Emperor had had it made for himself, countless maidens had been sacrificed with him and masons buried alive. Inside this menagerie were terra-cotta warriors, bronze horses, chariots; the common soldiers in battle tunics, legs in puttees, and the high-ranking officers in fish-scale cuirasses. Gave you some idea of what China was, in all its grandeur, while Europe was still a pebble pond. China was her favorite country, she loved the scale, the scope, of course not modern China with its little ant heaps of people spouting slogans.

The jeweled clock on the mantelpiece tinkled a dulcet tune giving the hour and she looked toward it with a seeming haziness, but within she had registered it correctly. Time to go. Calls to be made. Then her beauty sleep, which was quintessential. She kissed me profusely, saying it had been such fun, God what fun it had been, and who knows, she might even persuade me to come over to the finca. She would send her beau sailing one day so that we could have a gossipy lunch, and catch up.

7

In the less crowded bar, where I looked, half in hope of seeing Catalina, I heard my name called as D'Arcy assailed me with a bellicose welcome.

"Enter . . . enter . . . Druidess," he said, and before I could retreat he had spun me around to introduce me to his bosom friend, Gunnar, a Swede from darkest Malmö.

D'Arcy's face was flushed, wandering patches of vivid red as if cochineal had been poured on it, and he wore a white fringed dress scarf over his navy overalls, which gave him a jaunty look. Since early morning he and the Swede had been drinking and sounding, as he said, the depths of their pitiful souls. Despite the language barrier and relying often on the true Esperanto, they had covered many topics, ranging from the trace elements in mother's milk to *The Descent of the Locusts*. His spirits soared as he recited gleefully and fulsomely from that brimstone buddy Cardinal John Henry Newman (1801–1890):

"Brood follows brood, with a sort of lively likeness, yet with distinct attributes, as we read in the prophets of the Old Testament, from which Bochart tells us it is possible to enumerate as many as ten kinds. It wakens into existence and activity as early as the month of March; but instances are not wanting, as in our present history, of its appearance as late as June. Even one flight comprises myriads upon myriads passing imagination, to which the drops of rain or the sands of the sea are the only fit comparison; and hence it is almost a proverbial mode of expression in the East (as may be illustrated by the sacred pages to which we just now referred), by way of describing a vast invading army, to liken it to the locusts. So dense are they, when upon the wing, that it is no exaggeration to say that they hide the sun, from which circumstance, indeed, their name in Arabic is derived. And so ubiquitous are they when they have alighted on the earth, that they simply cover or clothe its surface."

"Cat's pajamas," the Swede said in a drunken blur and D'Arcy insisted that he tell again the story of the geese for my benefit. With mime and patchy words the Swede described how a flock of geese broke into a grainery where corn had been put to ferment, and how they devoured the fermenting stuff, glutting themselves on it, until they fell down dead. Their distraught owners decided to pluck them with the intention of selling them, even though Christmas was months away, but no sooner had they plucked them than the creatures revived, staggered up, and wobbled around the farmyard, shivering, stripped of their feathers, cackling and croaking, and in goosepimpled ignominy had to survive until the Christmas slaughter.

"Excuse me . . . my English no good," the Swede said apologetically.

"The best way to learn English is the mnemonic method," D'Arcy said, and spouted spoonerisms into his bewildered sweating face. They were drinking wine and local cognac and every few minutes the Swede would laugh and then give way to a bout of tears, which, as D'Arcy said, was bound to befall anyone who lived in the dark for eleven months a year and was suddenly exposed to decent sunlight. The Swede owned a sawmill, employed hundreds of people, but lamented his position, because he felt himself cut out to be a composer or an artist or even a ceramist.

"Tough . . . tough," D'Arcy said and muttered, "Bullshit," to me.

"Shit bull . . . bull shit," the Swede said, and made a gesture, parodying the toreador at the last intrepid moments. Was there a bullfight in the town, he wondered.

"You are not in Pamplona now, maestro," D'Arcy said as the Swede repeated "bull" and "shit" in a perplexed manner.

"Have you read Groses's *History of Buckish Slang*?" D'Arcy asked and when the Swede shook his head D'Arcy hit him rattily. Objecting to being treated in this lowly manner, the Swede rolled up his sleeves as if to challenge D'Arcy, who parried and said that the cheap drink was rotting their neutrons and why did they not order a decent bottle of good grog, since they were now blessed with female company. From the great array of bottles, a square black bottle was produced. It was wooden, with the wounds of wood painted black and the cork secured by a bright red seal.

"Napoleon's serum," D'Arcy said as he inhaled it proudly.

Glasses were filled and clinked ceremoniously.

"Cat's pajamas," the Swede said again, causing D'Arcy to do a study of the man's head, to see if there was a brain in it at all, or if the gray matter had been replaced with goat's pellets. Pummeling and pawing, D'Arcy rejoiced, said the skull bore a strong resemblance to the skull of Robert Burns, who as all the world knew had had a pre-Neolithic ancestor residing in a cage at Oban.

The madman who had invaded my sleep the first evening sat in a corner, a model of reticence, since it was clear that this night of prodigality belonged to D'Arcy and to D'Arcy alone. Suddenly Iris put her head through the door. She was wearing a black cloak with a russet lace mantilla and her eyes invited adventure. Soon as she saw me, she withdrew.

"Who is the veiled sybil?" D'Arcy asked, and ran to call her back. He fell over a table and spilled a bottle of red wine onto a German woman's lap, a faux pas made worse by the fact that she was wearing shorts and that she did not understand a word of English. The wine ran over her thighs, as D'Arcy bent to express his profoundest apologies. Then he ordered her another bottle and decided to regale her with a few lines from Robert Burns:

Ae fond kiss and then we sever!
Ae farewell, alas! forever!

The Swede put down his glass abruptly and went toward the open door.

"Norseman . . . Norseman," D'Arcy called, terrified that he was going to be landed with an enormous bill. By putting his hand to his fly, the Swede indicated that it was the call of nature.

"Paying tribute to Cloacina," D'Arcy told the German woman and then remarked on the stupidity of the Swede, who was wearing a T-shirt that not only was too small for him but had that most ridiculous of insignias: "I'm Greta . . . Try me."

"Greta who . . . Greta fucking Garbo," D'Arcy said and then

pulled me aside, to whisper a word in my ear. I was not to leave, I was not to abandon ship, he had a bit of business up his sleeve, a bit of business that would be better expedited by the ministering and loving presence of a woman. The Swede, he explained, had a wife in Malmö, one Solveig, who was a bit moody, a bit dropsical. He had seen a photograph of her earlier, at lunchtime, when they met and courtesies were exchanged.

"Intelligence has been received that he is loaded," D'Arcy said and vowed that ere night ended some of that money might end up in our coffers. In due course, we would repair to his studio and I would make finger sandwiches with anchovy pâté or strawberry jam or whatever.

Staring across at us was a man with curly brown hair and large gray eyes, like sheep's eyes. It was Scottie Jr., the agonized artist.

"That's our Scottie," D'Arcy said. "And oh man, he is now awash with freedom after his long night of autocratic sex . . . the truth has suffered to ooze out, wifey followed him hither, so he is enjoying a renaissance of conjugal sex." Beside him sat a largish woman, busily knitting. D'Arcy commented on her plaits, her flagellating plaits, and her hips, which he deemed fearsome, and begged me to feel some pity for poor Scottie, who had to pretend that he did not know any of those nubile visiting American girls on their bewitching grants.

The Swede came back, his face splashed with water, tears flowing from his eyes. Out there, under the moon and the stars, he had had a vision; he would sell his sawmill, he would move here and paint orchards.

"Bollocks," D'Arcy said, and added that there were enough orchards on canvases already, turgid bushes, hemorrhoidal gooseberries, and so forth. The Swede envisaged for himself and Solveig a perfect future: they would have picnics on the mountain, fall in love again, live like bohemians. D'Arcy shook his head at such fancifulness and said the Swede was to think one word and that word was "timber." The Swede admitted to having troubles, indeed his troubles had sent him hither, it was that or suicide. The factory was losing money, there was labor unrest, his salesmen were drunk by noon, whereupon D'Arcy butted in with a solution—the Japanese technique, the samurai induction where salesmen learned the rules. There was a place where salesmen went to learn the Sales Crow Song. He had read about it and now proceeded to indoctrinate the baffled Swede:

> The products you make with the sweat of your brow
> You must sell with the sweat of your brow.
> The products you make with your tears
> You must sell with your tears.

D'Arcy bellowed it while the Swede tried to repeat it after him.

"Pro . . . duct," the Swede said heavily.

"Loud . . . louder . . . accurate . . . sincere . . . these are the marks of a true warrior, a true selling samurai," D'Arcy said, then stressed the need for inner sincerity. Next he was reciting the businessman's breakfast test:

"A salary man must have breakfast, because without breakfast he will be lacking in health and energy. What happens if a salary man does not have breakfast—he will not be a good salesman. He will get ill and his family will suffer. What is the current condition of the salary man's breakfast—the current condition is that fifty percent do not have breakfast."

"Why not?" the Swede asked, at which D'Arcy foamed and said because they were stupid salary men who would not take the proper instructions from a superior, who would not perform the task as cleverly as a fox, as faithfully as a hunting dog, and as bravely as a lion. For the benefit of the swelling audience D'Arcy enacted the baying sounds of these animals, but soon an incensed woman, dressed in an overall, came from the rear of the bar and, without having to speak, conveyed to him that he was going too far.

"Descalzas reales . . . my barefoot princesa," he said and bowed, assuring her that he would not defile her esteemed posada. There was disdain in her back as she turned away. Japan, D'Arcy then continued, was where the future of mankind lay, the cornerstone of business acumen. He knew it. He had been there once. He had been stupid enough to come home but he would go again, and in a bank in London there was lodged a single ticket to Tokyo which he had purchased some years ago and which, alas, needed refurbishing. He took his hat off and passed it around, and for fun, people put ridiculously small amounts into it, which he tossed onto the terrace. It happened quite suddenly. D'Arcy was dilating on his own plight, his shag-artist plight, on the dreams that scald mankind, when he suddenly happened to say the name Vincent van Gogh, which brought ejaculations from the Swede as he folded his hands and genuflected to Vincent van Gogh, his brother, his hero, his saint. He believed that he was the reincarnation of Vincent and that one day he would paint like that, the gift would come to him. Moreover, if Vincent were alive now he would be in a five-star hotel, his atelier bursting with tubes of paint, all the canvases he needed, because he, Gunnar Helm, would see to it. His eyes brim with tears as he tells D'Arcy that at moments he is van Gogh, he has painted those boots, those matted chairs, those wild irises; in his head, that is; and now D'Arcy has an arm around him, clutching him, dragging him out of there, while at the same time exhorting me to sign the chit, to say we will pay on the morrow.

Down the busy street, careless of motorcars and motorcyclists, they go, arm in arm, with D'Arcy reciting: "Caesar and Lepidus take to the fields . . . wibbledy . . . wobbledy . . . wu . . . Caesar and Lepidus take to the fields . . . wibbledy . . . wobbledy . . . wu."

He advises me to wave a kerchief, red or white, as the case may be, to tell all passing cruisers that he and the Norseman have charge of the thoroughfare. Two oncoming cars scream to a halt as D'Arcy puts his head through the open roof of one, asking a disgruntled young man if he has been perusing the cosmos, Venus' pudenda, or the Milky Way's rectum. Taking a shortcut where there is no street lighting, they stagger and fall, regain their faltering balance, all the while D'Arcy assuring the Swede that a meeting such as theirs was made in heaven. We go up some steps, then along a ramp, and he advises me to find the door key by the side of the fonta.

"Enter Holy House of Mecca," D'Arcy says as he leads us through a room with Turkish cushions and Turkish hangings on the wall. Absurdly, the little round table is laid for breakfast, complete with packages of cereal, marmalade, and a silver-and-gold coffeepot. He warns us that the good people are in bed. We go down a hall, past some doors, to a room at the end, and as he pushes the door open and switches on the light I see a cluttered studio, mostly blue and violet nudes, several musical instruments, and a sign in bright red which says: "Abandon your reason all who enter here." But the miracle, the pièce de résistance, is none of those things, it is a painting on an easel, newly finished, so new that the thick paint is moist. In a light blue jacket and with bristling, upstanding, red-bronze hair is a portrait of van Gogh, looking like an amalgam of van Gogh and D'Arcy himself. He is wearing a pair of wide-winged tortoiseshell sunglasses and in the blue lenses are the floating orchards that he painted in the last fevered days of his life. The Swede is speechless. The Swede starts to roar, then he starts to cry. He goes toward it, overawed. He has never seen anything like it. It is a mirage. It is not a mirage. He will pay anything for it. He will pay the ticket to Tokyo and back.

"A weightier sum, if you please," D'Arcy says.

"Excuse me, my English no good," the Swede says.

"Bollocks," D'Arcy says, and tells the Swede in King's English, coupled with mime, that the fee is two thousand dollars and that I am at hand to witness it. The Swede grasps the figure, gasps, demurs, halves it, and eventually they agree on fifteen hundred and shake hands.

"It is yours, my warlord, my samurai, Vincent is now yours . . ." D'Arcy says; whereupon the Swede proceeds to pick the painting off the easel, but D'Arcy intercepts him.

"Money, my lord . . . shekels."

The Swede explains that due to the perils of travel, highwaymen, brigands, and so forth, he never carries such large amounts but that he will go to the bank in the morning and have Solveig wire the money by the afternoon.

"Hath not a Jew eyes . . . ears . . . heart," D'Arcy says, putting his hands out in the manner of Shylock. The Swede assures him that he is a man of honor and once again picks up the painting. D'Arcy grabs it, says it is not a matter of commerce, it is simply for art's sake; he wants to add a few finishing touches to it, especially to the revers of Vincent's jacket, which is too dun. The Swede insists that he loves the picture as it is, and begs to be let take it.

"It's yours," D'Arcy says, and to prove it he picks up a brush, dips it in a palette, and writes, "Sold," in a vivid blue-green. The Swede erupts, he cannot bear this defilement, this sprawl.

"Vincent wouldn't care," D'Arcy says, and torn between umbrage and drunkenness the Swede begins to laugh and says, "Vincent wouldn't care." Now the two of them are laughing, the bonds of friendship and brotherhood are renewed, as they salute Vincent, the Impoverished One.

Again the Swede tries to grab the painting, and grasping it, D'Arcy says that he would like to point out, as G. K. Chesterton before him has pointed out, that Irishmen are nifty with the practice of physical assault. They are each holding one end of the painting, with D'Arcy shouting, "Tomorrow and tomorrow and tomorrow."

"No . . . now," the Swede says.

"No such word, Swedenborg . . . no now means never . . . whereas tomorrow . . . dawn . . . Aurora . . . breakfast in your bedroom . . . knock-knock . . . genii arrive . . . I, D'Arcy with painting."

The Swede wrenches the picture from him and D'Arcy calls on me to bar the door because he intends to beat the bastard to a pulp. He grabs the Swede from the back and pinions him to a wall against the violet nudes. The Swede lets the picture fall as D'Arcy gives him a few preliminary punches. Blood pumps from his nose, and D'Arcy, sobering slightly, and fearing he might have lost the sale, pleads the artist's Fifth Amendment, which is that he must put the finishing touches to the work before bringing it to the hotel at dawn. Then he dabs the bleeding nose with a rag, says true friendship is always forged through fisticuffs, and tells me with an excess of sentiment: "Thou knowest that Gunnar, my brother, is an honorable man."

"Bibulous bastard and 'onclene beste' " is how he describes him after the Swede has gone and then he orders black coffee, but not the instant puke.

A mammoth task faces him before dawn. A complete new painting has to be done and why, why, because he, D'Arcy, cannot part with said picture, because in that picture lies his soul, his scrotum, the pipe dreams of his life; that picture and he will never be parted. Before morning there will be two Vincents, one bound for Malmö, and the other concealed in his studio, his for life. He pours water from a jug, into a metal basin, sinks his face in it, and asks me in God's name to talk to him, to talk to him, to engage him, to keep him from falling asleep.

A clean white canvas is set upon the easel and he starts to smear it lavishly with a yellow undercoat. He paints with a flourish, great bold crazed strokes, as he celebrates in advance the money in the palm of his hands, the journey to the capital to book a cheap flight to London, collecting his ticket from the vault in Brook Street, returning to Japan, and standing beneath the place where Yukio Mishima disemboweled himself, beneath the foothills of Mount Fuji. It will help exceedingly if I read to him from the Japanese. It will spur him on. He points to a pile of books between two sedate bookends.

"Anything . . . read anything . . . just don't stop," he says.

So, it was *White Snowflowers*, *Kanefusi's Hair*, *Brown Mimosa Seed*, *The Cuckoo Bird*, and *The Lover-Star's Reprieve*, all night, as D'Arcy envisaged the future with tinctures of sweet rice wine, plum blossom, and that wench, herself, one Ming.

"Little voice like a xylophone," he said as he mimicked her.

"So it's your ladylove," I said, tentatively. Ladylove! He grunted at the nicety but conceded that all scheming and dreaming on this planet concerned man and woman.

He twirls the brush in the air, he lets lozenges of paint drop onto the canvas, he jokes about the Swede's avoirdupois, even wonders if in the lenses of the tortoiseshell glasses he should paint different orchards, straggled orchards with blight; wonders if the bibulous bastard would notice.

It was dawn before the second Vincent was completed, clad in his blue jacket, his bristling hair wet as if Vaseline had been smeared over it. D'Arcy put down his brush to rest and suddenly he looked exhausted. He feared for the transaction, what with the daylight and hangover, feared that he had botched it. He saw it disappear, like thistledown. Picking the wet canvas off the easel, he looked at me with a look that was infinitely sad and infinitely resigned, as if admitting that the great windfall had eluded him and that in his perversity he had wanted it to elude him.

"The Tao that can be told is not the eternal Tao," he said as he went up the hall and hurried outside, presumably to remonstrate with the Swede, to beg.

8

The mountains in the early light were soft and misted, pearled orbs, before the day's break. I was setting out to buy lace and wrought-iron candlesticks at the gypsy market in the town, while in another part of my being I was thinking of not going home at all, but drifting, endlessly drifting. I will give the lace and the candlesticks and whatever I buy to my sons, or my friends, or their friends, I thought, as Wanda gabbled away beside me. She was going to collect a friend from the airport and had offered me a lift. Over the weeks I had met her in the shops or in the bar and always she was eager for conversation. I knew by now a little of her past, how she had come there temporarily, only to find that while she was away her husband had gone off with someone else, a dancer from Seville, and the two of them had set up house and a mail-order business in Southern California. Her son kept making tapes which he sent to his father to ask for the money to go to boarding school but as yet there was no answer.

"You'll miss him," I said.

"I'll miss him," she said, not really realizing it.

We were the only people out, the lorries full of provisions had not started on their rounds. The air was fresh, iridescent, terraces glowing with light, houses cloaked in their sunny slumbers, and church bells in their niches silent—matte with verdigris. As we drove along, the mist lifted from the mountains, like a veil being lifted from a face. Those mountains she was blind to for three years after he left, because of her blinding hangovers. She would stagger out, look at them, and, unable to see them, crawl back to bed and bury herself. But that was behind her now. She had had a few romances of course. In this place one met people all the time, people escaping from something or searching for something, people who had dropped out or half dropped out and were, as she said, smitten by the place, bewitched. There had been several pairs of men's slippers under her bed and endless eyeball-to-eyeball philosophizing, but as she said, before you know where you are, you're cooking for them . . . you're apologizing for your hair being a mess . . . you're begging your kid to call them Daddy or at least Uncle, and just when you think it's all working out, the bastard ups and leaves.

"Is there someone now?" I said, thinking in some other part of my mind that other people's heartbreak does not touch in the same way, simply because we're not prepared to look in at it, at the depths of it. Yes, there was someone, but he hardly counted. What am I saying, she exclaimed, there were two or three. More maybe. Somebody else's English boyfriend, who rang every day to say he'd like to play tennis or he'd like to pop by to discuss modern art. Modern art! There was, of course, *the* guy; he came by bus occasionally, spent the night, but as far as she knew lived with a woman on the other side of the island, an older woman, German, hardly ever went out, had phobias.

"So, I play tennis with one and footsie with another . . . but no número uno or número dos, for that matter," and she laughed with a twinge of bitterness. When she laughed, her gold bridging glinted harshly.

She was recounting a dream she had had and was still reeling from. It was of a man who kept all his women, herded, in a dormitory . . . no, not a dormitory . . . more like an institution or a prison. He wore a jockstrap and he came over each one but it was ugh . . . it was rusty . . . it was filthy. She, Wanda, was told to go to her cell, at the end of the corridor, and wait there. She would hear the others getting their gout of rust and she was to make herself excited, but not too excited, and wait her turn. Hell, she thought, do I want this, do I want him . . . and turning to me, and in a half-bashful voice, she admitted that he was someone she knew in everyday life and hadn't given a thought to.

"What do you make of that?" she said.

"I don't know," I said.

Something in me recoiled. It was as if she were taking my own hopes or half hopes away, hopes that had to feed themselves on nearly nothing, that clung to specters. I could not tell her of the man I loved because to tell her would be to adulterate my feeling, and yet I knew that she ached to know, the way women do, half in curiosity, half in mischief. As she dropped me off she wagged a finger and said I was a secretive one, but that I was not to forget that her apartment would be vacant in a matter of weeks and that I was top of the list.

"We'll play gin rummy . . . we"ll have fun," she said, giving me that smile, that coy, girlish smile I knew so well.

The market was not at all as I had envisaged it. It was stall after stall with a glut of knickknacks, mostly brass that smarted in the sun. I had expected something different, the lace, the wrought-iron candlesticks that Iris had boasted of. On her last day at the hotel she had got into the pool and even deigned to talk to another woman. They swam slowly up and down, in tandem, their heads covered in frilled bathing caps, their wrists adorned with jeweled watches. Iris was telling the woman of the bargains she had found at the gypsy market, the lace, the wrought iron, even a samovar, an eighteenth-century Russian samovar, can you imagine, for nothing, for a song. She had even cajoled the little man into packing it and shipping it to Paris. Marvelous, really, the things you can do with a bit of coaxing and a bit of artfulness.

All I could see were varnished wooden caskets and wooden scuttles of grotesque design, made to look unlike wood, cheap jewelry, and leather bags hanging and swinging from coarse nails. The gypsy women were laying out their wares and their flowers. They were strong, well built, their dark hair parted severely in the center and tied back with tortoiseshell slides. The flowers had just been delivered and each one was busy adorning her own stall, and putting flowers into tins and buckets. Here again, lilies, sweet peas, roses, pinks, gladioli, the women seeming not to care whether they had a sale or not, showing an indifference to their customers, almost a disdain. They had an uncanny earthiness as if the high-heeled shoes that they wore were merely plinths which connected them to the earth beneath, not just its surface but to the foundations where the sewer and the sap flowed, way way beneath to the earth's root. Suddenly I saw a figure that gave me a start. It was a young girl, her black hair wet and with a sheen. She was moving quickly, bobbing underneath the awnings of bags and tablecloths made of machine lace. My heart gave a little lurch because I thought she looked like Catalina. I did not want to meet her there, I felt it would spoil things. Each day she left a large fresh bouquet in my room, and often a little one by the bedside table, and when I bumped into her, I thanked her, but that was all. Some reserve had grown between us. Something in her manner had asked me to keep my distance, a fact strengthened by a conversation I had had with the head-waiter. I mentioned her name once, said how vivacious she was, how welcome she made people feel. He was behind the bar counter putting bottles on a shelf. I saw him smile behind his glasses, but it was an insinuating smile.

"Yes," he had conceded. "She is a very vivacious girl . . . also a little tragedienne . . . there is one in every village . . . our mountain Carmen," and by his turning to regroup the bottles, I knew that the conversation had come to an end. Yet, for me, to know that she was there, to know that she existed was a consolation in itself. In the evenings when I had a drink or two I would allow myself to think of her, as I might a painting or a beautiful garden. I would dwell on her body the way I never allowed myself to dwell on my own, exploring it with invisible hands, invisible eyes, touching her tentatively and without shame. Her skin I would see as the skin of the lilies, fawn, filtered gold, and her breasts like the oranges with perhaps a crescent around them, her arms like little oars from all the work she did, the heaving and the carting, her belly a dome ripe for child, and the hair, when it was not wet, like a burning bush. I would see her doing the flowers, or arriving late, or darting through the courtyard with her friends as if they were playing truant. One day I found her ironing her hair in the laundry room and she laughed and said it was the only way to get the crinkles out.

Another time she was at the bus stop and I paid her fare but we did not sit together as there was a bit of a squash. The next day, underneath the jug of flowers, there was a catalogue from a shop that made beautiful ceramic plates. She had guessed my taste.

I looked again but the girl with the wet hair had vanished and I felt relief. I was in front of a flower stall where a woman had begun to compile an arc of flowers. First she made the base of green shrub, rather like the base of a wreath, and then she began to build bloom after bloom as if she was building in stone or brick, stalk after stalk, each ascension calling for another and still another, so that soon it was this pinnacle which would be impossible to sell, since it would not fit inside any house and was too prodigal for any church altar. She talked to herself as she did it. A little man crept by with leaves and branches and without even turning around she shouted at him. He dropped all the branches at her feet and scampered. I ran, too. She did not welcome my staring at her.

A bell pealed in the distance and I thought for a moment it was an Angelus bell ringing at an awry time. A crowd gathered around the stall in answer to this ringing and I joined them. There she was, in blue jeans and a white blouse, looking far more suave than she ever looked at work in her tracksuit. It was a stall full of junk, bits of iron, bits of lead, stair rods, bedheads, and this one clay-crusted ample bell which must have come from an old monastery and which she was ringing impudently. As she caught my eye I looked away. She was smiling as she amused the assembly by ringing it boldly again and again and to different effect. The stall owner then snatched it from her and put it down solemnly. She came toward me laughing, her bare arms out in a gesture of supplication. She had been to the fruit market, to sell lemons, and her hands and arms were full of infinitèsimal little cuts, from picking the lemons. She made me look at them, pore over them. To make matters worse, her stupid father had climbed up into the trees and had flung the lemons down, damaging many of them, so that, instead of earning the estimated amount, she had got only half.

"I picked each one of mine, each one, carefully," she said, "but he, he just shook the branches and let them fall off." She rooted in one of the boxes of junk to find casters for her parents' bed. That was why she had come at all, she normally never came to this market, it was for tourists only.

"Like me," I said.

"You don't sit in the sun . . . you hide in your room and write in your journal . . . I want to read it," she said almost contemptuously as she picked up two casters which dripped with machine oil. She haggled about the price, and perhaps dreading that she was going to ring the bell again, he wrapped them in newspaper and gave them to her as a present.

We walked on, past stall after stall—chains, leather purses, leather pouches, blouses, tablecloths, and still more brass, an affront to the eye in the blazing sun. On one little makeshift table there was an array of nail varnish, each bottle the same color, a drained, unappealing lilac. She stopped and laughed and showed the vendor her overworked nails with not a sight of a cuticle. The woman ignored her. For the most part the vendors took no notice of their customers, they sat with each other, eating and talking, then glancing up slowly if someone asked the price of something. I stopped to buy a picture of a Madonna and Child but when she heard the price she dragged me away. Farther along she saw something she liked and winked to show me how one did the transaction. It was a tin plate which had been painted white and had little pink rosebuds on its scalloped rims. Some of the white paint had chipped away and the roses had suffered the onslaughts of rain, so these rinsed roses were cheek-to-cheek, their curves like the round dimpled cheeks of children on Valentine cards. She wanted it for the little boy.

"What little boy?" I asked.

"My sister's little boy . . . Carlos," she said evasively. Then she picked up the plate, looked at it with utter disdain, and began a rapid dialogue with the vendor. I could not exactly follow what she was saying but I knew that she was taunting him. She was asking him, more or less, if he was selling this item or if he had bought it to feed a dog, his own dog or a stray. She put it on her head like a helmet and drew a smile from the more well-to-do owner of the neighboring stall, who was surrounded by grandfather clocks and was busy polishing a brass weight with great vigor. He agreed with her. He said it was useless, belonged on a rubbish heap. He made a gesture to fling it away. She then held the plate forward and in English and Spanish she began to discuss its wretched life, the curs that had eaten off it, the cats that had drunk milk from it, the wind that had made it roll and roll so that its edges were battered, the rain that had washed it again and again, and the many other degradations which she would not mention. All this for my benefit, while at the same time herself and the vendor swapped insults and figures. The plate was pitifully cheap but it was clear that the pair of them enjoyed the battle and had even drawn a little audience. Eventually she took some coins from her crinkled white purse and gave them to him and shook his hand and wished him every happiness.

Walking along, she carried the plate like a breast shield. Where the stalls ended, there were fields full of tall yellow flowers, and beyond that, a series of high, mud-colored apartment buildings with television aerials, like birds' feet, askew in the air. She knew exactly what we must do. We must go to the center of the city to a beautiful old-fashioned bar and have coffee and English breakfast. We would have to take a taxi, because wouldn't you know it, her van, which was really her sister's van, had broken down and she had had to take it to the garage. Any profit from the lemons was now destined to cover the repair of the van.

"Bah," she said, but she was not peeved, just flirtatious, and full of bravura, as she went out onto the main road, whistling for a taxi. As we drove along she pointed out the sights: a school, a hospital, nightclubs, the cathedral, the university where she hoped one day to go.

Walking down the main shopping street, past the boutiques, she showed no interest in the clothes or the furs and only once allowed me to stop to look in a window where there were red, black, and amber mantillas spread out like gorgeous webs on which feathered hair slides lay pinioned like butterflies. I wanted to buy some, one for her and one for me, and was about to go in but she would not hear of it. She put her hand on the belt of her jeans and said she had no liking for finery. All that was for other women, different kinds of women, but not her. She would hate herself if she were seduced by such things. I looked at the shop front and thought I would go back alone. There was no number but I hoped that I would recognize it by the cobbled street and the one neon sign for a brand of cigarettes. The restaurant was just open, the waiters unfolding the stiff starched cloths and napkins. We stood at the counter and she ordered espresso and toast. Suddenly a levity overcame her and she suggested that we have cognac with the coffee. The waiter smiled at her indulgently and put the bottle on the counter so that we could lace it ourselves. We sat on high stools drinking this heady stuff while she ordered croque-monsieurs and said to add some mustard, for the piquancy. There were English papers on the counter and for a moment I thought that I would have to run away. They were a reminder of him. Any heading or any paragraph, though it did not necessarily concern him, brought me back to my own surroundings, the thought of him going to work, driving along the Embankment past the houseboats or the bridge with its little girdle of lights, resurrected many moments sweet or bridling as the case may be, as when he touched my necklace and in doing so touched the very lining of my being, looking at it earnestly, lovingly, his eyes the blue of forget-me-nots; and then another moment, a quite different moment, ugly, knifing, when in the throes of love he suddenly drew back from me and said, "You have too much power over me," and all I could hear was the revving of his car and then the roaring of his engine up the tree-lined street, a fugitive from me.

Catalina was rhapsodizing about their farm, their great estate, how her family did everything themselves, had their own fruit trees, their own olive orchards, their own vegetables, never bought meat, ate only the rabbits and chickens which they reared themselves and which her mother put in the paella. Her pride in it was like the pride of someone who owned dairies, butteries, pantries. She would never leave the land, it was in her blood, it was in her veins. She talked of how she dug the earth in the places where the plow could not reach, on the inclines of the terraces, on the headlands, around the house which they owned on the mountain and where she would one day live. She described the plow that they had bought as if it were a motorcar. She is not with me, or rather she is with me and I am the witness to her excitement as she describes putting the seeds in and weeks later the first little leaf, the first little nurseling above the ground. She talks of her father, how he tests her, how he bullies her, how he watches to see her strength ebb, how he cheers when she falters. That very morning, when it was still dark and they had hefted the bags of lemons onto the barrow and were bringing them down the path, he let go of his end, hoping the barrow would run away with her, hoping she would stumble and fall, except that she didn't, she clung on.

"Yesterday, when I was plowing . . . he did the same thing . . . he ran in front of the plow . . . and for what . . . to remove a little white pebble from the ground . . . no bigger than a bead . . . it wouldn't have broken the plow . . . he just wanted to break me . . . he always wants to break me," she said, and called him monster, actor, emperor, and clown. He was forever challenging her, asking if she could clear a terrace as well as he, if she could grow radishes as well as he, if she could prune orchards as well as he.

"Can I . . . can I . . . can I not," she said, excited now from the brandy and her surroundings. No sooner had she maligned her father than she felt a need to praise him. Like her, he loved the land, he cherished it, he knew every hectare of it, he knew if a leaf sprouted or if the goats had eaten a bud, it had been in his family for hundreds of years and since he had no son she had to be his son because her sister was ill and moped in bed, crying, sulking.

"So what would I do with nice dresses or mantillas," she

said, but I felt that secretly she had a yen for some of these things. I could picture her, indeed did picture her, in a taffeta dress the color of fuchsia, tier after tier of it, falling down over her shins, her feet like the gypsies' in the strong black court shoes and black stockings, stamping, wherever she trod. On impulse I took off my earrings and laid them on the counter in front of her. She pretended not to see them, chose to ignore what I had done. She was eating toast, and threads of melted cheese laced her lips as she asked the barman, sweetly, to put cognac in our second cup of espresso.

"Have them," I said.

"I couldn't," she said. They were long shell earrings mounted on silver and in the sunlight the dark exotic shells took on rivers of color, as if a rainbow flowed within them.

"Uno," she said. "Uno."

She took one earring and put it through her pierced ear and I took the other and put it through mine and then she shook her head and her hair as one on the brink of adventure.

"What do you do in the evenings?" I asked.

"In the evenings . . ." she said and shrugged. "In the evenings I milk the goats . . . I cook the supper . . . I read to my sister's little boy . . . I read fairy tales and then he and I fall asleep and we dream of dragons."

Later I sat in one of the big squares while she went to make a phone call. It buzzed with life. There were men with monkeys on their shoulders, others doing card tricks, and still others stopping people, trying to sell them gold rings or gold watches, ill-gotten goods. Near me, a fat man with a speech impediment sat on a barrel, selling raffle tickets, shouting his wares in a strange, spluttering voice. The sun blazed and emphasized everything, sugar crumbs on a plate which the previous person had left, the white gold of the watch, a parrot on its lead, its greenness seeming to vibrate and emphasize the gravity of the women in black, who like mourners crossed the square in a slow stately way. It was clear by her stance that she was talking to someone whom she enjoyed talking to. She moved about and I could imagine her saying saucy things. When she came back her cheeks were crimson and she bubbled over with excitement. She had borrowed a scooter and would be my chevalier.

"I can take the bus," I said.

"You don't trust me," she said in mock indignation.

"I do," I said, already dreading it, because I knew that she would be reckless, that the excitement of a relatively new scooter would be too much for her.

In the garage as she put on the goggles she was already zooming, breasting a Grand Prix. The attendant watched her with fascination. In the tiny room where he sat and made his coffee there were postcards and out-of-date calendars with views of Peru. He had come from there and for thirty years had been resolving to go back, except that he was penniless, and lived, as she said, in a hen coop in someone's back yard.

"We go together . . . Conquistadors," she told him proudly as they hefted the bike across the garage and out into the sunshine. A certain caution reigned as we maneuvered our way through the maze of cobbled streets and back alleys but once we came up onto the main road she found her momentum. My arms gripped feverishly, holding on to whatever I could, one minute it was the narrow belt of her jeans, the next minute it was her blouse that had ballooned out. I could not decide which was worse, the vertigo, the smell of burning oil, or the hot air that rose up from the road. From time to time she shouted words of enthusiasm, asked if I loved the wind or smelled the balsam or whatever. The sea which I saw when she took the corners was an upside-down version of sky, heaving crookedly, like water being sloshed about in a giant beaker. Far out there was a liner, a white liner that seemed to be gliding at a snail's pace. The corners were the worst. Twice she hollered at me as I leaned in the wrong direction and caused her to swerve.

"Lean into the turn . . . lean into the turn," she shouted, but minutes later she was uttering her satisfaction at everything and said how pleasant it was not to be interned in a car or van, to be one with the wind. I expected us to land into a lorry or a bus and almost wished for it, because at least the ordeal would be over. Farms, gateways, flowers came in swoops as if seen from a Ferris wheel at a fun fair.

"Smell the pollen, smell the balsam, smell the sea," she would say, her voice rising above the din of the tappets that were like some out-of-tune mechanical piano. I saw the high wall on a great swerve of road and thought it was only two more kilometers between life and death, only to be daunted afresh by her suggestion that we speed through the town and spend the day visiting other towns and port towns, enjoying ourselves.

"I can't," I screamed.

"Why not?"

"I have an appointment," I said.

She came to an abrupt stop outside the bar, our arrival causing something of a stir. Two girls in shorts sat on the steps and eyed us with a sort of disdain. She looked back at them and suddenly expressed the longing to be in some strange country, alone, free, independent, unfettered.

"Aren't you coming to the hotel?" I asked.

"It's Saturday . . . I don't work Saturday or Sunday," she said.

"Maybe you would like to have dinner," I said on the spur of the moment.

"You'd be bored," she said. "I'm a peasant . . . I'm an ignoramus," and a line came to me out of the blue—"Her heart amber and plump"—but she was already gone, leaving me with the anxiety that I was unsporting and that I lacked daring.

9

The driveway was long and winding. At times, it seemed like a well-kept private road, then deteriorated into a track, with old trees and old tree stumps out of which briars sprung. The taxi driver kept turning around to voice his displeasure. I had been summoned by Iris, and since it was a doleful Sunday, I agreed to go. Soon, as I heard the dogs barking and as the car swerved in front of a large house, I guessed it was the right place. The dogs were behind gates, but on the lawn itself a flock of peacocks strutted, their ghostly cries in contrast with their blue-green plumage, which at that moment splayed expansively.

An upstairs window was opened and Iris called out in a summary fashion that I was to keep the taxi. I walked about, wondering whether or not a maid would admit me. At either side of the big beveled door were two huge stumps of olivewood, like replicas of a Neolithic man and woman, guarding the entrance. The taxi driver made no secret of his impatience, and I stood, of two minds, wondering whether to touch the brazen knocker or to wait.

Eventually she appeared. She was not wearing a coat, not even a dress, and to my surprise she looked disheveled. She was wearing a long purple slip and her feet were bare. She gave me a little peck on the cheek and said that she would like to show me the house, or at least the courtyard, that I must see the roses, the roses were the only reason she had rented the place.

"He's in a bad mood," I said, pointing to the taxi. She ignored that, and I followed her through a dark shuttered hallway and then through vestibules also dark, into a huge courtyard where there were indeed masses of roses. They hung in bunches, in clusters, great traunches of them trailing over low-tiled roofs, covering window casements and in one place blotting out a window completely. The place had a neglected quality.

Soon we went inside and up a staircase to the first floor, because she said that the gallery was one of the features of the house and several centuries old. It was a long narrow gallery that looked out onto the courtyard and it was filled with chairs, many of them brown rocking chairs. For some reason, I imagined invalids sitting there looking out at the beautiful roses, plaintively. I did not want to be there, I wanted to be with Catalina; I yearned to be with her, on the scooter, on her farm, milking the goats with her, anything, because here in this deserted and luxurious place there were whiffs of despair, reminding me too pointedly of my own life.

By the way she staggered I saw that Iris was not well and that possibly she had been drinking. There was no music playing, no other voices, no sign of her South American houseguest, and no murmur of servants. We went through salon after salon in which there were huge paintings either of animals or of gouty ancestors; then long bog-oak sideboards on which there were laid single things such as a chafing dish or a ladle or a set of teaspoons. I kept admiring it, even though I found it dismal. We arrived at the end room, which was a little library where a wood fire had been laid. She went toward the telephone and spoke a message into the answering machine which was next to it. She said that she was out, said it twice in a muffled voice, and then rooted for the little pad to find the number of the restaurant to which we were going. Unable to find the pad, she quashed the message, lost her temper, opened several drawers of the desk, found some book matches with the name of the restaurant, and then proceeded to use the machine again. But first, she said, she needed a drink.

"Get me a vodka . . . on the rocks," she said and pointed to a bar, or at least a tray of drinks, in the adjoining room. The dulcet voice had gone and there was, instead, this abrasiveness. Yet as she taped her message she resummoned her seductive tones and said in the nicest voice that she was out, then gave the exact time during which she would be in the restaurant and the approximate time when she would be home, begging the caller to allow fifteen minutes in each instance for her to get to and fro. She blew a little kiss. I thought I heard the car drive away but then decided that he was merely turning around, and anyhow I felt too nervous to worry her. She donned a long satin dress—which buttoned all the way down, and seemed excessively chaste. From her handbag she took her makeup pouch and painted her lips hurriedly. Her shoes she hauled from under a chair. They were very high-heeled, suede mauve shoes, with an ankle strap, and I could not see how she was going to navigate in them. I was not certain what she was saying as she bent to put the strap through the diamanté buckle, but it was clear she was repeating something that enraged her, something the paramour had said—just give me time, give me time to think, all I need is time to sort myself out, you know I love you, I hate to do this to you, I hate myself for doing this to you, Iris baby, you don't deserve this . . .

She raised her head and looked at me bitterly as if I were the cause of it or in some way a reminder of it. Her South American friend had gone, and where had he gone, to Cannes, and why had he gone, because there was a film festival there, and whom did he hope to meet, cheap little bitches, starlets, pseudo-starlets, models, tarts, the lot. The memory of it, and the knowledge that he was there at that very moment, flattering God knows whom, made her demand another drink and this she did by picking her glass up and shaking the ice onto her lap, onto the dress, which was only half buttoned. She pouted like a child.

By the time we came out, it was dusk and there was no car. He had indeed gone, my hearing had not deceived me. She fumed. She said how had he gone without being paid. I explained that I had paid him as we came up the drive, as I was under the impression that I was having supper in her house. She almost struck me. Does one have a cook on Sunday evening when one is renting a villa. Where did I get such Pollyanna ideas. One was lucky if one got breakfast. In her high heels she flounced back in and picked up the phone in the hall. She couldn't remember the numbers of any of the taxis, so she sent me upstairs to find them. I met her as I was coming down with two printed cards, a fresh glass, a wineglass, in her hand, curses issuing out of her, at me, at taxi drivers, at the country she happened to find herself in, at the whole costly mess of it. She was paying a fortune for this place, a fortune for those imbecilic servants, and what was it, a morgue, a morgue, with syphilitic ancestors on the walls and a phone that went out of order every time you blinked. No wonder he'd left. It wasn't her he'd left, it was this cursed house, and she slammed the phone back and said there was nothing for it but to rustle up something and so we went together to the kitchen, which was down the main stairs and then another series of narrower stairs. It was a big white kitchen fitted with every kind of equipment and my first thought as I heard all the machines hum was that I was in a kind of hospital. She opened the refrigerator and took out two pitiful strips of parched veal, which looked to have been there for days.

"Vienna schnitzel," she said, laughing, and then as she went across to the very modern stove she hit her head on the several baskets and copper pans that hung from the low ceiling.

"I give up . . . I simply give up," she said, almost admitting to tears. It was up to me. I had let the idiot taxi driver go. I hadn't told her he had been paid and was therefore itching to escape, so I had better take my nice tailored jacket off and get down to business. She said she had better explain that none of the pepper mills worked and that if I thought of making a wonderful salade chaude to think again, because there wasn't any arugula in the house, or goat's cheese, and possibly only some wilting lettuce.

"There's these," she said, as from a cupboard she took a stack of tins and plunked them on the white table. She would of course help me but first she must go and erase her message and turn the machine off, because she was expecting not one call but several. She had rung everyone, literally everyone, even her masseuse in Aspen, Colorado, to come and bail her out.

"I'll be back," she said, very sweetly now, fearing perhaps

that I might desert her, that once her back was turned I might creep up the stairs and out the door.

I searched in the pantry and found a few things, onions, olive oil, herbs,and then took a long time in choosing one of the many pristine copper pans. I felt quite pleased to be cooking again and thought with a little rush of irrational pleasure what it would be like when I got home. I heard her once or twice but it must have been as she tripped over something or spoke to herself because the phone had not rung and neither had a light flickered, as it would if she had been ringing someone.

It took her so long to appear that I thought perhaps she had gone to bed. I would look at the kitchen clock, which was a drained white, like separated milk, and I would think, In another five minutes she will appear, and then I would squeeze a little more lemon on the cooked veal, which was already shriveled. When she did come she was beautifully dressed and beautifully made up and there was a freshness to her as if she had just wakened, as if all her annoyance and disappointment had been whisked away. She wore a different dress, it was velvet, burgundy-colored, and she had long earrings to match, which when she moved bobbed against her shoulders. In the most girlish voice she asked me to please forgive her, to please please excuse such awful tantrums, such awful breeding, such unforgivable behavior, and to put it down to a woman who when she had her migraines lost her marbles. She praised the dinner, said it was delicious, ate masses of the toast and said that we could patent the recipe for the tinned beans, because whatever I had done, they were très bon. Then she confided that she also was a good cook, something of an adventuress with the sauces, and that when she lived in New York she insisted sometimes on doing her own cooking and made all those hatchet hostesses green with envy. She asked if I had been enjoying myself in the hotel, if I had made friends, found lovers, or at least somebody very simpático, and before I could reply she was shaking her head at her own luck, almost too good to be true. She was staring into space with that fixed and pensive gaze of hers, which had become second nature, and which she knew flattered her immensely, gave her the look of a graven mystic. Her eyes were narrow and she blinked feverishly as she recalled the wonderful weeks she had had since she last saw me, so much fun, so much pleasure. Sorrow, rejection, loneliness, these were things she knew nothing about. She had of course quarreled with lovers from time to time, especially Reinaldo, her South American, because he was so fiery, so tempestuous, naughty boy, but then ten minutes later he was in her arms and they were doing a tango, all over the house, upstairs through the salons, into the garden, like midsummer's night dreamers. He was the most thoughtful of men, he always made up first, he was the one to ring straightaway, to ring from downstairs if she had gone to her bedroom in a flounce, to beg, to plead, and as for flowers, he sent them every day, did I not see, did I not notice those great arrays of flowers. She had had roses, actual roses, not the Interflora muck, roses from South America, and no bouquet had ever looked so ravishing. They had lasted weeks, weeks, they just would not die. In fact, come to think of it, she should order her flowers from South America in future and save herself a packet of money.

"I'm so lucky," she said and gazed ahead at some point in the reaches of the long dining room, as if the gilded mirror could absorb an image of her pensive, exquisite self. Yes, she was spoiled, she had to admit it, spoiled by men, spoiled by everyone, and moreover she could eat anything, she could stuff herself and not put weight on. To prove this, she took a piece of toast in either hand and ate each piece alternately, gobbling as a child would. We drank and talked, but all the while she kept fidgeting and when it struck eleven from the very white clock on the wall she jumped up and asked to be excused. This was when he rang, and they had their cuddles, so wonderful, so exciting, so naughty, almost as if he were in the room, undoing his robe, and they were about to do the "Cuadro Flamenco."

"Oh, I feel quite randy," she said, and put her hands to her lips, shocked at her own indiscretion.

"You will let yourself out," she added, sweetly, nonchalantly, as if we were in the middle of a metropolis. Then she told me to be sure to leave my London address because she wanted to dine with me and take me to the opera.

Each time that she was not using the phone I took the opportunity to ring a taxi rank, and each time I got a ringing tone. Then, soon as I replaced the receiver, the red light appeared again and I knew that she was trying to reach him. By midnight I had reconciled myself to spending the night there. I thought I would go upstairs and knock on her door and ask which room it might be suitable to lie down in. But when I went upstairs I hesitated, because I could hear her talking to someone, spelling his name very slowly and clearly, asking the operator to please try his room again, because she knew he was there, he must be.

There was a screen around her bed, a lacquered screen with pictures of birds and simpering ladies. I drew back and repaired to the study, where I had seen a sofa and some plaid rugs.

Sleep would not come, because I yearned to be in my own room in the hotel and because I was cross with myself for having been enticed. I had met women like her before, and they had frightened me; their brittleness, their heartlessness had made me cower. On the tape machine I listened to the voice of Maria Callas, the haunted, liquid voice that I loved, and fearing that it might be too loud, I pressed some button, heard a lurch, and then suddenly there was another voice altogether in the room, a young man, speaking desperately, calling, "Mother, Mother." I started, thinking someone had come in, but the voice was indeed from the machine.

"Mother," it began. "Are you listening . . . I hope so, because I want to get it all out. I have followed you around the world to say this, but what did you always do, you fled, you hid, you ran. You were so busy, Mother, with your lovers, your secretaries, your dressmakers, your charities, your friends, and your art collection, so busy that when I came home from school at Christmas I would find my presents on my bed, when each time I hoped, I prayed, that you would hand them to me, but no, there they were, the camera, the watch, the bottle of shampoo with my very own name on the label, on the pillow, along with another box of Irish linen handkerchiefs, but where were you, where in fuck's name were you. The housekeeper, the French one, or the Italian one, or the Colombian one, would always say that you were due back, you had been to lunch, but then after lunch you were tired and in need of your siesta, and then it was teatime and what's-their-names were coming, people you didn't really know but who might be useful, some dope that owned a museum in San Miguel or Lucca and then some earl was taking you to drinks at six and you would have to get into one of your creations. You had so many creations they would fill the *Titanic*. I can see them, smell them, those sweeping gowns of yours. I gave a scarf once to a girlfriend and you saw red . . . I had to go and humble myself and ask for it back, I had to lie and say it was not yours, it belonged to the Colombian. You bitch. Of course you would phone me in the early morning and ask how I had slept . . . Coo-coo-coo-coo. Ask what I would like for breakfast . . . ask me in a smattering of French and English . . . reminding me that I could have anything so long as it did not have to be cooked . . . I could have toast or bran muffins . . . fuck your muffins, Mother . . . hey . . . listen, why don't *you* do it . . . go on, have the courage. It's simple. I got the booklet. I swotted up on it and this is what you do . . . you down the bottles of vino . . . get the good stuff and then your bottle of Nembutals . . . you have them . . . I know . . . you send a driver specially to that chemist in Horsham, he gives you one hundred at a time and you hoard them like you hoard jewels. Splash out, Mother dear, splash out . . ."

Here the tape slid and there were only slurps, as presumably he drank. Then the voice resumed, except that it was softer, contrite. "Mother, do you know *The Seagull* by Chekhov? You must know it. You must have seen it often, there is a mother like you and a son like me. He goes down on his knees to her, he begs. All I ever wanted was to do something to make you proud of me . . ."

When the voice took up again, it was hazed, lost, already half dead: "Too late, Mother . . . it's working, eight cans of special brew and now the last fistful of pills . . . if only I knew where you were . . . are you out at some party . . . or are you having an evening in . . . your TV supper on a tray . . . I saw you this morning in the patisserie . . . I wanted to run to you . . . Too late . . . It's working. Maybe you will come through the door . . . maybe you will and I'll be pumped . . . All I wanted was time . . . ti . . . me . . . Dar . . . ling . . . Daaarrr . . . ling . . . Mothhhhhh . . . er."

The cassette had Iris's name written in capitals, was dated the previous June, and was signed:

YOUR EX-SON, ANDY

I felt a shiver, as if he had just stepped into the room. I imagined him pale, thin, I even imagined he had blond hair and blond eyelashes.

The moment it was light, I stood in the landing, outside her room, waiting for her. She came out, calling the servants:

"Conchita . . . Conchita . . . Pepe . . . Pepe."

When she saw me she realized that something was amiss and asked if I had seen a ghost, adding that the house was supposed to have the statutory ghost, a woman no less who had drowned herself in the artificial lake. I wanted to embrace her but somehow her coldness and her cleverness were deterring me. Half of me was saying, "Go ahead and tell her," while the other half was apologizing for having spent the night. I kept rehearsing it, I even saw her drop her defenses and weep, telling me some key moment, as where she was when she heard it, when the news was broken to her, and who she turned to.

"I played some tapes," I began to say.

"Don't you love Callas . . . don't you love that sleepwalking aria . . . her trance," she said.

"Another tape came on . . . a young man's," I said. She stiffened. All seemed havoc for a moment, the very center of her being smashed, and rage issued from her like the vapor from erupting lava. She knew.

"Pepe will take you home," she said and she called loudly, harshly, like a street vendor. I could see clearly her terror, her blue vitreous eyes, the bone of her nose aquiver, her morning gown voile, and I thought that if I could say it, something tender would occur between us and the stone inside her would dissolve. I thought of the blood of martyrs in churches in Italy which though solidified turns to liquid one day a year. The prayers of the faithful cause them to melt. All that was needed was faith. Even as I tried, I knew that I could not take those few but immeasurable steps between me and her, between me and life, and that in two or three minutes I would be gone, dispatched, and rubbing her hands she would order breakfast and shout out to herself: "Imbeciles . . . that's what people are . . . liars . . . imbeciles . . . ogres"—and walking to the breakfast room she would snap off the dead heads of the roses and think that in the future she must be more careful, she must take precautions, because one must, one simply must protect oneself from people, horrid, prying, inquisitive, thieving, stupid, callous people.

10

A wind was rising and along the road various boughs and branches had fallen. The driver did not speak, just exclaimed from time to time, said, "Sirocco . . . sirocco," and chain-smoked. As I got out of the car the wind whipped about my feet, its howl like the combined and furious seas of the world, while within it there was another sound, a shriek, as of doomed newborn infants.

In the hotel lobby, various telephones were ringing, but no one answered them, as both the desk and the switchboard were unattended. It was still quite early. The very young sleepy waiter rushed in, jumped over the bar counter, grabbed a bottle of brandy, and ran out again. I followed him as he hurried up the steps toward the pool. The wind had ripped the plants out of the terra-cotta pots, so that they lay with clods of clay littered over the steps, along with shards and splinters; the fallen pots lay on the ground like great Neolithic carcasses. I could hear voices and commotion.

A small crowd, including some guests and some staff, were huddled around a woman who was holding a little boy in her arms, talking to it, talking in a strange voice, as if hypnotizing it. It was the German woman whom I knew slightly, who wore a different bikini day after day, had a blue celluloid sunshade over her eyes, and frequently asked her husband to oil her back. She was holding the little boy, Otto, in her arms, talking to him. He looked safe, like a sheaf inside the big towel, but by her talking I knew that he was not safe. Around them were several people, including her husband, who fingered his wide bronze mustache as he kept saying, "We try to watch him, we try," hideously mixing past and present because it was clear from all the faces that the little boy was lifeless. The mother was speaking to her child, praying, waiting for his eyes to open, his pulse to beat again, his heart to start thumpety-thump. But the men knew it was all over, the waiters knew, and the father knew, because they had given him the kiss of life, they had done everything they could after the mother dragged Otto from the deep end and brought him to the metal ladder, screaming "Help" in three languages.

"He try to do what his sister do," the father said to the waiters, to the bystanders, and now to me. The storm had wakened the little boy, the clatter of things breaking and rattling had wakened him, unduly early. He had crept out of his cot while they were still asleep and had gone down with his water wings to the pool, had got in, believing somehow, in his dazed state, that his sister or his father or someone would follow. His sister stood looking up at her mother, expecting a miracle. She was holding a box of crayons which someone must have given her along with a jotter. Most of the people were in their night dresses with coats over them, which they clutched in the wind, but the mother was naked as the towels slipped, though the headwaiter again and again tried to put them back in place. She threw them off, not knowing what she was doing, begging her husband to give Otto life, to bring it back, while all the while her husband pleaded with her to take brandy from a spoon. On the ground and looking hideously garish were the blue-and-red water wings, one squelched and the other flat. So this was the little boy that I saw day after day, witnessed his pranks: he would stand on the first step of the ladder with his blue-and-red water wings already donned, simulating fear, doing oohs and aahs until his sister, Greta, lifted him in. He would call in his high childish voice . . . Greta Greta, and soon as he was in, he wanted to get out again, then ran to his mother or father to dry him and then back to the ladder to simulate the fear and do oohs and aahs until his sister lifted him in. The mother is speaking to Otto, half speaking, half singing, in a coaxing voice. When the coroner comes she breaks down completely, describing it in broken English, searching for the words and somehow finding them, the words that tell that she cannot face it, that she does not believe it, and that something must be done. She tells how in her sleep she heard the wind, she heard the voice of her little boy, the soul of her little boy crying, "Mama, Mama," and she wakened, looked, saw the empty cot, the covers thrown off, ran, and as she says all this, she is clutching the shirtfront of the coroner, who is a solemn man and sad-looking, sad no doubt from what he's called to do day after day, dawn after dawn. As she is talking, he is trying to write things down, but is impeded by her assaults. He alternates in her mind between friend and enemy, because at some moments she is talking calmly to him, reasonably, and at others she is shouting as if it is his fault, as if he has come to accuse them of being negligent, of not loving their little boy;

then she screams as she relives the run she made, down the stairs, down another stairs, across a courtyard and a shrub garden and to the pool, where she does not need to look; she jumps in and finds her little boy and it is as if he is not dead, he is sleeping, he is trailing . . . "He is not dead, he is sleeping," she roars it, for all to hear, and her husband puts his hand gently across her mouth, his ringed marriage finger looking absurd in this light, in this crisis. Her husband takes up the evidence for the coroner. There is something barbarous about the fact that it is all being written down, her waking, her running, her jumping in, her swimming back up, her relief that her little treasure is not dead, even though he is dead. He describes his own running to the scene, meeting a waiter on the way, the two of them assisting his wife, laying Otto out—he can hardly say the name—on the grass, trying to revive him with the kiss of life. He looks at the waiter with immense and useless gratitude as he says these things, then he, too, breaks down, but he checks himself and puts an arm, a needful, comforting arm, around his little daughter and says wretchedly, "Otto try to do what his sister do."

A young policeman arrives, shy and unshaven; he stands next to the coroner as if that is the proper thing to do. They are trying to take the sheaf from its mother, begging her to move from the spot, as if by moving she will feel less demented, she will admit the fact that it has happened and that it cannot be made to unhappen. I think of Iris with a mixture of rage and pity. What would she do if she were here; would she break down? Suddenly and to everyone's surprise the mother hands Otto over, like a little parcel, and then possessed of a whim of modesty she draws the towels around her and looks at me and shakes her head. I shake my head in return. We used to have conversations about the room we went to each week to have our hair done, a makeshift place, the owner's sitting room, where she used to have to carry the bowls of hot water in from the kitchen. We joked about it once, how primitive it was. The father carries the little boy and walks off up the steps, not knowing quite where he is going. The headwaiter tries to disperse the added crowd, some to weep, some to watch, some to mutter about how careless the parents had been. Most of all they watch the mother, the gnashing mother, who cannot believe that it has happened because it is a ghost happening, a ghost death, there is no grave to mark the actual spot where her little boy went down, down into that pocket of water that is no longer there, dispersed as it is by other pockets of water, and even as we look we hear cruelly the plop-plop as through the vents fresh water issues, bubbling, gurgling, indifferent; as is the cold windy surface with its impersonal little pleats.

Suddenly she is berserk again. She refuses to follow the cortege. By following she will have to admit that she is being parted from her little boy, whom in life, day after day, second after second, she took for granted.

"I can have no more child," she says, grasping the coroner's arm.

"You can," a woman says.

"I can have no more child," she says and the woman tries to comfort her by saying that God wanted him, that God wanted her little boy very much. She reacts to this with such rage, such frenzy, it seems for a moment that she is going to claw the woman's eyes out. She lifts her hands, draws them down over the woman's face as if putting a curse on her or else transferring the curse that she feels has been put on herself. She runs after them, snatches the infant back, shouting and keening over it, bringing her face to it, breathing, whispering, even putting it again at her cold breast to suckle. Her husband pulls her away, not quite so gently now, as the headwaiter tells the crowd that it is best to leave them, it is best to leave them alone to grieve.

We watch them walk away, a tableau of mourners and officials. Up to then, they were a German family who had brought their breakfast charcuterie down to the pool and picnicked, now suddenly they are the pitiable ones who have lost their little boy. The storm makes it worse, adds to the calamity, a hectic wind blowing things about, oranges fall through the air in a mad flourish and the stalks of flowers on the ground are oozing a white stuff. Someone says that the family are going back to Germany to bury Otto, are driving straightaway to catch the ferry. There is no way that one can imagine that drive, past ravaged fields, roads strewn with boughs, past strange towns, through a land where they must feel that fate had crushed them.

Later the headwaiter came among us and asked us if we would be so kind as not to tell newcomers since it might put a damper on their holidays. Without his glasses, his eyes looked hurt, not the hurt of the moment, but a bigger hurt. Then he rallied, looked at his big pocketwatch made of silver, and ordered the waiters about, and soon they carried baskets of breakfast to the various rooms, to the people who had slept through the tragedy and the others who had gone back to bed.

"How long will the sirocco last?" I asked the headwaiter.

"One day, two days, three . . . who knows . . . maybe you

never go home . . . maybe you are marooned here," he said, without laughing.

The poplars swayed like drunken reeds, poplars that would serve as wands to the unknown spot within the depths of the pool where little Otto had gone down.

11

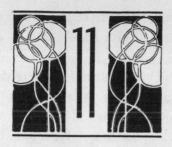

Catalina had not come, nor was there the usual heap of flowers on the table for her to arrange. The table itself had turned over. I stood in the courtyard looking at things, broken pots, ripped-off petals, and severed cacti that looked like disembodied crocodiles, waiting for her, eager for her, as if her appearance alone would dispel the morbid gloom. Even the hotel had lost some of its harmony, some of its allure, people skulking about, half fearing a fresh catastrophe. Eventually, when she did not arrive, I decided to go to her house, even while realizing that such a thing was precipitate. One of the other maids gave me instructions on how to get there, reminding me that there was her house and her grandmother's house, both bearing the same family name, but that her grandmother was very odd, shied away from people, and was thought by some to be a witch.

Along the street, people saluted or attempted to salute as they soldiered along or ducked to avoid a falling clatter of roof tile or gutter. Children ran about in outlandish clothes—curtains and tablecloths which they wore as togas. They were uttering some wild chant. It was an Arab chant in keeping with the sirocco.

"Shish-Kal-Abaam, Shish-Kal-Abaam, Shish-Kal-Abaam," they said in a shrill chorus.

A little group had gathered around one of the big houses and in the courtyard two huge white Alsatians were pacing and moaning. Here, too, tragedy had struck.

"Poor Walter . . . poor dear," Wanda said, pointing to the open door, through which I could see heavy brown furniture and vases of madonna lilies, which, having fallen down, looked weirdly libertine. Walter, one of the visiting Americans, he who days before, in the crowded bar, had boasted that the only thing that mattered to him was partying and that he would party with anyone, had had a heart attack. He had come down onto his terrace, like many another, to carry his plants in, when suddenly he keeled over and might have lain there to die but that his dogs raised the alarm by the ominousness of their howls. An ambulance had been called and he was being carried away on a stretcher, his dogs fretting; his boyfriend bulky, sullen, impassive. His boyfriend had not come home the previous night, had been playing cards in the next town.

"Poor Walter," Wanda said again and raised her eyes, implying that the heart attack was the result of unrequited love and not partying.

A woman whom I had never met before invited me to have coffee, and as I went through the door I recognized the Turkish hangings and the coffeepot.

"Doesn't D'Arcy work here?" I said.

"Work!" she said, admitting an impatience that was masked by infinite restraint and forbearance. D'Arcy had helped her husband to cast some sculptures, then had forgotten to leave, but he had promised to move out soon. As we sat there, eating currant biscuits and drinking very strong coffee, she talked about the winters, the damp, how she would like to go away in the winter, live in a big city and frequent the cinemas in the afternoon. The place was a paradise, true, but the winters wet and long and lonely.

"Maybe paradise is lonely," I said to cheer her. She had this wounded quality, as if at birth she had heard only one command: "Thou shalt go forth into the world and be a slave."

The front door burst open as the group of crazed children came in and circled round us, shouting: "Shish-Kal-Abaam, Shish-Kal-Abaam." Two of them were her children, changelings, out of place in the neat sad room. I excused myself on the grounds that I had to make an urgent telephone call and she stood in the doorway to try to detain me by reminding me that, due to the storm, the wires were down.

It was like walking through a heated void. The wind still thrashed and keened and in the distance I could hear the cocks crowing deliriously, which added to the displacement of things. The street was deserted and the road looked violated—carob pods strewn about like green bandaging, overturned dustbins and new tar in little heaps like oily turds. They had tarred a patch the day before. I went down the donkey path, and along the road, past the dried torrent and over the bridge, toward her house. Two acacia trees, like bridal trees, were in full flower, except that much of the blossom had fallen off and lay like limp garlands on the ground.

I could hear shouting as I approached her gateway and I was about to turn back, but I met a young girl who introduced herself as Catalina's sister, Rosario, and she told me to go on down, thinking perhaps that I had brought some message, some reprieve from the hotel. She was thin and shrewish, had none of Catalina's sheen or verve.

Through the open door I saw Catalina wielding a knife, then cutting bread in a businesslike fashion. A man, presumably her father, sat at the table, hunched but combative. He was waving a letter in his hand, a letter typed on official paper. She was different here, unwashed, unkempt, scruffy, bawling like a hyena. The kitchen itself was quite dark and full of clutter. Her father was the first to see me and as soon as he did he composed himself, raised an eyebrow without raising the lid, and made a finicky movement with his little finger, as if to say what a tawdry place I had chanced on, what a hovel. She turned, surprised to see me. She had put gel in her thick black hair so that it stood up in great swathes, and I could see that she was incensed. I heard myself mutter that I had been passing by, knowing that it was an idiotic thing to say. She rallied and in a sudden gesture of hospitality lifted a dishcloth and from underneath took a little tin cup that was filled with warm custard. She handed it to me, along with a buckled metal spoon.

"Eat . . . eat," she said, as if that was why I had come, as if starvation had driven me in. Its oversweet yet bland taste, its little curdles, its golden sugared crust brought to my mind the custards of long ago, when one was ill with measles or fever. A little boy stood near her, protecting her, stroking one spot on the calf of her leg, stroking it endlessly, round and round.

Knowing how I like tea, she put the kettle on, still sparring with him, matching every outburst and every fist of his with her own, emphasizing her fearlessness by standing near him, or prodding him with the end of a toasting fork, then returning to the stove and refusing to accept whatever barb he had just issued. At one point she ran and poured hot water onto the crown of his balding head and I thought then he would strike her. A woman, obviously her mother, came in carrying three eggs in her hand and by her expression seemed to say she was surprised that hens could lay eggs in a storm such as this. She held them out to Catalina as if to proclaim a miracle, as if they had been propelled from the hens' backsides by the havoc of nature. They were very white eggs. Because of where I was standing, she had not seen me, but the moment she did she gave me a suspicious look that said I had no business being there. She looked alarmed. I thought maybe she believed I had some connection with the hotel and had come to bring Catalina to work. Catalina spoke to her rapidly and in a low voice and I knew that she was explaining who I was and how she knew me. The mother looked at me again with a greater scrutiny, thinking probably of the privileged life I had, being able to travel, being able to stay in a hotel, my hands smooth, not like hers, which were worn and gnarled. Then she picked up two buckets and hurried out, presumably to fill them with water. A cat ran about the kitchen, rasping, looking under chairs, so much so that Catalina broke off from her duel, to explain that the kittens had been drowned that morning. They sparred and sparred, and either out of nervousness or to draw attention to himself, the little boy pulled his pants down and a great soft explosion of shit gushed from him.

"Diarrhea . . . diarrhea . . . my God," Catalina screamed, while in a gesture of disdain the father held his nostrils together and gave me a curious flirtatious smile. Catalina ran, returned with a half bucket of water which she sloshed on the floor, and then began to sweep vigorously.

It's all crazy . . . crazy," she said, her way of both apologizing and appealing to me. I stepped outside to avoid the splashes and waited, half wondering if I should go. The storm was abating and the sound of the wind now a heave, like the heave of a sated monster. The yard looked ravaged: fallen branches, fallen fruits, and the hens and ducks huddled together in earth baths, too frightened to move. Some toy trucks stuck up out of a bed of sand and I thought how she must have gone down to the sea and fetched it up. Hearing the row regain momentum, with now the mother's voice as well, I decided to leave. She caught up with me at the gate and thrust something in my hand.

"I've had it for years," she said. I looked down and saw a painted wooden blue eye, a protection against evil. The blue had been bleached by time, or else she had worn it when she swam.

"But it's your lucky eye," I said.

"Don't lose it," she said anxiously.

I loved her then, regardless of her unwashed body, her hair smeared with gel, loved the impulse that wanted to give me something, to make up for the absence of hospitality in the house.

"I had to come," I said, and she touched my shoulder, in a gesture of affection and forgiveness.

"I'm glad," she said, but presently she was running back toward the house, in answer to a fresh challenge. This time it was her mother, calling, and walking toward her with the incriminating letter. For some reason I imagined it was about money.

12

I got there early in case she decided to cancel. I dreaded the first moments when she would arrive, the clumsiness, not knowing what to say. It was Sunday, her day off, and I had reserved for lunch in another restaurant, under the mountain and overlooking the sea. Although it was daylight the moon still lingered in the heavens, it was not amethyst as D'Arcy had once predicted but a gray pockmarked embryo that shamed itself by being there. The light was shockingly, searingly bright, so bright that the cones in the undersides of the cypress trees stood out like very white knuckles, clear enough to be counted or to be smacked, one by one.

Geraniums festooned the surrounds, coral-colored, flagrant like cockscombs, tumbling out of terra-cotta pots, the incarnation and the emanation of redness that was not fire or flame but rather like a powder, a primordial rouge altering whatever it touched. Likewise the roses, thrilled and thrilling, the whole garden agog, the laid tables like altars waiting for their rite.

The water down below was a bright fidgety blue, but in two

places it was green where the roots of the two huge guardian rocks cast a shadow that had the amorphousness of cloud. Although I was expecting to see her come up a tall flight of steps, she came from the back through the garden, an apparition, a picture of radiance, herself a flower, a lotus, unfolding. It was as if the verve and prodigality of the geraniums had infected her. She wore a tapered, feathered earring, a white openwork blouse, and her pink muslin skirt had so many linings it looked like foam.

"I'm five minutes late," she said shyly.

The various waiters knew her and complimented her; and the headwaiter drew a vessel with his hands to show the outlines of a shapely woman. His wife, she whispered, was the local dressmaker, very fat, always complaining that her stomach was not like her clients' stomachs and wondering why this was so. She said that we would swim first, in order to get a big appetite.

"I won't," I said, too embarrassed to tell her that I couldn't swim.

"You must," she said, doing a little pout.

"Tomorrow," I said.

"Tomorrow," she said, and she was already removing her lace blouse, to show a knitted pink swimsuit underneath.

She ran down the steps and along the overgrown path, calling to one of the dogs to come with her. I saw her, then lost her, then saw her again as she went into the sea, a mermaid being carried away toward the patches of blue, going out as I thought to the spot where the rocks made imitation clouds, the dog along with her.

I felt lumpen, stranded, like the bit of moon, and I thought with longing of the two of us down there, hand in hand, together, plumbing the deep, my coming to know and trust the water through her, growing free, like seaweed, or reed.

People came with their children, their dogs, their swimming paraphernalia, and soon the waiters were carrying plates piled with calamari and chips thin as matches. One little boy made everyone laugh, because on seeing the rock, down below, which had a huge hole through its center, he asked if a giant had put his peepee through it. A beaded curtain divided the counter from the restaurant itself, and every time the till was opened, a little bell tinkled.

She came up the steps shouting with glee. She was mindless of the people around, as she called to me from afar, to look, look. She stood before me, dripping wet, her arms outstretched, proclaiming to have a blue body. Was she not blue throughout? The colors of the sea had got into her, the blue and the violet and the indigo had seeped into her like dye. They had. They had. She splayed her fingers, insisting on their blue surface and on the paler blue in the crevices. She was blue, upon blue, a creature Picasso had painted. Everyone stared, infected by her gaiety. It was as if she was determined to shock them.

"Do I look like a boy?" she asked.

"I don't know," I said.

"Take a look at me and tell me . . . Someone, some young man, down there, thought I was a boy," she said as she sat and opened the big wine menu which I had placed before her. The sun made little zigzags on her bare arm as she read aloud: "This much-favored wine comes from a region straddling the Gironde and the Dordogne, with strong British connections stemming from Henry II's marriage to Eleanor of Aquitaine."

"We'll have that," she said, and then asked the man if the gambas were caught that morning and how were they cooked and told him not to skimp with the garlic. First we would have spinach with cream and nutmeg. She was starving, ravenous.

She jumped up and grabbed a basket of bread from the next table. She hadn't eaten since the day before—another drama in their house, their crazy house. A stranger had called, in the evening, a dark, swarthy fellow with eyes that rolled round and round, a fact that convinced her mother that he was a drug addict. She herself was not there, but of course in the inquest that followed she had been given every detail, the rolling eyes, his menace, the certainty that he must be on drugs. He had arrived uninvited, had knocked on the open door, and had said her name: "I have come to see Catalina."

Her mother went berserk, and no wonder. Where was Catalina? No one knew. Her sister was already home from evening Mass but she had not seen any sign of Catalina there, Catalina had fled.

While she was telling me this, she put a present on the table for me, a gift from the sea, two beautiful stones perfectly rounded and looking so like biscuits that I almost put my teeth in them. One had a pale green coating like green icing and the other was like fudge. She took pride in telling the story of the stranger because this added to her sense of mischief, her longing for danger. Her mother, sister, and father knew at once that because he said her name, because he said Catalina, he must have met her, and that she must have tantalized him to the extent that he came and searched her out. She laughed as she described the scene, her little nephew bursting into tears and calling the stranger the devil. The stranger, it seems, sat there glowering, without being invited, his eyes going round and round but lingering quite often on the dish of warm paella that they were too frightened to eat. Each time her mother asked him what his business was, he blurted out, "Catalina, Catalina." Her sister swung her prayer book before his eyes and told him that Catalina was not there, asked him to please leave, since they were farming people who got up at five and would now like to eat supper. He pretended not to understand. He said the name Franco, which annoyed them further. The mother had to retreat to the bathroom a lot because his arrival had upset her stomach. The little boy cried and kept calling him Devil, Devil. When the mother switched on the television they learned the shocking news that there had been a rape in the vicinity that afternoon. Mother and sister at once came to the same morbid conclusion. Catalina had been raped. This man had raped her, because criminals always return to the scene of the crime. She laughed as she said this, laughed and ate ravenously. The gambas had come and she cracked the glazed shells with her teeth, then spit the shells out. The criminal had come to their house to expiate himself. Realizing this, her mother began to stagger, she always staggered when she was afraid. Her father, to show his importance, hit the plates with a big spoon, and the little boy followed suit. What were they to do, the mother asked her husband, who merely shrugged and said he did not know since he was not a woman and had never been raped and that, anyhow, women were the stupidest creatures on God's earth. He had no intention of attacking the stranger or defending the two women present if the stranger should strike again. It was up to mother and daughter. They repaired, it seems, to the back of the kitchen, where they hatched their plan. They offered him a repast. Rosario did it. She led him to the table, put him sitting with his back to the door. She ladled some paella onto a plate and begged him to eat. The two women then went to the well, filled a bucket of water, reentered the dark kitchen, crossed stealthily, and struck at the stranger as he was diving into the food. As they poured the water over him, they began to wail like witches, and then the little boy joined in, helping them to drag the drenched victim across the kitchen, out the door, and down the path, where he could sleep under the stars, before he was found, as he would be, by the police. Once inside the house, the mother began to ring people to ask if they had seen Catalina or if they had heard if she had been raped. She tells me all this, as if she herself had been there, party to every second of it. They pounce on her, converge on her as she arrives home, they maul her, thump her, question her about this man so that she has to admit that yes, she knew him, gave him a lift from the city that morning on her way back from selling lemons.

"In my van, in my van," her sister screamed. Catalina, refusing to be cowed by them, had picked up the little boy, who had fallen asleep, and gone to bed, hungry and surly. The stranger, as she said, was by now probably dying in a ditch from pneumonia. He had come from Wales, hoping to make a new life, to see a bit of sunshine, and what did he get but a douching.

Each time, before she lifted her wineglass, she dipped her fingers in the blue finger bowl, and once our fingers met in the cloudy, lukewarm water and I felt a current go through me, half fear, half desire, but when I looked at her she seemed oblivious.

"I often think of my mother and father when they were young . . . so young . . . so vital . . . my mother, strong and well built like me, in her black dress, her black shoes and stockings . . . a migrant . . . who had come from the other side of the island . . . with the workers . . . to pick olives . . . my father seeing her . . . deciding on her, flirting with her . . . lifting his eyebrow the way you saw him lift it . . . giving signals . . . at lunch

. . . when they all sat down, winking . . . making sure that she had the best piece of bread . . . and in the evening when she lay down . . . they all slept out of doors . . . they all brought their own blankets . . . my father going in search of her . . . finding her . . . bringing her somewhere very quiet and beautiful . . . to his own house, maybe . . . he owned the house and the land . . . he was the master and she was the slave . . . but he was the handsome master and she was the willing slave . . ."

Then she told me that she was going to tell me something she had never told anybody in her life. I flinched in case it was something too intimate, while in another part of my being I longed to share all her secrets. She believed that she knew the exact moment when she was conceived, that she was there then, there for the gasp and for the magnitude of it, but that she had not wanted to be conceived or to be born. The time was not ripe. I thought it a strange thing for one so young. This revelation came to her after she had taken some magic mushroom. She had taken it in another country, far from home, with someone else. She had seen strange visions, ravishing and frightening by turns. She had written them down and maybe one day she would show them to me, but then again maybe she would not. The man she was with wrote some of it, so that she was not certain which thoughts were hers and which were his. After lunch we sat and lolled, watched the people drift away, and the little mongrel dog, her errant escort, carry a bit of bamboo onto the terrace and wait for someone to throw it over the railing, allowing him to renew his mad canter.

The mountain was her bastion, the sea her passion, and she marveled at that surface that housed lions, calves, woods, flowers, fish; all subject to the most terrible transmutations. She loved the sea, she said, loved it in all its phases, she had lived looking at it for over twenty years and it was still a mystery to her, she did not have eyes deep enough to take it in, in all its depths. No albatross she.

Upstairs in the ladies' room she had grown lighthearted again. As we stood in front of our respective mirrors, she lifted her white lace blouse, geisha-like, and said, "I cleared two terraces to get this blouse." Her body was thin and wiry and for some reason made me think of a guitar. She had a little scar on her stomach, a zigzag knife cut. Music suddenly blared. With the luncheon guests gone and the headwaiter off home to have his siesta, the other waiters allowed themselves a bit of levity as they cleaned the tables and quaffed what was left in the wine bottles. Suddenly and without deliberation she put her arms out, as if weaving through water, and then she started to dance, a lazy dance, moving not just to the music but to some inner sway. Her fingers tapered and her shoulders went round and round with the ease of new tennis balls. She made me dance with her and carried away by her own boldness she led us out of the cloakroom onto the long corridor with floor-length windows that opened to the garden. I felt certain that we were going to levitate, while also fearing that I moved with the stiffness of an old perambulator.

"Let go . . . let go," she said in a whisper.

"I can't."

"Of course you can . . . first your feet . . . then your knees . . . then your head . . ."

"I can't," I said again. To make matters worse, the waiters had formed a circle down below and were clapping to show their appreciation. I prayed for us to stop, but on and on she went, over the slippery tiled floor, getting adventurous in answer to their catcalls.

"They're watching," I said.

"Let them watch," she said and from time to time she made a face at one of them as if to challenge him. He shouted some name up and her reply was a shrug.

"What is he saying?"

"He's reminding me of my past," she said, and added that he was a cheeky fellow.

Later, and as a reward, she said that I could come and milk the goats with her. Normally her mother and the little boy went, but for once her mother could sit at home and bathe her poor feet. I waited on one of the terraces not far from her house while she went off to get Carlos. It was a respite to come away from the naked glare of the sea light, to this bower, the eyes soothed by one green after another: the dark green of the flowering oaks, the silverish green of the olives, the branches of pines like feather, forming a screen between oneself and the world. It was as if I were being dreamed, as I sat there waiting for her, the tips of the young pine trees yellow-orange, votive candles ablaze in the golden afternoon sun. I thought that perhaps my mind was made up, that this surely was the place for me to stay, and moreover my friendship with her was no longer so stilted. At some moments the birds were singing and warbling and then again a silence reigned as if they had all been whisked away to one of the other terraces. I thought of poor Charlotte alone at Ca'an Pintada, hiding and weeding, and I resolved that I would write to her, ask her for a drink, make some little overture now that I was happy. Some children passed, their hair the color of molasses in the sun, and on the terrace just above me a man was pulling a donkey on a rope and playing with it, lasso-like, as if he were at a rodeo. They came, chatting like grown-ups. Carlos would say something and she would repeat it, or exclaim as if he had said something preposterous. He had obviously slept well, because his face was smooth and his hair newly brushed. He had a stick and with it he thwacked everything that he passed. at times adding a hearty admonishment. She didn't linger, she simply nodded to me and I took up my steps behind them. A feeling of delicacy overcame me, a qualm as if I shouldn't be party to their chatter, and moreover it set me off on another train of thought, memories of my own children as children. I smelled them there and then in the mountain air, a memory smell, quite distinctive, as distinctive as bread smell or a gardenia. I could see their little newborn wrestlers' bodies, being sprinkled with dusting powder, the powder bluish in the crevices, and how for years and years they adhered to me like limbs, branches growing out of me, wanting to do everything that I did, jumping into my high heels, or putting perfume behind their ears in imitation of me, and then the gradual stretching, burgeoning—chilling. Their spurts of independence, like choosing clothes that were in defiance of the slightly old-fashioned knitted things that I had togged them out in, then the motorbicycles and the scenes that were the prelude to their departures. I thought that perhaps it was their childhoodness, as much as his love, or my own long-vanished youth, that I mourned, or that they had all merged into a single prism of sorrow.

"What is he talking to you about?" I asked.

"He says he loves me," she said proudly and repeated all that he had been saying: "I love you, I love carrots, I love nuts, and

I love the goats," adding that it was a complete turnabout, because in the morning before she set out for lunch he said he hated her, that he hated carrots, that he loved chocolate, weapons, war, and killing. He had gone around the house and into the yard using his stick as a gun, assaulting flowers, trees, chickens, anything that got in his way. He was like that, full of moods. He would hide in a mud house with his imaginary friend, Giorgio, and they would plot terrible things—battles, raids, thefts—then in the evening he would relent and kiss her and go back to being an angel and ask for a fairy tale.

"Does he prefer you to his mother?" I asked.

"Sometimes," she said.

The goats came down to meet us, their bleats ahead of them, three generations of goats: a kid goat, its mother, and an old he-goat. They were off-white with speckles, their tongues the color of blueberries. She had brought a little corn in a pan to lure them, and their tongues ached to gorge on it. She said not to be duped by those soft tongues, they could eat anything, they could eat thorns, and did.

"Are you strong?" she asked.

"Why?" I said in reply.

"I want you to hold her while I milk her," she said and placed my hands on the crown of the goat's head, where I could feel the two stumps of wizened horn. The little boy was given the task of keeping the he-goat away. As she knelt she removed a cloth flap from the goat's teats, a necessary precaution because the other two would drink her dry. She had no illusions about family love, whether it was among people or beasts. She held the bottle slantwise and the milk came in little dribs as the goat bucked and reared, trying to escape and join her companions, whom the little boy was supposed to be herding. He lost interest in his task soon as a cat appeared. It was a huge fluffy white cat which kept watching the milk, like one mesmerized. At moments when the goat seemed about to break loose Catalina shouted, asking if I had never held an animal before. Determined to make the most of the journey, she seized the second empty bottle and began to draw on the pink shriveled teats. I held the tepid full bottle in one hand while the other tried to keep some hold on the goat, which grew more agitated as the last dregs were eked from her. Afterward Catalina gave her a sort of embrace, as a reward, then retied the cloth flap, stood up, and looked around as if she were seeing the place as a stranger might see it, as I might see it. All was silence, the olive trees with their gnarled roots and their distorted trunks seemed like figures in an enchanted slumber.

"I could live up here," she said, "with the goats and the grasshoppers . . . my own special little life . . . Carlos and me."

"Why don't you?" I said.

"Because fairy tales are things to dream about," she answered, quite abruptly, as if I ought to know that.

We stopped by a little house while Carlos fetched a plate, to pour milk for the cat. It was the tin plate that she had bought at the market. The house was only half finished and there were roof tiles and bags of cement lying about. It was called Ca'an Serra—House of the Many Mountains. She had built it so far, dragged the stones and the cement up, in a wheelbarrow. One day she would live there, she and Carlos would live there, then she would be independent. The two side posts and the lintel above the door were daubed with red. It was the blood of a ewe. Her grandmother had done it with a hyssop branch, to keep the

Evil One out: they believed in spells, in spirits, in incantation. They studied the flight of taloned birds and entrails for signs, signs in the color of gall and the symmetry of the liver lobe. Her grandmother had reared her, had told her many secrets, and together they traveled back in time to their bivouac days, to their Moorish ancestors. They saw what mortal could not see. "People think we are mad," she said with triumph. The cat watched us walk away, watched with a sort of knowingness; and darted through a window space to guard the house.

Where the paths forked we said goodbye. She seemed downcast, grumbling that she must go to sleep early because she was getting up at five. I watched her walk away, a little sad, a little disgruntled, and seeing the sag of her shoulders I thought of what she would look like when her children were grown, her body drooped from the toil and the years.

"I'll see you tomorrow," I said. She turned and looked at me with a baleful look. The tears in her eyes were so big they seemed like glycerine drops.

"Why are you crying?"

"Because I'm so happy . . . so happy," she said, but I could see that she was lying.

The letter was in my box the following morning along with the English-speaking newspaper. It was on ruled paper and written in capitals. It said:

SHE'LL DOE IT AND DOE IT AND DOE IT TILL DAWN.
—Robert Burns

My body froze, as I looked about, thinking that maybe the anonymous sender was sitting in one of the armchairs watching my trepidation as I read. I was suddenly afraid. People disliked her, there was something in her that provoked malice, envy. I saw the many glances when we were together, the looks, the nudges, the innuendos, and I thought how foolish to forget that I was in a small place where nothing, no matter how harmless, went unseen.

13

The flowers lay on the table, inert, some secured with rubber bands, all waiting for her ministrations, except that she had not come. By noon there seemed to be a consensus that she was not coming. She had not even resorted to her customary ploy, which was to send her sister, Rosario, with a note to say she had been taken ill. Her apron and her flash lamp were also gone. Rumors abounded, such as that she had gone to the rival hotel, or that she had joined a circus, and the burly hotel manager said that, wherever she had fled to, it was in self-interest, because she never did anything that didn't suit herself. The girl with the mustache said she believed that she had gone to work for the lady who had stayed in the hotel and who had had to have milk with which to wash her face. This I assumed to be Iris. I felt downcast, miffed. I took to the street, paced, in the hope that I might hear news of her. Eventually I found myself going up to the church, entering, genuflecting, uttering childish prayers in a singsong, distracted voice that was devoid of devotion. Without the phalanx of accusing women, I saw the various statues as fading and grotesque testaments to gore and suffering. The altar stripped of flowers looked bare and spartan, not at all the place for sacrament, or consecration.

As I came down the hill, a girl stopped me. She had grayish skin, like putty, and long hair which was severely and unremittingly drawn back. I thought at first that it was to discuss something about the church, or to ask for money maybe, but I soon saw the spleen in her expression. She asked if I realized that I was in a small village, a small community, where each person knew each other person intimately. Her lips were thin and met tightly like the leaves of a prayer book. Being English as she was, she brought to my mind those deserted country churches with damp weeping walls, unattended pews, a psalm on raveled embroidery, lesson books, and hand-printed signs appealing for things for the fete. How often I had slunk into them to mutter some appeal for him.

"I am a visitor here," I said, mustering authority.

"Visitors come here and try to taint the locals."

"Do you mean Catalina?" I said boldly.

"I mean Catalina," she said and in her eyes I saw an admission of love, buried, shocking—a love so intense, so intricate, she herself did not understand. I felt the color rise in my cheeks, imagining that she saw into me, saw my own desire mirroring hers, wild, inchoate, covert; a desire without precedent. To calm myself, I kept running my fingers over my room key, smoothing the metal as if it were flesh, trying to forestall one of those cloying berserk battles, which I had always envisaged, with a woman, at least a certain kind of woman, the ones who issue strictures or commands, who have replaced the milk in their paps with something tart and sour, the harridans. I dreamed of slapping her face again and again, pounding her, disfiguring her so that she became grotesque, a laughingstock to all who saw her.

"She is a free spirit," I said.

"She is a respectable girl, from a respectable family," she said and added that she and Catalina worked the land together, that their terraces adjoined, they went three evenings a week to water their crops, they worked like donkeys, they depended on each other. Her pride in telling me this was so great, so sensuous, that I felt that if she were to give vent to the passions within her she would swoon and lather like any medieval mystic. I thought of the several nuns who had taught me, nuns with the hushed footfalls who begrudged us our passage through the town each evening, where we could see streetlights coming on, or clothes in shop windows, and although we could not linger, we could hear men and boys talking or whistling as they mounted their bicycles or walked their greyhounds.

"The land is her life . . . not restaurants and scooters," she said, coming closer to me, as if to strike me, or at least tug at the collar of my jacket.

"I think you have made some very rash assumptions," I said.

"Not at all rash," she said, getting the last word, because presently she turned on her heel and went down some steps to let herself into a basement house, which I imagined to be hers. I wanted to run after her and continue the argument, while at the same time I pitied her, grizzled as she was with sorrow.

It had begun to rain, drops that did not get heavy but fell sullenly were eked from the sky. Because of the weather, the hotel lobby buzzed with people who sat and treated themselves to midmorning tea and midmorning coffee with slices of cake dense with cherries and green candied peel. Some kept pestering the girl behind the desk, asking her the price of the items of jewelry in the glass case. There were earrings, rings, and bracelets laid on twigs or on stumps of semiprecious stone. I decided on a spree. I bought a pair of earrings that were symbols of fertility, rounded and wholesome, silver ovaries.

From the landing that approached my bedroom I could see a tiny portion of mountain through bars, six iron bars with seven oblong spaces, showing me a patch of mountain, trees clinging to a breast of rock. Was this my life, was this my vision, as limited, as petrified as this, and through bars, from some unnamed prison. I thought of going back to search out the putty-faced woman, to violate her.

I thought of going to Catalina's house and warning her parents, I thought of confiding in one of the maids, except that I was not sure what it was that I wanted to say; in the end I rang the desk and told them that I would be leaving at the end of the week. By way of installing myself in my own house I rang my own number, and hearing it ring and ring, I traipsed around the room and saw objects that had in themselves become witnesses to my life, and in one of those moments of muddle I included certain objects that were no longer there, that I had thrown into skips or rubbish dumps because they had become reliquaries of him. I had thrown those cushions on which we had basked, and I saw, not with the scales of memory but with a palpability that overwhelmed me, that very first day when we had made love in my sitting room, a winter day, by the fire, on cushions, a bank of them, purple velvet cushions with gold lacings. There had been about it a detachment, a nonchalance, and I felt certain that I would not repeat it, or hunger for it. At the time it did not seem too important, did not seem like one of those brooches that, though pinned to the bosom, can sometimes accidentally go straight through to the flesh and the bone beneath.

Afterward I went to prepare lunch and he made some attempt at restoring order to the room, but he had done it so clumsily, in such an amateur way, that when I came back I laughed aloud, seeing the curtains only half drawn back, straggling on their brass rings, and the purple cushions in an ungainly mound on the chaise longue, dumped, allowing anyone, even a simpleton, to guess at once what had gone on in that room, in the daylight, with innocent snow falling outside. Seeing his shy pride in what he had done filled me with a tenderness that was not dissimilar to the tenderness I had felt for my sons when they were still very young and would do something ridiculous such as buy hats to make themselves manly, or in the case of my elder son acquire a walking stick, claiming as he did to be suffering from water on the knee. Imperceptibly I had admitted him, a seam had opened and he had joined the others, the very few others, whose bloodstreams I imbibed:

> And your blood in torrents
> Art O'Leary;
> I did not wipe it off
> But drank it from my hands.

Allowing the phone to ring and ring, I reentered my own room, opened the shutters, and looked out on my paved garden and the stone Buddha with its inscrutable expression. It grieved me to think that I had hurt myself by parting with my props, the cushions, the chaise longue, my glass lamp with a colored globe overlaid with segments of color, like the candied peel in the cake, and then it came to me in one of those dreadful little revelations that I had run away not because I loved him too much but because I feared I had not loved him enough, that I had not loved him in the selfless way in which as a child I had loved the saints and the martyrs, and that maybe now I did not know how to love at all. I was not capable of the sacrifice.

A few people sat around the pool with fawn towels over their shoulders, drinking hot chocolate that was exactly the color of the towels. Lights were being fixed inside the pool and the sleepy waiter had been given the task of going down with screws and disks which he was to affix at various points along the walls. Being a novice, he succeeded each time in dropping what had been handed to him and was to be seen diving deep into the water, his feet straight up in the air, as he rummaged around for things. Afterward, with a pleased sheepish smile, he came up to announce to the engineer that he had found some, but not all. It took an inordinate amount of time for each lamp and each saucer-shaped reflector to be fitted, so that the ladies and gentlemen kept complaining or consulting their watches and making sarcastic remarks. The engineer ignored them. From each large cardboard box he would take the equipment wrapped in plastic bubble paper, and open it in a leisurely fashion, often disappear and return without ever once acknowledging their fret. Then he would fit the wires and the flexes to the lamps and place them on a little table while he went off on some other apparently vital mission. Meanwhile, the young waiter sat on the edge of the pool in his wet trunks, shivering. They were very smart trunks and had the names of various French resorts splashed all over them. They could not possibly have been his own. Eventually he decided to treat himself to two of the hotel's fawn towels, and once secured inside this luxury tent, he assumed another expression, a sort of aristocratic bafflement, and presently he was smoking and calling to one of his companions to bring him a cognac and a café noir. His daydream was not to last. He was hastily stripped of his toga, and once again dispatched into the pool. People drifted off, telling each other and themselves that since the day was destroyed they might as well go for a drive or go to the glass factory or go and look at churches or any damn thing.

Around lunchtime, when I was called to the telephone, I knew for certain that it was Catalina. I could hear her even before she spoke to me at all, hear her confess that she had run away and was asking for my indulgence. I was certain that she had eloped with some man and thought that when we danced in the restaurant perhaps his name was the one shouted out. But it was Iris, asking me in the sweetest and most suppliant of voices if I would, oh if I would do her the teeniest favor, saying as she asked that she knew it was an imposition, and would I forgive her, please, prego, por favor. She had ordered two lamps and the stupid artisan had delivered them to the hotel instead of the finca. She couldn't trust a taxi driver on his own, since her driveway was a cart track, so would I bring them, holding them in my arms like the precious booty they were. She would give me tea, cinnamon toast, maybe a little glass of champagne, she might even find me a present, a trinket. By asking me, she had forgiven me, I felt, for having listened to her tape, and I was vaguely flattered, or at least relieved. Even before I said yes, she was thanking me, saying she would pay the taxi of course and give him a handsome tip. I could take him on to the port if I wanted to, have a joyride. I was to guard the lamps with my life. They were divine, simply divine, lapis lazuli, they were for her bijou apartment in Rome.

A servant opened the door and I could see Iris coming through the archway, hands out, to receive her trophies. She wore a worried expression. The thing was, she tried to phone me, but I had left. Plans had changed. She was leaving straightaway, we could not have a tête-à-tête. Her maid was packing and naturally she must oversee it. She took some money from her pocket and went out to pay the taxi driver. Then a whim of decorum possessed her and she said I must come up if only for a minute and have something, a glass of Vichy perhaps. She put me in the little sitting room that led to her bedroom, as she hurried in to say something to whoever was packing. She alternated between praising her one minute, then showering her with abuse, then coming into the anteroom to say some little pleasantry to me. She would say my name, slowly and languorously, then ask if I was having fun or if I had found a beau or if the hotel was still full of shopkeepers, estate agents, and anorexic upstarts from Battersea. The maid appeared, weighed down with two gigantic trunks. She was old and had unmatching brightly colored shoelaces in her canvas shoes.

"Nobody packs like her," Iris said, adding that it was a miracle to get her at all, since everyone wanted her, booked her weeks, even months ahead. She had a shawl draped over either arm, one was black, embroidered with red and white, and the other turquoise, its flowers embroidered in the same color, except the calyxes had a silver glisten to them, like thistles in frost.

"They would look so pretty on you," she said, and she allowed me to touch them, to feel the threaded pistils, and the little central nodules that someone had so devotedly stitched. Then she hurried back into the room and exclaimed because the señora had done something awful, something unheard of. Words passed between them and soon it was apparent that the señora was not a slave who packed for the rich but a virago in her own way, an artist who well knew how to throw a tantrum, because she was coming through the door, obviously threatening to leave. Iris hauled her back and from the pitch of the voices it was clear that they were both old masters at it.

Iris appeared in tears. Imagine it, the cretin was putting the lamps in, without wrapping them in anything, merely a tablecloth. She hated to do this to me, but she just couldn't sit with me because the moment she turned her back something disastrous happened.

"When I think what I pay her," she said, waving a fist toward the door. The señora came out with some more cases, smaller than the first. They were lizard and were a mottled gray-blue; they emanated a sort of menace, stationed there waiting for their dispatch. Somewhere in one of them, tucked perhaps in a scarf or a pillow slip, was the tape, the smothered secret. I rose to go.

"When will you be coming to Paris?" she asked and managed a girlish pout when I said that I did not know. I could hear a car turning in the front driveway and the dogs and peacocks resuming their frenzied cries. To my surprise, I saw D'Arcy get out of a sports car. He was in a white suit and boater and instantly put his finger to his lips to ask for my discretion. He did not know me. Iris rushed toward him, all composure and hauteur gone, and said, "You came, you came . . . my beautiful Lochinvar," and the last I heard was D'Arcy spouting about white Ophelia . . . her dreaming brow . . . her golden hair, as he spun an excited Iris round and round, while she begged to be put in her chariot, with her Pharaoh.

14

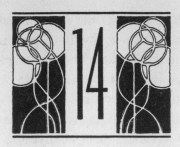

First it blew and then it snew
Then it friz and then it flew
Then it friz again.

It was only a few days later that I looked up from my deck chair to find D'Arcy, raw, unshaven, and full of animated bile. He managed a smile, however, as he put his hand out and said meekly, "The poor you have always with you." He was still dressed in the white suit but had discarded the boater.

"Situation dire . . . need shekels nunc," he said, calling at the same time for a drink to lubricate his scalding brain. As we went across to the bar he held my arm protectively, as a suitor would, and bowed to everyone that we met. At the counter, however, he erupted when the barman proceeded to pour his lager into a glass. Did the oaf not know, not recall, that Ignatius D'Arcy abhorred and eshewed other people's pusillanimous germs. The barman put the bottle on the counter and turned away to write the amount on my bill. D'Arcy drank quickly, pronouncing it a good gargle, a salve to the nightmare. His fling with Iris was over, abruptly terminated as he said, adding that Venus and Cupid had had some very rum jokes at his expense. He even apologized for the ungallant fact that he had snubbed me in her driveway.

"I seek neither truth nor likelihood," he said, "but I seek astonishment, as the blind Argentinian has said, and I tell you, brother, sister, there was no astonishment. If she had left me alone, it might have been all right, it might have been 'Awake, Iris, thou first amongst women' . . . libations pumped into her . . . but as it was, it was a question of suspension of all animal strength . . . desire vamoosed, nay knackered."

He asked very gently, very solicitously, if by any chance we could sit down and if he, D'Arcy, who had not eaten, could be permitted to suffer the enticements of an Armagnac. He carried the bottle across to one of the tables and pulled the chair out, ceremoniously allowing me to sit down. I thought, we will squander the money that he so badly needs, but I was too nervous to thwart him.

"Where is she?" I asked, dreading a swish of skirts on the steps, for Iris's umbrage I knew to be considerable.

"God forbid it . . . quoth he," he said and looked about sharply to make sure that nobody could overhear us.

"Kept me prisoner she did, we were in this gigantic suite—número 1503 and 1504, as I recall it; matching dressing gowns, little chocolados on the pillow . . . 'Isn't it cozy?' she said. Cozy . . . cozy . . . Jesus . . . of all the words in the vernac I abhor it most . . . it and sincere . . . a maggot is sincere . . . we have just stepped into the room and she bids me to perform . . . be Stud . . . little knowing that I have surrendered all intentions of same. As far as I am concerned, it is going to be bar-hopping and discoteca but no intergalactic sex on chocolada pillows . . . piece of meat in permanent purdah . . ."

He hit his forehead and asked himself in the name of Euclid and Pythagoras how he had got embroiled at all. A sort of rueful smile lit his features as he recalled their first entanglement—and spoke as if to himself: "She tried all the winsome, wonsome ways the four winds had taught her . . . She tossed her stumastelliacinous hair like the Duchess of Alba in her light gown spun of Sistine shimmer . . . half strumpet, half milkmaid."

Soon buoyed with drink and careless of those who passed by, he bawled out every detail of their rendezvous and his own sorry part in it.

"But you must have liked her . . . you eloped," I said.

"For a brief and shining moment I saw her otherwise . . . glimpsed the magic gnaw in her eyes . . . devilishly flattering light, plus devilishly flattering see-through gown, sharp-toothed necklace, jewels everywhere; blue, sapphire, amethyst . . . Over at her finca it was . . . candlelight, chicken au poivre, venerable wines, telephone calls from far-flung resorts, and I thought, this is it, D'Arcy . . ." and he knelt as he reenacted the proposal and called for slow music please.

Then he sat down, drank some more, shed some tears, and as if talking to himself relived every moment of the proposal and the theatricality of it: "I get off my chair, I get down on one knee, and lunatic that I am I beg for her hand. That was exactly eleven days ago. I need hardly say that she accepts, jumps up and down like a yo-yo, does a few pirouettes, Nijinsky-style, and says, 'You naughty man, you naughty man making a fool of an old woman like me.' I confess to undying love. We make a plan, a lifetime of plans, Cleo and Mark Antony on their barge, the world opening up before us, the Nile, the mouth of the Nile, the source of the goddamn Nile, and meanwhile in some small crevice of the cranium a thought is being deposited that I will give her a year, perhaps two, and then I am a free man, a man of means, that I will set out for Japan and track down that wench, one Ming who has lascivious powers over me, and I will even know if D'Arcy the spoiled priest has spawned an offspring or not . . . She asks if it can be a plain gold wedding band, nothing too ornate, something simple and chaste to match the sagacity of our years. She sees us walking under lime walks in our extreme old age. She omits to note that her old age has a decade on mine. I might have sniffed something fishy . . . a rich woman, alone in a finca with no friend, no husband, neither kith nor kin, but she fooled me . . . asked me not to trifle with her. She even demurred. She begged if she could think about it, said she had accepted too blithely, asked if she could give it the sagacity of a night, and Jesus, I fell for it. We were alone, two storm-tossed seagulls or barnacles or some other migratories . . . We could be a team, a team together, buffeting the winds. Crafty, the common touch. Buddies. Not man and woman but team. I did not lay a finger on her . . . I did not go up the twelfth-century staircase . . . She waved to me from the gallery . . . blew kisses, trilling kisses, a suite of kisses, flourished an embroidered shawl . . . 'tis but a spring to catch an impecunious cock like me as Jolls Joyce has already sagely noted. I came home. Pondered. Succumbed. Gave up my studio, Jesus, gave up my studio, and not long after, in fact two matins later, you saw me in her driveway, in white suit and boater, relics from my dandified days, and as you know we set out with an army of luggage, enough to go up the Nile or to pitch a tent in the Sahara Desert. First stop, Barcelona, and I tell you it was not 'Yon Duomo San Colón,' but hosiers, seamstresses, furriers, jewelers, and crimpers . . . it was yours truly in tow, as Iris tried on one gown after another in some midget-size boutique. Iris caparisoned in purple, in gold, in turquoise, and in eau de Nile. Then it was back to the boudoir for the grand toilette and our first bathe together . . . Up to the big suite in the deadly silentest of lifts . . . down a glittering corridor . . . She plonks the "No Molestar" sign on the door and claws at my starched shirt in her haste to remove it. Jesus, I'd rather be taken with an apoplexy like Gustave Flaubert or suffer the blind piles like the Irish friars than go through that fiasco again. She undresses to show a good example. Her waist and her thereabouts, white as lard . . . never saw sunlight or even lamplight . . . Acting like a little hussy . . . saying things . . . endearments. I cannot stand endearments, words like 'sweet' or 'sweetie pie.' I cannot stand the oils or perfumes she has lathered herself with, and I cannot stand those thin white arms barnacled in bracelets, but oh, the voice, the voice is the worst . . . like gunge. Stump in a sulkato. She bids it to rise . . . to be gallant . . . to show its prowess . . . Mark Antony and Cleo tousling. It declines, visibly shrinks from her sight, like a retard. In my thigh energy not only a serious depletion but revulsion, puke. She begs me to allow her to do a little coaxing, a little somethinging . . . I consider strangling her, but think better of it, and ask to be excused, to be allowed out, to stand on the terrace, to breathe refreshing fresh air, to which she says, 'But of course . . . but of course,' changing from Cleopatra muse to Florence Nightingale nanny, even, dare I say it, fashioning two pretty little poxy tears. On the terrace I see the harbor, I see ships in the harbor, and express the wish to be the lowliest cabin boy, signing on. She has put music on . . . Edith Piaf . . . I listen to the Paris linnet while addressing the shriveled member and wait. The appelate decides to ignore me. Case clear. Phallus Banjax. She cannot wait . . . she puts her hand out, draws me in, while in her other hand I see Vaseline. Title of reaction—Puke. The Roman version.

" 'Oh, you little Roger, you little scamp,' she says, applying this unction, under the impression, false impression, that her solicitude is going to incite me, member and all. Murder crosses my mind once again, only this time more strenuously. I think I will crush her with a pillow. I will do same without any of Othello's oscillations. When she sees that I am beginning to flip, evidenced by an open mouth poised for curse and imprecation, she has the presence of mind to ask if there is something wrong. 'Something wrong? Darling . . . darling?' she asks. 'Nothing wrong,' I say. I tell you I would not live those moments again for all the money and bishops' palaces in Ferns, Swords, Limavady, or Termenfechin . . . Old Edith choking away on the arrows of love while yours truly announces that he must have champagne and that it must be Crystal.

" 'But of course, but of course,' nursie says. While waiting for it to be sent up, she gives me the pukes by telling me that she understands, she quite understands, she mentions lovers in several continents, earls, counts, Knights of the Garter, all laid low with prostate hernia or some other hardy affliction. For some reason that I will never understand I tell her a story that could only be calculated to offend. I tell her that Sir Isaac Newton was so absentminded that once and only once, when he loved a young woman, he sat smoking silently, then at length took his pipe and seized her hand, and she, expecting that he was about to kiss her, got the shock of her life when he stirred and cleaned his pipe with her little dainty forefinger. Jesus, she was up, clawing, screaming, Lady Macbeth instantato . . . was it a young girl I sought . . . was that it . . . was I one of those middle-aged men who needed a young girl to stroke his ego . . . If so, why had I led her this far, because after all we had both embarked on this, we had signed the contract. Contract! I was under house arrest." He reenacted the arrival of the champagne, a scut of a waiter, black trousers too tight, like a ballet fopper, tearing the dun-gold paper cork, holding the bottle with a pink napkin and opening it quietly and with conceit, then waiting for the emolument which she was loath to give. In the end she gave a pittance.

"Do let's talk," she had said, soon as the waiter went out of the room.

"I cannot speak more plainly" was what he had said, and to prove it opened the cord of the chenille robe, which he had knotted before the flunky came in. He roared with a mixture of rage and shame as he recalled her expression, her alarm, which grew so great that she wondered aloud if she should call the manager and ask him to send up the hotel doctor; and putting her hand to it and not finding a fraction of elasticity she jumped and said he would have to do something, he would simply have to do something, as this was not good enough. Yes, she would call the doctor, he could get an injection of some kind, she was not putting up with this, this ignominy, she who had danced with the crowned heads of Europe, she who could be in Monte Carlo at that very moment, being toasted lavishly.

"Thunder and sparables," D'Arcy said, reliving his ire. "I mean, there is nothing wrong with me that a young girl or a young woman could not cure . . . I find a young girl pulling turnips and I'm around her with my tricolored equipment . . . but not Dame Iris . . . oh, no . . . Dame Iris, now petitioning if she should sit on my lap, if that is it, if maybe I am just a teeny-weeny bit kinky, if she could entice me therewith; and while staying my rage I do some serious thinking . . . I think poison is the last resort of a Hannibal . . . the dagger the last resort of a Cato . . . incision of the veins the work of a Seneca . . . but to this lapsed Christian poxy, silence, exile, and cunning. So I tell her that I must take a walk . . . I am the brooding type . . . If I walk along the harbor I will become myself again, my fundament restored to me. She deliberates. She agrees. I go to the dressing room and put on my white suit and my boater. I am now able to hum a little ditty. I come out smiling. She slips her hand into my inside pocket and relieves me of my wallet, in which there lurked a few mangy dollars that I had oggled out of her to toss to menials. 'I'll hold on to this,' the cow said, reiterating her suspicion that I will go to a bar in search of eighteen-year-olds. On my exit she wags a dragon fingernail and tells me to hurry . . . to come back within the hour so that we can dine and then boogie-woogie. Eighteen-year-olds! I haven't a fluke. I walk out of there penniless. I do not trust myself to use the lift, lest she should follow . . . I take a back stairs littered with banana skins and muck . . . I am broke, hungry, humiliated, but I tell you that I feel like Clint Eastwood at the moment in *Dirty Harry* when he throws his police badge into the river."

I used the moment to ask him how much money he needed to borrow. I dreaded that it would be more than I could afford. The light had faded, and the first star, that never-failing emissary, had appeared in the shallow font between the two ridges of mountain. Also, by his shuffling, I knew that the barman was waiting to close the outdoor bar in order to go down and work inside.

"Anything . . . ten dollars . . . twenty . . . fifty . . . even a hundred," he said, putting his face in his hands to hide his shame.

"I bought some earrings here . . . I can return them . . . They were two hundred . . ."

"No readies," he said, or rather muttered.

"I'll see," I said and hurried off, not in the least worried that I would have to part with the earrings, or put the refund toward my bill.

In my room I signed his name on two of my traveler's checks, colored checks with lilac tints in them. They seemed to be more like paintings than money. When I got back to the terrace the bar was closed, the metal grating down, and no sign of D'Arcy. I thought maybe that he had gone across to the pool to have a stroll and I called, expecting to see his figure, but all I saw was the restless sheet of dark water, and the poplars as always, sentient, keeping guard. I called his name a few times, and then, as I went down the steps to search for him in the lobby, a young waiter came running toward me and handed me a note. I read it by the light of one of the lanterns. It said:

> Only friend . . . not a word of truth
> in anything I said . . . All for your
> amusement . . .
> Con amor por amores . . .

"Oh, D'Arcy," I said aloud and to no one. The waiter was already disappearing, his white shirt in the dark like a flying banner as he hurried to his next charge.

15

I found Catalina on the top step of the stone stairs that led to my room. Her head was down and her hair spilled over her face, covering it completely. At first I was not even certain if it was she, then I recognized her by her pink running shoes, and she looked up, desolated, haggard.

"I'm back," she said lamely, admitting the mistake she had made. She hated the city, had to share a room, an attic room, with her friend Teresa, who lived like a mouse. Teresa's little girl, Aurora, laid low with whooping cough, barked all night. She came to see me first to gather courage because she was afraid to go home. She would be punished for weeks and weeks. Then she ranted on about family ties, family chains, family madness. Baby birds, she had read, never build a nest within ten miles of the parent birds, and she could see why. Equally she should not have gone, she had made a fool of herself.

"In what way?" I asked.

"There's only one way," she said and nodded. Yes, it was a man, and she threw herself at him; he was someone she had met the previous summer at an English-language course, and she who believed that she would never fall in love again had fallen.

He was cold and austere but the coldness was only a mask. She sensed that the first time she had set eyes on him, on his sad, El Greco eyes and his long, beautiful El Greco face. They were staying in the same guesthouse and on the last night they all drank, students and teachers together, and afterward when she went to her room she couldn't sleep, because she knew that he was waiting for her, and on impulse she pulled a coat over her shoulders and went across to the main building, where he was sleeping. She knocked on his door, surprised him, told him that she knew it was rash but could they talk, could they talk. He got dressed while she waited in the hallway and then together they went down into a big old rustling garden that lay above the sea, and between the sighs of the sea and the rustle of the bamboo they talked, talked about everything, love, marriage, children. He confessed to her that he had dreamed of her on each of the three nights since they had met. The next day being their last, they walked in the garden again and she gave him a black pod full of black seeds and he told her that he had never told anyone the things he was telling her. He told her that he loved his country yet longed to leave it, that he liked teaching yet dreamed of being free, far out at sea, alone, that he loved his wife and children but they were ropes around his neck, that marriage was a jail and life itself nothing but a purgatory. For a year she had thought of him and twice she had written, and then one night, one fevered night, she telephoned him, wakened him, and he had said yes that he was happy to hear from her and that he would be happy to see her. Thinking it meant more than it did, she gave up her job, lied to her parents, said that Teresa and herself were going to run a boutique in the city, and even left the little boy.

"I hate myself," she said and lamented the misery she had caused, then regretted losing her job, and as she looked around she remarked that the flowers in my room were not profuse enough.

"Maybe they'll have you back," I said.

"They won't . . . they hate me . . . they think I'm reckless . . . just like he does." Thinking of him afresh she burst into tears, recalled going to his rooms in the university, finding the door open and waiting for him in his office, his coming in, his surprise at seeing her, his attempt to brush her off by looking about for books and papers, his postponing the moment before he kissed her and then doing it so suddenly that their noses collided and they drew apart shocked by the current between them. Soon after, terse things were said. She should not have come. Yes he remembered the garden and the night they had spent talking, a coat thrown over them, yes he remembered the black seedpod, and yes he had lost it or thrown it away, he was a different man now. Up there in the north, he had forgotten his responsibilities, reneged on his true feelings, he had been another man. Nothing she said would make him admit either to the sweetness or to the shiver of what passed between them. He was telling her to come to her senses, to study, not to waste her life as he did, as so many did; to waken at forty or fifty to find that they had missed the boat. Finally she asked him one favor, one small favor, and innocently, or else to get rid of her, before his secretary came, he said yes. She asked him to give her a baby. He looked at her as if she was possessed. She went down on her knees and begged of him and here she began to cry, repeating her words, her shameless beseeching, his voice as he said, "I can't give you a child . . . I can't . . . I cannot . . .It would be milk . . ." thereby telling her that he had had the sterilization that he had threatened the night in the garden, that he had actually gone and done it.

"Why would you want a baby?" I said, aghast.

"Because I want him."

The movement of her lips, rapid, uncontrollable, told me that if she were to speak she would break down completely, she would own up to a sorrow greater than any she had known before. I longed to be able to tell her something that was not true, such as that it would be all right, or that he would change his mind, or that she would get her job back, anything to console her. From her bag she took a miniature rocking horse that she had got in a junk shop. It was painted red and white, and there was glue on the face, where a beard had been. It was for the little boy. He, too, might not forgive her for a week. It was growing dark outside, slanting pillars of darkness filling the courtyard, swoops of it invading the room, and far below, those crepe shivers, settling over the sea, presaging the cold at the oncome of night. There was nothing to be said. Each time she touched it, the horse sidled back and forth on its frame, giving a strange animal-like mewl, and now that it was dark she allowed her tears to fall and asked all the whys: why she had not met him years ago, before he married, why he had given her to believe that there was something between them, why he was afraid of her, why, why, why.

16

"We'll be up there, far up," she would say, making me queasy as I looked through the window of the bus at the jagged summits and the dizzying tree-clad slopes. Ranges of mountain appeared before us in a broken sequence as the bus furrowed its way over the narrow, winding road. At times we had to stop to give way to another vehicle, but the driver, accustomed to such inconvenience, was cheerful and gave way to everyone. She had quarreled with her sister, quarreled with her parents; ever since she got back they were all surly with her, terrified no doubt that she would go again. Even the little boy refused to speak to her, called her a devil, and would no longer sleep in her bed at night. Her sister refused to loan her the van because it was Sunday and she was seeing a friend.

"Friend!" Catalina exclaimed, and then, looking down at my green espadrilles, her anger spiraled. Did I think I was going to climb a mountain in those things?

"They're flat," I said.

"It's steep . . . it's rocky . . . it's full of thorns and bristles

. . . it's a mountain . . . you have heard of such a thing," she said, giving the people around us the benefit of her invective.

"We needn't go," I said, feebly.

"No, we needn't go," she said and decided to devote her attention to a little dog on a leash who was eagerly trying to break away from its owner. I looked through the window at the road, bits of wall, and the sea down below still gray, a gray shimmerless net. I feared the mountain. Something told me I would fall or disgrace myself, or that we might quarrel. She was scowling, eyebrows puckered, and I could easily see why her little nephew called her a devil. I could barely trace in her scowl the memory of the girl who had put flowers in my room or had danced with me languidly.

In the town, we got off the bus in silence, and still smarting, I followed her foolishly up the street. Behind us an English group were planning their day and it was lamentably clear that the younger couple wanted to go off alone, while the older couple did everything to cling to them. Eventually, when it was confirmed that the young couple were going to take a steam train to the city, the others capitulated, and the woman, making the best of it, said, "On your camels, then . . . on your camels." Catalina could not resist a smile, a sort of sad smile, as the woman, to hide her disappointment, spoke formally, and to no one, of the beauty of the place, and then addressed some chummy chastisements to a stray dog who was slinking in near the wall. I still felt it was unnecessary to buy walking shoes, since I had a pair in my cupboard at home. I could see them for a moment, all those shoes, cleaved and cluttered together, a jumble of black suede, brown suede, with straps of gold and silver, and my thick, ungainly walking shoes, with padded insoles, shoes I had bought in America in order to be able to walk along the Atlantic coast and pick stones and think about him, as if thinking about him would induce him from afar to think about me. In the shop, she knelt and tied the laces of my new shoes, making big bows because of the laces being far too long.

"I'll have to take a photograph of you in these," she said, trying to humor me. She had brought her sister's camera but there were only two shots left on the film.

Next door to the shoe shop was a cake shop, and it being Sunday, the confectioners were prodigal. There were wide pale buns, like hollowed breasts, into which cream and custard had been poured. The cream was whipped and looked substantial, whereas the custards were softer and spilled over. On a revolving, three-tiered glass cake plate there were little cakes dusted with castor sugar, their upturned alert wings like cat's ears, agog. There were tarts of every kind, some filled with jam, red and dark purple; others with an amber filling like opaque honey, all of them latticed with pastry. The smell floated out. It was both sweet and airy and cloying, and reminded me of the magic that I had invested cakes with, as a child, one in particular, an orange cake that seemed like a moist full moon. Catalina ran in, waving her cloth bag to show that she was going to buy something. On a cake tray, covered with wax paper, was the local cake, yellow, made with almonds and egg whites and spread with lemon curd. She bought two slices, each one resting on its own sheet of waxed paper, and assured me that it was not fattening. I bought another cake, which had many leaves filled with purees of jam, which she predicted would melt on the mountain.

"What is it like?" I said.

"It's like Mars," she said. "It's rusty, like Mars."

Going down the street, we ate the slices of almond cake. One of the waiters from the hotel shot by, tall and proud on a new scooter as if it were a steer.

"Where did you steal it?" she called after him, and he turned and grinned, pleased to have made her jealous.

We looked in the various windows, as there was time before the next bus. All the cups and saucers were bordered with deep blue, the blue I came to regard as being the color of that place and of her—wild, vivid, cobalt. Beside them were glass ornaments of animals, absurd and funny, with twigs of glass like whiskers sprouting out of their noses and their mouths. There were pots in every shade, wide amphora pots, some brown as if they had just been lifted out of wet, boggy earth, others painted in blue or green and frosted on the inside, as if sprinkled with saltpeter.

We nearly missed the second bus, and when she heard it and saw it approaching the monument, she ran, shouting "Pare, pare." I ran after her, thinking how the cake was getting squashed, and half hoping we might miss it, so that we could sit in the square and have tiny cups of bitter coffee, then at lunchtime have grilled gambas and wine, and later rest in the shade under one of the big trees where the people sat, talking and fanning themselves.

We drove along an exceedingly narrow road with houses and orchards on either side. The orchards overlapped, to form an endless canopy, light filtering through the leaves, giving a calm and muted quality to everything, as if the world itself were one vast dappled orchard. It was like being in a cradle, or a horse and cart, jogging along, our shoulders touching, our eyes soothed by the greenness that was enriched by the tinted window of the bus. She had pinned her hair up with two unmatching combs, one white and one diamanté, out of which some of the specks of glitter had fallen. Every so often she took a tube of cocoa-colored ointment from her pocket, unwound the screw, moistened her lips, and offered me some as if it were a lozenge or a cigarette. She was asking me what I had on my dressing table at home, if I had round pink bowls for powder and perfume sprays with crocheted nozzles and velvet flowers and caskets of jewelry. She had seen such things when she worked for ladies, visiting ladies, or when she had given them massages.

"You do that, too?"

"I have to do everything," she said haughtily.

I described my room: a big bed, an old mirror, and cream wallpaper with garlands of rosebuds teetering on thin gold threading; a bow window that opened onto a garden where an owl nested in the old fig tree and kept me company at night by hooting softly a lullaby. Why was I not there now, why was I in flight? What malady possessed me? I thought of a strange custom of my childhood which had to do with warts. To be rid of them we rubbed them with stones, then put the stones in a bag at an appointed place, for the fairies to take. Surprisingly, the spell worked and the warts did go. I had been chasing from place to place to bury some affliction, to leave it somewhere, except that no fairies came to the rescue and it dogged my every journey. At least now I was preparing to go back.

"Maybe you will come one day," I said. She looked rueful and said that she doubted she would travel again, it always brought nothing but trouble. She was destined to be a drudge on the farm. She painted a heady picture of her decline.

Getting off the bus, she took a folding timetable from her

pocket and confirmed the time of the last bus with the driver. He seemed to know her, or else it was that he was attracted to her, because they shared some joke which I did not understand. Over one shoulder she carried a cloth bag in which she had everything for safari—bread, cheese, salami, olives, a bottle of well water, and the family wine. I hid my espadrilles at the side of the road, under some scorched grass, and we had a bet as to whether they would be there or not when we returned. The tinted window and the drive through the orange groves had been misleading, the sun was boiling and streamed down as if from a molten funnel; it grazed and pierced the eyes; it leaped off the specks on her hair slide, and seemed to assault the cake through the white box with the absurd cerise ribbon. I felt as if I were being consigned to some oven, like white dough about to harden and bake. I wanted to turn back, but cowardice and reticence drove me on. We took a path that zigzagged between the spindly trees and bushes and I envied the lizards hidden in the thorny brake. She took a squashed straw hat from her bag, laid it on my head, and debated whether she should use up the film then or later.

"Later," I said, every nerve in my body raw, rebellious.

The path was overgrown with scrub and thorn but underfoot it felt sandy, with here and there bits of loose pebble and shards of rock. We passed empty houses, then one where dogs that were chained did everything with their snarls and their muzzles to get to us. She knew their names, she seemed to know the owners of all the houses, had worked for them or done piecework from time to time, such as digging their gardens or clearing their terraces. She moved like a goat or a young colt, darting from one boulder to the next. Some of the boulders were intact, but others, torn in two by storm or lightning, had seared orange centers. Now and then she would pat an olive tree as she might a friend. The olive was her favorite because of the way it lived and survived in aridity. The oaks, of course, were not your English oaks, they were the runt of the species, but nevertheless they provided acorns for the pigs, charcoal for the fires, tannin for the hides, and shelter for the shepherds and the charcoal-burners in times gone by. The world down below already appeared far away, the cars moving like toy cars at an ordained speed, and the steeple of the church was a long needle growing invisible in the glare of pure light. There were flowers, single flowers, mostly blue and pale purple, and once a butterfly flitted by and she ran after it, with cupped hands, to catch it in order to introduce it to me. Pointing to the oaks, she said that the young boys and young men used to catch the thrushes, wait for them as they hurried home at dusk, and catch them in their big nets, but that they would not do it again, because since Chernobyl the thrushes of the world had been contaminated and hoteliers would no longer buy them as delicacies for the guests. She said in its way it was a good thing that the tragedy happened, it made people realize that the world was one planet, countries were not separate, as they thought they were, but vast families joined by something far more important than creed, or politics, joined by nature; and answerable to one another.

We came on a little ruin that was covered with wild grass and brushwood. A few gangly blue flowers sprouted from the roof and in the near wilderness it looked like a fairy fort. She ran inside and called me excitedly. It was almost dark except for the points of light through the holes in the roof; in one corner there was a bed made of grass and leaves and beside it a stump of red Christmas candle, half burned.

"Home," she said with a flourish, designating the place as

our cave, with gongs, tapestries on the wall, deer being roasted, skins on the beds, us women and children huddled together as our knights rode off to war. She had read part of a book about things like that once. She had liked it but in the end found that it was too fantastic. "So you do read . . ." I said, remembering how she had once chided me for sinking myself into my books. She said yes, that she liked fabulous tales about gods and goddesses, and that her heroine was Gaia, the Earth Mother, who even when she lost everything was not vanquished. It was the only reference to her recent and doomed escapade.

Outside, I faltered at the sight of the steep bluffs, stone and still more stone, obelisks of boiling ocher, and the summit far up, too far.

"Why are we doing this?" I asked.

"I'll show you," she said and she pushed me forward with prodigal strength. Soon I forgot the heat, all of my mind geared toward the danger. I felt powerless to go on yet equally powerless to go back. At times the sheer rocks were almost perpendicular and we had to scramble on all fours. When we came to a ledge that was a mere rim, overhanging a ravine, she said not to look, to just hold on to her. I stared straight ahead at a circular peace sign that had been stitched in black on the back of her T-shirt. Very slowly we went across, and when we had made it, I saw that she, too, was trembling. There was sweat on her upper lip and she put my hand to her heart, to feel its agitation. It was beating fearfully, like a bird trying to break its way through a window.

After that, we came to an olive grove, the trees clinging together, holding each other up, like bowed witches. There was a ruin, some columns and a beautiful archway, a summer abode which an asthmatic king had built for himself. "Cadira del Rei . . . the walk of the king," she said, as she strutted on. The worst was over. The last bit of the climb was a sheep track and far less daunting. It was odd and comforting to see the sheep scattering before us, thin sheep, scattering deftly, more like fawns, not bleating, as if they'd taken a vow of silence. I felt elated, reckless. The first thing she did when we got to the top of the mountain—itself a fairly inauspicious sight—was to let out a holler, to inform the world that we had conquered. Then she took out the water bottle and we drank from it in turn and with gusto. She thrilled to be offering me a feast, her first as she said, and she would wink as she produced each thing—hard-boiled eggs, the salt already smeared on them, a chunk of cheese, very red salami that was thin and spindly, and little custards in tin cups. She poured the wine into other cups, added water, and we drank ceremoniously to Beauty, to Risk, and to Mars. She produced her little knife and began to cut the bread and the salami. It was a Toledo knife. She had found it on a wall and had called it Fritz, after a character in *Swiss Family Robinson*. She apologized for not bringing a paella. Her mother's paella was the best in the world, tender, their own rabbits and poultry. As she said it I recalled seeing them, in their dust baths, peppering, on the day of the sirocco.

"Has she forgiven you for going away?" I asked.

"Half and half," she said. Her mother didn't address her in the house, but when they went to milk the goats, she said a few rough words and that signaled forgiveness. She lay on her stomach then and began to eat, her face full of animation, a red shawl over one shoulder, and I thought that this was the picture of her I would carry away, her talking, eating, confiding. It was not the first time she'd left home. She had run away at eighteen, gone to Turkey; she'd had an adventure there, many adventures.

Once at sundown, or rather before sundown, she'd left the little town to go into the hills. Some children from a gateway ran to greet her, her shorts and bathing suit a fascination compared with their older sisters and mother and grandmother, who were swathed in scarfs and veils. The children had dragged her in. It was a sort of courtyard where the women sat, on one long form, knitting. Underneath their swathed rags they wore floral pantaloons. They thrilled to see her and posed while she took photographs of them. The children clambered over a big red motorcycle, a Jawa, with wide handlebars and headlights like the eyes of giant insects. Each time that she took a photograph, they insisted on giving her a present—flowers or single petals, pink and white and pale rose. Then they gave her a little bag of golden fruits.

When she was leaving, the father, who had joined the group, asked if she would like a ride on the Jawa, and she had said yes. Instead of heading for the town, where her companion waited, they went up into the hills, away from the sea and away from his ramshackle farm. It was rough road after rough road and then across a stone field, until at length on a huge promontory he stopped the bike and got off. She had to get off, too. She sat on a stone and he came and sat next to her. He tickled her kneecap and said words in his own tongue. When she moved to another stone, he followed. So it was, from stone to stone, with her trying to pretend that nothing untoward was going on, and above all trying not to offend him. He took the bag of fruit from the saddle, handed her one, and with gesticulation begged her to eat. She kept pointing to the village and the sea, the cobalt sea down below, where she wished to be. He pressed the fruits on her. He ate one himself. He put a stone on her throat so that it slid down inside her bathing suit. It was small and shiny like a brown bee. She could not show fear. She tried to show indifference. She began to scrape the ground with a piece of flint, to write the one word, "town." After an hour or so of this he attempted to put an arm around her. She curled up as small as a lizard. Eventually and in a big sulk he went back to his Jawa and with head down she followed. In the town he dropped her outside the church, said nothing in the way of a farewell, and revved off. In the one shop-cum-tavern her friend was waiting and he slapped her in front of all the Turkish men and brought her home, to the house which they had rented. He wrapped her in huge carpets, where she sweltered and choked for two days.

"He was a carpet dealer," she said wryly.

"Was he the professor?"

"Of course not . . . The professor was the one who was going to save me . . . make me forget him."

"Where is he now?"

She shrugged, said she hoped he was in jail and said it was my turn to tell of my travels, but that I could save it, since it was time for her siesta. Then she turned and put the shawl over her face, like a cowl.

The world seemed to pause under a great silencing weight, every bit of stone motionless, the air suspended as if holding its breath in a silence so vast it seemed to produce thickets of silence. My travels did not have the daring or the adventure of hers. I saw parts of America, I saw television screens with pizzas being dragged across them, voices on the radio that said depression could be treated and in the next moment talked of floor shows, fine dining, and a city dedicated to pleasure and fun. I remembered how in the evenings I would go to that corner of Central Park where the horses and carriages were, for a whiff of the homeland, byres, milk smells, and the stirrings of birds about to roost in the big lonely trees. There would be people hurrying to the subway, barricades of moving people that seemed far less human than the horses, who emanated some little flourish, some little breath of humanity, the plumes of their breaths like chimney smoke, the carriage lamps red on one side, a dancing gold on the other, and then the hooves prancing as a pair of lovers were conveyed into the park; horses indifferent to the chaos and traffic all around them, piebald horses, black horses, and my favorite, the chestnuts, among the throngs, glistening, their haunches so solid, their breaths so fine, spiraling, and snug inside the carriages, a tartan rug or two, a spray of flowers, even a horseshoe, and in all of it a memory of country roads that, though I could not return to, I yearned for, and I thought how hard it is to part with anything, even the things that hurt most, especially the things that hurt most.

When she wakened she said that she had been dreaming of the East. She and the little boy were walking in Gethsemane, the little boy eating melons, eating and eating the striped green skins and the soft lime-green pulp, then the seeds, devouring them so that his teeth turned into seeds and were no longer the little square sturdy white teeth with sharp points but yellow and flaky, crumbling in his mouth.

"My grandmother will have to translate that," she said.

"Does she translate your dreams?" I asked.

"Yes . . . it's always the same thing, that I'm going to make a very long, beautiful journey, but she doesn't say where . . ."

"Maybe she will translate mine," I said. She said she doubted it. She said I would be lucky if ever I saw her grandmother, because she hid most of the day and only came out at night, at night she was often called to houses to comfort the dying, those timid ones who are afraid to go.

We were so early for our bus that she decided to use up the film. Nearby was a field, dense with poppies, dense, flowing, it was like a lake; a swaying redness, on and on; more and more, heaving like a quilt, or a sea, a hallucinatory couch to lie down on. After the mountain they seemed ravishing, tender. We climbed the gate and went in, walking first along the edge; then, halfway down, a path appeared between the rippling petals and on tiptoe we followed it, across to a tree. She set the timer, put the camera a distance from us, and then together we squatted on the grass, waiting for a click that was so silent we were not even sure if it happened. As we were waiting, we heard the bus and she jumped, careless now of the sea of poppies, trampling over them, hollering, but even as she ran she saw the bus come, pass, swerve around a corner, and as she climbed over the gate she shouted after it.

We hailed the first car that came, but it passed, and the next two were full of passengers, and the fourth stopped but the driver could bring us only part of the way.

"We can take a taxi, then," I said.

"Muchas gracias," she said to the driver and then turned to me and beamed. We both thought the same thing, that the day was too enthralling to bring to an end, and that possibly we would never spend another like it. Yes, yes, we would go back to our little cave and bivouac. Going back up, she planned the menu. She threw in everything. Paupiettes de saumon . . . Petit tournedos de boeuf sauté bourguignon . . . Swordfish . . . Gazpacho . . . Gambas and langoustines . . . Bouillabaisse . . . Mélange de soufflé et sorbet Marie . . . Gourmandise and café splendide.

It was dark by the time we reached the cave and the sky was pelted with stars, stars so bright and so fervent it was as if they spoke, as if each little grain of glitter conveyed a meaning; a signal. Numerous as they were, each one seemed to reside in a languid space, so that in looking up at them the eyes themselves expanded and swam in the wideness of the sky, marveling in the velvet darkness. She bustled about, first having to find the candle, then light it cautiously since she was using her only match. She pared the dry wick, begged it not to falter, not to fail. Soon as it had taken, and the flame became steady, she left me to gather grass and leaves for our bedding and wood for our fire.

"Our fire?" I said.

"Of course," she said. How else were we going to roast our venison, our potatoes and chestnuts?

I stood there looking at the little wan blaze from the candle as it skewed hither and thither, thinking what a bleak place it would be without her, what a dungeon, but her presence gave it the glow and ritual of a palace. I felt elated, as if set down in some faraway universe.

She came back with grass, branches, and an armful of wood, for the fire.

"Will your parents be cross?"

"No," she said. "They'll think that we went to a restaurant, and I'll be home in the morning before they get up . . . The first bus is at five . . . Anyhow, my mother thinks that you are a very respectable lady." There was a little glint of mischief in her eyes as she said this. What was she thinking? Did she know that I had moped day after day when she left, that I had waited for her to come up the stairs and tap on my door, that I was certain that she would ring me from some strange town, or some railway station, just to tell me where she was, and that twice I had dreamed she was in an accident?

She knelt and prepared the fire, putting thin little twigs on first, then heavier ones crosswise, and then reaching for the candle and lighting the wood, before piling on any more. The sticks caught fire, expired, all went dark for a moment as she pleaded and prayed, then a little spurt of flame issued through, retreated, then by a miracle attached itself to a thin piece of wood, which fired a neighboring piece, and soon the sparks began to crackle and the flames made leaping shadows on the mortar wall.

We ate outside so that we could look at the stars. She knew several by name and her favorite was Sirius, the Dog Star, the brightest fixed star in the sky. We had some bread and salami from lunchtime and there was of course the much-derided cake. She opened the sides of the cake box ceremoniously to form a tray and then she cut big oozing chunks with her knife, Fritz. It tasted synthetic, full of almond essence and mock cream and various jams, but she pronounced it delicious. We ate slowly but we drank heartily, toasting each other in whatever language we could think of. She knew far more languages than I did and knew the swearwords in all of them.

"Yegiba . . . Yegiba . . ." was the swearword in Yugoslavia. She would say them only in foreign tongues, not her own.

"Red or white, madam?" she would ask, becoming more daring with each draught. She had worked in a restaurant for two years, boasted of all the dishes she had dropped, the octopuses she had retrieved from the floor, timbales of crème brûlée she had eaten, scandals she had witnessed. One night in the restaurant a young man had gone berserk, attacked his father with a knife because his father had flirted with his new girlfriend. The waiters took the father's side, since he was a very important man, convened on the son, grabbed him, put him in the water trough, and ran the hose on him until he came to his senses, disgraced and shivering. Soon after, he went to the asylum, driven by jealousy. Had she been jealous? Yes, often, but she knew how to deal with it, the same man that tied her up in the carpet had made her jealous, again and again. They were in Madrid once, a whole party of them had gone to the flamenco. She had brought her friend Carmen. Carmen was pretty and knew it. Carmen had a long back, which she made sure everyone saw, because she wore low-cut dresses. She made her own dresses, copied the designs from ones she saw in grand shops. The moment he laid eyes on Carmen he was smitten. She knew it by the way he looked at her, by the way he asked her what she wanted to drink, by the way his hands shook when he poured the wine, then all through the dancing he kept looking to see if Carmen was enjoying herself or if she was bored or if she needed a cushion or another drink. At the interval he made a right fool of himself, ran out into the street and bought roses for all the girls, expensive bunches of red roses, spent everything they had. That night in bed she tackled him. He said yes, he loved Carmen, but only from afar, he worshipped her but he was not worthy of her, not worthy to tie her shoe.

She asked him what he loved about her and he said everything, everything about her was beautiful. She pressed him as to what was the most beautiful and of course he said her back, that long, honey-colored back that glowed like amber.

"I love her hands," she had said.

"Her hands," he had said, puzzled, trying to visualize them, asking if they were long or not long and if Carmen had painted nails and how deep were her cuticles, and together and in a spirit of fierce competition they traversed every inch of Carmen's body, with Catalina surpassing him in detail about most parts of it and capping each facet with boundless admiration, so much so that in the end he turned to her and had to admit that he loved her, that he loved her more than anything; Carmen was a dream but she was a reality, a bundle in his arms, and he held her and made love to her more ardently than he had ever done. However, she had the last laugh—the next day she left him a bunch of flowers that she pretended Carmen had sent, and the dolt believed it.

"Have you ever been jealous?" she asked.

"Not like that," I said, recoiling at the nature of my own jealousy, which by contrast was impotent, feeble.

All of a sudden she started to sing. It was in her own tongue. It burst out of her in a great unbridled flow. The whole mountain was filled with it, so that the sheep in their sleep could hear it, as could the distant peaks. At times I thought it was addressed to a man or a woman, certainly a loved one; at other times it meandered like a long Arabic chant. I knew that in it were expressions of pain and longing that cut right down to the bone of the heart, to the bone of night. She did not finish as much as she allowed her voice to trail away, barely audible, then inaudible, yet I felt she was singing a last fragment of it inside her head, a last plea to God, or man or nature or whatever.

"What is it about?"

"It's about an instrument . . . a musical instrument . . . that when pleaded to will bring the bread and the needed woman."

"Or the needed man," I said, and saw him flash across the outskirts of my mind, as I had last seen him unbeknownst to him behind his upstairs window, in a red pullover, a Christmas present I reckoned, as it was Christmas time. I even thought he might look out and be startled to see me skulking there.

"Now it's your turn to sing," she said.

"Long before Christ, there was an Egyptian sphinx lying on her belly . . . head up . . . bearing two cups toward life . . . a cup of poison and a cup of love." It was one of those dictums that clung to me, along with another in direct contrast about the special bird having no particular voice, or no particular color, in short being dun and self-effacing.

"I want to learn it," she said. "I want to learn it," and quietly she confessed that she knew that accretion of poison and love; she bore it in her breast for someone.

Later she took warmed leaves from around the fire and placed them on the bed one by one as if placing patchwork squares of linen roses on a quilt, and as she unpinned my hair and watched the pins fall helter-skelter on the floor, she hurrahed. She had wanted to do that for weeks, in fact every time she saw me—my hair was too neat, too groomed, not savage enough.

She asked me for a story; one from my own land, an ancient story.

> "My father gave me a province of Ireland, the province of Cruachan, which is why I am called Medb of Cruachan. And as to being asked in marriage," she said, "messengers came to me from your own brother, Finn, son of Ross Ruadh, king of Leinster, and I gave him a refusal; and soon after that came messengers

from Cairbre Niafer, son of Rossa, king of Teamhair; and from Conchubar, son of Ness, king of Ulster; and after that again from Eochu Beag, son of Luchta, and I refused them all. For it is not a common marriage portion would have satisfied me, the same as is asked by the other women of Ireland," she said; "but it is what I asked as a marriage portion, a man without stinginess, without jealousy, without fear.

"And I gave you good wedding gifts," she said, "suits of clothing enough for twelve men; a chariot that was worth three times seven serving maids; the width of your face in red gold, the round of your arm in a bracelet of white bronze. You are nothing of yourself, but it is in the pay of a woman you are," she said.

"That is not so," said Ailell, "for I am a king's son and I have two brothers that are kings, Finn, king of Leinster, and Cairbre, king of Teamhair, and I would have been king in their places but that they are older than myself."

"You know well," said Maeve, "the riches that belong to me are greater than the riches that belong to you."

"You astonish me," said Ailell, "for there is no one in Ireland has a better store of jewels and riches and treasure than myself, and well you know it."

"Let our goods and our riches be put beside one another, and let a value be put on them," said Maeve, "and you will know which of us owns most."

"I am content to do that," said Ailell.

With that, orders were given to their people to bring out their goods and to count them, and to put a value on them. They did so, and the first things they brought out were their drinking vessels and all the things belonging to their households, and they were found to be equal. Then their rings were brought out, and their bracelets and chains and brooches, their clothing of crimson and blue and black and green and yellow and saffron and speckled silks, and these were found to be equal. Then their great flocks of sheep were driven from the green plains of the open country and were counted, and they were found to be equal; and if there was a ram among Maeve's flocks that was the equal of a serving maid in value, Ailell had one that was as good. And their horses were brought in from the meadows, and their herds of swine out of the woods and the valleys, and were equal one to another. And the last thing that was done was to bring in the herds of cattle from the forest and the wild places of the province, and when they were put beside one another they were found to be equal, but for one thing only.

It happened a bull had been calved in Maeve's herd, and his name was Fionnbanach, the White-Horned. But he would not stop in Maeve's herds, for he did not think it fitting to be under the rule of a woman, and he had gone into Ailell's herds and stopped there; and now he was the best bull in the whole province of Connaught. And when Maeve saw him, and knew he was better than any bull of her own, there was great vexation on her, and it was as bad to her as if she did not own one head of cattle at all. So she called Mac Roth, the herald, to her, and bade him to find out where there was a bull as good as the White-Horned to be got in any province of the provinces of Ireland.

"I myself know that well," said Mac Roth, "for there is a bull that is twice as good as himself at the house of Daire, son of Fachtna, in the district of Cuailgne, and that is Don Cuailgne, the Brown Bull of Cuailgne."

"Rise up, then," said Maeve, "and make no delay, but go to Daire from me, and ask the loan of that bull for a year."

"It's beautiful," she said, and yawned. "It's very beautiful . . . I want to hear it again," but even as she was talking she fell asleep. Her limbs softened as her bare feet reached to the end of the sagging bed. The candle still guttered and there were spurts of light from the fire, but otherwise the silence was engulfing. She breathed lightly and gently and there was in her, in sleep, a fragility that she never allowed in daytime, the artless trustingness of a child. Her mouth was a little open as if, in a dream, she was talking to herself. As I lay beside her I could feel, not our bodies, but our hair touching, ribs of her hair touching mine, charged with inner current. She had left a comb in and the specks of diamanté gleamed in the firelight, like glowworms. I lay there stiffly, quietly confiding to myself that I wanted to hold her, be held by her, but in her sleep, so that our night selves might reach out and give each other that thread of sustenance that we craved, the invisible sustenance, not what we sought from men, something other-womanly, primordial. I feared that she might rebuff me, might move away in horror. I feared, too, that once I'd touched her, something would alter in me. I remembered once coming across a dusky girl, in a café, a café where I had gone to read and to stay as long as possible to fill time. Striking up a conversation, I went home later with her, to a huge flat that overlooked Hyde Park and from which one could see the saucered disks of the Post Office Tower and the incline of Parliament Hill. Standing by the window very close to her, I slowly began to undress her, astonished that the lace of her slip was exactly repeated in the lace of her pants, and then I laid her down on an extremely white sofa. Everything was white: the leather sofas, the floor rugs, even the upright piano. All of my advances she received without either dismay or flutter. Throughout, she remained courteous and did not seem in the least nonplussed by my touch, but then within me something occurred, some balk, some dread, some hesitation, and I knew that I could not go through with it. In fact, I began to weep. She was kindness itself, stood up, fetched a dressing gown, escorted me to the bathroom, and later gave me several of her cards. She had an apartment in Paris and another in Beirut. Out on the street there was a diminutive man sweeping the gutters, his broom far taller than himself. I threw her cards on his little heap, and seeing I was a bit perturbed, he felt obliged to voice the philosophy that no man was worth it.

In her sleep Catalina sometimes stirred and her breath was becoming quicker and more anxious. Dreams. Hosts of them. I will watch over her, I thought. I put my hand across her face, but without touching it. I allowed my hand to hover and thought of the hawk that we had seen that day hovering in the transparent sky. Her eyelids were soft, beautifully soft, like disks of fawn shell; they could have been ornaments. Her cheeks stirred to my near-touch and then I waited and it was like seeing the tremors of an animal beneath the ground, a mole maybe. She turned and wakened and there was a kind of quake in the heave of her surprised sigh as she realized where she was and who was next to her. Then I felt the thwack of her arms around me and the clasp of her hands, and I stretched out and cleaved to her, through her opening to life; arms, limbs, torsos joined as if in an androgynous sculpture, the bloods going up and down merrily, two bloods, like mercury in a heated thermometer, even the cheeks letting go of all their scream and all their grumble and their thousand unspent kisses; tenderness, rabidness; hunger; back, back in time to that wandering milky watery bliss, infinitely safe like wine inside a skin or sap inside a tree, floating, afloat; boundaries burst, bursting, the mind as much as the body borne along, to this other landscape that was familiar yet unfamiliar, like entering a picture, or a fresco, slipping through a wall of flesh, eclipsed inside the womb of the world, and throughout it all, her words, faint, sweet as vapor.

In the morning she fetched two bottles of water and without

even asking she poured one over each of us so that it streamed down onto our faces, our bodies, a baptism at once reckless and cleansing. She had brought leaves as well and she pressed them all over me like poultices or face flannels.

It was a little thing and I don't know why it occurred to me but suddenly I was telling her. I had been in Madrid a long time before, twenty years before, and had gone to a bullfight, it being the season. It was my first bullfight and I was taken by some very smart people. From time to time I would say something, something innocuous or ridiculous, just to let them know that I was there. Afterward, as they all gloated and discussed moves and the various passes, I agreed, like a sheep, except that I was bleeding, bleeding from the spectacle. I bled for the entire week, in sympathy, with either the bulls or the horses or the young picadors or the strutting daring matadors, or the whole ritual, which by its spectacle, its terror, and its gore brought to my mind too vividly Christ's bleeding wounds and the women I knew, including myself, as if Christ was woman and woman was Christ in the bloodied ventricles of herself. Man in woman and woman in man. The impossible. And during that week, one of those nights when we ate very late and drank jugs and jugs of wine and then peppermint frappés, a woman in our party, an Eastern woman with black brilliantined hair and an amber choker, decided to read the coffee cups, and when it came to my turn, when she read mine, her face flinched as she turned to my friend and said, "She hasn't done it right, she's not doing it right," and like a fool I reached for my cup, thinking I had not shaken the dregs of coffee enough or allowed the grains to settle in the right way. But it was too late, what she was telling me was that I drank and ate and lived and perceived life the wrong way. She looked at me with scorn and I knew, as I had always feared, that I was only scraping through and that death would be my only redemption.

"No tinguis por . . ." Catalina said.

"What is that?"

"Don't be afraid," she said, then she kissed me and the kiss was a seal. Her face was beautiful and not beautiful, it was a little swarthy and wet from the baptism. Our night was something not to fear either, but to carry within us, not as a memory of debauch, but as a constant, like one of those streams or rills that one hears when walking along a country road but that one does not see, simply knows it to be there.

Outside, the world was enveloped in mist, the topmost points of the mountain like gray carbuncles. The trees and the bushes were baggy, caught in this mist, and a herd of blue-black goats that ran in front of us were like phantoms. She ran on ahead, making sure that this time we would not miss our bus. She was brisk, probably already in her mind tackling the day's duties, while I wondered if I should get a chance to see her again. As if she read my thoughts she broke off a huge spray of lilac up at the bus stop.

"Show them that in London," she said, both a farewell and a reprimand for resuming my city existence.

17

I was happy to be going home, full of that little flutter that the prospect of a journey brings. I saw corners of England that I might glimpse from a train: a field of corn, bronzed; black-and-white cows with enormous pink udders wading in a stream, the crows rising, settling, then rerising like bits of black gauze in the sky, taking flight from a single tractor that seemed as lonely as a spaceship. I had left her a note and a little money to put toward buying a scooter. I had left it with the nunnish girl, the girl with the mustache, who because I was leaving had capitulated somewhat, even said, "We will miss you . . . It is our hope that you will return."

That evening and for the second time in my long stay I ate in the big dining room. It was very solemn, eating alone like that, baroque music drifting from the gallery, big stout beeswax candles, church candles, their flames veering this way and that, trying to break from the blue interiors that formed webs around the wicks. The wineglasses were so wide and deep they were like finger bowls, and drinking from them, I felt pampered, giddy. Afterward I took an amaretto and sat in the garden. The lights along the wall were covered with pink roof tiles which transmitted a shower of radiance, the lining a frailer pink, not like stone at all, but like flesh, and something about these colors and these exquisite drained tints reminded me of her and of him, as if love itself was a beautiful warm glow, a lamp inside of one. It was late when I left the garden and as I came through the hotel I lingered for a moment in the salon. The photographer from Cologne, Charlotte, Iris, they whisked through my mind like living ghosts, people I would probably never see again.

At dawn, someone burst into my room. I thought perhaps that I had overslept and that it was the young boy come with my last luxurious breakfast. Hurriedly I reached for a dressing gown, or a shawl, only to hear a girl screaming at me, calling me "Puta, puta . . . Whore . . . whore." I thought at first that it must be the putty-faced woman who had accosted me on the way down from the church, but soon, as I clicked on the light, I saw that it was Rosario, Catalina's sister, wild, demented, her hair uncombed and her eyes full of raging tears. I had ruined her family, I had destroyed their honor. "Honor" was the word she spouted most as she repeated the story again and again. They had been asleep, her father had got up early to go out and smoke his pipe and had seen it. It. It. It. "Lesbos" had been painted on their wall for all to see. I saw it in terrifying and graphic reality. It was black, as she said, and bold, as she said, and it would not wash out, or scratch out, and anyhow it was too late. Everyone had seen it, her mother, her aunt, neighboring women, all aghast at what they saw. Aghast and ashamed. Was Catalina capable of such a thing, such violation. Their own bodies no doubt partook of her shame and curdled in horror. I imagined them swarming into the hotel and stoning me.

"Do you see what you have done?" she kept saying. She described each second of it, her father getting up, going out, seeing some young boys up a tree and thinking they had come to steal the apricots, then suddenly seeing it.

"Lesbos Lesbos Lesbos!" she shrieked, as if I had not already heard, then she described his going back into the house, wakening them, dragging Catalina from her bed, her having to fight him with her bare arms, still half asleep, shouting, "What? What?" because of course she did not know.

"We're ruined . . . ruined!" she kept saying. Each time I tried to reason with her she would counter with another accusation. She had seen it coming for weeks. Her father had seen it too, her mother being too busy and too overworked to see anything. I had deliberately destroyed their good name. She could have foretold it. They were one of the oldest families in the parish and I had usurped their honor in one swoop. Her command of English was great and I remembered that Catalina had told me that she had worked in London for six months but had had to be brought back because of her homesickness. They were decent people, as she said, frugal, they worked the land, she allowed herself one packet of cigarettes per week; yet whenever they mixed with strangers it led to trouble and disaster. Why the presents to Catalina? Why the lunches and dinners? Why go to the mountain, why insist on staying all night? Why? Why? The shame was killing her. Her mother, she said, had fallen down in a faint. Her mother who not only worked the farm and the house but took in washing, so as to save for the little boy's education.

"How is Catalina?" I said.

"How is she!" she shrieked. I ought to know that she was black-and-blue, that she had gone to her bedroom and locked the door and most likely she would never come out. Her father had beaten her savagely, in front of the neighbors, and but for her grandmother he might have killed her.

"It's all lies," I said.

"Then prove it," she said. "Prove it," and she almost struck me.

"I'll go to the priest," I said, feeling myself hauled right back to that state of childhood, trying to brazen out some terrible confrontation with adults while quaking within.

"You had better go . . ." she said. "You had better . . ."

"Leave me," I said with as much authority as I could muster, and even as she was leaving I had my hand on the dial to ask the girl at the desk to change my reservation on the airplane.

Ripped-off petals of geraniums lay all along the ground in pools, looking like those vivid scarlet hearts painted onto Valentine cards. The outdoor trestle table made of driftwood was drenched, but in places the sun had just begun to suck the moisture from it, so that its surface was dappled like a lake and its unshaven edges jutted like cropped fur. Young vines on the terrace were an artificial green, as if they had been treated to one of those essences with which people dye cakes or icing; their delicate stalks curling upward, threading their way flawlessly through a lattice, to the light.

I had waited until a reasonable hour to call on D'Arcy, in his mountain abode, only to find him in a wild agitation, kicking oatmeal all over the floor and screaming obscenities. Each time he kicked, he coupled the obscenity with a world leader, a dynastic figure who was personally responsible for this most recent wallop of excruciating fate.

"What's for breakfast—Bacon is off,
fuck the Queen.
"What's for brunch—Eggs Benedict is off,
fuck Reagan.
"What's for tea—Muffins is off,
fuck Thatcher.
"Croissant, brioche, and baguettes is off—
fuck Mitterand, de Gaulle, the Little
Corporal, and the syphilitic Louis.
"Spuds is off—fuck Fianna Fail and fuck
Fine Gael."

He ceased from his barrage to acknowledge my arrival. The kitchen, or what passed for a kitchen, was in chaos, tins of paint and paintings everywhere, including the two van Goghs facing each other, with what seemed to be galling contempt. He said that I might at least have warned him, apprised him of this unprecedented visit, might have sent a calling card, a bush telegram, anything. Yes, he was in a foul humor, and he would like to say, and he would like posterity to note, that he had been revolving around the fucking universe on his arse and his axis for fifty-seven years and that he had had enough . . . Basta, basta, basta.

The reason for this excess of rage and for oatmeal scattered everywhere was that he was being evicted, having already lost his studio in the town. This little casita which he had inhabited for two years was an annex of a big house higher up and he had just received a letter from the piss-arse absentee owner that all was sold to a fucking foreigner, Hitler's valet's illegitimate grandson or a Zimbabwe arms dealer no doubt. He was used to spartan living as he so gloatingly said, but he was not used to being told to scarper at a moment's notice, and worse, he would have to leave his garden, his pride, his paradise, where he had planted marrows, corn salad, arugula; where he had spent wholesome hours treating that soil to care and fondnesses that he had never treated a woman to.

"Where to fucking go?" he asked as he vowed to dig up every little seedling, every bean pod, every sprout that would have been a potato or a flourish of potatoes; he would dig them up and give them to the animals as swill. He asked Christ, Judas, Simon Zealot, and sundry martyrs why he was cursed so, why like Branwell Brontë did the muse once attend, then subsequently forsake him. He, too, was a child prodigy and could write in two languages with either hand and moreover could read Walter Pater at six or seven, could say Mass in Latin.

"Every day, or every other day, I stagger up to that fucking graveyard and I speak to the dead . . . any old dead, and I say, 'Help D'Arcy to turn over a new leaf . . . no more drink, no more debauch . . . no more pipe dreams . . . Let D'Arcy drink of the milk of human kindness instead of this goddamn putrid whey . . . let D'Arcy's pulse beat with a merry rhythm,' and does it happen . . . no . . . no . . . no . . . it's Eviction, Bankruptcy, Ridicule!" and he hit his head savagely against the stone of the unplastered wall.

I thought of leaving but I had only to remember Rosario's screams and hisses to me to "do something." I blurted it out.

"Down McQuarie Street, were ye?" he said, adding that he had always thought that I was still snooping about for a young Lochinvar or a not so young Lochinvar, a Byronic bastard.

"Did ye use a catheter?" he asked gleefully, his temper leavening as he rose to the challenge. He wished to know the color of the graffiti, the approximate size, if it had been done by a hack or in a legible hand, was bold or trompe l'oeil.

"I haven't seen it . . . I've only been told about it." He doubled over, laughing, said it would titillate the town for a week, bars would be full, he D'Arcy would get free drink, might even get to shack up somewhere with someone, and as he enthused, the color came back into his cheeks and the blue, galvanized eyes grew moist with tears of laughter.

"I love it . . . I love it!" he said and he ran around the room, offering me now sodden biscuits from a packet, proffering an empty beer bottle, simulating largesse; then suddenly from under a knitted tea cozy he pulled a little mouth organ and began to play with fervor. He sang a line of the song between each bar of melody:

. . . On Boulavogue, as the sun was setting . . .

Oe'r in the bright May meadows of Shalemiler

A rebel hand set the heather blazing . . .

He had a solution that was Einsteinian, Archimedian . . . mind-shattering, would boggle the biddies and the bastards, keep them guessing and cogitating until Michaelmas.

"What is it?"

"Suffice to say that it involves the decorative arts . . . so now leave me to reconnoiter, and then to execute it, and by this time tomorrow your name will be cleared . . . Up the Queen, up Reagan, up Thatcher, and up Fianna Fail, Fine Gael! . . . Forget the Frogs . . ."

He played very fast then, signaling me out the way a gypsy disposes of an admiring crowd in a restaurant. He wanted no remuneration until the deed was done and then I could see that he was made a Chevalier or given the Legion of Honor but please no OBE or CBE, which sounded like a kidney complaint. Outside, the sun was blazing, and seeing it flow back into everything was like watching blood being transfused back into a corpse. The air was suffused with light, the earth soaked with it, as were the plants, the trees, the stones, the vegetation, even the little bed of parsley that he proudly pointed to.

"You came to the right man," he said and assured me that the task ahead would give him immense satisfaction. As an afterthought he added that it might be a good idea if I were to call on the ecumenical-minded priest.

"You are a very villain else," he said and warned that I give him a handsome sum, a nugget. However, he thought it most fitting and most laudable that I had come first to David Anthony Ignatius Donne, the unfrocked priest who might now be a missioner in clink or a paunchy curate in Ballinasloe. He ruminated about his long years in the seminary, a vocation that he wrestled with, and how the Fathers tried to keep him against his will except that he bested them, got the runs at all hours, fouling their quarters, giving their incensed corridors a whiff of bog.

"You never told me," I said.

"Must I," he quoted, "must I ravel out my weav'd-up follies." Like all lonely people, but particularly those who revile their loneliness, he would not let me go, but sent snippets, bulletins along the terrace, finding story after story to regale me with.

Later, walking along, I was douched with water and when I looked up I saw that my assailants were two youths, who sniggered.

"They're only youngsters," I said but already I had begun

to walk very fast and my feet in their canvas shoes seemed to traverse the rubble of the path without actually touching it.

The priest's house adjoined the church, but I waited until the church door was barred for the night and the faithful had gone home. His door was opened, not as I had expected by a housekeeper, but by a very young boy on roller skates. Down the length of the long, dark hallway I could see into a room, where there was a party in progress, with other young boys whizzing around on roller skates. One of them had put a hand over the priest's eyes to stop him seeing something on television. On the screen, in a black-and-white film, a couple were kissing, the woman bent back like a reed. Wanda's son was beating egg whites with a fork. He said my name, to show the others that he knew me. The priest was not nearly so cordial. He was in white trousers and red turtleneck sweater and finding me in the room came as a jolt to him. He composed himself as much as he could by pulling his sweater down over his protruding stomach. He was holding a currant biscuit, which he endeavored to disguise by curling his fingers around it. He was no longer young, and it was obvious that his appearance mattered greatly to him. He wore a brunette toupee that was lighter and finer than his own hair, and not being ample enough for his large head, it looked more like a skullcap. He rose and put his hand out, signaling me to return to the hallway, refusing to receive me in his kitchen.

The audience was in a very dark and somber room filled with heavy pieces of brown furniture. In a toneless voice he greeted me, asked in halting English what he could do for me. I replied in his language, having learned the phrase over and over again. I had come to ask to have a Mass said, to have it announced, so that the whole village would know. I had the money ready. He took it almost daintily, as a fat man might take a sugar cube from a tongs. He made some attempt at a smile but it was more like folds over his bucolic features. For something to say, I admired the room and its somber contents. He said yes, that his old chest and his mirrors were very dear to him and that of course they did not fade as a woman fades, even the prettiest woman. Suddenly he asked if I wanted him to hear my confession and as I was taken by surprise I said yes. He opened a drawer and pulled out a purple stole, which he donned over his turtleneck sweater. I knelt, and while I was muttering generalizations, two of the little cupids popped their heads through the door, and the absurd spectacle of me kneeling and him presiding over me sent them rushing to the kitchen, squealing and laughing, to tell the others. He became quite theatrical as he spouted the absolution and afterward, as he saw me out, he corrected me on one matter of history, said that although there was a large statue of Saint Sebastian in the church, he was not their patron saint, their patron saint was John the Baptist.

"No arrows," he said. And I was not sure whether that was offered as some sort of consolation or as a reward for the lavish offering I had given him. I imagined him putting it into one of the big brown chests, then hurrying back to the friskiness of the kitchen, where the egg whites would have been whisked to a magic foam.

18

It was midmorning and the lorries were arriving from the town, bringing crates of beer and wooden boxes of fish laced with thin icicles. The village buzzed with it. Many laughed, but those on whose walls it appeared were incensed. The postmistress, flushed and fuming, paced with a coat over her nightgown and a look of bloated indignation on her sallow face. It was as if she might explode, or a glut of violence might come bursting out. She would stand and point to it, the blond stone of her harmless house on which the black obscenity had been scrawled: Lesbos. Lesbos. It had been perfectly and legibly sprayed, for all to see. D'Arcy had done a superlative job. At times she shouted, then at other times strode back and forth talking to herself, mulling vengeance, calling to one of the other women to help her, to come to her aid, in this brazen heathen time. One of the maids from my hotel reported that it was on two other walls and was rumored to be on the main wall before one arrived in the town, the wall that had "Welcome" on it. D'Arcy had not been sparing. The offending word, perfectly sprayed, graced the wall of the post office, a private house, the Mayor's garden wall, and as this girl said, the gateway to the town. D'Arcy himself was nowhere to be seen, but I reckoned that he would appear by lunch, suave, shaven, chuffed at the brilliance of his scheme, and that as he sat down to eat with me, or stood at one of the bars to quaff, he would discuss it with the others, and debate as to whether it was of Roman or Byzantine influence. The little cupids that I had seen at the priest's house sought bribes so they could ride out of town and count how many other walls it appeared on.

At lunchtime I went to the restaurant owned by the two sisters and felt a little triumphant as I entered. The ladies welcomed me with a feigned cordiality, but at least they did not bar the way. I ordered a bottle of the local wine, and the local soup, which was clogged with bread, vegetables, and specks of brown so simmered that they were either mushrooms or shreds of rabbit meat.

"Gusta . . . gusta," one of them said as I looked at my soup, reluctant to eat, waiting, hoping that D'Arcy would come, my eye on the stairway that shelved directly up from the street. On the other side of the restaurant was a bar, where there was laughing and roistering, no doubt the customers, the foreigners that is, using the excitement of the morning to drink a little more.

Wanda came up the stairs and ran to my table, excited. Had I heard? She was opening a new boutique, in no time she would be flying to major cities to buy fashions and accessories.

At first she would stock just local stuff, embroidered blouses and knitwear, but in time she would have designer clothes, she would buy from the small designers, she would travel, she would go all over the world . . . she would call her boutique Zara.

Hearing that I was leaving, she said it was a pity that we had not become friends, particularly as she was the one to have met me that first morning. The puppy that her son had kept was bigger now and even in heat and would probably soon be propositioned by her father or her grandfather.

"Talk of vice," she said and declared the place to be a Peyton Place under the sheets.

She, like everyone, had seen the postmistress's fulminations, and laughed as she recalled that at the church fair the previous Christmas the postmistress had bought the only baby-doll nightie and matching knickers.

"To burn them?" I said.

"Maybe not," she said with a half smile. "Maybe she's keeping them in her bottom drawer, just in case."

"How's your son?" I said.

"An angel," she said. "I went in last night to give him a little peck and he had a cabbage leaf on his pillow to catch the ladybirds . . ." As she said it her features dissolved into a radiant smile.

"I saw him at the priest's house."

"Oh, yes . . . they go up there and watch TV and make whoopee," she said. Then she confessed that she had been a little hurt that she had not seen much of me, that I had given my affections elsewhere. I imagined she was referring to Catalina and that she was intrigued by the rumor, and would have loved to pry.

"I'll come back," I said, on an impulse. I even asked her to keep her eyes out for a little place for me, a holding with a terrace and a small orchard. The mention of it brought tears to her eyes. It was as if in this promise, rashly given, I had made a bond with her. She would keep her eyes open, she knew all the properties: people moving in, people moving out, she knew where to find a bargain, way off in the hills; moreover she knew auctions, markets, flea markets, everything, we could furnish it for a song. Then a youngster came in to tell her that the water man was at her house waiting to be paid, and she ran out, imploring me to come back before the end of the summer.

Not long after, a young man came in, dressed in black, black sweater and worn black velveteen pants. One of the sisters bowed to him, but it was a formal bow, not a greeting. Under his beard, his face was very pale and there was something pent-up about him. Over his shoulders he wore a black overcoat which he allowed to drop off, at the same moment as he stood by the sideboard and helped himself to some red wine. His hair was so shaven that he looked like an embryo; his eyes vortexes of hurt and rage. No one spoke to him, although it was clear that they knew him, as there was the occasional nod in his direction. He sat alone at a long table and ate ravenously. He was cosmopolitan and had a little tattoo on his wrist, it was an eye, a purple eye with swooping lashes. I thought perhaps that he might be an actor with a troupe of traveling players, or that he made jewelry or ceramics, which he had come to sell. At moments he would turn around as if he knew that I was watching him, as if to challenge me, and his stare was at once insolent and begging. He was proud of the way he allowed his body to swivel, and when he waved a hand to one of the sisters to bring him another glass of wine, he gave the impression of being a ventriloquist, as if something might drop from his sleeve. When he heard that the coffee machine was broken and he looked at her with such disdain and then laughed riotously and said, "La máquina kaput," he expected us to laugh with him, but no one did. She offered him instant coffee, which he declined. Then he thought for a moment as if lost in some reverie, stood up and looked around, sneeringly, as if he were looking at a bunch of sheep not worthy of his slaughter. He slipped the coat over his shoulders capewise and went down the stairs slowly, like an actor going onstage.

"Who is he?" I asked one of the sisters.

"He come here . . . sometime . . . he travel," she said.

"Is he a gypsy?" I said, and she smiled at my simple notion of supposing anyone eccentric to be a gypsy.

"He not gypsy, he heself," she said, but I knew that she feared him and also that he had not paid his bill.

D'Arcy did not appear and eventually I left, saying goodbye somewhat ceremoniously to the sisters and the remaining guests. Outside, the street was so empty it might have just been sacked, it had that desertedness of streets in Westerns just before the fatal shoot-out. The shops were closed for the siesta, and even the big brown unglazed pots seemed to have surrendered to sleep. I would sleep too, in my beautiful little room that had changed from being a cell to a haven with its flowers and its candles and its emanations of her. I went up the hill to see the sea, to have a last look at it. It was a sheer blue, with wavelets, like gulls' wings tilting upward to form an unending blue frill, and the soft green patches of cloud-like water underneath the rock with the hole in it. I stood there wondering if I would come back, wondering what it was that sent me to this place rather than any other, believing, knowing that it was she. The mountains seemed nearer too, more amenable, as if one could reach out and touch them. Somewhere up there was the spot where I had lain with her, and I thought, even after we are dead, places carry emanations of us, wisps.

A young boy of about ten or eleven came up behind me on

a scooter to deliver a message and hand me a bunch of dried flowers. She wished to see me after dark at the little casita . . . Ca'an Serra.

"Why has she not written?" I asked.

"She is afraid," he said very earnestly, and then added, "I am her cousin," as if in that simple remark there resided every guarantee of sincerity. Then he was gone as quickly and as stealthily as he arrived, and soon I saw his bicycle down on the track that led to the sea, bouncing and bounding like a surfer. It had to be she. Who else would be sending me dried flowers, flowers such as we had seen on the mountain. But even if it was not she, I would have to go, for her sake.

The afternoon dragged on. I repacked various glass ornaments, put them into nightgowns and sweaters to keep them from breaking. Anything to make time pass. At four I ordered tea and the rich fruitcake that I had so often and so willfully declined. Long before it arrived, I was feasting on the big green shreds of candied peel and the moist glacé cherries. They rang from Reception to ask what kind of tea I wanted and later they rang to ask if I would be settling my account by check or by banker's card. Both times I jumped. Yet I could not confide in anyone, the whole thing having become so clandestine. Foolishly I thought of writing to my sons, saying the trenchant things that I had refrained from, but this too I thought to be a bit extreme. I knew that in an office in Lincoln's Inn Fields was the will I had made, and immediately chided myself for being so superstitious, so timorous.

At sundown I set out, reckoning that it would be dark by the time I arrived. The mountains were tapestries now, dun-gold and russet. I did not take the donkey track but went along the main road, where I met a few people, the couple who owned an art gallery and from whom I had bought the glass ornaments, an excitable visitor in a dark suit with a soft brown hat, carrying an open bottle of wine and talking to himself. I passed various gateways, some shut for the night, others open, with several cars in the drive. As I walked, it grew dark, and once I got onto the terraces, I felt less sanguine. To calm myself I tried to imagine the waves coming in on the broken chain of seashore, coming in slowly, softly, then breaking into shreds, like guipure lace, then receding to allow for the next swoop. As I climbed higher I got out my little torch and would look in the other direction, expecting to see hers, which for economy's sake she would keep flicking on and off.

The door was not locked, and as I pushed it in, I heard a thud and thought perhaps that my worst suspicions were founded. By the light of the torch I saw that it was the cat which had jumped from the chair to the door and which meowed with hunger. In all the dramas, the goats had probably not been milked. Sidling back onto a chair, it decided to ignore me. As I shone the torch about the room, something in me petrified. The place was untidy, seeds and bulbs all over the table, and a little hand plow in the center of the floor. I felt that somehow she would have got there ahead of me to move these things. In one corner there was a baby's high chair with beads that stretched across it. I touched them, allowing them to clonk back and forth on a piece of plastic cord. Occasionally I went outside to see if there was any sign of her. The young moon was a mold of silver with a greenish hue to it, and not a single person moved on any of the terraces either above or below. She was perhaps biding her time. She had to come. I could feel her presence, her voice, her warmth. Inside the house I thought of going into the other room but suddenly conceived this dread that there was someone in there waiting for me, waiting for us. I talked to myself, talked reams to banish these fears. It may have been a quarter of an hour or it may have been less, but suddenly I heard a roar followed by a splutter of roars, so awful it was as if a herd of swine were being slaughtered again and again. It could have been a man or a woman, the gender being impossible to tell because of the pitch and the delirium of it. The cat jumped, leapt through the air, like a crazed monkey, and clawed at the door to get out. There was a supernatural energy to its movements and as I pulled the door open I was sure it flew. The roar had subsided to a murmur, more like a prayer or a series of prayers, and I thought maybe it meant some sort of procession and that the locals had come together to pray for their crops. I ran to the terrace, higher up, the one that I thought would bring me by a more direct route to them. Instead, it led me to an incline where there was a sheep dip, which I scrambled over, hoping to find a path beyond. Then the torch gave out. Plunged now in darkness except for the light from the moon, I ran hither and thither, seeing the same things, paths, trees, the sheep dip, heaps of stones, again and again retracing my steps, so that in the end I had to hang my scarf on a tree to serve as a landmark. I could hear the sounds of cars coming and going, car doors being banged, and I knew that there had been some accident.

Eventually, as I neared the main road, I heard the bells, two bells in steady and alternating sequence, one deep and pounding, the other lighter in tone, both with a sense of portent. I knew it, a second before I could have known it, that it boded death, yet I hesitated before running to ask.

"Campana grave . . . campana aguda," the voices said. Voices talking rapidly but in a hush, talking and blessing themselves, then waiting for the next peal.

"He do by knife," a woman said, and shook her head at such barbaric rites.

"Who is it?" I asked one of the younger girls.

"Pimpinella . . ." she said, and for a moment I believed it was a stranger.

"Catalina Espert . . . the daughter of Tomás and Conchita Espert," an older woman added, and then began to ream off the names of grandparents and great-grandparents from both sides of the family. The young girl cried openly, wildly. They were friends, she and Catalina, they had been at school together, acted in plays together. Catastrophe strikes the body first, long before it reaches the brain. I felt as if being gouged.

"He kill her at last," a younger woman said.

"Who killed her?" I asked, thinking that maybe it was her father, still livid from the disgrace over the graffiti.

"Her husband . . . Juan," the young girl said, and turned away.

The headwaiter was coming down the street, his jacket over his shoulder, his gait nonchalant, and I ran to him as if he could avert it.

"Her husband . . . he cut her throat," he said calmly.

"Husband?" I said.

"Infante Juan . . . She maybe never told you . . . She keep it a secret even from most of us in the hotel . . . but I know . . . We close our doors to him way back."

"Who was he?"

"A punk," he said. "From the very south . . . hot blood

. . . He try to kill a waiter in the hotel over nathing . . . He think the waiter flirt with her."

"So the child was theirs, too?"

"Yes . . . They go to court over him two times, they have bloodtesting," he said, his dry words in contrast with the bedlam.

Not long before, the women had seen Juan being brought to the police station, a blanket over his head, crying out that he loved her, that he wanted to die with her.

I knew he must be the man I had seen in the restaurant and I believed now that it was he and not she who had sent the message by the little boy and that the little boy must have panicked at the last minute and told her. She had gone out to meet him, to meet the fate that was meant for me. I ran from one place to another, as if running could undo it. What did I know of death—nothing. What did I know of life—nothing. The bar was empty and so was Wanda's house. Cats were on the table gorging on a bowl of chocolate mix. They looked grotesque. Everywhere people were talking, hurrying, children being comforted as they believed that they, too, were about to be murdered. I caught up with the women that had started down the donkey track, linked to keep each other from falling or fainting. Each new disclosure killed her afresh, so that by the time we got to the bridge she had died a thousand times.

"He donta care . . . he donta look for a way to hide her . . . he carry her . . . he drink her blood . . . he say I lave her . . . he carry her to her mother's house," a woman said to me. She was the woman who coiffed my hair each week and who was normally a model of reserve, sweeping the shop floor or stringing beans as I sweltered under the wobbling dryer, but now charged, unfettered. She and her aunt laid out the corpse, all in a short space, because mourners started to arrive once they heard the commotion.

They were the last to carry on the tradition. She spoke of their task with a mixture of pride and revulsion. She had had to run home to change. The blood was everywhere, even under her nails she said, holding her hands out. Still, they had done a good job, they had made her look beatific . . . "beata, beata." She longed to say more, to wallow in it.

Where the road forked near a tavern, there were a few men backing out of a house, carrying an invalid.

"Enfermo, enfermo," the woman whispered. Under the hazed shower of light from the streetlamp I saw a man's face, thin, wizened, mouth agape. They were taking him to the house to taste death. Death for one meant death for all. Their sorrow bound them together.

"La voz de Dios . . . la voz de Dios," they said as he stared up at them. Catalina had been a friend to him, she bathed his sores sometimes when his married daughter could not come.

As we neared the house, I saw Charlotte at the gate, smoking. She looked very tall and incongruous in her jeans, her face blurred. It was she who had found them, on the way to the village to sell her Walkman. She ran and clung to me like a long-lost friend. She was shaking, stammering, repeating the events as she had repeated them to the family, to the police, to the priest, to the coroner, to endless neighbors, and now to me, how she had met him, how he had a wild excited look in his eyes, how he had told her to get out of his way, and how she had hurried off in fear. Soon after, he met Catalina and she had heard their raised voices and their first bitter exchanges and she ran faster, not wishing to overhear. When she heard the roar, Catalina's roar, she knew what it was, what it meant, and again she relived the moments herself; pausing in disbelief, in horror, then running, tripping over the knife that he had dropped, picking it up, its feel warm and wet, like bloodied flesh. Here she breaks down completely, recounting the ghastly minutes that followed, his trying to give Catalina the kiss of life, her having to run on ahead, finding the mother in the yard rounding up geese, the mother refusing to believe it, then having to believe it once she beheld the gruesome tableau, his blood-smeared face, his voice crying to his Maker. She clutched me then, said she had heard some of the young men talking, they intended to take me for a drive, their brother Juan would have his honor restored. He had been drinking with them all afternoon down at the sea and undoubtedly they had filled his head with tales. He had had a rendezvous with me.

"They can't do anything to me," I said.

"They can . . . on a night like this they can do anything," she said. Nothing would deter me. My fear had been replaced by stunned horror and a scalding shame. Had I never come to this place, had I never met her, she might now be sitting down to her supper or washing her hair, and for the cruelest of seconds I saw her alive as on that first morning, full of arch gaiety, throwing flowers about like wet fish.

There was a crowd in the garden, mostly men, talking and drinking, but in the dark I could not distinguish them. I saw D'Arcy, his back turned, standing over the invalid, holding a jug of wine. From the room came the prayers and the oration "Decanso eterno . . . Lux perpetua . . . Eternal rest . . . Perpetual light . . ." As I went through the door her sister rose to bar the way, followed by three others, all in black. Her mother was closest to the bed, the women standing over her, weeping, like extras in one of the Stations of the Cross. I could not see Catalina's face, only the very white covers that reached to her chin like wadding. Where was her soul now? I recalled those books that I had read, depicting that long journey after death, sphere after sphere, before reaching the final destination. Death took root in me then, as for so many years love had, and to such excruciating purpose, but who in their right minds would not exchange love for death?

"Get out of here . . . get out of here," her sister screamed, the others repeating it exactly as they pushed me out. It was what the men in the garden had been waiting for, this cue from the women, this call for revenge. They gathered around me, heated, obstreperous. There were about ten of them, some recognizing me and telling the others who I was, the whore, the foreign whore. One of them tapped my chest, quick insolent taps as if it were a drumskin or a tabletop. They made no secret of their wishes, jerked their heads and said, "Vamos, vamos—let's go." Hatreds that they did not even know of glistened on their faces, hatreds fueled by their drunken spunk.

In jest one of them lifted my hair, gave a lewd sniff, and then pulled me by it to the gate. I saw a van and saw us go toward it. A young man got in and turned on the headlights and in the swoosh of light I saw their legs and their feet in high-heeled leather boots, then their faces, some chalky, others with sideburns and mustaches. My assassins.

D'Arcy came rushing toward us, his drink in his hand. He spoke to the ringleader, said his name, "Pablo . . . Pablo," while one of the others pushed me into the van, next to the lascivious young driver. They formed a huddle around D'Arcy, several of them talking and shouting. They seemed to disagree on what they had to say because some would push others aside and go close to him to air their version. Then one of them shook hands with him. He must have said something mocking or insulting because all of a sudden things escalated. Pablo, grabbing D'Arcy's glass, smashed it on the mudguard, to use the splinters as weapons. I saw D'Arcy open his shirt, challenging them, goading them, and soon he was on the ground as they converged on him. Charlotte ran up the pathway, dragging Catalina's mother, who looked as if she herself had been called from the dead. She was like one of those trees felled in a storm, its roots naked, obscene, gaping helplessly back at life. She moved among them shouting and they drew back, suddenly compliant, ashamed. Pablo put his folded hands toward her in a gesture of clemency and then he spoke to her rapidly, obviously trying to persuade her to let the men settle the vendetta themselves. At the same moment the driver started the engine and accelerated and I knew with certainty that he was going to ride over D'Arcy, crush him to death. With one hand I pulled at the handbrake and with the other grabbed the steering wheel and we tugged and wrestled over it, as might two people in a bumper car at a fun fair. It careened all over the road, then lurched to one side and dropped like a wounded beast.

D'Arcy was speaking to the mother, and I crawled out and went toward them to say something, though I did not know what. The look she gave me was pitiless. It was a cold look that said, "You may not have killed my daughter but you were the precursor of it, the Bad Shepherd." I put my hand out and she stared at it as if it were a leper's, then she turned and said something to Charlotte. It might have been a stone oracle that spoke, so stilted was her voice.

"She's broken . . . She's completely broken," D'Arcy said.

"I have to speak to her," I said.

"Speak. Bull," he said, with a savage glare, as if I should know that we are each alone with our crime, unable to bear it, unable to give it away. Then, less harshly, he proposed that we make ourselves scarce. Yes, he was saying as he put an arm around me, yes, it had all begun so blithely that Easter morning and it had come to this. As we walked, I heard the gate close with a clang, like a cemetery gate when the mourners have gone. I was too mortified to turn round to wave to Charlotte.

"Upon my vesture they have cast lots," he said, making light of his wounds and joking about his tattered shirt. Scuts they were, hardly even knew Juan, whom they so proudly defended. Nor was it any use accusing myself. It happened, it was in the cards from the very first day he and Catalina met; Infante Juan, led by a polar star, spouting Nietzsche—"The City reeks of the slaughterhouse . . . I am joyful in my winter sorrow," and so forth—elopement, bambolino, hostilities, the old story . . .

"It had to be," he said with a kind of awful compassion, then he reeled toward the low wall of the tavern, calling his friend, "Kevin . . . Kev." He said that the sooner I scooted the better, as passions might run amok again, indeed would, once the hearse came.

"Calle aparta . . . Parting of the ways," he said. In a way, it was the worst moment of all, the dismissal, the final banishment.

Going down the road, I saw a figure appear out of the darkness. I thought it was one of the young men but turned to see a little woman, a wisp of a thing. I knew it was the grandmother. She was wearing a threadbare black coat which flapped on her as though on a hatstand. She handed me something in a scarf. It felt warm. I thought it was a dead bird or entrails, a curse, but as she undid the knot I saw Catalina's hair, so vibrant, so alive it was as if her face still adhered to it. Under the moon it glistened, black for the most part but red where it was matted with blood. She put her lips to it.

"Muy precioso . . . muy precioso," she said, her voice cracked and choking. But it was with a kind of ecstasy that she gave it to me. Take it, she was saying, for to love one must learn to part with everything. Then she was gone, hobbling like an unfledged bird or a creature on stilts.

The road grew dark and bright at one and the same instant, and for the last time I set out for home.

THE GO-BETWEEN

BOOKS BY FREDERICK TURNER

Redemption: A Novel

In the Land of Temple Caves: Notes on Art and the Human Spirit

1929: A Novel of the Jazz Age

When the Boys Came Back: Baseball and 1946

A Border of Blue: Along the Gulf of Mexico from the Keys to the Yucatán

Spirit of Place: The Making of an American Literary Landscape

Of Chiles, Cacti, and Fighting Cocks: Notes on the American West

Rediscovering America: John Muir in His Time and Ours

Remembering Song: Encounters with the New Orleans Jazz Tradition

Beyond Geography: The Western Spirit Against the Wilderness

The Go-Between: A Novel of the Kennedy Years

EDITED BY FREDERICK TURNER

Into the Heart of Life: Henry Miller at One Hundred

The Portable North American Indian Reader

Geronimo: His Own Story

For Susan —
Love & all the best in the new year.

THE GO-BETWEEN

A NOVEL OF THE KENNEDY YEARS

Frank

FREDERICK TURNER

Mariner Books Houghton Mifflin Harcourt
BOSTON NEW YORK

First Mariner Books edition 2011

www.hmhbooks.com

Library of Congress Cataloging-in-Publication Data
Turner, Frederick W., date
The go-between : a novel of the Kennedy years / Frederick Turner.
p. cm.
ISBN 978-0-15-101509-2 ISBN 978-0-547-52032-2 (pbk.)
1. Journalists—Fiction. 2. Exner, Judith, 1934–1999—Fiction. 3. Kennedy, John F. (John Fitzgerald), 1917–1963—Fiction. 4. Presidents—United States—Fiction. 5. Giancana, Sam, 1908–1975—Fiction. 6. Sinatra, Frank, 1915–1998—Fiction. 7. Mafia—United States—Fiction. 8. United States—Politics and government—1961–1963—Fiction. I. Title.
PS3620.U765G63 2010
813'.6—dc22 2009036908

Book design by Melissa Lotfy

Printed in the United States of America

DOM 10 9 8 7 6 5 4 3 2 1

This is a work of fiction. Names, characters, and incidents are the product of the author's imagination, except in the case of historical figures and events, which are used fictitiously.

For
Robin Straus

THE GO-BETWEEN

1

PHIL

LOOK, I KNOW I COULD tell you this straight off, and it would entertain you, too, like the campfire yarn that goes, And then, and then, and then—right through to the finish, where the hero gets the girl or dies. But if I did it this way, you'd forget it, or at least you'd forget the things I want you to remember. So in order for this to have a chance of sticking with you the way it has with me all these years, I have to go against the way I learned my trade, which was to buttonhole you quick, so to say, and then hold on to you until I was done. In the newspaper business this wasn't very long, even when I was starting out, which was damn near sixty years ago. And it's gotten a hell of a lot shorter nowadays, what with the carpet-bombing of twenty-four/seven news. A print reporter now is lucky to get even the top of the reader's eyeball for two whole minutes. In that respect, I'm glad I'm out of it, though I'd be lying to you if I said I didn't miss the hurly-burly of the newsroom, the clackety-clack of the big old black machines, the cigarette smoke and swearing, the pints of sauce the older guys kept stashed in the bottom drawer of their desks. These are probably clichés to you, but before they became that they were the way we lived, and underneath that tough-guy, front-page pose we privately thought being a reporter was pretty hot stuff. I know I did. Even when we were telling each other this was one hell of a way to make a buck—busting your ass to write a story that would be used that evening to wipe up the puppy's poop or wrap the garbage in—still it was exciting to try to intervene in people's lives, *arrest* them, even if it was just for a few minutes, with your story, your version of events. When you come right down to it, that's what was truly exciting about journalism. It isn't enough for me now, though. I want more of you than that.

You know how every once in a while you'll be walking along the street, minding your own business, and suddenly you'll get a look from a complete stranger, and you'll take *meaning* from it, even if you can't put your finger on just what this is? You walk on, but you can't get that look out of your head. You keep seeing those strange eyes boring into you, and you keep wondering, Why me? And, What the hell was he trying to tell me? Well, what I want to do here is more like that than the news story I used to write or the campfire yarn.

But right off the bat I have to get something straight between us, which is this: some of this stuff didn't happen exactly the way I'm going to tell you here. That's not to say that I'm making it up; I'm no blogger. I have my sources, and they're an important part of the story. Sometimes I think they're almost as important as the story itself, as you'll see in a minute. They took me as close as anybody's going to get to the truth of this thing. They witnessed some of the events they talk about and took part in many of them, but they didn't see the whole of it or even know the whole of it. Nobody knows the whole of it. I wish to God there had been some all-seeing eyewitness and that I could have gotten hold of him or her. But there isn't, and anyway eyewitnesses, who are so highly prized in precinct stations and newsrooms and lawyers' offices, are actually often a good deal less reliable than you might think.

I was tipped to this years back, when I was just a squirt trying to catch on steady with the *Daily News* and hanging out at precinct stations on the South Side after the war. There was an old lieutenant at the South Halsted station called Rawhide O'Meara who took kind of a shine to me, maybe only because I was so goddamned green it was funny to him. When I met him old Rawhide could smell the barn, and he was ready for it: his feet hurt, his back hurt, and he was tired of the beat's relentless bullshit. He couldn't be bothered learning anyone's name anymore, so I was Mac, same as everybody else he hadn't known for at least ten years.

One afternoon I was asking him about a filling station knock-over where there'd been a bystander who positively identified two brothers named Brady as the perps. "See here, Mac," he said, "that don't make this any automatic. Not yet, anyways. Sure, we rely on these eyewitnesses when we can get 'em, and we try to use 'em to make the case, don't ya see. And sometimes they do, if we use 'em right. But there's a lot more to most cases than meets the eye." He liked that and haw-hawed, elbowing me hard in the ribs. "There's a lot more holes in these eyewitness deals than you'd think, and a defense lawyer who knows his stuff'll find 'em."

Well, as you see that comment stuck with me, though if I'm going to be completely candid with you here, I should add that I thought old Rawhide had plenty of holes in him, too. He never shut up and claimed to know everything there was to know about police work. Still, as I say, his comment stayed with me, and it came back to me later when I went to a lecture at John Marshall. I don't make a habit of going to law school lectures at night, but I wanted to hear Phil Keneally and see him in action.

Keneally was notorious. He was an absolutely brilliant criminal defense attorney who not only worked for the Mob but eventually married into it. That night his subject was supposed to be evidence and its uses and misuses. But it turned out to be almost exclusively about eyewitnesses, and he used a case tried by Lincoln in his downstate days. Lincoln appeared for the defense, and if I remember correctly, an eyewitness claimed to have seen his client stab a man to death one night in a field. Well, in his questioning, Keneally said, Lincoln led the witness through the woods, so to say, right up to the edge of the field, where he had him peeping through the trees and witnessing the murder. At which point Lincoln broke off to ask the guy if the moon was pretty bright that night, and the guy says, "Bright enough to see what I saw." So then Lincoln springs his trap and produces a *Farmer's Almanac*, or some such, to show that there wasn't any moon at all that night—black as the inside of a cow's ass—which sure as hell cast the shadow of doubt on *that* eyewitness's testimony. When I heard that I thought back on old Rawhide, whose funeral I went to not long ago. I'll come back to Phil Keneally, because as you'll see he's a big part of this story, but for now I simply want to say that history depends a lot on eyewitness accounts when it can get them. The full truth of most human stories, though, is a lot harder to get at than just having those firsthand reports and involves other considerations.

My eyewitnesses are like everybody else's. They tell what they saw and what they think they saw. They tell what they heard. They tell what they remember. They almost never tell you what they forgot or later realized they'd completely misunderstood. So to this extent history—written history, that is—looks to me kind of like a high-stakes gamble, something more or less carefully assembled, depending on the skill and conscience of the historian, and then kind of shoved out there like you'd push a bet through the hundred-dollar window at the track. So here's my point: I'm betting that what I've put together here is a plausible and even probable reconstruction of a very murky story. But I want you to keep in mind that it is a reconstruction, an attempt to reconstruct events and people from the past, bring them back to life in the present. That's what I've aimed for. Nothing more, nothing less.

A guy like me, trying for that plausible reconstruction, begins the same as the guys who win the prizes. The pros, the Pulitzer types who write the big-time official histories, will ride their firsthand sources as far as they can, then switch to secondhand, and finally go to other written sources, both published and un-. They don't deal much, if at all, in barebacked speculation, in hunches, in it-must-have-beens, though I think there was a writer a few years back who did just that sort of thing in a bio of Dutch Reagan. He got reamed good for it, too, if I'm remembering the incident correctly. I'm no different from the pros here. I'll ride my firsthand sources as far as they'll take me. Then I'll go to my secondhand ones, and finally to the books, and so forth. But then, here's where the difference comes in. A guy trained like I was, he'll probably handle all his sources a little more *freelance*, so to say. He'll be a little looser with them. He'll be kind of juggling them in his hands, feeling for their weight and heft and shape, like schoolkids of my generation used to work with their marbles out in the yard.

I don't really have the words for what I'm trying to describe for you, as you see. But I'm wondering if an old term my auntie used might possibly come close. Auntie Helen used to say that if you were trying to get inside a fact or around behind one to see it from that angle, you might have to look *asquint* at it. That meant you kind of looked past it almost, instead of square-on. You saw it, all right. You didn't ignore it. But you were looking for other things as well. How hard was the fact, really, and did some other party have an interest in making it seem like solid cast iron when it might turn out to be terracotta? Were there other facts surrounding it that cast a different light on it? What did the person look like when he was telling you his fact? This way of looking, it seems to me, inevitably leads you up to and probably across the borders of the Land of Hunch, which is where I might possibly have an advantage over the pros, because for some years I made a kind of living at what's nowadays called "investigative reporting," though we didn't have that term back then. The investigative reporter has to learn the terrain of the Land of Hunch, has to learn it by trial and error, by developing instincts, because there aren't any maps: an awful lot of it is simply *feel*, learning when and how to go beyond your sources and then hoping you're going to end up at the right spot, somewhere your sources alone couldn't have gotten you.

That's what I did here. I followed my sources until they gave out, as you'll see they did. And then I went on, trusting my training. I'm pretty sure that most of the time I tell you when I'm operating on a hunch, a feeling; or, if I don't come right out and say that, you'll be able to figure it out for yourself from what I say—and what I don't. Anyway, I try to keep things as straight as I can, though you must have already guessed I don't think there are that many things in this world you can take straight—unless it's a belt of Maker's Mark at the end of the day. When you have that, you know it's true because it hurts.

But don't get me wrong here: if this was *all* hunch or even mostly that, I'd be like those bloggers we have with us now, who get to claim absolutely anything they want, the wilder, the better. I'll bet you didn't know that LBJ had Jack Ruby poisoned in prison. Well, now you do, because you just heard me say it. And so forth.

So I have my sources, as I said. First and foremost are the diaries. Without them there wouldn't be any other sources for me, for the simple reason that if I hadn't seen them, I would never have known there was a story here, lying in wait behind the headlines of half a century ago, and no idea where it might lead me. Put another way, you can't play hunches if you have nothing to play with. No marbles, no game. There are—or were, anyway—at least twenty-nine of them. There might have been more, many more maybe. But I only had my hands on twenty-two, and I only got a really good look at sixteen. You could call them "volumes" if you wanted, but that in itself would be misleading, and there are sure as hell enough false leads and red herrings to this story without adding another. The diaries aren't the same size, and they aren't the same length, either, a couple of them being just a few pages long while others are filled to the margins and have tiny scrawlings all around the edges. And there was one completely different, but I'll get to that.

Not one of them has a date on the cover or inside on the flyleaf. Some of those I looked through but didn't get enough time with didn't seem to have any dates at all, while others had dates scattered here and there. The earliest one I saw has entries from 1948, which would make Judy Immoor, as she was then known, fourteen. It's a girly-girly book, physically: fat, padded leather covers, fat leaves, big spaces between the ruled lines. But she filled up those pages, all right. It was like right from the start she seemed to know that she had a story to tell and that there would never be anyone who would tell it except herself. And so here again you see what I mean about history, what it's made up of and what's left out. Of the uncountable billions of humans who've walked this planet, only a tiny fraction of them ever tried to tell their own stories, and an even tinier fraction of their diaries or journals or actual autobiographies survived war, famine, fire, rain, roof rot, rats, starving dogs, and simple neglect. So in that sense, too, history is a gamble based on fragmentary evidence, like a racing form where you don't get a look at the records of all the entries.

Maybe it's just as well. I mean, just imagine for a moment what history would sound like if each one of us had tried to tell our stories as seriously as she did. My God! What a Tower of Babel *that* would be, those millions and millions of voices crying out, *"Look at me! Look at me! Don't believe anybody else! This is the truth about how I lived!"* But she kept at it, off and on, with a kind of deep doggedness, from that first fat book all the way to what looked to me like the last. By that point she was very sick and was going as Judith Exner.

She was never what you'd call an accomplished writer, a pro, and I doubt she ever even thought about that, though she did think of herself as a practicing artist and seems to have really worked at painting for several years. But she was accomplished in other areas. She could bowl a good game, play gin, give the guys a run for their money on the golf course and hit off their tees. In the sack, she played in the biggest league on earth, and from what I could tell she held her own there, too.

But I don't have a full-length view of her talents, her strengths. I'm not even sure I have a full-length view of her character, though I know what I think of her, all right. Partly this is because I never got to spend time with all the surviving diaries. Partly it's because she wasn't much for blowing her own horn. And partly it's because I only met one person who really knew her in any depth, and he was never about to open up to me about her. I doubt he has ever done that with anyone, and I doubt he ever will.

But the other thing here is this: she played her cards pretty close to her chest, if I could put it that way. Nothing unusual here, for sure. You meet many people in life who're like that, never letting you know much about what they're thinking, much less what they're really feeling. But you'd think if someone was going to take the trouble to keep a diary and keep on keeping it, year after year, she'd let it rip in those pages, wouldn't you? I mean, what else could be the point—why withhold information from yourself? Sometimes, though, I get the funny feeling that this is just what she was doing, that she wasn't being completely confidential with herself. There's a kind of evasiveness there, especially where you'd expect her to be completely candid. That's not to say she *never* lets it rip; she does. But not with any consistency and not always just where you'd most want her to.

But then I think of her life, particularly once she gets into the deep waters, and I find myself wondering who she thought she could really trust. Maybe she came to feel that there was *nothing* of hers that was permanently hers, that it could all be taken away by somebody, every bit of it, even her thoughts, and so she held on to some of them.

This accounts, I think, for that feeling of opaqueness I got so often in reading the entries. It wasn't simply that she wasn't a very good writer—how many of us are? But there I was, reading along and trying to find out what really happened in Hawaii with Sinatra, in Chicago with Sam Giancana at the Ambassador East, up on the second floor of the White House with Jack Kennedy—and it really isn't there. Oh, it's there, all right, but there's no *substance* to it, if you follow me. To put it in the terms of my old trade, if you were a feature writer and turned in copy like this, you'd get it back in your face if your editor was on the ball. "For Christ's sake!" he'd say. "I could get crap like this off the goddamn wire service! Give me some meat on these bones." You might have gotten the who and the what and the where, all right, but you hadn't gotten the reader into the human reality of the situation, whatever that was.

She rarely does this, and so a lot of the time I have to try to do it for her. I quote her own words when I can, when they seem to do a justice to the situation, but much more often I have to try to make the things she lived through come alive because she either didn't want to or couldn't, or maybe she thought she would come back at some later point and flesh these things out but never got around to it. So I have to try to put some meat on the bones of her life. When I began working with her diaries, I didn't see a problem with this: "Hey, the chick was no Shakespeare, so I'll have to tone her up a bit"—that sort of thing. But later on, as I got further into it, it came to feel a bit more complicated. I was, after all, trying to give a dead person a fuller voice, a more realistic one, and who was I to try to do that? Was I in fact burying the very story I had set out to bring to life? Was I posthumously violating her privacy, which had been violated so dreadfully in her lifetime?

I can't give you a figure for the total elapsed time I had with the diaries—not a figure, anyway, that would do you any good. The first time I saw any of them they were the property of Judy's adopted son, Ed. She had a blood son as well that she gave up for adoption, but I doubt that kid ever knew about the diaries. As for Ed, he kept them in a Kellogg's carton in this rec room he had in the basement of his house in Evanston, with its top ripped away, just piled in there in no particular order, 1955 resting on 1950 or whatever. They must have come to him after Judy died, and I'm convinced he only looked into them enough to know what they were. That randomly piled box told me that in headlines. But he probably did understand that he had enough dynamite in there to blow a hell of a hole in the liberal political establishment of America and make obsolete a lot of the books written about JFK.

Oh, sure, there are plenty of references in books and magazines to Kennedy's womanizing. The guy was one hell of a swordsman by all accounts. But as far as I know there aren't any other firsthand accounts by women who went to bed with him, at least none that have survived or else aren't under lock and key in some Georgetown mansion. Likewise, there are printed references to the connections between national politics and organized crime, but none I know of that can take you beyond the generalities, the it-must-have-beens, to show you how things were done and exactly where the money changed hands, and she had that down, too.

As I say, Ed had to know at least some of this. Now, how much he knew and how he knew it are questions I don't have good answers for. How much he got from her and how much out of the headlines I couldn't tell from his very few comments about his mother and the life she led. He said almost nothing specific about the diaries.

If I had to get money down on this, here's what I'd say. She felt forced to give her blood son up for adoption because her own notoriety was so ferocious she thought the kid stood a better chance at life with another family and a different identity. Then, early on, she gave Ed her maiden name, Immoor, to try to shield him a bit from that same notoriety, which shadowed her all the way to the grave. Now, if she did these things, why would she subject Ed to a bruising, face-to-face description of all the stuff she'd had to go through, all the stuff she wrote down in those diaries? No. I think she probably told him only as much as she thought he needed to know and then left behind the diaries she still had so he could fill in some of the blanks if he wanted to.

Being around Ed as I was for a brief time, I have to wonder now if he'd ever thought much about the diaries at all until William Safire wrote this column after her death, all about poor Judy being a "tragic footnote to history" or some such crap. I looked up that column in the morgue later, and of course it wasn't about her tragedy or her being a footnote; it wasn't about her at all. She was only a cudgel Safire could use to beat Kennedy and the liberals with. Which wouldn't have surprised her in the least, because she knew what it felt like to be used—oh, she knew that in spades. But to the extent Ed had thought about them or glanced through them, I don't think he knew what to do with them. Probably the last thing he would have thought of was to have them published. That would have been like digging Judy up and dragging her corpse through the streets all over again. He respected her way too much for that. So they just sat there, year after year, in that box. I think the only reason he even let me look at them was that he was stoned out of his gourd. And this brings up another thing you need to understand about Ed. Despite the fact that he'd started out in life with something of a handicap, being an orphan and all, things came easy to him. He was a big, handsome guy with what's called a winning personality. He was a scratch golfer—Judy had him out on the course when he was very little. But to me there was something kind of indolent about him. He wasn't big on persistence, and if it didn't come easy, he wasn't interested. That was my take on him, anyway, and aside from the fact that he might easily have had a natural reluctance to read certain details of Judy's life, I come back to this trait as a better explanation of why those diaries just sat down in that rec room all those years in a Kellogg's carton with its top ripped away.

At the time I'm speaking of I was working as a legman for G. Katzen. That name won't mean anything to you, but back then it might have, because he and his younger brother, Arthur, collaborated on a series of very popular books about American cities. The Katzens were Bronx guys who had tried a number of other things before they wrote a book called *New York Confidential*. It hit big. So then they did *L.A. Confidential* and then *Boston Confidential*. These were supposed to give you the inside dope on these places: who really ran things and how to cut through the red tape at City Hall to get to the guy you needed. If you played the ponies, they'd tell you how often favorites ran in the money in stakes races at the various tracks and whether the going was a little deeper on the three inside posts at Aqueduct. If you wanted a really good steak, they had the restaurant for you and the headwaiter's name, plus how much to tip him for a table without a reservation. Enough of this stuff was accurate so that if you were going to L.A., it could be a help. And even if you weren't, it was kind of a gas to read about what went down in Manhattan and how if you tipped Angelo a tenner at Locke-Ober in Boston, he'd see you got a table in the main-floor dining room, where the local sluggers ate and drank, instead of a seat upstairs in Siberia.

In every one of these towns the Katzens had their legmen, guys who were native and knew the kinds of stuff the brothers dealt in. Of course, once the Katzens got hold of your copy, they'd generally give it a pretty good massage. Still, as I say, the books were factual enough; they weren't fiction. The brothers knew when to quit, so to say, but still deliver enough dirt and gossip to make for a very satisfying package.

I was their man in Chicago, and I had three stringers working under me, one of them a girl in J-school at Northwestern who was nervy as hell and tough as nails. She was also scared to death her profs would find out she was moonlighting for the likes of me and the Katzens, so I made it part of my business to make sure they never did. She needed the money, and she was worth it, too. So in that way I guess you could say I helped put her through school. Later on I saw her byline in a pretty classy magazine, far better than those I got into myself. As for the Katzens, they never had any literary aspirations at all, and after *Chicago* they took their money and bought some retail space below Fourteenth Street in New York and did very well with it. I doubt they ever wrote another line, either of them.

I never learned what the G. stood for. He went by it, signed my checks that way, and if you should happen across one of those *Confidential* books at a yard sale or in the unsorted bin of a used bookstore, you'd see on the title page "Arthur Katzen and G. Katzen." I asked him about that one time. We were having a drink at the Tip Top Tap at the old Allerton on Michigan. G. didn't drink much, but he did go for the Moscow Mule they served up there—vodka and ginger beer in a copper mug with a sprig of mint. It sounded disgusting, but then, I never had one. When I brought up the subject of the initial, he just stared at me through his foggy spectacles a long moment and shrugged.

"Why isn't it good enough for you?" he said. "It's enough for me."

That was that. The money was good, the checks were solid, and I had no reason to piss him off. He always made it pretty clear what he was looking for, as much as you can in a situation where you yourself don't really know the terrain and want to give your man his head. When I delivered, he was professionally appreciative. In that line of work you can't ask for more than that. A guy like me makes a living—or tries to—being curious and persistent, but at the same time he needs to develop a feeling for when not to be either of these things, so "G." was fine with me.

When *Boston* hit the bestseller list and I was running stuff down for him on the Chicago number, G. surprised me one day. He was a pretty low-key guy in his personal style: midrange hotels like the Allerton; ready-to-wear suits; chopped steak instead of sirloin; public transportation. Yet on this occasion he told me he wanted me to research a new car for him—an MG convertible, no less. I knew he had a wife and kids back in the Bronx, on Arden, where he and Arthur were born, so when a guy steps out of character like that you have to figure he must be getting around on his old lady.

However that was—and I never learned—I went to work on the assignment, and that's how I happened across Ed Immoor. He had the MG dealership in Evanston and another outfit in Skokie that handled late-model used MGs, a good number of which he'd sold new over in Evanston. His customers were mostly North Shore types, and Ed knew them like a veteran tout knows a track or a stable—quirks, tics, vanities, pressure points. It just sort of came to him, I think, and what with his looks and personality he was a talent, all right.

The showroom was on Chicago Avenue, right by the tracks, all glass and lights and Formica, but when I went in there on a late February afternoon, one of those days that can give you the feeling that death couldn't be any worse than this, I thought the mood was pretty low. I'd done my homework and knew Ed was the guy to see. Sometimes when you shoot straight for the top you'll get snotty treatment from the flunkies, and if the head man isn't available, you can't expect any favors when you're forced to move down a rung or two, if you know what I mean. But on average the brass-balled approach is worth the gamble, as it was here. When Ed bounced out of his office onto that gleaming floor, well, the place came alive and the ceiling lifted.

Right off I let him know I was serious, that I wasn't any window-shopper. I told him exactly what my boss had in mind, and shortly he had me driving around the neighborhood with him in this terrific-looking green number with an off-tan top. I loved the ride of it, wondering to myself if G. could really appreciate it the way I was, tooling so smoothly around the gray suburban streets with here and there some lines of old slush in the gutters, looking like filthy fleece. In the MG, though, you felt insulated from everything, like nothing out there could get in to where you were sitting in such tight luxury.

I told Ed my boss would be happy with this very car, and later, in his office with its color photos of Ed posed with various golfing groups and him bent over his desk working out an offer sheet, I let it drop that my boss had a brother who was sure to want one just like the green convertible, only probably a different color. Ed was filling out some standard stuff about extras and service specials, but when I threw in my own extra he glanced up quickly and without hesitation scratched out a set of figures and put down some others.

"This," he said, still writing something below the new figures, "is off what I was going to offer. Good offer, too. But even if the brother doesn't end up doing this"—he smiled and shrugged those broad, flat shoulders he had—"this is my thanks for bringing him onto the floor. When you line it up like that, what I knock off here"—tapping the papers—"is, ah, minuscule."

I knew the word, all right, though I can't tell you I ever used it in conversation. I know I never used it in print. I wasn't looking for it from him, and it kind of bumped me off stride, making me wonder whether I'd sized him up right. I don't know if he was a college man. I doubt it. For what he seemed to want out of life college wouldn't have been that necessary, and as I've already said, Ed liked shortcuts if they were available. But maybe he'd acquired one way and another a stockpile, so to say, of heavyweight words he drew from on occasions like this. I don't know. In the short time I knew him I never heard him use another like it, but then we never did automobile business again.

I'm pretty sure he didn't get it from his mother. Judy was no dummy, that I can tell you, despite what you might have read about her and despite what her first husband told reporters; Billy was no Einstein himself. But judging from the diaries, I'd say her vocabulary didn't run to fancy words. It was pretty much meat and potatoes but did the job she apparently wanted done. Since I never met her, never heard her voice, I can't tell you how she came off in person, how she presented herself verbally and socially. I have to believe, though, that on top of her shyness, the deep insecurity that no number of private visits to the White House or evenings out with Sinatra and the Rat Pack could ever quite wring out of her, she could hold up her end of a conversation anywhere. And then, of course, there's that universal credit card she always carried: she could flash that brilliant smile and it would be worth any amount of chin music.

I did, however, catch a glimpse of her in action, and I'll be surprised if it doesn't stay with you awhile like it has with me. This was in a blippy, faded home movie where the only sound came from the mechanics of the production techniques—whirring noises, grinding, clicking of wheels, etc. All quite primitive by our standards now. At the time I saw this footage, though, I remember thinking that the noises were oddly more realistic than voices might have been. They kind of took you back, if you see what I mean. In this movie, anyway, she says one word. That's to say, you see her mouth move once, and the word she says looks a lot like "*Hey!*"

The movie was shot in color at poolside somewhere. Could have been Chicago or Miami or Las Vegas or Southern California, these being the places she hung out with Sam Giancana and his pals. He's in it, too. But even though it's his show, his cameraman and so forth, she's the star, the focus. She walks past the camera in a black tank suit, but she's so close you can't see that much of her. The camera guy—some hood probably more comfortable behind a wheel than a camera—jerks the thing around to follow her, and so then you get one of those dizzying, wheeling sequences of empty sky and umbrellas and pool water that looks like it's rushing uphill before he finds her again and adjusts the focus. And when he does get the range right you can understand why he might be in such a hurry. She was a knockout. There isn't any other way to put it. Big girl, beautifully put together, with broad shoulders like Esther Williams, narrow waist, long, clean legs. When the camera guy gets up to shoot her climbing the ladder to the high board, you can see her calf muscles at work, and they are definitely not minuscule, to borrow from Ed.

Well, she gets up there and stands with her hands on the rails, and while she's that way the camera guy scurries back to his original position so he can catch her in profile. And even though, as I say, she's wearing a tank suit without any cosmetic scaffolding, you could tell she had plenty up top, too. She must have worked out, is all I can think, though this was before the days of personal trainers, ladies' gyms, weights, and all that. The kind of life she was leading then was hardly designed to keep you in condition, but she was all of that. It makes you wonder where she found the time. I know I never came across any references in the diaries to workouts, but that doesn't mean they aren't in there; or even if they aren't, it wouldn't mean she didn't do laps or the like. Every gorgeous woman, which she definitely was then, has got to have a streak of vanity in her somewhere, don't you think? But vanity about looks doesn't just happen; it's got to be *worked* at and preserved in private, I think. In her case, I know this from the many references she makes to the hours she spent putting herself together for a night on the town.

But there she is, up on the high board, and the camera's on her steady for a good minute or so before it swings back to the ladder. And there is Momo Giancana himself, in his bathing trunks, making a big show of stealth as he climbs the ladder, putting his finger to his lips, broadly pantomiming *"Shhh,"* taking big, high, cartoony steps until he's up there behind her. And still she doesn't appear to notice him.

When I rerun this movie in my mind—and I've done that many times—I come back to just this moment, wondering what the hell she could be thinking about not to have noticed Giancana and his goofy antics. And here the lack of sound becomes a kind of problem if this question interests you. Because you'd like to know what was going on at poolside just then, whether there were lots of others around, whooping it up, music playing and the like, so that she could kind of lose herself in her thoughts and Momo's approach could get lost in the general hubbub. In some of the footage you can see another woman in the background, wearing sunglasses and a broad hat with a scarf tied around it and under her chin. She's wearing a swimsuit that might have been orange, but the film is so faded that it and the scarf look more like washed out pink with orange around the outlines. So that would make at least four of them there, and somehow or other I have the feeling there were more than that, that this was a party. This is one of the hundreds of details to this story we'll never know, along with what thoughts she was having up there—clearly a more important matter—while she looked down into the deep end.

Then here comes Momo, creeping out onto the platform behind her, and his stealthy, hunched approach is creepy, coming up like that behind this statuesque, unsuspecting girl. And when he gets within striking range he makes this big pounce and rips down the straps of her swimsuit, and in that instant you get a look at her before she grabs herself and crosses her arms and whips around to face him. That's when she says that one word. She had heavy eyebrows, and in this instant she brought them together in a frown while she uttered that single word, which maybe wasn't even a word but only the voicing of the sound of surprise and outrage and, yes, even disappointment. Later on, when I try to tell you something of her story, you might find my use of this word positively weird. After all, you might say to yourself, how could a girl like this, living this terrifically fast life, possibly be *disappointed* by the behavior of the men she ran with, from JFK down to Giancana? You would have to think that life could hold no surprises for her, that by the time she climbed that ladder she knew what the deep end looked like and the shallow end, too. Disappointment can only come out of what we *don't* yet know, wouldn't you say, not what we already do?

But from what she wrote I have to think that almost to the end she still believed. In what? you're asking. Well, there you have me. But *something*. Some ghost or glimmer. Some far-off call or close-up whisper. Some quick glimpse of what I guess I can only call *possibility*: the possibility that everything she was living through—all of it—had some better meaning than met the eye: the glamour and the glitz that were meant to blind you so that you couldn't really tell what garbage it was made of, like Frankenstein, who was made out of garbage, if I recall. She wanted to believe, I think, that there was a meaning, for her, in all the endless restlessness of travel on planes and trains, in limos and taxis and fast cars driven by big-time wheel men. Wanted to find a way to accept the featureless hotel suites with lamé bedspreads and deep-pile carpeting—and cigarette burns behind the nightstand and a suspect stain on the loveseat's cushion. Wanted to go along comfortably with the pervasive falseness of all the arrangements of that life—fake identity papers, fake business cards, fake names, hotel registrations, itineraries that said you were in Chicago on such-and-such a date when you were actually in Las Vegas. Wanted to believe, too, in the necessity of fake guards who looked the other way while ushering you into rooms almost nobody else on earth was supposed to enter. And finally to accept the brain-killing pace of the partying—daiquiris with Jack, champagne with Frank and his flunkies, martinis at the Armory Lounge with Sam, and then the sun coming up on the silver wing of a private plane on its way to somewhere and the passengers still skunked from the night before. And there would have been as well the necessity of learning how to bear the constant sudden passes trusted men made at you, to think of these as tributes to your physical beauty, which, I guess, they were in their own grimy way: those bodyguards and gofers fumbling at her chest when all she'd really asked for was a lift back to her room after another night-into-day.

After years of this, I think, she still somehow clung to possibility. Using that word again, I hear it loudly and wonder if it's truly the one I want. I can only tell you it's the one that keeps coming at me when I think about her life. And so for now, at least, let's let it stand. Maybe you'll come up with a better one on your own. But then, you might find that you don't share at all this hunch I have. There were plenty of people who knew her who didn't. To them, Judy was nothing more than a high-class whore whose luck ran out when her boyfriends got whacked: tough luck, toots, and so forth. I can't feel that way about her, and you might as well know it right off.

I think it's quite possible that even her boyfriends—Frank and Jack and Sam—might have thought of her as a whore. They were all users of women, and they certainly used her in the most intimate way possible, as well as in very practical ways. And they knew her in a way I never would. But I came to know her in a way I doubt they did, a way probably nobody else did, including Ed, who most likely hadn't done much more than riffle through the diaries she'd left him.

Oddly, he had looked through the one written in code, because he told me so. It was the only direct reference to the contents of any of them he ever made to me. It was written, he said, when she was very sick. Actually, she was on her way to death, and so maybe she wanted to talk out loud to herself in total privacy, if you see what I mean, at the very end willing to write out everything she'd been holding back. She didn't get very far with the project, though. I should have written down the number of pages there, but I didn't. Couldn't have been much more than a dozen. After that there were a few more scratchings that looked pretty hesitant, as if she didn't remember anymore how the code went. And then the scratchings just trailed away into blank pages. Talk about being confined by responsibility to your sources! A set of diaries written over the years that ends in code and then silence: if this doesn't tell you anything at all, pal, you're in the wrong racket. Now, *what* it tells you may be quite another matter, and as I've already said, I never could make much of anything of the code. Maybe there at the end she couldn't either. Was it the key to or the summation of all the others, a bottom line she wrote to herself about what her life had meant? Or was it a reaction to the years of relentless surveillance by the FBI and the CIA, the Secret Service men, the Mafia mugs, the Senate committees, the paparazzi, down to the garden-variety stalkers who somehow found out who she was? Or was it a side effect of the illness that killed her and the treatment, which was pretty near as bad, as far as I can figure it? I'd show you a couple of lines I copied out, but they might have a chance of making a little more sense to you later on, when you know her story, or as much of it as I can tell you. Maybe at that point you'll see something I just haven't. You know how it is: you look at something long enough, you see less and less, until you don't even see the obvious anymore, which a fresh pair of eyes will spot right off. It's like looking in the mirror every morning and not seeing how you've taken on age.

How I got a look at the diaries Ed had was this: he liked me. That and the dreary aspect of that February day, sales slow, and then in walks an easy one, right down Broadway. So that had put him in a good mood, and afterward we had a pop—single-malt Scotch—back there in his office and got to gassing about this and that.

"Sometimes I think I wouldn't even bother with this stuff anymore," Ed said, nodding at his glass and then swirling it a bit. "It's the long way to heaven, that's for sure." He went on to clarify his meaning, telling me that if he could find a reliable source for Moroccan red hash, he would stick with that and just drink tonic water or some such on social occasions. But his supplier had been nabbed recently by the port authorities in New Orleans, and now old Duke was doing a good stretch in the stone house. "Duke was my guy," he said sadly. "Nobody else can get the real McCoy."

Several things came to mind all at once for me here, the first being that Duke, whoever he was, wasn't the only hash importer left in North America. I knew a man in Blue Island who could get it. I'd run across him in working for G., and after I'd interviewed him about what vestiges remained of Capone's old organization, I'd pressed some folding money into his hand. He looked at the bills without counting them, smiled thinly, then invited me back to his office in the rear of his sporting goods store for a friendly pipe. I only took one hit, just to be polite, and it was the real McCoy, all right. It gave you that almost-instant illusion of a perfect, hard-edged clarity where you think that *finally* you've arrived in the real world out of that fuzzy fog you've been stumbling through like a West Madison Street bum on a bat. It's a hell of a high, I'll give it that. But what I don't like is how heavy it hits and how long it stays with you. If I'm having my drinks, I know pretty much where I am and how I got there, and some of the time I know when to quit, too. But with this stuff Ed seemed to like so well, it was already too late to quit with your first lungful.

Did I want to be Ed's pony? I asked myself. The errand itself of running a pancake for him up from Blue Island to Evanston would be relatively risk-free, I thought—but not entirely so. What if some clown should sideswipe me on the Dan Ryan or the Kennedy during those few minutes I was "in possession"? Highly unlikely, sure, but how many times have you read in the paper about the serial killer who was stopped for a routine traffic violation and they find the mask and ropes in the trunk?

What the hell, I thought. I told him I had an acquaintance on the South Side who had the goods he seemed to be talking about. So right there we made an arrangement for me to bring the stuff up to his house, which I did late one afternoon about a week later.

Down in his rec room—full bar, mounted buffalo head, deep couches—he went right to work on the hash, getting out his little collection of brass pipes and asking me if I wanted a hit. But I said I'd stick with a Maker's Mark if he had it, which I felt sure he would: the room was obviously set up for entertaining clients and business associates, and so shortly I had my drink, and then we settled down with our vices.

At first there was some talk—the Cubs and what their chances looked like for the new season, and then the auto business, which was slow just now. But then it got quiet, and I was beginning to think I'd fulfilled my function in Ed's life and should scram. But just then he broke the silence to tell me he had something that might interest a writer like me, and more to be polite than anything else I said sure, I'd be happy to have a look at whatever he had to show me. He went back behind the bar, rummaged around a bit, and then brought out a Kellogg's carton with its top ripped away and set it down at my feet.

"These were my mom's," he said, pulling out a diary at random. "I guess you couldn't call her a writer—not like you, anyway—but she led a fairly unusual life and wrote some of it down in these diaries."

Well, I was in the man's house, and I wasn't so far along that I could miss the past tense he'd used in speaking of his mother. What the hell could I do except pretend interest? So I flipped open the diary he'd handed me, and there in girlishly rounded script, complete with little circles for the dots of the *i*'s and the *j*'s and the periods, was the name Judith Eileen Katherine Immoor on the flyleaf, but no date or place. Inside it, I found her whining on for some pages about not being allowed to go with the other girls to Sacred Heart or His Precious Blood or some such school but instead being tutored at home. Perfectly legitimate complaint from a teenager, but what the hell—you know what I mean? I could tell that Ed was already up a bit, but I hadn't figured the hash had turned his brain to oatmeal. Still, as I've said, this was a situation I was in, so I kept on a bit, skimming over longish comments on an uncle who lived in Balboa, figuring I'd slowly page through the rest of it, maybe pick another one out of the box, glance through that, and leave. Ed wasn't watching me, or if he was, it was intermittently from a long way off, and my hunch was that he would be pretty indifferent to my leaving.

I read through some more entries about that Balboa uncle, who seemed to give young Judith nightmares, and then I carefully replaced that one and fished out the next that came to hand. I opened it in the middle, and before I'd read a sentence I knew it had been written some time later. The handwriting had lost its girlish roundness, as if Judith had lost her own roundness, what they used to call baby fat when speaking of adolescents who still had chubby cheeks and asses and tummies. Also, those circles that had floated like clouds above the *i*'s and so forth—they were gone. Just black dots now.

I read the entry for the day that had fallen under my thumb; it didn't have a date. But Judith was watching a football game on TV with somebody named Billy, so that at least gave me the season. There was mention of a Bob Wagner at the end of the entry, evidently a friend. I went quickly through a few more pages, watching Ed out of the corner of my eye, some more references to Bob Wagner bobbing up along with the place name Hollywood, and so I thought about asking Ed if this Bob Wagner could possibly be the Robert Wagner who was married to Natalie Wood when she went overboard. Common name, of course, but at the very least my question would show interest and at the same time might justify Ed's claim that his mom's life had been unusual. But when I glanced over at Ed I could see that he was out there, and so I didn't ask but instead turned back to the flyleaf. And there in clear, bold script was the name Judith Campbell. Somewhere between that girly-girly diary with its rant about home schooling and this one, Ed's mom had acquired a new name—marriage, most likely—and I wondered why it sounded a faint, tinny bell in my head.

You know how it is in these moments: that far-off bell tells you *something*'s there, but what? And if you're a curious guy like me, you start riffling through the card catalogue of your memories, and sometimes you get lucky right off. But most of the time you have to work with it a little, tease it out, so to say. If it's a name, you try to hook it up with something, some event or place or time. Me, I try to visualize it in print. Sometimes you might have to fiddle around with the name itself—with its sound—and that's what I did here, changing Judith to Judy, which gave me Judy Campbell, and the tinny, tiny bell became a huge gong.

I had to try.

"Well, Ed, you're right," I began, trying for the conversationally casual. "These are interesting." He swung his head slowly in my direction and gave me a long look. It was that stoned stare dope will give you, but there was something more beneath that. I can't honestly tell you that even if I'd been stony sober I'd have been able to identify what it was. Now—*now*—I think I can. It was an immediate, instinctive defensiveness that came over him when the subject of his mom came up. I mean, it was okay if *he* mentioned her, as he had when he'd said her life was "unusual," because he was in control there, if you see what I mean. But here it was me who was bringing her up again and making a kind of judgment, even if it was really only a repeat of the one he'd made himself. But like I say, this is hindsight, and at the time what I was thinking was only that suddenly he wasn't easy, affable Ed the car dealer anymore. Different guy: you can't ever tell what direction dope will take a man, though I guess the same might be said of the sauce. Even so, I thought I had to go on.

"They make me wonder if she's the Judy Campbell that knew JFK," I said, and in saying those words my own voice sounded strange to me, like someone was applying pressure around my neck.

"*Yeahhh,*" he drawled in a suddenly weary tone. "Right. That one."

A moody silence fell between us. Ed put his pipe down and stared off across the room. I thought maybe he wasn't going to say anything else, and what with that look he'd given me and those four weary words I wasn't sure I wanted him to. He raised one hand slowly and began to stroke his lower lip.

"But let me set you straight, pal, she wasn't anything like they painted it."

More silence then, and me sitting there with my hands on the diary and all my fingers feeling that what I was really holding was a stick of dynamite; that if the pages in these randomly piled books covered the right territory, this was the scoop of a lifetime, right at my feet. Because this Judy Campbell was the woman whose face had been plastered across the covers of magazines and tabloids years back, the dark-haired beauty said to have been used as a go-between by Kennedy and Momo Giancana. And right then I found myself wishing more than anything ever in my life that I had been sober and clean as a whistle, because all my reporter's instincts were instantly alive to the possibilities here. But they weren't *sharply* alive, and a false move in this situation could queer the deal forever. I fumbled around a minute for some kind of comment that would break the silence, which was getting thicker by the second.

"This Bob Wagner," I said, gesturing in Ed's direction with the diary and not going straight for the target but for something next door to it, "would that be the Robert Wagner in the movies, by any chance?"

Ed didn't answer. He must have been stuck back there with the rumors about his mom, the ones that made her out to be a moll.

"Whatever you *heard*," he said finally, "it isn't what I *know*. She was a real lady, and she was a great mom to me. She was strict as hell." Saying this, he lolled his head back against the sofa cushions and looked at the ceiling. Then he brought his head back down and almost glared at me. "But she always encouraged me in whatever I wanted to do."

"That's a good combo for a parent to have," I said, and meant it.

"You're damned right it is. I never knew a one of my friends who had it as good at home as I did. Not a one. She saw to it I had a damned good Catholic upbringing, and it wasn't farmed out, either. She saw to it herself. But you never hear about this. Goddamned vultures. All they wanted to talk about was the Kennedys and the Mob."

I was thinking you could hardly blame them, and also that I myself was one of them. To be completely honest here, that was all I was interested in at that moment. That's to say, if Judith Eileen Katherine Immoor hadn't become Judy Campbell, the notorious go-between rumored to have been making it with the most powerful and glamorous man in the whole world and at the same time with the shadowy, vicious vice lord of Chicago, who the hell would care how she'd raised her kid? Who *did* care? Did I, really? And if the answer was no, did this make me just another in the flock of vultures? I've asked myself this question a number of times since then, trying to come up with an answer that isn't influenced by all the stuff I later found out about her. And what I've come up with is only this: *at that moment*, the one I'm trying to tell you about, she could have sold her son into slavery or scrubbed floors to put him through divinity school, and no writer I know of would have cared much either way—me included. No, the red meat here, the blood that gave it that color, was the connection she'd had with JFK and Giancana, and what I wanted just then was to sink my canines into this juicy mass and just *gorge*.

I don't know how this sounds to you. But we all know that if there's a fire, arson sells a hell of a lot more papers than faulty wiring, and here was a five-alarmer with a wad of oily rags at its center. So whatever I came to feel about Judy Campbell later—and you've already heard me say something about that—down in that rec room waiting to see what Ed's next move might be, I quickly consigned the Judy-Ed relationship to the back burner, the *far* back one, like you might have seen on one of those big old Wolf commercial stoves. Life, as one of the Kennedys famously said, isn't fair. Neither is the writing of history, which runs a lot closer to the tabloid headlines than we like to believe and would rather deal in mayhem than mothering. This was a fact of life I picked up early in my career, and it's stayed with me. You can make of it what you want, but if you're honest, you won't be able to say it isn't true. So you see, you're implicated, too, in a way.

Now here's something else that's true about me that you need to factor into this situation. As a writer I've always been what you'd call in racing or boxing a ham-and-egger. This is a term, I think, out of the Depression. It means a guy who knows his trade, all right, who has the skills to keep busy at it, but who's a full cut below first-class. In racing, your ham-and-egger generally gets mounts that are just that, too. He isn't going to get up on Kelso or Secretariat or ride in the Arlington Million, though he'll get stakes horses once in a while. In boxing he'll be a step above being merely an opponent; he'll be the guy who'll take a licking from some kid on the way up or else one from a former contender on the way down who's hoping for one more good payday. But he won't beat a good fighter on a normal night.

Unless he gets lucky. And what came to me in Ed's rec room was that here at my feet could be the break I wasn't even looking for anymore, simply because I'd been on my beat long enough to stop looking for it and settle for what I was. Saves you some heartbreaks that way, and some heartburn, too; sometimes your body will tell you what your head won't own up to.

It's the nature of the terrific break that you almost never see it coming, until it's handed to you like cosmic room service. But then you have to be ready. Remember way back when Jersey Joe got in there with Joe Louis and damned near cleaned his clock? Jersey Joe was the walking definition of the ham-and-egger, if ever there was one. But he was ready for his break, and it changed his life. Sure, he lost. But he got another shot—which he also lost—and he kept on getting shots until finally he caught Ezzard Charles on a bad night and was the champ at last. He saw some real money then, got his name in lights, even got into the movies. These diaries, if they covered the right territory, could do the same thing for me. And they had to cover at least some of it, or why would Ed have made that remark about Judy's unusual life when he'd handed them over?

But it's one thing for a guy to let you have a glance at something and a whole different thing for you to ask him if you can *appropriate* it, so to say, which is just what I'd be doing if I said I'd love to copy some of this stuff down. He'd just made that crack about the press, and so maybe in handing me the box he'd been telling me that this was strictly between friends and completely off the record. Stoned though he was, I didn't think he was stoned enough to have forgotten what I did for a living. He had stopped even glancing my way but was staring at his shoes and every once in a while shifting them slightly, as if he was admiring the shine somebody had put on them. So I thought, What the hell, and took the plunge again, asking him if he minded if I copied down a few things—hell of an interesting story, and so forth. He just waved in my direction, still admiring facets of his shoes, and I pulled my dog-eared spiral pad from my pants pocket, snapped my ballpoint, and copied out that entry about Judy and Billy watching football on TV. Here it is:

> Sat—
>
> We slept late. Then Billy said he wanted to do it but we'd have to hurry—the UCLA-Cal game was on tv and he had to watch—Jackie Gibbs being so great. When he was finished I got us some chips and onion dip and Billy got beers and we watched. B had USC on the radio too and it was confusing to me. Afterwards he started fooling around and said let's do it again and we did right there. About 6 John Agar called and wanted to come over to talk about Shirley. B's really worried about John's drinking and sure enough when John got here he was already about half bombed. B. tried to get some coffee down him but he was too upset for that and we had a couple with him while he talked about S. and who she was seeing.
>
> Went over to Bob Wagner's for supper. Pretty much fun. Billy talks behind Bob's back though and that makes me sad—I've known R.J. a lot longer than him.

When I think back on this, a part of me is astonished. I mean, I was no rookie reporter, a wide-eyed jerk out of J-school. I'd been around the block a few times, and I ought to have had a fairly well-developed sense of what was at least potential pay dirt. Yet the morning after when I had looked at this entry, it looked an awful lot like just dirt, a waste of a precious chance. But then, remembering the circumstances, I kind of let myself off a bit. Might have been a really dumb choice of a passage to copy out, but pardonable. But here are a couple of odd things. First, I've come to think of this as a bit of dumb luck, because I think I see here something pretty important after all. Oh, not in terms of the story's red meat. But more in terms of giving me an early understanding of who Judy Campbell was. It would be unfair of me to say more than that here, because it would be kind of like coaching the witness; I'd rather you get further into the story before you start forming opinions about her. But you might want to come back to this and give it a closer look. I'll try to come back to it myself.

Anyway, there I was the morning after, like I say, looking at that note and the few others I'd scribbled with Ed on the next couch and sinking deeper into a mood, until finally he'd glared at me and then shifted his glance down to my notepad where I'd just been making some frantic scratches about how his mom had chanced to meet Peter Lawford and Pat. That glance, hostile as it was, told me it was time to get the hell out of there before I ruined whatever my chances were of ever being invited back so that I could dig into that box in a systematic way. So I'd left, and now here I was in what felt like a very bleak morning light, looking at my little notes, which wouldn't take me anywhere unless I could get another invite, which seemed pretty unlikely given that last glance: it was like he'd completely forgotten that it had been his idea to let me look at the diaries, that somehow I'd gotten my mitts on the sacred coffin and was pawing through it like a grave robber.

But while I was sitting there feeling hopeless the phone rang, and it was Ed, wanting to know whether he'd paid me and whether I could get him some more of that "dynamite stuff." He had paid me, I told him, but as to the other matter, I'd have to check with a friend of mine. I wasn't eager to continue this part of the conversation, because Ed's end of it was hardly Navajo code talk. It was pretty transparent. So even though I dearly wanted to keep him on the phone awhile so that I could work around to the diaries, I felt I had to ring off, telling him I'd get back to him as soon as I knew something. And that's what I tried to do, immediately calling Mario, the Blue Island guy who'd sold me Ed's pancake. He wasn't there, and every few minutes for the rest of that day I kept trying, but no dice. Same thing the day following.

The short of it was that it was a week before I had the goods and could tell Ed that, and when I reached him his tone scared the bejesus out of me, it was so flat and coldly distant. He wanted the stuff I had, all right; he made that clear. But it would have to wait. There were other, unspecified things he had to take care of first, and when he had these cleared away, he'd call me back. I'd been counting on him being hot to get his hands on Mario's stuff, but obviously he wasn't hot anymore. Neither was I when we'd hung up. I was in a cold sweat because I had the feeling, like doom, that he'd take delivery, yes, but then he was going to drop the nickel on me about my access to the diaries.

In fact, the hunch was so strong that before I got on the Edens going north to Evanston, I dropped off my notepad at my girlfriend's apartment. Lucy and I had known each other for years but had only recently become involved, when both our lives had changed. Handing her the notes for safekeeping, I suddenly was very aware of how pitiful they must look to her—this little dog-eared pad that I considered so terrifically important. I doubted she'd actually open it and read it after I left—that wasn't her style—but if she did, then it really would have seemed pitiful to her, with my frantic scribbles and cross-outs, the margins crawling with half-finished thoughts. And there was absolutely no order to it: that was a luxury I hadn't had time for. Driving away toward the North Shore, it felt to me like I was never going to get that luxury, either.

I was right, too—about the nickel, I mean. I knew it the second

Ed answered my ring. No easy, country-club Ed here, and the way he was looking at me, he couldn't have *given* away an MG to the hottest prospect who ever walked onto his floor: he looked that sour. "Hi" was all he said, and even then he was turning his broad back to lead the way to the kitchen, so my outstretched hand grabbed nothing but air. Maybe this has happened to you sometime in your life. If it has, you won't have any trouble remembering how foolish you felt. Finding that your fly is open in public trumps this, I guess, but not by much. So what could I do but drop my hand and follow him? I felt like the guy taking the last long walk to the hot seat.

In the big, airy kitchen we made the exchange right off, and for some odd reason I remember a pink sponge lying there on the tile-topped counter and Ed tossing it into the sink while muttering something about his "spic" maid. Meanwhile I'd begun to silently curse myself for not thinking about what I was going to do when he did drop the nickel, which I knew he was about to do. Instead of working out some sort of response, some kind of strategy on the way up there, I'd spent my time pissing and moaning about how he was going to ruin my big break. Not very smart, I know, but then I think I probably have lots of company in this useless habit.

So there we were, with Mario's little package on the counter and Ed's cash in my hand, and he was giving me that hard look again when he asked how much I had copied down from the diaries.

"Not that much," I told him, which was truer than I could have wished. "More like notes to myself about how I might write your mom's real story the way it deserves to be written." I didn't think it was a real question. That's to say, I don't think he cared what my plans were for the story. It was what *his* plans were that was the issue, and his plans were to get rid of me as quickly as possible and then stash that box somewhere good and safe. Probably he'd already done that.

"What exactly did you have in mind?" he asked, fiddling with Mario's package.

"Well," I came back, cursing myself again for not having rehearsed at least something, "you told me your mom led a pretty unusual life, and from the little I've read, she sure did. Amazing stuff, really. Totally unique. What I'd like to do is tell her story—tell it the right way, I mean. Her side of it. How she felt about those things. I think she deserves that, don't you?" Believe me, I could hear how lame this sounded, and even more, I could *see* how it sounded, looking at her adopted son's face.

"Nah." He shook his head, looking off down the hall, probably measuring off the steps back to the front door. "Nah. Can't be done."

I don't remember exactly what I did at that point—whether I simply gaped at him, or shrugged as if I didn't understand, or asked what he meant by that, or whether I even claimed I could do it the right way. But whatever it was, he filled in all the blanks of that single short statement.

"Can't be done. It's too late. The damage has already been done." He took a deep breath, those big, flat shoulders rising with it. "All those lies, those—*ahhh . . .*" He lifted his hand from Mario's package to make another of those dismissive gestures I knew well enough, but this wasn't one of those slow, stoned ones I'd seen downstairs. This one had some force to it. And the accompanying sound was like he suddenly had a foul taste in his mouth. He probably did, thinking of how his mom had been so widely portrayed as the sinister moll of a Mafioso godfather or else as an anonymous high-priced spread for handsome Jack. And right then what popped into my mind was the literal image of his mom as a moll.

If you remember her at all, chances are you, too, might be thinking right here of that once famous photo snapped by some lucky news hawk who caught her in fur coat and white gloves, either going into some club or hotel or coming out of one. Clearly she isn't at all happy about the encounter. Those heavy brows are knit, just like they were in that bit of movie footage I was telling you about, and she looks . . . Well, she doesn't look tarty—not to me, anyway. She does look, though, like she's acquainted with nightlife, if you see what I mean. Put another way, you wouldn't think, looking at that shot, that she's on her way to a Junior League benefit. Anyway, that's the image that came to me just at this critical moment, and it's a good thing Ed couldn't read minds. But now, telling you this, it occurs to me that it's possible, given what Ed was talking about—his mother's public image—that he himself had that same photo in mind. It was famous—or infamous—in its time, that real brief, flashing instant we call "time" when you're thinking of current events. And trying to trace Ed's thoughts here, I wonder how you can correct an *image*, especially one like that: beautiful, dark-haired, dolled-up woman emerging into the night and the glare of the cameras? In that particular and peculiar sense, Ed was right. And the bitch of it was that it was just her startling beauty that here became a kind of fault, if you follow me. I mean, if the shot had been of, say, Mamie Eisenhower, it wouldn't have been such a big deal, right? Who cares how Mamie might have looked coming out of some state dinner or fancy ball?

Well, I'll never know what Ed might have been thinking at that moment. But the conclusion his thinking had led him to was perfectly clear. "I don't want you to write anything" was what he said. There were probably quite a few ticks on the second hand before I asked him what had changed his mind. I didn't want to beg—though that's what I really felt like doing—mostly because I felt sure it wouldn't do any good.

"I didn't change my mind. I never had it made up. I don't know what in hell I was thinking about then, letting you have a look through them. Probably wasn't thinking anything." He tapped Mario's package and raised his eyebrows. "But like I said, it's too late to clean up all the crap that's been spread around. Way too late, especially now that she's dead and gone. She knew that herself. She made a stab or two at it and gave it up. She even let a guy ghost-write her life story, which just made everything worse. I want her left alone, simple as that."

That's how I found myself out on the street—literally—with Ed's door closed in my face. It was humiliating, just standing there, looking at the brass knocker, a horse's head. It might as well have been the horse's ass, and I felt the eyes of all of his neighbors boring into my back. So I drove my car to the end of the block, turned the corner, and parked. My chest was heaving and my temples were sweating, but after a few minutes I began to settle down some, at least enough to steer, and I drove over to Howard Street and the Tally-Ho at the corner of Winchester. It was a Saturday afternoon, and there were some college kids at the tables drinking beer and some neighborhood types doing more serious work at the bar, where I joined them, determined to get blind. I took down a Maker's Mark, and I took it fast, too, and ordered another. But then as I sat there, staring at its swirly brown depths, something came over me. I don't know what to call it, whether it was a reporter's instinct to try to think this thing through while still reasonably straight, to see if there wasn't a way to salvage something out of this awful wreckage, or whether it was something more basic, like not wanting to get legless up in Evanston and then have to somehow navigate back to the South Side: that had the potential of making a bad situation considerably worse. So I didn't have that second belt. Instead I drove slowly down to the city along Sheridan and Lake Shore Drive, turned off at Melrose, and parked.

The day had changed, as if the weather was tracking my mood. When I'd dropped off my notes at Lucy's it had been a classic midwestern spring day, lots of wind and high, puffy clouds and the sun darting in and out. Old leaves skittering around and a real nip in the air, especially over here near the lake. But now the clouds had massed and the gray sky felt like it was sitting on top of my head as I walked down through Lincoln Park, kicking those skittering leaves and hardly looking up at all, which can be a hazard, since the cyclists tend to whip along there without too much concern for walkers or joggers.

I found a bench behind the Theater on the Lake and flopped down on it, my hands jammed in my pockets. The theater's red neon light announced SUMMER THEATER TONIGHT, but the building looked so dank and dark I didn't believe it. I stared off in the direction of Navy Pier, but a fog had swiftly settled there, and I couldn't even see the top of the Ferris wheel. I don't know how long I sat there, trying to line up my options. One I knew I didn't have was to try to make another run at Ed. There are times when even if your dearest hopes are set on something, you know it's no go. So when I started back up through the park I had that image of Ed's closed door for company, and I knew there was no way I'd ever get back down to that rec room and that box with its jumbled collection of diaries that would've changed my life forever, if only I could have mined them.

That's not to claim that it was then and there that I succeeded in putting this out of my mind forever. Far from it—especially in the following months, which were unusually hot and muggy. During that time I thought constantly about Ed and how I might get another look into that box. I'd think about calling him and making all kinds of ironclad promises about what I'd write, but mostly about what I wouldn't. Once I even got into my car and started up to the showroom on Chicago, but I hadn't gotten far when I saw how foolish this would be. I didn't take Ed for a violent man, but I did sense he had a lot of anger in him on the subject of his mom, and I didn't want to put myself in the way of it.

I never exchanged another word with him. As far as I know those diaries are still down there in that box—unless he's burned them, which I definitely think he's capable of. I do think this: if he hasn't burned them, he will destroy them somehow before he buys the farm. Then it'll be just like they never existed, as if Judy never wrote all those words of recollection and explanation. You'll just have to take my word for it that they once existed and that I had my hands on them.

Sometimes I think sobriety is overrated. That April afternoon in the park turned out to be one of them. Yeah, I'd pulled back from the bar at the Tally-Ho, but when I got back to my car on Melrose

I had zip for all my sober reflections. So over on Halsted I called Lucy and we met for drinks near her place. Then I had that second bourbon, all right, and a bunch of others along with it. And after that we ended up in the sack, where I wouldn't exactly say I was a standout.

Actually, there wasn't anything I did during those following months that was outstanding, unless you want to count bumping up my bourbon consumption to heroic proportions, and the cigarettes, too; or maybe the increasingly lousy meals I cooked up for myself when Lucy worked late or went out with friends. I was feeling sorry for myself, stumbling around with my half-scoop like a kid who lets his ice cream cone droop and drops the ball. He still has the cone, all right, but not much of a scoop.

On many mornings during this slump I didn't feel so hot. I'd drunk too much, eaten too much, and my throat was raw with yesterday's smoke. Also, I arose with the growing impression that Lucy was growing weary of this mopey man—not nearly what she'd signed on for when we'd moved from friendship to romance. One night we went to Ed Debevic's, where I hogged down a huge meal in virtual silence. Afterward, Lucy poked my belly with a finger that felt very hard and said, "That's a nice little alderman you've got going there"—Chicagoese for a potbelly. That unsubtle prodding turned me back to my pathetic notes, where I thought I might somehow recover a bit of self-respect. But there was nothing there to build on. There wasn't anything for me to do but go back to my old beat as best I could. I was quickly running out of dough, and Lucy was getting pretty short in the patience department, too. Something had to be done before my life completely disintegrated into a pool of liquor, fat, and nicotine.

I knew a kid who had a photographic project going, a portrait of the Wrigleyville neighborhood. He lacked depth of background, though, being from Michigan. I signed on as his guide and then supplied the text for what became a pretty decent book. Then there was a friend from New York who used me to get him an intro to Deborah Norville, whom I'd known in her Chicago phase. He ended up having lunch with her and writing that up for *Chicago* magazine. I got some change out of that. I did a couple of straight-up reporting jobs for the *Trib*, but I knew that wasn't going to lead to anything: those conservative guys have long memories and remembered when I'd worked steady for the *Daily News*—hell, they're still trying to get back at the liberal press for Watergate and Robert Bork. Studs Terkel said he might use me to run stuff down for a book he had in mind on Western Avenue, a sort of sequel to the one he'd done on Division. But while I was waiting for that call I was "eking out a living," writing copy for a neighborhood rag called the *South Side Enterpriser* that was delivered free, whether you wanted it or not. "Eking out a living" is a term meant to cover your near acquaintance with poverty, like a shrunken overcoat that tries to cover your ass in deep January: if you're eking, you know how close to not eking you actually are.

One late-summer evening, having nothing better to do, I went up to a Sox game and afterward drifted into a bar on Shields called the Bullpen: blue-lit, divey place, the kind where you can order a Schlitz, if you have a memory long enough to recollect that brand and it suits your pocketbook. That was me, all right, and I was on my second and wondering if Schlitz had always tasted like soap and sugar and how it had all come down to just this. These were not big thoughts, you understand, only the sort of numbed, lazy ones everyone else around you was having. Which was why I glanced up as little as possible. Every time I did, though, there was this kid right in my line of sight, at two o'clock around the angle of the bar—sunglasses pushed up on his slicked-back hair and a long-sleeved T-shirt that said he loved New York. It was clear he was waiting for someone, but when I glanced up the next time, the seat to his right was overflowing with a guy in a suit but no tie, and I was sure this wasn't who he'd been expecting. Maybe he'd gotten tired of saying the seat was saved and was now peeved at his tardy friend, because when I looked that way again, I saw him say something to Mr. Big, who turned to answer. When he did that I caught a glimpse in the different slant of the lighting of what I hadn't seen: a huge dent in the man's right temple. There was only one guy I'd seen in my life who carried such a marker. It was Phil Keneally I was looking at. I wouldn't have recognized him without it.

The dent was as big around as a silver dollar and maybe a quarter-inch deep—hell of a hole. The story was that he'd picked it up in the Solomons in the war's last days, and they'd done some amazing sort of surgery right there in the field that saved his life. He got a Purple Heart to go with the Bronze Star he already had. But as I say, without that dent I wouldn't have recognized him. The Phil Keneally I'd heard give that night school lecture on Lincoln had been a red-faced, handsome man who looked very much like the star fullback he'd been at Notre Dame before the war. He still had those shoulders, all right, but the rest of him—well, from my angle it looked like he'd been subject to some special law of gravity; I mean, everything about him seemed to be sagging toward the floor, and it was only those shoulders that saved him from collapsing into a shapeless heap of suet. I knew he'd fallen on hard times—messy divorce from Annette Giancana, disbarment, even a prison stretch. Still, the effect of seeing him like this was a shocker.

And that shock was obvious, too, because when he looked across at me I could tell from his eyes that he'd caught me staring; he hadn't lived the life he had without acquiring the necessary skills. He made me right away, too, fixing me with his light blue eyes and nodding that jowly face so that his cheeks and chins bobbled. I nodded back and raised a hand to signal *Hi*, and he excused himself from the kid who loved New York and made his ponderous way around the bar to where I was sitting.

"Newspaper guy," he began, winking an eye and pointing at me, index finger out and thumb up like a pistol. "Give me a second, and I'll have it."

I saved him the trouble, and he sat down, smooth enough and already ordering a Scotch. "I would have fuckin' had it," he said when the drink came. "*Daily News.* Worked for those Jew boys on that Chicago book. That was a while back." He flicked his pale eyes over me, managing to make his meaning clear. "So now what?"

"Well, you know," I came back, "this and that."

"Oh, *yeahhh,*" he said, raising his eyes briefly ceilingward as he swirled the Scotch. "I know all there is to know about 'this and that.' I could write a book about it—but then, that's your bag. I can't really write, not the way I can talk." He made the flapping-jaws gesture with his thumb and fingers. He looked at me searchingly, as they say, as if inviting confidence or even a full-length confession, and I thought right off, What the hell, this guy's down even further than I am. But right behind that thought, almost treading on its heels, was the realization that here at my goddamned elbow was a guy—no, *the* guy—who knew the whole terrain of the Judy Campbell story, maybe better than anyone else still alive. He'd been married to the Mob, though now some years divorced from Annette Giancana; he'd been their legal mouthpiece for years before that and would have to know the guts of the entire operation. He'd even taken the fall for them in a jury-tampering case, and it had cost him his license. If I'd searched the entire city for the one person who could truly understand what I'd had my hands on and then lost, here he was. I don't believe in fate or luck or serendipity, or whatever word you want to stick in here. What I thought then and later on, too, driving back down to Morgan Park, was that this was nothing more and nothing less than two guys down on their luck and looking to forget about that for a few hours. These two guys would naturally find themselves in a dive just like the Bullpen. So there you are, and there we were.

For the next twenty minutes or so I told Phil Keneally my version of "this and that," and I saw no point in trying to put any makeup on it, besides which he'd have seen through it right away. Even in my sorry-ass, self-serving rendition it wasn't that long a story.

He heard me out, this huge, misshapen, dented, damaged man

who had no doubt listened to hundreds of sob stories in his line of work. And he heard me out in silence, too, sipping his Scotch right along, signaling for another, never once interrupting with a question or objection. Must have been a trait—this control—he'd had to learn when listening to his criminal clients lie to him. When I'd finished, he nodded, staring straight ahead, then signaled the bartender. He still hadn't said a word. When the bartender came over, Keneally asked if I was sticking with the Schlitz, and I said not if he was buying. He shook that massive, jowly head with its tarnished badge of honor.

"No, no, no, *you're* buying, ass-wipe," he growled, pointing a finger at me, though this time not with the thumb cocked, the bartender standing above us in his short-sleeved shirt with his tattoos faded to green on his forearms. "You're buying, and I'm selling. Bump me up to a Grant's," he told the bartender. "Suddenly this has turned into a lucky night. And bring him another can of that horse piss."

I guess I have as much pride as the next man, but among other things I knew about Phil Keneally was that he had a famously salty tongue and wasn't particularly careful who he used it on. A story got around about him telling Charlie Fischetti to go fuck himself and his guinea mother, too, when Fischetti was his client and had said something Keneally didn't like. If you remember who Charlie the Fish was, you know this was very risky talk. So I didn't take it too personally that in the last few seconds Keneally had called me an ass-wipe who drank horse piss. Besides, he wasn't that far from the mark in his description of the Schlitz. So I said nothing, tried to look as if I hadn't even heard his remarks, thinking I'd stay another round to see what it was he was up to here, what it was he was offering to sell me.

When the bartender produced our drinks, Keneally leaned toward me and said in a conversational tone, as if we were discussing tomorrow's races at Arlington, that I hadn't really missed my scoop, because from the sound of it what Ed had in that box was much too early to be of any real use. "Who gives a fuck how she grew up," he growled. "The point here is she fucked JFK and Momo both—probably at the same time. You don't have the real beginning of this thing. You were wasting your time down there in your friend's rec room. The story starts here"—tapping the blackened, sticky bar top with his finger so that it sounded oddly like a judge's gavel, and I thought the guy's troubles with the bottle had unhinged him.

"Here?" I asked. "*Here?*"

"Not *here,* you sap," he said. "Here in Chicago, at the County Building, in February of 'sixty." Now it was he who was looking at me, wondering whether I was unhinged or never had hinges to my frame to begin with, whether I could keep up with him or was only a hopeless hack. He paused a long moment, like he was considering whether he was wasting his time on me. If this was what he was doing, then you see again in this situation how *accidental,* really, history can be. That's to say, suppose he'd just dismissed me? He might have, easily enough: seedy-looking guy in a crappy bar, whining about missing his big break when all he had to show for it was a jumble of anecdotes that kind of circled around the center of the story. And he himself with a famous temper on him.

"I have the real story," he said then. "I have the notebooks Campbell had Momo stash when the feds were all over her ass. They were just about the only things Toinette got after they whacked her old man. What happened to the rest of it—the loot and so forth—I don't know. Only the family does."

The instant he said it I knew it had to be true. So far as I could figure, there wouldn't be any point in his lying to me. Looking into his face, I wasn't seeing it so much as I was seeing in that bleak, blue light how it all made perfect sense, even if I didn't have the facts that made it add up, if you follow me here. So I asked him how many more books there were.

He shook his head. "I haven't looked at them in a while, but it's got to be a dozen, anyway. Toinette almost threw the package of them at me." He grinned in rueful recollection. "She was one fiery bitch, I'll give her that—that's one thing she got from her old man he didn't quite stamp out. But otherwise he did a pretty fucking thorough job on her personality. Where was I?"

"The notebooks—diaries."

"Right. Anyway, after they found him her family got whatever was down there to get, and after that, then they called the cops. They left the shit for Toinette—some tie clasps, a rosary, shit like that. Not a dollar. They told her there wasn't any. Bullshit. The guy was keeping millions—that's *millions*—right there in his safe. I know that because I helped him put some papers in there one time, and I saw it with these baby blues." He pointed at his eyes with the forked fingers of his hand.

"But they hated her ass, and the truth was she'd caused them all a *huge* amount of trouble when she was a teenager." That rueful grin came to him again. "'Here are his whore's diaries.' She said that when she heaved them at me. 'If you want to find out how many times they fucked, be my guest.' There they were, big package wrapped in brown paper and her first name in the upper left-hand corner—in his handwriting."

"Well, did you," I asked, "look at them?"

"Not really. I glanced through them some, and then, what with one thing and another"—he flicked a glance at me out of the corner of an eye, a reference to my own "this and that"—"I stashed them and forgot about them. When she came back in the headlines with the Church Committee investigations, I remembered them. But shit, it was old news to me, and I thought, Fuck it.

"But if your real question here is, Do they have the goods?—the blow jobs, the payoffs, that shit—the answer is yes, in spades. They've got all that, all right, the stuff you need." He swirled his tumbler some more, and I sensed he was getting ready to order up another. Big as he was, I could tell the stuff was starting to take hold: his face had that sheen you get when the whisky starts cooking your insides. He wasn't slurring his words, but I thought his pronunciation had lost a bit of the courtroom crispness it had had when he'd sat down next to me. I don't doubt he would have come up with my name when he'd first come over, as he claimed; I wondered if he would have now, though.

Wouldn't this be a hell of a note, I thought, if I had my hands back on this thing and then had my man drift off into an alcoholic stupor? Who could tell what might happen to him? He might just blow up with a stroke or heart attack this very night, the way he was going, or, more likely, have a fatal smash-up on the way to wherever it was he was living.

"Anyway," Keneally suddenly continued, tapping the bar again with his finger, "they've got plenty. And what they don't have, I do. So"—again that insistent tapping—"you came in here with shit in your wallet, and suddenly you've got yourself the two crucial sources you need to write your story. If you can't put it together after what I'm handing you, you're a bigger asshole than I figured." He let go of his glass and clawed at the dirty air with his meaty hands. "Oh, Christ! If only I could *write!* Then I wouldn't have to fuck around with fifth-rate minds. If *only* . . ." He dropped his hands and leaned into me so that I got a good load of what he'd been drinking. This plus all the other drinks he'd had in places like this and worse; also the better ones when he'd been mobbed up and the Boys in the White Hats (as they used to be called) were buying and often enough owned the joints where they all were drinking. His breath smelled hot and awfully stale at the same time. If history had a breath, it might smell something like this, and I wanted to draw back but didn't.

He was dramatic, yes: that was part of what had made him so spectacular and successful in the courtroom. Probably was his nature, too. But I had to believe him. He would have taken those diaries and shaken everything out of them that was important and written it up himself if he thought he could do it. So that part of the drama with the hands and all, that was genuine. Whether I had a fifth-rate mind might be another matter; if you're comparing mine to his, maybe he wasn't that far off the mark, which would make his comment not so much insulting as rude. That's a pretty big difference, no matter where you're sitting. Even on this night, with all the Scotches he'd gulped, even after that stretch in the stone house, the loss of his license, the lower layers of life he was drifting down through—even after you've thrown all this into the calculation, he was still a brilliant man in his way. You couldn't miss that. Maybe he wasn't the guy I'd seen that night at John Marshall, but then, he didn't have to be to deserve, in my mind anyway, that word *brilliant*. He was.

"But here's the thing," he said, his tone altering just slightly. "Here's the thing—you can. I've read your stuff. Read that *Chicago* book. You're okay. And I can tell you now, if this thing's done right, we won't ever have to come into a shithole like this. Ever. We'll be drinking Johnnie Black, eating at Charlie fucking Trotter's, and our girlfriends'll be farting through silk, to quote a famous source."

I didn't get the reference, and I didn't care. What I wanted, what I was driving toward as best I could, was making some kind of deal, right here and now. What was in it for him, I asked, for him to be so generous?

"*Half*, you shit-eater. *Half*." He glared at me saying this, his great, glistening mug jammed up to mine with that breath on him.

"Sounds okay to me," I said, trying for the professionally cool while knowing full well that what I'd already confessed to him had destroyed any pretense of leverage. I had none, and he knew it. "When do we start?"

"Right here," he said, shifting his ass on the overmatched barstool. "Right here, right now."

"Jake," I came back, reaching into my pants pocket for my ballpoint and little pad. "But—" I couldn't finish before he had those meat hooks outspread between us.

"But what?" There was impatience of a high order here, as well as a pretend puzzlement. "*What?*" Still, I had to plunge on and ask the question.

Looking back, I'm a bit surprised I felt even so early on this kind of urgency about it. That's to say, what I should have done then, what a reporter's gut should have been sending up to his brain with all bells and whistles full on, was this: okay, let me at it. Instead, I heard myself asking whether he'd ever met her. And I wasn't surprised when he tossed his head toward the ceiling, as if he thought the question was asinine—which it probably was under these circumstances. But he checked his impatience for some reason. He was one really impatient guy, as I've tried to indicate. Remembering this, I've wondered why he didn't just let it fly: after all, he'd called me a fair number of unflattering things already. Why stop here? But that isn't what happened.

When he brought his head back down and nodded at the bartender, he answered me in a different tone. *Soft* isn't the word I want, but there was an edge that had dropped away. "Yes," he said. "That is, I saw her. Twice. Once when I had something to talk over with Momo at his house.

"Our arrangement was for me to call him when I got close. Usually I'd do this from over on Harlem. I did that. He told me to come on, so when I came around the corner on Wenonah, there she was coming out the back, by the garage. She didn't even so much as glance in my direction, just got in one of those shitty little Fords he used to drive, about one step up from a golf cart, and backed out. Didn't look either way, but I could see her face in profile inside the car.

"The other time was about the same. I had some business to discuss with him, and he told me to meet him at the Armory. When I got there, I parked in back, went in, and there she was in the booth with him, and he says something to her, she gets up, walks past me, doesn't look. Then she's gone." He smiled, for the first time, I think, since we'd glanced at each other across the bar. He had long, broad teeth that looked like they'd been cared for once upon a time.

"Yeah," he breathed, nodding twice for emphasis. "Yeah. They didn't lie about that part of it, at least—she was a dish, a bombshell, a smoking babe. That was true." The new drinks came, and he took an enormous hit of his, wiping his mouth with his fingers. "She made an impression on you. But you know what I thought about on that occasion when I saw her coming out of the house on Wenonah?"

I shook my head.

"Well, this is Christ's own bare-balls truth. I thought to myself, Why is *she* fucking *him?*" He glared again at me, this time with what I took to be a simple feeling of stud rivalry. We've all felt that, right? But I've come to think there was more to it than that—though there's an awful lot of troublesome and important stuff wrapped up inside that, isn't there? Maybe I never would have come close to it—if I have—if I hadn't seen that bit of movie footage I was telling you about. Of course, I hadn't when he and I were sitting cheek by jowls at the Bullpen. That wouldn't happen until months later, because it was Keneally who showed it to me. But when I was watching it, that was when it came to me that it wasn't just stud rivalry, though it was probably that, too. No, what it was was *outrage.* Outrage at what he took to be a kind of cosmic mistake, or an insult, if you like, to the way things ought to be if the universe was going to make any sense. And this coming from a guy who had seen everything the show has to offer and then some. But looking at that footage, it came to me that you couldn't feel any other way about it: this banana-nosed guy the color of old, raw liver, at least in that faded film, with his back all hairy, creeping along like a beast of prey, and this beautiful, statuesque girl, staring down into the deep end and just unconscious of what was about to happen to her. If that didn't give you the instant feeling that *Hey! Something's wrong here!* then I'm telling all this to the wrong party, because you haven't got a heart in you, only a timepiece.

Anyway, back to the Bullpen and Phil Keneally, who had pulled himself back from wherever he was to tell me that this was way too big a story to get paralyzed by pussy—his words, not mine. "This began before her and it goes on after she'd left the scene," he claimed. "Yeah, she's a player, and she has some firsthand stuff you won't find elsewhere. But we're hunting elephants here, my friend, not fucking gazelles. *Elephants.*

"The story starts in the County Building"—nodding in the direction of the Loop—"and I'm sitting in the chambers of William J. Tuohy, chief judge of the Circuit Court of Cook County. We're waiting for a friend of Judge Tuohy's to show. It's after hours, and the place is pretty still, just a few sounds, far-off. Then we hear footsteps, and they keep on coming our way, on through that empty courtroom." He made walking legs with his fingers along the bar, and such was his dramatic talent that at that moment the background noise of the bar dropped away and I was *there.* "Then the door's pushed wide, and in walks Joe Kennedy, the old man. *That's* where your story starts, pal, not with some shithead recollections Judy Campbell had of her childhood."

2

JOE, JUDY, AND JACK

HAVE YOU EVER done business at the County Building? Well, it's a pretty impressive place. Half is City Hall and half County Court House. Runs between La Salle and Clark and Randolph and Washington, so just in that physical sense you can see how impressive a pile it must be. Huge. *Grim* is a word you could use, and I might have done so myself, it being handy like clichés are. But truthfully, I never felt that way about it. To me it's still exciting after all these years: those vaulted ceilings with their swirling moldings and the big brassbound lamps that drop their light on the marble floors they keep at a high sheen. Of course, administrations are always changing, but no matter who happens to be in charge, they keep that place spotless. Even at six P.M.

At that time of day, when the building's pretty much emptied out and the action's done, there's something else that takes over. I don't have the words for things like this, but then, who really does? But it's like something *settling*, you know? Something coming down over the whole building, over the hallways, the emptied-out courtrooms, the judges' chambers, the crappers, everything: it's like the building's reasserting itself, reclaiming its territory; like it's saying it's seen 'em come and it's seen 'em go and it's just keeping watch, like God or history or justice, which are never the same thing.

At this time of day the black guys are out in the halls with the push brooms and mops and rags and polish; and the guards are gassing with each other, and one of them is starting up again with fat Alice, who's laughing but probably not buying his line yet; and the guys who run the little concession stands are pulling the cash out of the drawers and setting the trash baskets out and rolling down the mesh gates and snapping-to the locks—and it's then that Phil Keneally is sitting in Judge Tuohy's chambers, and Tuohy is very unhappy.

Tuohy was a guy of complete probity, solid right down through the core of him. You could have a beef with some of his rulings and opinions and so forth over the years. If a man sits on the bench long enough, he's got to have his critics. Hell, Learned Hand had people take exception to him, enough, I guess, so he never made Supreme Court, and Learned Hand looked like Norman Rockwell's idea of earthly justice incarnate. So William J. Tuohy had people who had long-standing beefs with him, didn't like his style, thought he was arbitrary. There were Jews—lawyers—who used to tell you you couldn't get a break in a carload with Tuohy up there if your opposite number was a Mick.

But what you never heard—what I never heard, anyway—was that Judge Tuohy was on the take, and this despite the fact that he came from the same family as Roger Tuohy—Roger the Terrible, as he was known back in the Roaring Twenties, when Chicago was Murder City. Well, that's the family, and it's known a hell of a lot more for crime than justice, and so in this city you'd assume, naturally, that a judge with that name could be had. You never heard it. When the feds ran that number they code-named Operation Greylord, they scooped up a lot of dirty judges, but not Tuohy. I tell you this much to position you to understand why such a man could be so upset waiting in his chambers on a February evening in 1960 with Phil Keneally. Because he was waiting for Joe Kennedy to show up for a meeting with Momo Giancana, and he, the judge, had put this thing together.

• • •

Tuohy and old Joe went back a ways, to a time before Tuohy was a judge and did some legal work for Kennedy in connection with the Merchandise Mart. They may have had some social connection as well, but if they did, I don't know how deep it went. But when Kennedy called him just before Christmas, asking for a favor, right off Tuohy said sure: old client, friend, former ambassador, fellow Irishman. So, Hell yes, and what is it? And here old Joe dropped this *bomb* on his pal. I want to come out there and meet with Sam Giancana, he told Tuohy. Jack's going to get the nomination, and Illinois looks to me like it just may be the state we've got to have in the election. Giancana can help get the union vote out for us. Can you help me on this? And so forth.

Having already said yes, the best Tuohy could do then was to say something like, Well, I don't really run in that individual's company, but let me think about it and see what I can come up with. And who he came up with as a middleman was Phil Keneally, for reasons you already heard.

I don't know how deep you go in Kennedy family lore, but if it's only to refresh your memory, let me just say here that at one point Joe Kennedy was a big-time crook, right up there with Longy Zwillman, Owney Madden, Frank Fay, and Frank Costello: did business with all of them in the twenties and thirties. Now, I'm not telling you he was a killer like Madden or Dutch Schultz, but if you're a bootlegger, which Kennedy was, you have to get involved in a lot of rough stuff. I'd be totally shocked to learn he was ever present when somebody got whacked. He was way too slick an operator to let himself get connected with that sort of thing. But he knew how to play rough, knew the hazards of the trade, where people came up missing all the time and others went to Dannemora or wherever, and customers went blind and batty on a bad batch. So when he went out to Hollywood to get into the movie business in the thirties, he was no patsy the California sharks could dazzle and separate from his money. They found that out pretty quick.

You could argue, though, that Hollywood changed him permanently. He learned to love the glamour of it, and part of that glamour was *power*, which goes a long way toward explaining what he was doing meeting with Giancana in the judge's chambers. He loved having the ability, the authority, to say, Let's make this picture and let's have him and her and him star in it. He loved having the strange, remote thrill of knowing that because of him thousands and thousands of faceless, anonymous folks from Kansas and Ohio and Arkansas were putting their coins and wrinkled bills through the wickets, having saved up for the picture show, to watch what he, Joe Kennedy, had caused to happen. It was like being a kind of giant puppeteer, hanging over America and making all sorts of people move about doing the things you wanted. That's power, man, the glamorous kind, as I say, and you could make a very good argument that it turned his head around, even that he got drunk on it, like his customers got drunk on his bootleg booze and then later, after repeal, on his legitimate Scotch and Gordon's.

If you were making this argument about old Joe, then I think you'd have to go on to say that it would follow naturally that the old man would imagine a progeny of his, Joe Junior, becoming president someday. Because here would be an infinitely greater, more glamorous high than making movies: having the whole *planet* acting out your designs, so to say. Well, as we know, that master plan crashed when Joe Junior did, and so then it had to be Jack. And the way to figure just how ripped old Joe was on this power trip was to look at what he was asking his friend Judge Tuohy to do for him.

This wasn't, let's remember, Dick Daley Joe Kennedy wanted to meet with. He wouldn't have had to go through Tuohy to get next to the mayor—and I'll say more about Kennedy and Daley in a minute. But it's enough to say here he knew Daley on a first-name basis. This wasn't some Cook County power broker, either—J. J. Duffy, say. Not even a union boss who could directly give him the help he wanted. No, this was a man so powerful he went around with a business card in his wallet that said NO BUSINESS, NO ADDRESS, NO MONEY, RETIRED. Momo Giancana, in other words, advertised himself as a nobody, and any man who can afford to do that has got to really be a somebody. Which he sure as hell was, so that what the judge had, with the utmost reluctance, put together in his chambers was like a meeting of evenly matched champion sluggers who both knew the ropes and just where the belt line was and how to hit beneath it when necessary.

Some cops I've talked to will tell you there wasn't a particular person named Sam Giancana, only a collection of disguises. There's even a dispute about his real name. Judy clearly believed there was a person behind all the aliases, the sunglasses, the phony business card, the bodyguards, toupees, and ratty-assed two-door cars he drove around in: a genuine man with a set of very traditional values she could count on. I guess I don't have a problem with this aspect of the relationship. After all, here was this girl moving with men who showed up at clubs and restaurants every night with a different dame on their arm, who were thickly protected from the public, and some of whom went by different names in different places. Momo was different, at least when it came to her. He was devoted to her. From what I can put together he treated her respectfully—most of the time. I say "most of the time" because you'll recall that bit of film I mentioned with its footage of his high jinks up on the high board—not exactly what you'd call respectful treatment. But that episode is balanced off and then some by this: when Judy gave him her diaries for safekeeping, she packaged them up and made him swear he wouldn't read them. He never did, because when Annette Giancana—Keneally's Toinette—practically threw them at Phil Keneally, they still had the wrapping paper and twine around them, though she had torn enough of the paper open to see what they were. Momo didn't know *precisely* what was in those books. But why would Judy ask him not to read them if there weren't things in there about her and Jack that she didn't want him to see and that she feared the feds were after? He would have guessed that much anyway, and probably guessed as well that she'd written about their relationship, too. Still, he honored her request, and I'd call this serious respect, wouldn't you? He had to know there was incriminating stuff in there.

Notice I didn't say that Momo was "nice" to her, because I don't know that he had it in him to be nice to anybody, including his daughter Annette. But he tried in his way to treat her as he thought she deserved. He certainly piled on the presents—and please spare me your judgment that this makes her just what the government gumshoes always claimed she was: the high-priced spread. What woman have you known really well who wasn't sweetened up even temporarily by a piece of jewelry or a fine silk scarf? You show me that dame, and I'll show you Miz Flintheart. But as far as this goes, I'd say she turned down as many presents from him—and from Jack, too—as she accepted. When she ran with the Rat Pack for a while there in '60 she basically paid her own way—which angered Sinatra no end. Where did that kind of scratch come from? My answer is, I don't know. She said in one of her diaries that she was always told it came to her as an inheritance from her granddad Immoor. But then she went on to say she wasn't exactly sure about that and thought it might actually have come to her from her father. I don't know that it makes much difference which. The point here would be that it came to her from her own family, not from the men she saw. I guess you'll have to decide for yourself whether what I say squares up with what I tell you about her life.

So this was a hell of a match-up the judge had put together, and of the two, Joe Kennedy was by far the most exposed, so to say—the presidential candidate's father discovered meeting with the city's boss of bosses. Which brings up the obvious question: if the old man believed this meeting was critical to his campaign strategy, why in hell would he hold it here, of all places? Maybe Wrigley Field or Michigan Avenue in front of the Tribune Tower would be more public, but the County Building's right up there. Why not hold it in his suite at the Drake or the Palmer House, or wherever it was he was putting up? Or why not out on Momo's turf in Forest Park or Cicero? Here's what I think. I think that when Kennedy called Tuohy, he already had in mind getting Tuohy to hold the meeting in his chambers, where the old man would feel safe. In the judge's chambers there couldn't be anything like a gun accidentally going off while Kennedy was cleaning it or an unfortunate fall from a window, the kind of things that could happen even in the ritziest hotel or in some ratty joint out in Forest Park. And even if at the last minute Tuohy had had information that the deal had somehow gone queer, he'd have found a way to let the old man know—maybe through one of those janitors the old man would have to walk past at that hour and who might just push a broom in his path and say, "I wouldn't walk that way, sir."

No man alive knows exactly what went down in the judge's chambers that day. Phil Keneally never knew, and he was there when Kennedy shook hands with Giancana. And as for Tuohy, once he made the introductions, he couldn't get out of there fast enough, and he took Keneally with him into the empty courtroom, where they sat in the jury box, and he said he never wanted to hear another word on this matter. Then he sank into a silent gloom and stayed in it until Kennedy came out about an hour later, and he and Tuohy went off together, clickety-clack, down the hallway. When Keneally went in to collect Momo, he was sitting there with a little smile, but he didn't say a word, just glanced at his watch, and out they went. He never did say anything to Keneally, either.

Now—*now*—it's not that hard to make a solid guess that what the old man offered Giancana in exchange for an all-out union effort in November was a kind of protection from the Justice Department under Jack, one where they'd go after other targets but not mess with Momo's interests. Joe Kennedy could make an absolute guarantee on this because if Jack won—which Giancana could help insure—then Bobby was going to be Jack's AG, which, of course, is the way it turned out. Within that family, what the old man wanted was done. From the time Jack got into politics in 1945 until the old man's stroke at the end of '61, nobody who knew Jack Kennedy can remember a major instance when he dared to cross his father.

To Giancana such a deal made perfect sense. It was a classic example of organized crime—which he never would have called it—doing business with politicians. Here in Chicago it's called one hand washing the other, and it has an old and honored history, dating back at least to the days of Hinky Dink and Bathhouse John, when the mobsters *were* the politicians. But then the city was more obviously a frontier town than it was in 1960.

There was another piece of this whole thing that got put in place at this same time, though it had nothing directly to do with either Giancana or Tuohy. In telling me of the meeting in Tuohy's chambers, Phil Keneally made a passing reference to Kennedy and Dick Daley, how well they knew each other. It was nothing more than that, and as dumb as I was at the time about the shape—the scope, so to say—of this story, I didn't think much about it. But then, when I began trying to plow this thing the way you do when you have the time, I thought back on that reference. The more I did, the more probable I found it that Kennedy and Daley visited during Kennedy's Chicago visit. It's even possible that Daley already knew what Tuohy had done for Kennedy before his own meeting with Joe took place. But when Kennedy and Daley met, they wouldn't have so much as mentioned Tuohy. As I just said, in Chicago one hand washes the other, and one of the reasons that technique works so well is that when the washing's going on, the principals confine themselves to a particular piece of business and what it'll require. Way in the back of his brain Dick Daley would have wanted to know just what old Joe and Momo had to say to each other, but the forefront of his brain would have told him he would be better off not knowing. The man who might be called upon to testify on certain matters can be a hell of a lot more convincing when he claims ignorance if he really is ignorant. So I think what old Joe and Daley confined themselves to was Adlai Stevenson and what to do about him.

After two losses to Ike, Adlai was worthless to Daley, who never liked him anyway and thought he was a faggy egghead. Still, the man had a power base within the party, and that had to be taken into account. Daley and old Joe were so successful because they always took *everything* into account when considering their moves, and they were always thinking three or four moves ahead of the other guy: If he does that, then I'm gonna do this, and when he does this to counter me, I'll do that, which basically exhausts his options, and he has to come to me. Here, old Joe would have predicted what Adlai would do if Jack came to the convention without the nomination sewed up. In that event, he thought Adlai would go to Daley and ask him to hold the Illinois delegation for him as a favorite son. After that, anything might happen. And so what Kennedy wanted from the mayor was his assurance that Illinois would stay Jack's and that Daley would tell Adlai that he was going to back Jack all the way. Without this piece, what Kennedy had worked out with Giancana might not be worth a shit, you know?

Of course, Daley would take Jack over Adlai any day, but he wasn't going to jump on that bandwagon until he saw that it had real good wheels. Not his style at all. Much later, when it was all over and it was time to write the history of it, Teddy White said that the Kennedy brain trust wasn't any too keen on Jack entering the Wisconsin primary, that state being sort of an extension of Hubert Humphrey's Minnesota, kind of like New Hampshire was of Jack's Massachusetts. Minnesota had a western tier of counties that were Protestant farming communities, and these could spell big trouble for Jack, who was trying to project an image of inevitability even this early. The fact that Jack announced he would enter the Wisconsin primary once old Joe got back home says to me that Daley told the old man he'd have to see how Jack did in a tough contest like that one before he made any commitments. Show me a win in Wisconsin, Daley said, and I'll hold the delegation for you. This is all speculation, sure, a hunch. But to me it makes perfect sense.

I get this picture in my mind here, of old Joe in the mayor's office, looking at that meaty puss Daley had on him and those little eyes that were like chips of ice, and thinking, Well, this is the best I'm going to get right now, and come to think of it, I've done okay for this trip. I've got Giancana's unions in November, and I've got

Daley's delegation if we can run off a string of wins in the primaries, beginning with Wisconsin. We've got to go to Wisconsin.

When I think of it now, with the hindsight I've acquired and all the years piled up since these events, I can't get away from the feeling that just about everything that could be lined up to put Judy in Jack's path was in place by the time Joe Kennedy left Chicago that February, far-fetched as that would have seemed at the time. If you think of this story as a chess board, then by this point the pieces have been moved to where Jack almost has to meet Judy, though neither would have known that. Let me try to explain briefly.

Joe was going for broke on this deal. He'd already gone to organized crime for help, and he'd gone to his other power base, too, the movie industry, where his daughter, Pat Lawford, had been canvassing Hollywood since the fall. She'd married Peter Lawford, you'll recall, a bosom buddy of Sinatra's, so she was tight with the inner, inner circle out there. Which brings us to the next development. I don't have a date for it, because Judy didn't give one, but it's fall '59, as near as I can figure it, and even though chronologically this takes us back a couple of squares, we have to make the move to see what I mean about all those pieces being put into the right places by the time Joe Kennedy left Chicago.

The scene here is Puccini's in Hollywood, and Judy's out to dinner with a group of friends. Sinatra was at another table and he glances over, does a double take, and then he can't take his eyes off her. After a while it got to be funny to Judy and her group. Finally Sinatra started to laugh, too, and then he kind of helplessly got up and went over. They made room for him, and he sat down next to her and was all over her like a cheap suit. If anybody was starstruck at that moment, it was Sinatra, not Judy, and it'll help you appreciate the irony of the situation to remember that in '59 there wasn't a bigger name in entertainment than Old Blue Eyes, and I'm not just talking about here in the States; I'm talking about the planet, man. And here he was, falling all over himself, telling her he knows her from somewhere but he can't quite place it, and is she in pictures, because she's such a knockout, and won't she please tell him her name and how he can get in touch with her, and so forth. "It was funny enough before he came over," she said, "but after he sat down and gave me this line, then it got really funny. I'd seen him before at big bashes and knew he could be pretty obnoxious. But he laughed right along with us. I told him I wasn't in pictures but my sister was and one in the family was plenty. He asked for my phone number so I gave it to him. Won't hear from him—that's the way these spur-of-the-moment things go. You're a knockout tonight and in the morning you're yesterday's knockout."

But he did call the next day and asked her to go to Hawaii with him. In this tight little world they don't waste time with preliminaries like you and I might; they get right to the point: you're either in or you're out. She's in—she told him, Okay. But right from the start she signaled that she wasn't going to be a standard-issue player. He wanted her to fly over with him in his private plane, but instead she told him she'd meet him there. There was a silence on the phone, and then he made some kind of odd noise and said he had a room reserved for her at the Surfrider, but he didn't sound very cheerful about it. What girl said no to Frank?

Well, she had said yes to him, more or less on her terms, and she went to Hawaii without ever having been out with the man. And so here we need to look at this a bit, ask the question, What kind of girl would say yes to such a proposition on any terms? My answer is, if you're asking about the world of that time, a lot of girls of all kinds. Maybe the better question might be, How many would say no? And then, if you're restricting your question to unattached women, which she was then—having finally had it with Billy Campbell's betrayals—I'd say the answer would be almost all. Still, these kinds of questions don't cut deep enough, because this episode takes us back in a hurry to Ed Immoor and his smoldering fury over what he thought was a totally unfair picture of his mom as a "scarlet woman." It was such a bell-ringer for him because it was so completely different from the person he knew.

She certainly had to know the score about Sinatra's invite, what it would involve. She wasn't being asked to go over there and play shuffleboard. Sinatra was asking her to come over and party with him and the terrifically fast crowd he led, and that meant she'd be asked to go to bed with him—again without too many preliminaries. What she would say when the moment came would be something else again, but she had to know it would come.

Remember a while back when I was trying to tell you something about what I thought made Judy tick, and I said she seemed to believe in what I called *possibility?* I could hear myself then and knew the word wasn't quite the right one, but still I stuck with it because it seemed closest to what I was reaching for there. Well, now I'm going to reach again, reach even further out and use the word *virginal,* in the sense of a woman who got around a lot but who was in some way *impervious* to some of her own experiences. Not that they didn't mean anything to her. On the contrary, I think maybe they meant too much to her, considering what they might have meant to the men she went to bed with.

Yeah, she made it with this guy and that, just like they had it in the tabloids and the gossip columns and the trashy magazines. At one stage, working through the diaries, I decided to make a list. But then I stopped—and not because it was getting too long. I stopped because in this view I'm trying to tell you about, it was basically pointless. What would the final number mean, whatever it turned out to be, if the woman in question kept her virginality, if that's a word? Because the way I'm using this word doesn't have to do with the *act,* with the condition of being entered. What it does have to do with is the woman's state of mind. That's a place no man can enter, my friend, I don't care how he's built, because it isn't a physical place. I've come to believe that as long as a woman is in touch with the center of herself, where she truly *lives,* then she can't be violated by any man, not even if she's raped. If a man is inside her and is thinking to himself that he's *fucking* her, he isn't. He's only fucking himself. We've all had to do that at one time or another, particularly in adolescence, and so I know that you remember how empty an experience it can be, how when you've finished off, you feel more alone than when you started.

Now, I'm not trying to tell you that every woman can feel virginal forever in the way I'm thinking of. I've been around the block, same as you, and I've been atop a few who didn't act virginal at all, and didn't feel it either. And then there are those situations where you, and the girl, too, know that you're *only* fucking, that's all. Nothing wrong with that: a good old-fashioned animal tussle is fine, as long as the girl knows what she's doing and why she's doing it. If she does, then in my view she keeps that virginality, and if that isn't a word, it ought to be. I wonder whether something of the sort can be said of men. I mean, I wonder whether we ever really know what we're doing when we hop in the sack. Whoever said that a stiff cock knows no conscience had it about right. And by this same token, we've all had to listen to guys telling you they really know women, how to turn them on and so forth. I have to wonder whether they aren't kidding themselves, even a legendary swordsman like Sinatra or Jack Kennedy. Take a look sometime at photos of Sinatra with Ava Gardner, and tell me he knew what she was about: the guy looks completely lost to me, in way over his head. Maybe he did have other women figured out, starlet types and so forth. But Ava Gardner was the love of his life, and I don't believe he ever had so much as a clue there. We know this much for certain: he never got over her. Whether she ever got over him, I don't know, and whether she kept that sense of her vital center, so to say, is another question. She was by all accounts a very complicated lady, and my money says she did keep it. After it was over, she had an interesting response to a guy who was running Sinatra down, telling Ava he was nothing but a skinny wop who probably didn't weigh more than a hundred and ten pounds. Yeah, she came back, but that ten pounds was all *cock.* Might have been. Judy said he was one terrific guy in bed. But for my money he never really made her.

• • •

Sinatra's Surfrider suite was rented by the year. Today the cool style of this wouldn't make us raise an eyebrow. The scale of what the famous sociologist called conspicuous consumption has become so extravagant we might not even notice if some teeny star *bought* the place, you know? In fact, a while back there was a movie star who bought an entire town somewhere out West; I don't remember whether she kept it or not. Back then, though, to rent out the top floor of a swanky hotel—that was flying high.

He had it decorated in his gangster style: big furniture, deep cushions, shank-high shag. And all of it—*all*, even the artwork—was done in orange and black. This is what hit Judy when she walked in, all that orange and black glaring at you like you'd walked into a tiger's lair, which was probably the point. Moving around it were Frank's people. Chauffeurs. Gofers who had specialized missions, like the ones who went to liquor stores for Jack Daniel's and Bacardi and those who went out for pasta and seafood salads. Guys who made phone calls to the cleaners, restaurants, and clubs. Other guys who placed calls to numbers nobody else had. And two or three heavyweights who weren't in civvies but in suits that looked dark but then shiny when they moved into the sunlight, which caught the folds of their sleeves and shoulders. These were the guys Frank needed most, more than his drivers and reservation makers, his tailors and masseurs, his agents and sound personnel. Not so much because he actually needed what they did but because they were the ones who made him feel like Frank. These were his hoods.

Sometimes it almost seemed like Sinatra was sorry he had so much talent, because it interfered with what he really wanted to be, which was a wise guy, a guy who hurt people. After all, when you think of it in a certain way, there's something *menial* about entertaining people, right? I mean, you're *serving* them in their leisure hours. A guy who shows up, though, when you haven't redeemed your markers—this guy commands your complete attention when you're called out of a business meeting or your doorbell rings in the middle of the night. Frank's men were there to cover his ass and to put yours in a sling if that's what was needed. They were on duty to pin your arms while Frank took a swing at you outside a club at four in the morning, or else to step in and stop a fight he'd provoked but didn't really want to get into. It's like the tiny dog who is secretly happy he's on a leash so he can't rip the jugular out of that Great Dane who's crossed his path in the park.

Living around the Hollywood scene as she had, Judy'd brushed up against the fact that there were shady types who associated themselves with the entertainment business. You couldn't miss that, unless you had a reason to. But to see all these hoody guys who could have snapped Sinatra over their knee like a twig bowing and scraping like serfs, this was a real eye-opener. She thought the name of the hotel ought to have been the Serf-Rider but didn't say so to him. If Frank made any sort of observation, there was a murmuring chorus of yeses that ran around the room. If he wanted a cigarette, it was instantly produced and lit for him, and there came a moment when Frank wanted another cigarette, and some bruiser fumbled the lighter and dropped it, and the great man called him "Mr. Fumblefuck." Everybody had a laugh about that, though it was obvious to her that the man had been nervous.

When she made her entrance, she turned heads, of course, but Frank himself was fairly casual about it, going over to give her a quick peck but then turning to talk to someone else. Then she had to more or less fend for herself a little, though a man did get her a drink and stood talking uneasily with her awhile—"How's Hawaii treatin' ya? Some swell place, huh?" That sort of thing. She thought Sinatra might be giving her the distant treatment to punish her for flying over on her own. But then suddenly he made his way to her side, his famous blue eyes twinkling now, and put his arm firmly around her waist. Then he glanced around to make sure everybody registered the significance of his gesture. After that people began deferring to her, not like they did to him, but still there was this difference. Here was her crash course in the tribal laws of the in crowd, and she found it privately amusing. Soon enough she would learn that these same laws applied in the highest reaches of American politics as well. In both, the chief, the don, the president demanded an unwavering fealty that extended all the way up and down the chain. As far as Sinatra's crowd was concerned, she was to learn that the only person exempt from the workings of this law of absolute fealty to power was Dean Martin, who enjoyed a special immunity from Sinatra's tyranny. It might tell you something about Judy to learn that of all of them, she liked Dean best.

Everybody drank Jack Daniel's all that afternoon, because that was what Sinatra was drinking. Then a nap, which by that point she was in some need of. Then the long makeup session in the suite that was down the hall from Sinatra's. Cocktails in the tiger's lair. And this time when she made her entrance the group had shrunk some, because the gofers and other ass-kissers were gone and so were the phone men. The driver was there, and so was the beef trust, though they'd changed to civvies—loud, loose-fitting print shirts hanging over slacks—but the heavy dress shoes were a giveaway. While she stood there, taking in the scene and feeling very shy and exposed, she noticed some newcomers, a couple emerging from somewhere in back and Sinatra with them: Pete and Pat Lawford, just in from somewhere. Sinatra spotted her right off and came over, the bodies making way for him like the Red Sea or something, and introduced her. Judy thought Pat looked awful, her hair dry and carelessly combed and her linen shirt wrinkled and worn over a pair of faded jeans. These were, you'll understand, the observations of a girl who was fresh from hours of meticulous preparation for just this moment. (I can't tell you how many hours I spent, total, reading through her descriptions of these private sessions of hers, learning about how to put yourself together for a long evening on the town, and I'm certain Judy would be horrified to learn that I did read all this stuff and even more so to learn that after a while I actually developed a kind of interest in all of it. But then, history has made me into a sort of accidental witness to all kinds of private moments—which is a bit different from being a peeping Tom.)

At dinner the Surfrider staff was at full attention and Pat Lawford was in full monologue mode, explaining just how Jack was going to capture the nomination and who the political figures were who would have to be won over, one way or another—the county commissioners and registrars, the ward heelers and sheriffs, down to pro-tem mayors of obscure towns nobody had ever heard of but that the Kennedy machine already had in its sights. This was clearly an impressive national strategy—no house of cards here or cocktail-hour bullshit—and the whole time Pat Lawford was talking exclusively to Sinatra, because the Kennedy machine had him in its sights, too. The others might as well have gone for a stroll on the beach. Sinatra could function for the Kennedys as a cutout, moving between the worlds of megastar entertainment and the unions with their shadowy associates. And all the while Pat was talking, Sinatra just sat there in total silence, didn't say a word—except when one of the staff leaned over to ask him if anything was needed and he snarled at the guy and told him to shut up until he gave him a signal. Because Sinatra knew the score, too—or very quickly figured it out. This civics lesson wasn't to make up for his deficient high school education. No, Pat Lawford was talking exclusively to him because the Kennedys had decided they could use him, and that was fine with him. It's a ticket to the White House, baby, and that ain't bad for a dago guinea wop from Hoboken. So by the time Pat had finished he was ready to pick up where she'd left off. He signaled the staff into action—more drinks, menus—and told her he knew guys all around the country who could hardly wait to back Jack.

Late that night up in the tiger's lair Frank and Judy sat on one of the big couches, with Frank still going on about all the help he could give the Kennedy campaign, repeating with emphasis and detail the claims he'd made downstairs to Pat Lawford, telling Judy he had guys all over the country who could turn out voters for a primary or the general election: California, New Jersey, West Virginia. All he had to do was pick up the phone and it would be done. There was one guy, though, he couldn't deal with on that basis. He was way too big for that. For him, Sinatra said, thinking out loud, I'll have to go to Chicago. Either that or invite him out to Vegas or Miami—Miami might be best. But when she asked who this big shot was, Sinatra turned toward her, raising his hand, and those famous blue eyes suddenly looked very cold. Slowly and with measured emphasis, he told her never to ask someone for a name, because if it wasn't volunteered, it was better for her if she didn't know it. That was fine with her; she didn't have that much interest in knowing the names and numbers of all the players. What was interesting to her was how eager Sinatra was to sign on as a helper, to be a real team player—this after a day watching roomfuls of people falling all over themselves to satisfy his tiniest wish. Here was another lesson in tribal anthropology—the hierarchy of power that you had to understand and respect. Whether she ever learned as much as she needed to about this is a question that haunts me still.

Power had never been a big deal to her. This was partly because of how she grew up and where. She'd been raised in a twenty-four-room mansion on the edge of Hollywood, where it was nothing to say hi to Bob Hope or Greg Peck or Bert Lahr or any number of other big-timers of that day, though for you some of these names might seem a bit quaint. Saying hi to Lloyd Bridges, which she regularly did, might not strike you as a special privilege; me either, but then, I wasn't a fan of his, except for his part in *High Noon*. Anyway, it was probably next to impossible to grow up there without developing a sense of how much of everyday life was about power, *juice:* who had it and who had more of it. But if you're a kid, you don't take this all that seriously, like a good many other things grownups are concerned with. Later on, you might: this general kind of process or evolution over time must be pretty common no matter where you grow up. But in her case, for reasons we'll never know, she seemed to stay in that childhood indifference to power, and it became a part of the person she was. She simply wasn't impressed or cowed by that sort of thing. Since we've become so punch-drunk on celebrity culture that even the local TV weatherman can make a maitre d' cringe, that sort of nonchalance might look like pretense or else just stupidity. Maybe it did back then, too, even if it wouldn't have been quite so glaring. But when I try to get a handle on her life, the turns it took, beginning with the moment she accepted Sinatra's invite to Hawaii but paid her own way, I find myself coming back to this attitude and wondering how much of her trouble was caused by it. For sure, it brought her trouble quick enough with Sinatra and the Rat Pack. Later, I think it caused her to make some pretty crucial miscalculations in her relationships with Jack Kennedy and Momo. I'd really like to know how the Camelot crowd saw her and how Momo's boys did. Did they think she acted in the nonchalant way she did because she was simply a bimbo, stupid and self-absorbed—that she was a fool who imagined that a great pair of knockers and a brilliant smile was all she needed? I mean, in those days she was moving through a world where millions and millions of dollars were in play in one scheme or another and the lives and destinies of uncountable others were at stake in matters she appeared to breeze through, worrying only about whether the ass of her Dior dress had gotten wrinkled while she waited in a White House anteroom for the president to take her away for wine and roses. If they did see her in this way—and I think they may have—this might account for the treatment she got later on, especially after Dallas. I don't think it would be that extreme to argue that a lot of what happened to her was a kind of revenge, as if the suits were saying, Okay, toots, you laughed along, now cry some. It seems like one of the things powerful people can't handle is someone who fails to recognize just how powerful they really are. Peculiar, I grant you, but true enough.

Well, after Sinatra had finished rehearsing what he was able to do to elect the next president, he wanted, naturally enough, to turn back to himself, his own power, and to exercise it on this beautiful, offbeat broad next to him. He got up, blade-thin in the baggy fashion of those high-end resort clothes, and put on one of his albums. Romantic stuff, soul-senders, Sinatra selling you the sentiments of songs like "A Cottage for Sale" and "Violets for Your Furs." This wasn't "Come Fly with Me" or any of that high-hearted fluff designed to lure you onward—"In llama land there's a one-man band," that kind of crap. No, this was music sent heart to heart.

And the message got there, too; at least it did for him. Because when he heard himself singing "Here's That Rainy Day" he seemed to huddle into himself, so much so that when the song ended and the needle arm ratcheted inward an instant before retracting, the singer just sat there, slumped and staring off into the orange-and-black vista he'd created. Then she felt a wave of sadness from him come washing over her shore, and she reached over and took his limp hand. She thought he might have been thinking of Ava Gardner and wondering what had gone wrong. Whatever it was, he was able to shove it aside, because he kept her hand, then stood up, pulling her gently with him, and led her silently into the bedroom.

Frank wasn't one of those men who expects to be made love to, she said. Instead, he was very "active," very romantic, and they went on "quite a while." If you're waiting here for more intimate details, I don't have them for you, except the ones you've just heard, which are enough for me. I can imagine the rest. She did say he kept his arms around her until they drifted off. Then later he awakened her and they made it again. Same thing in the morning, so you'd have to say the old rumors about him seem to have a basis in fact, judging from this episode. I don't know about you, but I'd have to say that was pretty good going. I mean, three times in maybe five, six hours and him having taken on quite a cargo of sauce during the long day before. Makes you wonder what feats he might have been capable of if he'd been in top-drawer condition. Just when you're thinking you'd like to hear from Ava Gardner on this score, you think at the same time, Forget it—they were both probably bombed every time they got between the sheets. For safety's sake, maybe this was for the best.

When they finally got up, Frank made breakfast, standing there at the range in a blue silk robe with orange piping. Scrambled eggs with tomatoes. And after Judy had gone back to her suite to freshen up they went out shopping, just a guy and his girl, holding hands, laughing softly. Beautiful day with a light breeze to keep things fresh. Nobody seemed to notice them. When Frank said he wanted to get back, to work on his tan, she continued on to find a record shop that had most of his albums, and she bought a copy of each. When she got back Frank's place had filled again, though not with quite so many as the day before. He was out on the terrace working on his tan, and she caught a glimpse of him lying out in the bright sun, all the planes of his face visible as well as those old scars on his neck from where they'd yanked him out of his mother, Dolly. In that instant he looked frail and vulnerable, but then Pete Lawford came out and started bantering with him, and the moment passed. When she looked out there again, Sinatra had his sunglasses on and was sitting up, and she went out with the albums in her arms and presented them to him. Behind his shades he seemed genuinely touched, smiling slightly while he shuffled through the stack, touching the heavy cardboard sleeves, making a remark or two about this one or that. At lunch he seemed abstracted and didn't do much but push at the edges of his seafood salad and take a couple of sips of an Italian white wine, saying very little, the others watching him warily, trying to gauge his mood: where was the Man going next? All except Lawford. Without Pat around he was doing a bang-up job with the sauce, and as he drank along he began sending longer and more meaningful looks Judy's way, trying to hold her eyes with his. Sinatra didn't seem to notice.

Sinatra's mood kept cocktails and dinner subdued, and afterward, up in the lair, it was just Judy and Pete trying to keep a silent Sinatra company, until finally Sinatra announced he wasn't feeling too sharp and was going to turn in. So then it was just the two of them, and the scene was perfectly obvious to her, with Pete urging her to drink and keeping right on with it himself, edging closer to her each time he returned to the couch with a refill. She was wondering what she should do when he made his move, which she thought would be soon, but he solved the problem for her, asking her to take a stroll on the beach. "I jumped at this," she said, telling him she was going to her room for a wrap and would join him downstairs, but when she made it inside her suite she locked the door, took the phone off the hook, and doused the lights.

They had a ten-thirty tee time the next morning—Sinatra, Lawford, and Judy. A couple of the heavies were along to make sure everything went smoothly. She got some whistles when she walloped her first drive long and straight off the men's tee. She must have had one sweet swing. She shot eighty-eight that day, better than either of her partners, and might have gone a bit lower if Lawford hadn't begun drawing Sinatra aside more and more often on the back nine, putting his arm around him and giving him some sort of earnest advice she couldn't hear. It began to make her nervous and cut into her game. Whatever it was, it didn't improve the Man's game either, nor his mood, which was darkening quickly, like a tropical storm moving over water, and by the time they reached the clubhouse he was shooting her some very venomous looks. Up in her suite for her long preparations, she wondered whether Lawford had been telling Sinatra some bullshit story about what supposedly happened down on the beach the night before, but when she dialed his suite to try to clear the air, a flunky growled that Mr. Sinatra wasn't available.

Cocktails and dinner were a trial: Sinatra froze her out completely, directing his talk to a large party that now included Joey Bishop, one of the Rat Pack regulars. At the long evening's end and with the party beginning to swing into another gear, which would take them on toward dawn, she drew Frank aside to ask him what she'd done wrong, but he only snarled "Nothing" and turned his back on her. That was quite enough for her, and the next morning she packed and took the first flight out.

She didn't hear from him for well over a week, and when he did finally call she let him have both barrels. He kept trying to explain between blasts until finally he just began to laugh and she found herself beginning to laugh, too. When that was over he gave her what she took as a sincere apology, though a vague one, and he ended up inviting her out for a long weekend in Palm Desert.

To begin with this was a carbon copy of the way things had gone at first at the Surfrider: lots of company, lots of drinks, lots of laughter and talk about "clydes" and "ring-a-dings" and so forth. Mostly she tuned this stuff out, not wanting to bother with breaking the boys' club code. Joey Bishop was on hand again, and Dean Martin this time, but no Pete Lawford, for which she was grateful, convinced by now it had been Lawford who'd poisoned the well in Hawaii with all his hush-hush business on the back nine.

That first night, too, was like the one at the Surfrider, with Frank being very active and romantic and patient with her. She was always "slow to ignite," she said, but he stayed right with her until it happened. And like the time in Hawaii they had another predawn go. When they finally got up, Frank cooked breakfast for them and then spent much of the day on the telephone, which was fine with her. He was still on it when she left for her long work-up, but she felt reassured that things were good between them, because when she paused at the door and turned back he shot her a brilliant smile and winked one of those sea blue eyes. On that she sailed down the hallway, thinking that even if she wasn't at all sure where this was going, she was a lucky girl, because Frank at his best was a beautiful lover and a great artist. Maybe Hawaii had just been a freak thing after all, an example not so much of Sinatra's well-rumored mercurial nature as of Pete Lawford's mischief. Soaking in the Jacuzzi and gazing out at the desert, she found herself feeling a weird mixture of calm and excitement. The brakes she always applied when she found herself getting carried away and racing too fast toward something ahead weren't working that well. But for the moment, anyway, she seemed content not to worry too much about it, because the ride felt wonderful.

I copied out a few lines from that entry, though I have to say I don't know *exactly* when they were written, only that they appear below her comments on the day and how it seemed when she'd left Frank. I doubt she was writing any of this while she was in the Jacuzzi, though I guess even that is possible. It's possible, too, that all these lines were written once she got out and before she joined the crew down the hall for another long evening: plenty of time for that. You wouldn't think they could have been written *after* the events of that night, because what happened between her and Sinatra when all the others had left changed their relationship for good. After that they were never lovers again and not even particularly good friends. But I guess I'd better give you the lines:

> *God.*
>
> Never known a guy like this one with so many sides to him. What does it add up to. All my life I've been waiting for one thing to be really seen but I haven't found the man patient enough to find the Judy that hides beneath the clothes and all that.

Okay. Keep these in mind a minute while I tell you what happened between them after the others had left.

She goes into the bedroom ahead of him, and it's very dark when she closes the door to get undressed and into bed. She waits there, and after a bit he comes in and glides in next to her. They start to snuggle, but just then she gets this funny feeling that something's wrong and she starts to tense up while he's making soothing noises and movements. Then she sure as hell *knows* something's up, because another person's getting into bed on Sinatra's side. It's dark in there, as I said, but not so dark she can't make out that it's another woman, a dark-skinned, long-legged woman, who proceeds to go down on Sinatra while she—Judy—lies there "frozen" with fear and humiliation, listening to the sounds of their action until the other woman brings him off. So then it's the three of them lying there together in the dark, breathing hard for what seemed to her like hours. Finally she pulls herself together, enough anyway to say, "Oh Frank, how *could* you?" She crawls out of bed, gropes for her clothes, and leaves.

While she's trying to think what to do back in her room there's this polite little knock on the door, and it's him, asking if he can come in and talk with her, just for a minute. But while he's trying to sweet-talk her she finds herself screaming hysterically at him, and so here, too, it's become a kind of carbon copy of the Hawaiian caper, only this is much worse—much—and she knows at that moment that whatever it was that might have been between them, it's over forever.

She was far too upset for sleep and spent the next hours getting ready to go back to L.A.—and by the way, when she did, Sinatra sent her in a limo—and I have to wonder whether this isn't when she wrote those lines.

Does it make that much of a difference? It does to me. Because I think that what you've got here is someone who still believed in possibility, like I tried to explain a while back, who was still looking for depth, meaning in life, even after a scene like the one Sinatra had set her up for. This is a hell of a lot different from some moll with a hide as thick as a rhino's and a brain to match. I look at this passage, and I compare it to that one I copied down from an earlier diary—the one about watching football on TV with Billy?—and I see a woman who's still taking her knocks from the men in her life but who hasn't given up on possibility. She hasn't found what it is yet, but she still believes in it.

That, as I say, was the end of the romance but not the end of the relationship. He kept on calling her, inviting her out to Vegas, where he was filming *Ocean's 11* and appearing nights at the Sands with the Rat Pack. After turning him down numerous times, she went. It was fun, exciting: the drinks, the dinners, casino-hopping with that fast crowd, watching dawn come up on the desert. Joey Bishop could be hysterically funny doing improvisational routines on the street or in a hotel lobby. She saw a lot of Dean Martin. There was something about his personality she found restful; he didn't seem to take too many things seriously, including himself. Sinatra was always around, of course, pestering her with public questions about her strange behavior, repeatedly asking her when she was going to wise up and quit being so damn square. But I get the impression that he'd actually given up on her and was merely doing all this for show. It couldn't have been that he needed somebody warm to get in bed with, so what I think is that what Judy had become for him wasn't an actual romantic target anymore but only a challenge he couldn't quite let go of. But then the relationship changed dramatically. This would have been at the very end of January or the first days of February 1960—impossible to date such things with that bombsight accuracy the historians seem to set such store by. But then, a lot of important things can't be dated, and not because we've lost the records but because there never was a way to pin a date on them.

Oh, sure, you can do that with some things, like D-day or the assassination of Lincoln, but a lot of stuff that later appears as fact, solid, agreed-upon fact, begins as something as shapeless and trivial as a stray thought—a daydream, if you like. I'm hunting here for an anecdote from history to show you what I have in mind, a story about a huge battle that was lost just because the king's horse threw a shoe—you know the one I mean? Well, it's no matter; let me go on, and let's see if I make my point.

Let's just say that the day before the battle the royal blacksmith was thinking about the girl in the kitchen who scrubbed out the pots, and so he missed a few strokes with his hammer while he was shoeing the king's horse. *Bingo*—the king's thrown and captured and held for ransom and the battle's lost. Then, much later, the historians arrive and gas on about the battle and why it went the way it did. They talk about superior numbers or the kind of bows one side used—oak, say, versus yew, or whatever—and then, of course, about the king and his horse, which they all agree to discount because it's much too simple to be really accurate. But it could be that here the truth is much too complicated, that it could have been that smith's stray, horny thought about the scullion girl that caused him to do a sloppy job with the stallion. What I'm trying to do is paint in what may have been the background of Sinatra's idea to offer Judy to Jack Kennedy, a gorgeous gift that would make the giver even more welcome at the White House than his connections with movers and fixers all around the country.

Sinatra was a first-rate user, especially when it came to women, and once Judy had made it clear she wasn't up for his kinky kind of action, he must have felt used himself. That kind of personality doesn't seem to understand any other standard of behavior. Well, if he could figure out how to set it up, she'd make a terrific gift, not only because of her looks but because she was a game girl, a trait in women that Sinatra and his bunch highly prized: kind of like the affection you feel for a boxer who can take a punch and keep coming, or a horse that can go a mile and a quarter and consistently get you show money. If that sounds to you close to liking a girl because she could take a certain amount of punishment with style and a smile, I think you're on the right track and will have a better understanding of the scene Judy was into. And here I mean not just the Rat Pack but also the Kennedys. All those girls had to be game, too, up for just about anything, at any hour: pump out litters of kids; play touch football on the beach; throw a cocktail party at a moment's notice; do grassroots campaign work out of dingy hotel conference rooms in towns they otherwise wouldn't stay the night in; black-tie events, blue-water sailing. And maybe once in a while some special attention paid to an especially important man—nothing excessive, you understand. Sinatra could see Judy fitting a number of Jack Kennedy's requirements.

True, she wasn't quite the standard-issue broad and could be unpredictable, stubborn at times, and with a tendency to go her own way. But hell, nobody was perfect, and if she had these defects, let Jack find them out for himself. By that time, Sinatra must have realized, he himself would be an established figure in the Kennedy operation. If Jack should ever come to him and say, Frank, what's with this Campbell chick, anyway? he'd be able to say, Well, Jack, I never quite figured that out myself, but I thought you could. Which would cork Jack's bottle, because he wouldn't want to admit that he, too, was baffled by Judy.

Sinatra was hardly a close friend of Kennedy's at this time, but he'd been around him some. He'd met him through Pat and Pete, and it's possible he may have kept Pete around just for this access. Judy had a low opinion of Lawford's character and talent, calling him the weak link in the Rat Pack's onstage presentations. In another place she refers to him as a steer. Anyway, there were two things about Jack Kennedy Sinatra did know, and they were very useful things to know, too. He knew the senator got around on Jackie a lot, and he knew Kennedy was as fascinated with him and his world as he was with Kennedy and his. Which, of course, takes us right back to the old man, who passed along these things to his sons, almost like a social disease. They all had it, Jack the worst. So when Pete told Frank that the senator was going to stop over in Vegas on his way to the West Coast, all the tumblers fell into place for Sinatra, and he called Judy to invite her out. If he told her Jack Kennedy was going to be there, it isn't down in her diary; doesn't mean he didn't, but, juggling all the marbles, I doubt he did. He had more to gain through the element of surprise, I'd say.

Here's a place, though, where it's useful for us to have a date. She said she met Jack Kennedy on February seventh of 1960. At that time he was already campaigning in the New Hampshire primary, but it wasn't a serious race: he had the state in his pocket all the way. None of the other big hitters were in it, and his only opponent was a guy who sold ballpoint pens or some such. So it was a perfect situation for him, because it would give him a quick, easy win, get his name in the headlines, and meanwhile he was more or less free to hop around the country, making himself more visible while polishing his approach and his speeches, which he needed to do. At this point he wasn't that terrific a speaker. I looked at some video footage of those earliest days of the campaign, and while I have to say he was a cut above average, he wasn't the speaker he became later on. He had those hand gestures we all remember. He had the occasional stick-out phrase reporters could copy and editors would be grateful for. He was "telegenic," a word that might have been minted to describe what a natural he was in what was at that time really a pretty new medium. But his speaking style needed the work he was giving it. He spoke very quickly, trying to cram in statistics, trends, grand sweeping visions, and it was too much. He hadn't learned what you might call drama but what might better be called pace. But even so, you could tell he had a first-class mind, and as we now know, he learned to play his audiences like a rustic virtuoso playing one of those real long saws they used up in the North Woods pineries—lots of tones and held notes, that sort of thing.

On this hop he was on his way to poach on the territory of the maverick senator from Oregon, Wayne Morse, looking ahead to a late primary there, and his pal Sinatra had set up a cocktail party in his honor, followed by dinner and the show, where Sinatra, Martin, Bishop, Lawford, and Sammy Davis Jr. were nightly playing off each other and all of them at least half in the bag. So this was the big scene that Judy walked into, dressed to the nines and unsuspecting. Dead ahead of her as she walked into the party was handsome Jack, and I hope I don't have to emphasize anymore how unaccidental a meeting this really was.

She had seen his pictures in the papers, of course. Still, she wasn't prepared for how radiantly handsome he was in the flesh, how dashingly he carried himself, all those Irish teeth, as she called them, that thick, reddish hair. And wherever he'd picked up that tan, it was rich enough to make his host and all the other Hollywood sun worshippers green with envy. Right away Sinatra made the introduction, but then he said, Jack, you wouldn't believe it just looking at her, but this gorgeous gal's got a heart like an iceberg. I've been trying to date her for what seems like years, and all I got to show for it is a bunch of turndowns. My heart's beginning to feel a bit like the *Titanic.*

Well, you shouldn't have too much trouble imagining what the effect of this would be on the senator. It was the verbal equivalent of

Spanish fly, is what it was—an incredible turn-on: being introduced to this movie-star-like beauty who's advertised as an iceberg. What would Jack Kennedy want more right then than the opportunity to turn on all the heat of his charm and have this iceberg melt into his arms? We'll never know how long Sinatra worked on this line, but I doubt any of his writers could have improved on it for sheer, brilliant strategy. It had everything: seduction, challenge, mystery, the whole shebang.

What she thought of it, I can't tell you. In one obvious way it was a lie, of course. She and Frank had been bed partners, as you heard, so the impression Sinatra was conveying here wasn't accurate. But she could hardly correct it under the circumstances; she couldn't do anything except let it stand. But I wonder whether she just left it there permanently because she felt it was *essentially* true: she had turned Frank down. And more than that, she'd always reserved a deep part of herself from him, so that when he pulled that midnight trio trick she was in some way ready for it, if you follow me. Sure, she was humiliated by it, and angry, too, and she never forgave him, either. But she was hardly one of those strung-out broads that hopelessly followed Sinatra around until he told them to get lost—permanently. She still had her inner self intact, her virginality.

Now, whether this ability to escape pretty much unscarred from intimate relationships shows a deep selfishness could be a question, I guess. If you're always holding something important back, that could be an emotional miserliness. And if you wanted to work this line of thinking out some more, I guess you could go on to say that it might be the reason why she got hurt in the first place—that the men in her life sensed she wasn't giving it her all and so they turned on her, first Billy Campbell and most recently Sinatra. But a kinder interpretation would be that it shows a shrewdness, that she sized up Sinatra for what he was. Same, I think, could go for Billy Campbell, who was a user and a playboy who betrayed her uncounted times before she finally had enough and left him.

But then, here comes another question: did she ever let *anyone* in all the way? And if the evidence you have says, Probably not, then you go on to ask, Why not? Was she hiding something way in there? Was she hiding *from* something, and was that something inside herself? These questions get to seem like a Chinese box, you know? You keep pondering them, year after year, and the boxes get smaller and smaller, but you never seem to quite get to that box where the answer lies. But here's something I got out of the later diaries. See if it answers any of these questions for you.

When she was a teenager and living in that parental pile on the edge of Hollywood, she was up in her room one afternoon with her door open, singing along to some record. It just so happened that downstairs her parents were entertaining a big-time producer and his wife, and when he heard that voice he stopped short and said, Who in hell is *that?* When they told him, That's our Judy, he begged them to let him talk with her. Well, they brought her down and he got a look at her, and right then and there he told her that he thought she might have what it took to be a star in movie musicals. Could she come to the studio for an audition? She said okay, but by the next day she'd changed her mind and said she wouldn't do it. The entry goes on a ways and has a lot of back-and-forthing, which isn't very interesting, but how it ended up was that she finally said the producer could come back to the house and she'd sing for him there. Which is what happened, except that when he got there she wouldn't come down and said she'd sing from where she was, up there in her room where he couldn't see her. By God, he agreed to that, too. So they waited down there in the hallway or vestibule or whatever it was, the producer, an associate, her parents, and her older sister, the one who was in pictures. And they waited. Finally a voice told them, "I can't do it. Nothing will come out." Which was literally true: she'd been up there trying to sing, but when she'd open her mouth, nothing, no sound. Natural shyness? Stage fright? Could be either of these. But the really odd thing is that she says she never sang again, ever, not even to herself in the shower.

Much later I happened to come across a quote from a singer—I think she sang Latin jazz, but it doesn't make any difference—and when I did, it caused me to come back to this episode. The quote ran something like "What is singing but the sound of someone dreaming out loud?" Maybe what we're looking at in this story is more complex than anything like shyness or stage fright. Maybe there was something way down in there that she didn't want anybody else to discover. I'm no Dr. Freud, but this singing business is so weird—*never* to sing again?—that it stands out, almost like it's asking you to make sense of it in a deep way. I'm not telling you that I have, only that it intrigues me enough that I've kept trying.

When I went to work on the diaries Phil Keneally had, I asked him one afternoon his opinion of this. He was living at that time in a crappy apartment on Washtenaw—junk and bottles and dirty laundry all over the place, really disgraceful for a man of his brilliance. Anyway, I told him the story and asked what he thought. Among other things Keneally had a reputation as a guy who was a very shrewd judge of character; he could size people up with an uncanny quickness. This was one of the things that once made him so successful in the courtroom. Here, though, he just looked at me, and after a long silence he said, "Huh?" like he couldn't believe the idiocy of my question. Here he'd put me next to this dynamite material and I was asking him why some teenager refused to sing for a stranger years and years ago. "Are you *nuts?*" he asked me. "I didn't know your syphilis was that advanced. What possible fucking difference could it make to what we're trying to accomplish here whether she had a great voice or a mediocre one or none at all? She had a *mouth* that was in good working order, though—she gave great head. *That* we can use."

Well, that answer wasn't really what I was searching for when I asked the question. As you see, I have a lot more questions about this whole story than I have answers. But you can't say I didn't warn you right at the start.

After Sinatra disappeared to get ready for the show, somebody asked the group, Who wants dinner? And right then Jack signed to Judy that he wanted her along. It ended up with Lawford, Teddy Kennedy, and Gloria Cahn joining Jack and Judy in the Garden Room of the Sands. Jack made sure that Judy had a place next to his, but Gloria Cahn, whose husband was the songwriter, wasn't about to let this nobody have Jack Kennedy all to herself and so proceeded to monopolize the conversation with a ceaseless string of political questions and observations. At one point Jack glanced at Judy and made a little gesture of resignation, like he was saying, What can I do? That made her feel suddenly warm, because she took it as a sign that he'd rather be talking with her than listening to Gloria. But nothing really changed when they went into the Copa Room for the late show. She and Jack shared a small table with Teddy, and you couldn't really talk over the uproarious laughter. All she got of Jack was the whites of his teeth through the smoky gloom as he laughed along with everybody else, especially at a joke at his expense. Still, there was something else going on here, something she felt didn't need to be communicated in words. Jack was sending it across the table: his strong interest in her. It was thrilling, but it felt dangerous at the same time, that being, I guess, the nature of thrills. After all, here was this man with his eyes set on the White House, married to a beautiful woman who was more and more in the news alongside him as the primary season came on. Also, Judy had very recently been down this road before, with Sinatra, whose attentions had seemed genuine until she'd found out she'd have to share him—literally—with another woman.

There's a gap in her entry of this first meeting with Jack Kennedy, because the way things were looking between them you'd have wanted to get money down on them ending up the evening together. It didn't go that way. She ended up with Teddy—barhopping, I mean. But she doesn't say how this happened or where Jack went, only that she showed Teddy the town and that the longer the night went on, the more attentive he became, until at the end of it she had to gently but firmly push him out of her hotel room. Even that wasn't the last of it, though, because he called her at dawn to say he wasn't leaving on campaign business that day but was going to stay over to see her. She thought this was pretty irresponsible given the stakes involved, but she didn't say that to him, only claimed she was fully booked. In any case, a few hours later she was glad she'd said no to Teddy, because Jack called, asking if they could have lunch. She said yes to that.

When she arrived at the appointed hour there was Jack, surrounded at poolside by reporters, giving a press conference, relaxed, witty, smiling. Clearly he had these guys eating out of his hand—as he did all through the White House years, and even posthumously, come to think of it. But when he saw her come through the double doors into the pool area, he half stood and called out to her, I'll be right with you, Judy. And while she tried to hide her amazement that he'd be so public about her, all the reporters turned to see what the candidate had suddenly found so compelling: a glowing young woman in a burgundy-colored knit dress with a black belt to match her hair. Nowadays I don't think they wear knit dresses like they used to in the fifties and sixties, which I think is a shame, because if a gal has any kind of a figure, they'll show it to good advantage. So I think it would have taken a real hard-boiled, front-page type to just throw her a quick glance and then turn back to ask the candidate a probing question about the balance of trade or whether he thought there really was a missile gap between America and the Russians.

Well, Jack didn't keep her waiting very long. He wrapped that session up pretty quick and joined her, suggesting they have lunch in the privacy of Frank's suite, where they could talk over some matters about his campaign—this to a woman who up to that moment had never asked herself whether she was a Republican or a Democrat. When she confessed this later that afternoon, Jack just laughed and said, "We'll change that."

Their lunch on Sinatra's patio was private, all right, only a single waiter there, and as the hours went on—four by her account—even he disappeared and they were alone together. Finally it was she who ended it, telling him she had to get herself ready for the evening. By that time she had felt the full force of the man's charm, and it was something she never forgot.

After all the stuff that's been said about him, I can't think of a single other source that gives you as good a look at Kennedy's personal effect on others as her diaries. Sure, you get some of this in Sorensen and Schlesinger and Goodwin and Ben Bradlee. You get it, too, in the footage of his news conferences, where he was just flat-out, untouchably brilliant; even in some stills, photos—have you ever seen the one of him with Princess Grace? Well, look carefully at that one when you have a chance, and you should get a hint of what Judy experienced on that February afternoon in Vegas. Nobody got as close to him as she did—nobody, that is, who left a record of it. The one exception might be a woman in Washington, but we don't have her diaries, so it's pointless to try to compare them, whatever they might have been, with hers. I'll come back to her in the right place, but for now I simply want to emphasize that Judy's portrait of him trumps all those by the pro writers, despite the fact that there are hardly any amazing images or eye-grabbing descriptions. She simply wasn't that kind of writer. It's more of an accumulated thing, showing him in this situation and that, his characteristic mannerisms and tics and obsessions. But above all else, like I said, what she gives you is the immense—no, the *intense*—charm of the guy.

That afternoon he was totally present for her, leaning forward to catch every word she uttered, his head slightly tilted, quizzing her on the smallest details of her life, interests, beliefs, hopes. And it wasn't an act, either, because in the months to come she was astonished over and over by his total recall of these details. If that's an act, it's so successful that the actor believes in it himself, in which case the act crosses over into the authentic—there's no difference anymore, kind of like Archie Leach becoming the elegant and witty Cary Grant. He made her believe—and *feel,* which is maybe more important in a situation of this sort—that she was the most important person on the planet just then and that what she thought was vitally necessary to him, that he was going to remember it and draw on it in the future. That's a hell of a talent for a man to have in any situation, and Jack Kennedy had it in spades: everybody who knew him and talked about him—woman or man—testified to this ability.

She'd wanted somebody to be able to see through to the real Judy hidden behind the beautiful presentation she made in public, and here was someone who had. The fact that there's a comic irony in this is beside the point—the handsome Lothario who is able to see beneath the burgundy dress to the real girl hiding there. The point is that she completely bought his pitch, and he must have bought it himself in that moment.

And it turned out that he really did have something he wanted to talk over with her, that it hadn't been just a line he'd given her at poolside, and this was the issue of Catholicism and American politics. How he could have learned beforehand of her Catholic background I have no idea; maybe he had a number of topics ready for any occasion and trotted this one out when she told him she'd been raised Catholic. But in a way she really was a perfect person for him to talk with about a problem he now had to face. She was intelligent, thoughtful, and had had the standard parochial training, complete with the scare tactics, the bullying, the brainwashing. She could give him a solid, usable view of your average American Catholic looking at the upcoming election, someone sensitive to the historic anti-Catholic attitudes of the country but having at the same time genuine misgivings about the Church getting a say in national politics. How, in fact, should he approach this?

In case you don't remember your American history, in 1960 no Catholic had ever been elected president, and after Al Smith got the crap kicked out of him in '28 it looked like none ever would be. The Republicans sure weren't going to run one, and after Smith the Democrats weren't exactly itching to try it again. In fact, Catholics had been leaving the Democratic Party for the GOP since 1952, and in '56 Adlai only got something like 51 percent of their vote. So Kennedy had a hell of a problem here: how to convince the Protestant majority he wouldn't be taking orders from the Vatican while at the same time wooing defecting Catholics back to his party. They talked about Catholicism for some time, Judy telling him how frightened she'd been of the priests, the forbidding nuns, and the confessional booth, and Jack saying, Yes, yes, but that sort of thing was fading away and that it was his judgment that Catholics today were a lot more receptive to reason than to medieval superstitions. He said he was planning to appeal to this trend and to make it clear to Protestants and Catholics alike that he firmly believed in the separation of church and state. He even auditioned a good line he delivered sometime later when he told her, chopping the air with his hand, that here on earth God's work must be our own.

By the end of the afternoon he'd made a convert of her, and this was prophetic, really, because the basic approach he tried out with her was the one that worked so well with the voters. There, you may remember, he made no bones about his Catholicism, but he presented himself as very much a modern Catholic whose political priorities could be shared and understood by any American. You'll recall, too, maybe, that by the time of the actual election, Joe Kennedy's influence on Jack was more of an issue than the pope's, something crusty old Harry Truman had predicted months before. "It's not the pope I'm worried about," he told reporters, "it's the pop."

And I know that right now you're sitting there thinking, Well, sure he made a convert of her: he was *romancing* her, for Christ's sake. True, he was: at the end of the luncheon he gave her a bunch of telephone numbers where she could reach him and made it clear he wanted to see her often, whenever his schedule permitted. But the point I want to make here is that this was JFK's true style: he was *always* a romancer. He romanced the whole damn country that year and a lot of the rest of the world in the years following. That was the secret of his success (and the success of other leaders who had huge, emotionally charged followings). Look at FDR. The people who didn't hate that man *loved* him, were nuts about him. They didn't even see the leg braces, you know what I mean? We hear the word *charisma* all the time now, but if it has any meaning left, which I doubt, it's got to be right there in that romance thing. You've got to feel the heat.

She must have. But even as I'm telling you this, I also want to stick in a kind of qualifier. There's a quality of reserve in her that runs along with the obvious admiration, same, I guess, as there was with Sinatra. She was clearly drawn to Jack Kennedy, but from the first I don't think she was headers for him. What I find in her words is that admiration—plenty of it; fascination, too. Also a deep pleasure in being taken seriously. But no gushing.

Well, you might say, don't all of us want to be taken seriously, to be valued for what we are? Sure. But then think of how many of us surrender this desire under the right circumstances. Think of all the flunkies clustered around Old Blue Eyes, some of them pretty big names in their own right but happy to be counted as members of Sinatra's court. Think of O'Donnell and Powers and Sorensen and Schlesinger and Galbraith and all the rest of the Camelot crew, thrilled just to be there. Think of the dozens of women who threw themselves at Jack Kennedy because he made them believe in him. They bought the romance, all these dames, from Grace Kelly and Marilyn Monroe on down to those two secretaries who swam naked with him in the White House pool and were happy to be known simply as Fiddle and Faddle. One of them was supposed to have had a degree in comparative literature from Johns Hopkins.

Yes, JFK and Judy had a love affair, if that's the term you want to use, and I have no doubt that there were moments during it when she was carried away by him. But I've wondered often if, after the initial impact of his appearance and his personal magnetism, it was those high ideals he expressed that really drew her to him. I've said she seemed to believe in some possibility, something that might somehow redeem the present. Maybe that's really impossible; and maybe, too, those high ideals are impossible. Does that make her life a tragedy, or does it make it a kind of farce? The answer might depend on what we make of our own lives, it seems to me, whether we believe in some possibility.

They met again in early March, in New York at the Plaza. Really a classy place. I had a drink in there once, in the Oak Room, and as

I recall, they had a big painting up behind the bar that showed the fountain that's out front and a crowd of high-toned people coming toward the hotel entrance. Perfect spot for Jack to rendezvous with her—both of them real lookers and always beautifully turned out.

He was fresh from winning the New Hampshire primary, which, as I've said, was a walkover. Not to her, though. She was thrilled with the win, and this feeling helped her a bit with the nervousness, which she was definitely feeling, because she had a sense of what was on the line here. Waiting for him up in her room, she had time to ask herself if she really wanted to get involved, knowing what the next step must be, and knowing, too, that if she took it she'd be into something serious and that this was precisely what Jack wanted. She couldn't have known what "getting involved" would turn out to mean, and it would be a long time indeed before she did begin to understand just something of that. Even so and at this level she felt herself poised on a sort of fulcrum.

She had plenty of time to think about it, too, because he was pretty late. There was a small marble-topped table over in the corner of the room with a bottle of Jack Daniel's, an ice bucket, and two highball glasses, and as the minutes dragged by it was so still in there she could hear the ice cubes shifting and was tempted to have a drink, but she didn't want him to smell liquor on her breath. Killing time, she began to leaf through a couple of fashion magazines, imagining herself in this outfit or that. Then there was a quick, sharp rapping at the door, and when she opened it there was Jack, brilliantly handsome, flushed, and slightly out of breath. Later she wondered whether he'd sprinted up the back stairs to dodge reporters, of which there would have been a good number the day after New Hampshire. But that thought was later, and now they practically fell into each other's arms. Then he pulled back to arm's length. "Let me just look at you," he said, his Irish teeth flashing. "Turn around." She felt self-conscious but did it anyway. "God, you're beautiful," he said, closing in again, and in that moment he made her feel that way, too. When he held her tight she could feel his excitement. But she was feeling something else as well: she wasn't ready for what he clearly was.

"Let's have a drink, shall we, Jack?" she managed.

"Oh, sure," he said, dropping his arms. "Sure."

His disappointment was easy to read as she stepped over to the marble-topped table to fix the drinks, and when she turned back to face him it suddenly seemed as if the bed had inflated to a size that took up almost the whole room, and she had to force herself to look away from it. Jack had slung his suit coat over a chair and was loosening his tie. He seemed in that moment suddenly very weary.

"God, I've missed you," he said as she handed him his drink. "It's been really rough."

She told him how proud she was of him for winning in New Hampshire, but he shrugged that aside immediately, as if she was missing his point, and maybe she was. So she asked him about Wisconsin, how that race looked, but clearly he wasn't up there to talk politics with her; that he could do downstairs with his staff. He kept fidgeting in his chair, glancing over at her, twirling his glass while she kept slugging away at hers, hoping for that courage we've all looked for in a glass or a bottle, most of the time in vain, and trying not to look at "that damned bed." Suddenly Jack stood up and put his glass down with a sharp crack.

"Judy," he said, holding out a hand, "come here." What could she do but take it and let herself be pulled up? Then he led her to the enormous bed, which she still wasn't ready for. With one arm around her waist and the other on her chest he gently pushed her downward.

"Jack," she found herself saying, "I just can't do this."

The look on his face was just like someone had hit him from behind: first that blankness you have when what's happened hasn't registered upstairs yet; then the flood of disbelief; and finally the pain of it. Except what she remembered was that the pain didn't seem to be there, only deepening disbelief: he couldn't believe that a woman was telling him it wasn't going to happen. *What the hell is this?* he must have been thinking. Here they'd made all the arrangements just for this purpose, and he'd carved out the time from a ferocious schedule. But there was more to it than this, of course. There was the history of his conquests over twenty years or more, and by this time he'd had so many women he couldn't remember some of their names, even when he was in bed with them, and so had adopted the safe strategy of calling them "kid" or "kiddo," like Babe Ruth, who had so many people around him at all hours he called everybody "keed." You have to wonder if the last time a woman had turned him down was at the prep school prom—and then only because she was having her period. But here was Judy, telling him it wasn't going to happen, at least not just then, and so he pulled away, straightened up, and asked her what the problem was. The only thing she could come up with—and she implied this wasn't really an explanation of what she was feeling then (or wasn't)—was to say they hadn't been around each other in weeks, not since Vegas, and it just felt rushed to have a quick drink and then hop in the sack. But we've been on the phone almost every day, he argued, which makes you wonder what those conversations were like and whether they were, for him anyway, a kind of foreplay. He stood there looking down at her and then buttoned his collar, pulled up his tie, and went for his jacket. She said she felt a sense of helplessness watching this and knowing that if he left the room, it would be over between them. She still didn't know exactly what she wanted out of this relationship, only that she didn't want it to end like this. When she called to him he already had one hand on the door handle and his jacket in the other. But at the sound of her voice, he turned to look at her over his shoulder.

"Jack," she said, "come here, will you?" He did, and she put her hands gently on his arms. Maybe even at that moment she might not have known what she wanted to happen, and so maybe kissing him on the lips—a long, full one—wasn't so much strategy as it was instinct, which has to come before planning. It was the first time they'd kissed, and after it they sat on the bed (which must have shrunk some in its proportions by then) and talked through it, with her doing her best to sort out her feelings while voicing them—a tough enough trick under any circumstances, let alone in a high-pressure situation like this. As for him, he claimed he hadn't been trying to rush things. It was simply that he always had to have time somewhere on his mind, as he put it. I take this in more than the strictly literal sense of a candidate whose every waking moment must be scheduled. No doubt it was meant that way, but those who knew Jack Kennedy well all said that he gave the constant impression that he was haunted by time, or, more pointedly, by the lack of time, the time when for him there would be no more time left. He'd felt death brush close when his brother went down in the war, and again on his PT boat in the South Pacific. In 1947 he'd been so sick on a transatlantic voyage he'd been given last rites. And the year following that, his favorite sister, Kathleen, had been killed in a plane crash in France. No one lived forever, and for some few life was fated to be very brief indeed. "Live like hell," he once said to one of his hard-drinking, skirt-chasing cronies. Maybe that was the innermost motto he lived by, why he took all the chances he did.

So they sat there on the bed for some time, not having it out but exposing something of themselves to each other, if I can put it that way without bringing up the sexual connotation of that word. And by the time they had said what needed to be said, Jack had long ago laid his jacket aside, disregarding time for the moment, at least. And then they turned down the covers and went to bed.

Now, you tell me, was this a classic example of a legendary Casanova merely making another of his numberless conquests, strategically overcoming the woman's reluctance in order to get what he came for? I'll tell you what I think. I think it's more likely a classic example of a man—here it just happens to be Jack Kennedy—*imagining* that this is what happened and probably feeling a little smug about it all, when what had really happened is that the woman, for her own private reasons, decided to let the guy in and was willing to let him think whatever he wanted. I don't know that it made any practical difference what Jack was thinking once they got under way. Whatever it was, he took his time with her—nothing rushed—and she found him tender and attentive and ardent.

Afterward, she fixed them drinks and they sat up in bed, holding hands and talking, Jack with a sofa cushion propped up behind him to ease his back. Now she found him eager to talk politics. He'd shifted quickly into that gear, though he still dismissed New Hampshire and said Wisconsin would be the big test, maybe the biggest. It wouldn't be enough just to win. He'd have to "crush Hubert's nuts," as he put it, and he'd have to do it in Hubert's backyard. Nothing less would convince Eleanor and Truman and Daley and Sam Rayburn that he could win anywhere. He seemed to her exasperated that he would have to show these people, particularly Eleanor, whom he'd been carefully courting for some time, telling Judy he didn't know what the hell more she wanted from him. "I'm not her goddamned husband," he said, and anybody who tried to campaign on that famous model was dead—like FDR Jr. He let go of her hand to saw the air for emphasis. "You can't improve on the old man." And when he said that, he laughed and clinked his glass with hers. As for Truman, he said the old bastard would have to come around sooner or later; there was no place else for him to go. "He can't stand Adlai after 'fifty-two and 'fifty-six, and he's got to know Symington doesn't have the nuts of a toy poodle. Who the hell else is there?"

Since their meeting in Vegas, Judy had begun to follow the campaign closely, so she knew Humphrey was already complaining to the press about having to run against so huge and wealthy a clan as the Kennedys, comparing himself to the corner grocer trying to compete against the supermarket down the block. So now, with Jack beside her, doing his own kind of complaining, she teased him a little, saying Humphrey, too, had his problems. "Poor old Hubert," she said. "One man against all you Kennedys."

"Screw Hubert," Jack said, asking her if she really thought that if Hubert had the money, he wouldn't use it. That was such a bullshit argument. And in fact, he told her, he'd already let Hubert's people know that if Hubert wanted to talk about establishing some sort of spending limit, he was willing. But it was easier for Hubert—and maybe more advantageous, too—to go on whining to the press and trying for sympathetic support.

"But you've still got your own plane," she persisted, "and all he's got is a bus. And you've got your whole family out there working for you, and all he's got is Muriel."

"Yes, yes," he came back, with that Harvard accent that made *yes* sound more like *yeah*. "Yes, I've got the plane. Goddamned handy, too. And the family, all the brothers and sisters and in-laws. And then there are the grandkids coming along. Who knows?" he said, grinning over at her. "Someday we might just take over the whole world."

That was the beginning of it, and now she was involved, all right, though there's no way she could possibly have understood just what that meant—that it would come to mean a hell of a lot more than just a brief romantic affair. Maybe at that point he didn't understand either, though with Kennedy you always have to consider the possibility that he was thinking ahead to other ways this girl could be helpful.

Before they went their ways they talked about how they could stay in touch, and he gave her some more phone numbers. She told him she was on her way down to Miami to catch Sinatra's opening at the Fontainebleau. Jack said he'd be sure to call her there; he wanted to hear about everything that was going on. She thought it was funny and also a little odd that this brilliant man who was taking dead aim at the most powerful position on earth should be almost childishly intrigued by the things she herself thought were almost ho-hum. Later she teased him about this, saying, "Jack, why does this stuff interest you so much? What you need to do is buy yourself a movie magazine and read all about it." I wonder how this kind of ribbing went down with a guy who by most accounts was a lot more comfortable dishing it out than taking some of the same himself. I don't know that this makes Jack Kennedy that unusual. Most of us, I'd guess, are built along similar lines, and those so-called roasts celebrities give each other are oddly public recognitions of this fact of human nature. I mention this exchange between Judy and Jack mainly because I see it as another illustration of the fact that a lot of the time Judy didn't seem to quite understand the league she was playing in: how thin these guys' skins really were and what long memories they had. Most of them—JFK, Sinatra, Momo—would have made an elephant seem like a victim of Alzheimer's.

Well, he did call her a lot down there, pestering her with questions about Frank, who was with him, what they were talking about, and in one of these conversations she mentioned that Sinatra had some of his mysterious friends around and that he'd introduced her to a couple of them.

One of these intros happened shortly before Sinatra was to go on, and he'd asked her to come up to his suite. She walked into a room that was practically empty—only the Man himself, his valet, and another guy sitting quietly in the corner and wearing a straw hat and dark glasses. Judy the clotheshorse noted that his suit was pretty shiny, "like it was made of metal almost." But it was well tailored, and the guy had a mannerly air about him. She couldn't tell much about his looks with the hat and glasses, but at least he didn't leer at her like some of Sinatra's entourage did, so that was a restful change for her. Sinatra himself was subdued, standing there quietly under the hands of his valet, who was straightening, tugging, smoothing, then giving the star a final whisking. On impulse Judy stepped up to Frank and smoothed his tux jacket over his shoulder blades, and he turned to her with a look like he might have given his mother way back in Hoboken when Dolly had sent her scrawny son out to conquer the world, a mission the son himself had only half believed in. Then he looked over at the quiet man in the corner.

"Joe," he said, "what do you think of this Campbell chick—pretty nice, huh?"

"Beautiful, Frank," Joe came back. "Very beautiful."

"Judy," Frank said to her, "say hello to Joe Fish."

She gave Joe Fish her brilliant smile, and he nodded and touched his hat brim in a kind of "European way." The name meant nothing to her, and even if she'd been a Chicagoan, it probably wouldn't have, because it was only one of a hatful of names Joseph Fischetti went by. Joe was the brother of Rocco and of Charlie—who I mentioned to you when I was talking about Phil Keneally's bad temper. The Fischettis were cousins of Capone and pretty rough customers in their own right. Joe had been tight with Sinatra for years, since way back when he sang for Dorsey, and the folklore was that Joe had been one of the guys who made Dorsey that offer he couldn't refuse—the phrase *The Godfather* made so popular. It's only a funny line on the screen, though. If it's in real life, not reel life, it isn't funny to get one of these pieces of Mob generosity: it's your business or your life, and if you're fool enough to refuse, it's both. So Joe Fish's presence at the Fontainebleau meant that he and Frank were still doing business.

All this passed over her head, of course, as did the other intro Sinatra made for her a few minutes later down in the lobby, where a phalanx of his friends were waiting for him when he stepped out of the elevator. There was a lone guy, though, who wasn't part of the crowd that closed in on Sinatra, fawning over him, eager to be seen shaking his hand, patting his back, but who hung back, waiting. He knew his business, too, because as soon as Sinatra spotted him he grabbed Judy's hand and went over to him, while all the others quickly got out of the way.

"Sam," Sinatra said, and they hugged. "Sam, this is the heartbreaker I was telling you about. No kidding there, as you see." He kept her hand while saying this, but at the same time he was taking a couple of short steps back so that she was at arm's length, like a prized possession. She said she almost felt as if he wanted her to twirl around, like she had for Jack, or maybe even curtsy, which she probably knew how to do. But she didn't do either of these things, and when Sinatra finished that bit he told her that this was his valued friend Sam Flood from Chicago.

Sam was a balding guy, big nose, sad eyes, and he was instantly all eyes for her. Here's what she wrote down about their first exchange:

> He told me a girl as beautiful as I was had no business wearing junk like the brooch I had on. It's true it was costume jewelry but I like it with that outfit and anyway who the hell was Sam Flood to tell me what I should or shouldn't wear. So I just said a girl like me wears what she wants.

That brought Mr. Flood up short. He stood there a long moment in silence, just staring at her while Sinatra was swiveling his head back and forth from one to the other. But then, slowly, Sam Flood smiled, a big, generous smile, and then he cocked his head and laughed. "Okay." He laughed. "Okay." Then Sinatra laughed as well and put his arm around Sam Flood and they moved across the lobby to the lounge for drinks. But as they were about to enter the gloom, Sinatra dropped back to Judy and grabbed her arm and hissed in her ear, *"For Christ's sake!"* That was the last thing he said to her that night.

Just short of noon the next day she heard from him. She thought it was early for him to be asking her to come up to the suite, but she said she would when she'd gotten herself together. When she did make it up there, she found him alone with a tall, dark-looking bloody mary. Without asking, he fixed her one just like it, and they went out onto the balcony, where he looked down at the pool without saying anything. She knew his mercurial temper well enough and wasn't about to lead with her chin. So she sipped and watched him out of the corner of her eye, waiting. Then here it came.

"You know, Campbell, you're so beautiful it's a crying shame you're so fucking stupid," he said at last, turning ice blue eyes on her. "Let's leave aside that your crack down there could've got both of us whacked. Let's leave that over here"—making some sort of gesture. "You're just stupid, which I never figured on, and the thing is, you're not getting any smarter, which means you're getting stupider. That's dangerous."

She said something like, Gee, Frank, you really know how to flatter a girl. Glad I came up. But he ran right through that.

"You know what that intro I made for you was?" he asked. She'd seen him in a fury, but somehow this was different. He was just intense, with that major vein working in his neck. But he was in control of himself. "You know what *I* am?" She said she knew very well who he was, that he was a singer, a great artist, but he was also a man with a very bad temper, and if he was working up to another one of his tantrums, she was going back to her room. He ignored this, too.

"I'm an *opportunity* that's come knocking, baby. And that was another one, down there in the lobby. These are *doors* that are opening for you, but you don't walk through them because you're so fucking square."

She told him that if you had to have a small crowd with you when you made love, then she didn't want to be a swinger, that she'd much rather be a square or stupid, if that was a different thing. He came right back, claiming that she was missing the point.

"You only go around once, baby, and you've got everything it takes to have one hell of a whirl. Why not wise up and loosen up and live a little? You'll have more fun, and so will we." He muttered something that she thought was "Might live a little longer, too," but when she asked him what he'd said, he just said, "Skip it," and then smiled a small, tight smile that seemed to take some effort and abruptly changed the subject, asking her how she thought he'd sounded last night: somewhere he'd picked up a slight cold and had sounded nasal to himself. She was glad to reassure him that he'd been his usual fabulous self.

I doubt she reported this conversation to Jack. But she did tell him about meeting Joe Fish and also that she'd met a Sam Flood, a nice enough guy, though his crack about her costume jewelry was in poor taste.

"Oh, you met him?" Jack asked. And she said she had, and did he know Flood himself?

"Oh, sure," Jack said. "That's Sam Giancana. He works for us."

Get that. I'll tell you, when I came across this I kind of fell back into the ratty chair I used in Phil Keneally's apartment and stared up at the ceiling, which was painted a tired dogshit brown and was one of those old-timey stamped tin ones you can still find in that Logan Square area. I just sat there for some minutes, not actually thinking, not working through the implications of Kennedy's casual admission. I guess I wish I had that kind of mind, the kind Phil Keneally still had, despite his bad habits and troubled history. You know, where you just *seize* the fact, whatever it is, and begin to dissect it until you have it spread out in all its parts, and you examine each of these from every angle? I didn't do that, just sat there, staring up at that stamped tin ceiling, and if I was thinking anything at all, it was only the obvious: that here was independent confirmation of the arrangement made in Judge Tuohy's chambers between Joe Kennedy and Sam Giancana. Not that I really needed it: I'd never doubted Keneally's story from the moment he began it at the Bullpen when we'd bumped into each other after the ballgame. Still, coming across it like I had, it packed a wallop, and I was stunned enough to be sitting there, looking up, when Keneally came back from the crapper with a newspaper under his arm. He glanced at me but didn't ask what the hell I was doing, just slouched over to the street-front bay window and dropped massively into the chair. I was glad of that, of course, because I don't know what I would have answered that wouldn't have exposed my ass to his withering fire.

The rest of that particular entry wasn't very interesting—what Judy wore, who sat with whom at the show that night, where they went afterward, and so forth. But the entry for the next morning had some real juice to it: she got a call from the front desk telling her that some flowers had arrived for her and were on their way up. Four dozen yellow roses from a Mr. Flood.

This wasn't merely Momo's style, of course. It's the style of a Mob guy, and you can spot it anywhere they hang—Hollywood, Vegas, Chicago, Queens, New Orleans. I don't know where it comes from, but it's part of a kind of bundle—a bouquet, if you want to stay with the roses. The houses the Mob types choose to live in, the neighborhoods, the cars they drive—all of these are quite often pretty inconspicuous, and for every mansion like Big Tuna Tony Accardo's up in

Lake Forest there are dozens of small bungalows in lower-middle-class neighborhoods. Other things are different, though, quite different. When it comes to presents, to clothes, to funerals, these are expenditures where price is no object and extravagance is the rule. While their wives often live middle-class in many respects, the boys like to rain presents on their girlfriends. And by sending her all these yellow roses, Mr. Flood was telling Judy that that's just what he wanted her to become.

3

JACK, JUDY, AND SAM

JACK WANTED HER in Washington when the Wisconsin results came in on April fifth. Jackie would be out of town, he told her, and they could see each other on the sixth. She flew in on the night of the fifth and put up at the Mayflower.

He won it, all right. He beat Humphrey in his own backyard, which was what Daley and the others had been waiting to see. But it wasn't New Hampshire. It was a tough trip through alien territory where winter was still hanging around like it does up there, and if you've ever been in Rice Lake or Trade Lake or Balsam Lake in March, then you have an idea of what the young man from Massachusetts was going through in the western part of the state, where he had to devote much of his energies. I know these towns a little because I once did a feature on ice fishing for the *Daily News*.

He'd start out in the still-frozen dark of morning, pumping hands in diners and in the parking lots of meatpacking plants and dairies, at fraternal halls, even in high schools, where the kids couldn't vote, of course, but where he might light a spark that some of them could carry home to tell the folks around the kitchen table that they'd met John F. Kennedy. In one diner he introduced himself to the wool-capped geezers with their hands cupped around their coffee mugs, telling them he was running for president, and one of them said,

"President of what?" That'll take the press out of your pants, day after fourteen-hour day.

Humphrey was doing it, too—you've got to say that. But this was home to him. He knew these folks, especially in the western part of the state, and he knew farmers, which Kennedy definitely didn't. And there was this as well: despite the fact that Humphrey was an older man than Jack Kennedy, he was actually a healthier one, though, as you may remember, Kennedy's public image was one of Vigor with a capital V. His family and handlers went to great lengths to hide his various physical problems, but even this early in the campaign his back was giving him real trouble daily.

Still, like I say, he won it, won it with 56 percent of the vote, and you look at that number and think, Well, that's pretty good going. Except he lost every one of the predominantly Protestant districts, and that was what Daley and Rayburn and the rest of the hardasses would have been looking at. When Daley told the old man, You show me a win in Wisconsin and then we'll talk again, I doubt he was more specific than that: just win, baby. But this kind of win wouldn't have convinced them of anything except that they had to keep their options wide open. Maybe Symington would have to be their man, or maybe even Humphrey.

Nobody knew this better than Jack Kennedy himself. Up in his Milwaukee headquarters, when the district voting patterns were broken down, one of his sisters asked him what this meant, and Teddy White—who was in the room at the time—wrote that Kennedy replied bitterly that it meant they'd have to do it all over again, in West Virginia and Indiana and Oregon, and win all of them, right up to the convention. There wasn't going to be any early-round kayo for him; the Wisconsin results had ended that hope. Early the next morning he was in his plane and on the way back to Washington for meetings with his strategists—and with Judy.

At that time Jack and Jackie were living in Georgetown; Judy had the address as 3307 N Street Northwest. She took a cab over there on the evening of the sixth, wearing a black dress with what she called a simple strand of pearls, and when Jack got a load of her standing on his doorstep, his eyes bugged. "*Wow*" was all he said. He led her into a dimly lit drawing room, where a big man in a dark suit sat by the fireplace. The whole scene was so dim she had trouble making him out, but Jack quickly introduced her, a servant brought her a drink, and then the two men went back to their conversation. They talked in low tones, bending toward each other. Eventually they all went in to dinner, where she discovered she wasn't in the least hungry. Butterflies, she knew, brought on by being in this house surrounded by furnishings—too many for her taste—collected by Jackie. Here she was, a stealthy visitor in Jackie's home, and she found herself thinking that as difficult as the marriage seemed to be—and virtually the only thing Jack had said about it was that things hadn't worked out as they'd hoped—still, Jack and Jackie were man and wife. And so while Jack talked about what he kept calling the "goddamned religious thing," she was more and more feeling like a very bad Catholic girl who was here to commit a sin and to enable Jack to commit one as well. By the time the guest had left she was feeling almost sick to her stomach, and of course completely out of the mood for romance. This was looking very much like a repeat of the situation at the Plaza, but she felt powerless to tell Jack this as he took her hand and walked her through the rooms, including the bedroom he shared with Jackie, and then at last into a smaller bedroom with a fireplace that was glowing against the rush of the air conditioner. They sat down on a loveseat, Jack still holding her hand and smiling steadily at her. "You know," he said reflectively, "if I don't get this thing, Jackie and I will probably go our own ways, and then I'm going to take you to a little island I know about in the Caribbean, and we'll just lie around in the sun and make love all day." She giggled nervously at that and told him to tell her another. But he said he really meant it and went on in detail about the island and how much he would love to watch her body soaking in the sun. "No clothes for either of us," he went on, "at least not for you. I'll have to struggle into some pants once in a while, just to go into the village for supplies—rum for our daiquiris and that sort of thing." By the time he'd finished spinning this out at some length she found her butterflies had flown away, and the transition from the loveseat to the seat of love, as they say, was completely natural. There was nothing in the least rushed about it. Jack had absorbed the lessons he'd learned about her style at the Plaza, and she felt it was more wonderful than that, which had been completely wonderful.

Afterward, while they sat up in bed, Jack talked about what it was like out there on the hustings, a term he liked to use, partly, I'd guess, for ironic effect, gesturing vigorously with his hands. And for her, suddenly, it was oddly like she was watching him on TV. He was good and warmed up by now, fully switched into his political mode, and it was thrilling to her to be there next to him, watching history being created, enacted with those hands molding and shaping phrases that soon would be heard by millions. Talk about a ringside seat! Even Ted Sorensen, the ultimate JFK insider, never had a seat like hers.

After a while—and by this point it must have been late—he turned to her and asked, "Do you think you could love me?" And she answered, "I'm afraid I could." Which led to a discussion of the ways they could see each other while the campaign was on: difficult, he told her, but not impossible if she was willing, which she assured him she was. For his part, he said he wanted to see her as often as he could, and if you're trying to assess the true nature of this relationship, I think at this point you pretty much need to take his claim at face value. He went on to say he wanted to pay for her plane tickets and hotel rooms, this man who had a well-developed reputation as a tightwad, but she told him she paid her own way. "He looked so awfully disappointed at that," she said, "and said that there was so little he could do for me, wouldn't I at least let him do that. But I still said no." A few minutes later, though, when she was in the shower and he was in the bathroom of the master bedroom, she began imagining him over there feeling hurt by her refusal to let him pay her way and wondering what she could do to make that up to him.

She didn't have to wonder long. When he reappeared in his bathrobe, he said he'd been thinking of something important she could do to help him with the campaign—that is, if she wanted to become a member of the team. This I think you need in her words:

> He didn't have to tell me what it was—I jumped at it. Here I'd just been thinking about how I could make that thing up to him and here it was. So I said sure. This was my chance to be part of the Kennedy team. I've never done anything yet in my life that's been terrifically important and here is this wonderful exciting man asking me if I wanted to help him get elected president of the country. What an honor! Of course I said sure. But he wanted to sit me down and talk it over before I agreed. I said he didn't have to do that I was ready whatever it was. He said to wait there and excused himself and when he came back he had this attaché case very expensive looking and he sat down with it in his lap. It was very important to the campaign to get this into the hands of Sam Giancana—Mr. Flood—as quickly as possible and if I was willing he could make all the arrangements for me to go out there tomorrow (which was really today). I said I would do it that I would be happy to do it.

Jack asked if she didn't want to see what was in the case, but she said she didn't care. He appeared to hesitate over that, then told her he thought it would be best if she knew a bit more about her errand and after she did, if she decided she didn't really want to do it, he would completely understand, and it wouldn't change a thing between them. She laughed at that and asked, "What's in there, a gun?" Then he showed her, unlocking the case, and it wasn't a gun, but it was loaded, all right, with stacks of thousand-dollar bills bound with thick rubber bands. This, he explained, was for Giancana's help with the campaign.

Clearly it was. But was it a down payment for the help Momo had promised old Joe back in February, or was it for some new favor the Kennedys now found they needed? I looked over at Phil Keneally and told him what I'd just discovered. He asked the date, and

I said it was April sixth, the day after Wisconsin. He thought a moment, but not longer, and said, "Then it was for West Virginia. Illinois was strictly a quid pro quo deal—my votes for your protection. For West Virginia it had to be cash. That was strictly a cash-for-your-vote state." He was sitting over there by the window as always, and now he kind of leered at me with those long yellow teeth he had. "Not altogether unlike what we're up to here," he added. "I find your ass for you, and then you pay me my whack." After another moment he tossed his magazine aside with a "here we go again" show of resignation, which I think really was mostly show. Don't forget what a dramatic guy he'd once been in the courtroom. But he didn't have anything more important to do on those afternoons in the apartment on Washtenaw than to try to help me by answering my questions. He rarely went anywhere while I worked with the diaries. He might go back in the bedroom to sack out if he'd taken on a particularly heavy load the night before. Once in a while he'd go out for cigarettes or to the laundromat on the corner. But the rest of the time he'd be over there in one of those loungers where when you tilt back the footrest comes up. Reading. I mean, always. There's a saying about some public figures with big-time problems, addictions mostly: he battled his demons. Well, that's what Phil Keneally was doing over there by the window. He was disbarred and disgraced, yes, and clearly his money was running low or he wouldn't have been taking this long shot with me. Still, he kept himself mentally active. He read his law journals. He read an enormous number of magazines and newspapers. He had only one small bookcase parked in the hall between the bedroom and the bathroom, but it was jammed with what little was left of his library, and piled on top of it were stacks of books from the CPL: he'd had to sell his books to a dealer up in Evanston, and so where he'd once bought, now he borrowed. I never saw him take a drink while I was up there. He just sat there and read and waited for my questions, and to me the spectacle came to seem admirable despite—or is it *because of?*—the awful way he was living.

Anyway, he gave out that big sigh and tossed his magazine aside.

"Here's the way that state operated," he said. "Pay attention so I don't have to go through the fucking thing again.

"I never knew how they got the cash to Momo until just now. Pretty neat. At that point nobody knew who she was, so she could come and go anywhere. Later on, J. Edgar had his boys all over her sweet ass, and she couldn't step outdoors without being accosted by them with their questions. He did the same thing to Jean Seberg, and it drove her so fucking nuts she killed herself."

He asked me how Judy delivered it, and I said she took a train. He nodded and said that left less to chance.

"The cash had to come from the old man. Momo could have handed off to his friend Skinny D'Amato out east, but that would've involved another cross-country transfer, and they obviously felt there was a time issue here. So what he did was get in touch with a friend of Shriver's here, a guy named Jimmy Coffey. I knew him: another Mick, good guy. Could tell a joke, had plenty of stories, sang Irish tenor.

"By that time Jimmy ran his own coal company and was hooked into City Hall with a contract to deliver coal for the public schools. But before that he put in his years as a buyer for V. R. Killian down on Vincennes. He was their man in West Virginia, and he knew the territory. I mean, he knew every fucking sheriff and deputy sheriff and committeeman in every fucking rotten-assed hamlet and hollow in the state. Up at Michael Deasey's on Catalpa, which is where I used to run into him, he told hilarious stories about the gene pool morons he'd run into down there, guys who were an eye short or had one too many, and how that was what you came out with after three generations of fucking your sister. He could do their accents, stuff like that.

"Now, I'm going to simplify this for you: The ballots down there used to be hellishly complicated, ran on for maybe a dozen pages sometimes. It made you wonder how those gene pool types could ever figure them out. The answer is, they didn't. The committeemen and the sheriffs did it for them. They drew up what were called 'slates,' and for the right price they'd put your man's name at the top of the slate. A little less dough would get you second place, and so forth. They never would tell you exactly what first place would cost you, so competition stayed healthy. And to eliminate the possibility of double crosses or other kinds of misunderstandings, when they handed you the slate, they'd go into the booth with you to make sure you got it right. A fact. Oh, maybe the sheriff himself didn't, but his deputy would. These guys, the ones who went into the booth, were called the Lever Brothers, a wordplay on the soap company and the service they provided, pulling that lever for the candidate of their choice.

"The people coming out now with books about how the Kennedys invented the modern presidential campaign? That's horseshit. The Kennedys didn't *invent* anything. What they did do was raise the stakes and fine-tune a process that they had found and that they understood from way back. In West Virginia they tapped a man—*the* man—who knew the state and how it functioned and who he had to get next to."

Keneally began rummaging around his bloated, disheveled person for a light, his cigarette bobbing unlit in the dead center of his lips while he went on about how it had been Jimmy Coffey who had put the West Virginia deal together and how Jimmy was just as happy to let Skinny D'Amato run his mouth, taking the credit. Jimmy's ultimate reward was that contract with the public schools. In fact, Keneally said, he was pretty sure Jimmy's older son still did business with the city. By this point, though, he'd begun to get irritated by the persistent nonappearance of the matches, and rather than risk one of his blowups I went over and gave him a light that he didn't acknowledge in any way except to draw in a lungful and then let it out while running his fingertips gently over that big dent he had in his skull.

As I watched that repetitive gesture, my mind skipped away from the subject at hand to that terrible wound he'd gotten fighting for America, for democracy, the people's freedom to choose their own officeholders. Yet here he was, talking in what sounded to me like a completely neutral way about how the sacred process could be totally corrupted by money, and I had to wonder what the paths were that had led a highly decorated vet to accept the corruption of the very system he'd shed blood and bone to defend; and not only to accept that but to actively work toward its further and deeper corruption, which, of course, is what he'd done by setting up the Joe Kennedy–Giancana meeting. I think he was right in what he'd just said: that there was nothing truly new here, and the Kennedys hadn't invented anything any more than Keneally had. What they did was to put the whole shebang on a new basis, a meticulously planned, carefully calibrated basis that must have struck the West Virginia folks like the changeover from the horse and cart to the mass-produced Model T, putting crisp lettuce in every petty pol's jumper in every hollow and village and crossroads town that now, with Eisenhower's interstate system in the works, could entertain dreams of one day becoming a sure-enough city.

And they just *flattened* poor old Humphrey, wiped him off the map. I mean that almost literally, because there was a while there—not very long, it's true, maybe only a week or so—when Humphrey looked like he might have a chance in West Virginia. But then that attaché case arrived in Chicago in the gloved hand of a beautiful courier, and within just a few more days Jimmy Coffey and his helpers arrived in West Virginia, and the Humphrey signs began to come down, and the Kennedy signs went up where only last night the Humphrey signs had stood. And they said the Hump's men were just bewildered, because they'd been buying the same sheriffs and committeemen who now were working for Kennedy, but they'd been buying them earlier and not as dearly. And really, what was a man to do in so hardscrabble a state but accept the way things were now? Who were they to go against what felt like a rip tide of history? Sure, they'd taken Humphrey's money, but then here came the tide in the persons of those they knew well, telling them, "Hell, boys, we got the wrong danged horse. You can keep that money, but this here'll go some further, and they say this Kennedy kid is going to do something for miners and their families."

I listened carefully while Keneally ran all this down for me, and I never thought of asking him how he felt about it, not just about the West Virginia business but the whole process. But since that afternoon I've thought back on it quite a bit. This story will do that to you. And you know, despite all the hoopla and ticker tape and confetti after we'd won the war, there was actually a good deal of resentment on the part of some of the GIs who made it back to America and took a look around at what kind of a country it had somehow become while they were off getting shot at. There was a fair amount of disillusionment and a cynicism that took different forms. I didn't have any of that myself, but then I never got out of the navy yards in Oakland. I was still there when they dropped the bomb, and when they did I was happy as hell. Hooray! I don't have to get buried in a sand hill in the Solomons! I didn't have to wear, either, that sour look you got used to seeing on the faces of some of those returning vets. But if you're counting up the casualties, I've come to wonder whether you need to factor in another kind in order to account for a man like the one Phil Keneally became. Maybe he was a casualty not only because of that dent in his dome but also because the America he found back home did something equally harsh to his heart.

That was it for the Hump. Jack's win in West Virginia left no doubt about that, nor much about who the Democrats' big dog was. Symington said as much. Lyndon Johnson had been weighing his chances, but after West Virginia he decided his best bet was to remain on the sidelines and wait for Kennedy to make a big blunder. Eleanor had Jack to lunch (not dinner yet) and issued a guarded endorsement, saying she had found him to be a young man of promise, a little quick to form judgments, but then young men were like that. When Jack reported this on the phone to Judy, he made a sarcastic comment to the effect that old ladies were like that in their endorsements. But the meat of their conversation was his satisfaction that things had gone so smoothly on her errand to Chicago. But he didn't have to learn this from her, because he had a firsthand report: he'd put a tail on her from the minute she left the Mayflower to the moment she handed the attaché case to Momo at Union Station. He even knew she'd eaten dinner in her stateroom instead of in the dining car. Of course, he didn't tell her that, and I don't know that she ever learned it, at least not about that tail. But I wonder if it might have made a difference if she had. I mean, in the sense of putting her in a better position to understand the power, the sheer *juice* of these men she was now involved with. They might love her glamorous looks and court her, sure, but the game they were playing involved such enormous stakes they left absolutely nothing to chance if they could help it. In this particular instance you have to wonder whether Jack had the tail set up even before she said yes to the errand. That may have been a silent part of what he meant when he said he could make all the arrangements for her trip.

I suppose you could make an argument that it wouldn't have made any difference to her if she had known. From that diary entry it's clear she was hot to be of help. And there's context here, too. If you wanted to go back to Sinatra, to her quick decision to go to Hawaii to party with him and his pals, you could go on to say that that's the same kind of dame who would agree to take a train to a strange city, hand off a huge amount of cash to a mysterious man she barely knew, then spend the rest of the day hanging out with him. You might want to use the word *reckless* here, or even *foolish*. I wouldn't, and here's why.

First, she trusted Jack Kennedy not to put her in jeopardy. Considering what came down later, you could say that trust was misplaced, but at the time it would've seemed perfectly justified. Remember that millions and millions of people who really didn't know anything about him were placing their trust in Jack Kennedy, too. And here she was, someone who knew him in the most intimate way possible. Second, even if Sam Giancana, a.k.a. Sam Flood, was mysterious, even shady (which she thought he was), he actually had pretty solid connections as far as she was concerned: he was a close friend of Sinatra's, and he did some sort of work for the Kennedys. He wasn't going to harm a friend of those people. Again, it comes down to the matter of juice, and at that time she had too much of it behind her to be put in harm's way. So the riskiness of the errand on the surface of it turns out on a little inspection to be only apparent, if you follow me. But there's something else involved here, I think: I think Judy would have gone on the errand even if there had been genuine risk. I think she was looking for adventure in her life and knew she probably would have to take some risks in order to have it.

Oh, I don't mean adventure pure and simple, like somebody who decides to take up skydiving or mountain climbing. That's more like *distraction*, it seems to me. What I've got in mind is some activity or some *action* that you know involves risk but that you decide to do because you think it might lead to freedom from whatever kind of prison your life feels like, whatever dead end you've strayed into.

Up to the moment Jack Kennedy asked her to carry that cash from Washington to Chicago, I don't think there had been anything in Judy's life that had given her what I sense she was looking for—and I'm aware here that the word I've been using, *adventure*, might not be quite the one I want. But by way of a fuller explanation, let me just add that there are times for all of us when you're doing something routine and deeply boring, and you find yourself thinking, Sweet Jesus! This is my *life* I'm spending on this! Maybe you're waiting in line on a Saturday morning in summer at the Division of Motor Vehicles to get your license renewed. And the line's long, the place is incredibly dingy, the air's bad, and the clerks and examiners are just as pissed to be there as you are—maybe more so—and are moving so slowly they look like they're under water. And you're thinking, This can't be real; there's *got* to be more to the show than this. Like I say, all of us have these moments. Some of us, though, have them more often and more strongly. I see Judy as this type, and I think that everything from Hawaii to this day in Chicago with Giancana was an adventure she hoped might turn out to be the doorway to freedom.

If I'm right here, I don't think it's necessary to go on to theorize that she'd thought through where all this was leading. That sort of long-range thought process isn't really a part of what I'm trying to describe for you. You aren't thinking, Gee, if I do this, I'll get that. What you're thinking, if you're thinking anything and not just feeling, is, Well, I'm gonna try this door and see what's behind it, because none of the others have led anywhere interesting. When you think about it, every time you grab the handle of a strange door there's a little moment of risk, and maybe a tiny part of your brain, way in back, is saying to you, Well, here goes . . .

Often enough, of course, what's behind it looks so goddamned ordinary your heart sinks down to your shoes. That might have been Judy's reaction that day in Chicago when Momo zipped her around the Loop in one of his ratty two-door rigs and then said he was going to take her to a spot where they could get some good Italian cooking. Her thought about this was that she liked first-class Italian food—but not for lunch. And then the place Momo had in mind turned out to be a crummy-looking one-story joint way out west on Roosevelt, beyond Harlem. It didn't even have a sign. When they pulled into the parking lot, he told her that before they ate he was going to have what he called a "meet" with some friends but that it shouldn't take too long.

He took the attaché case in with him and casually gave it to the man behind a little desk at the door, then led her to a scarred booth in back, where they sat down. Instantly men gathered at the booth, but nobody else sat down until Momo looked at two of them and nodded. Then they slid in opposite Momo and Judy. Whoever Sam was, in here he was a king.

At that time the place was called the Armory. I don't know what name it had when it was a Capone speak. It's still there—and Capone's still parked a few blocks from there—though the last time I was there its name had been changed to Andrea's. The Armory's owners of record were Angelo and Ruthie Idella; she did the cooking that Momo liked so well. Angelo was the guy at the desk, and he came over to take an order. The martinis were good here, Momo told Judy, and he ordered two; the two men opposite had nothing, not even water. Then they talked to Momo, who listened but said very little. After a few minutes he turned to her and smiled.

"You don't understand a thing we're saying, do you, honey?" She admitted she didn't. "We're talking Sicilian," he explained, "and it's better for you that you don't understand. Life's complicated enough, you know?"

She said she was going to sign up for Sicilian at Berlitz, and when she said that there was another of those suddenly charged silences like the one in the Fontainebleau lobby when she'd come back at him for his remark about her jewelry. The guys opposite clammed up quick while Momo stared at her a long moment, then finally cocked his head, muttered something she didn't catch, and laughed. When he did the two guys went "Ha, ha, ha," just like they were reading from an unfamiliar script, and that was that.

That night, when Momo dropped her off at the Ambassador East, she had a message to call a number she recognized as one Jack had given her. When she reached him, they skipped around through this and that while the feeling grew in her that there was something on his mind, and so finally she asked him what it was. He repeated that he was glad things had gone so well for her out there and that what he called "the message" had gotten to "our friend."

"Now there's something else you could do for us—for me," he said, "—before you leave. I'm going to be in Miami on the twelfth, and we could see each other there. I think it would be helpful if you could set up a meeting with our friend while I'm down there." She said she'd ask the friend and get back to him with the answer. She thought this coded kind of conversation was exciting. It made her feel a part of something that was secret and very important. So this was how the first known meeting was arranged between JFK and Momo Giancana, and Judy not only put it together, but it took place in her suite at the Fontainebleau.

When Jack showed for it he was all business, and shortly she excused herself and went out window-shopping. She never saw Momo, but when she finally returned it was obvious a meeting had occurred: the empty room smelled strongly of cigar smoke, there were the stubs of two cigars in an ashtray, and there were two water glasses on the table. At the beginning of the seventies, when a lot of stuff on JFK was beginning to leak out, a woman working for Jack Anderson was sleuthing the much-rumored relationship between him and Giancana. But she was obliged to admit that nobody had yet been found who would say they had ever been seen together. But we do know, she wrote, that John F. Kennedy was in Miami on April 12, 1960, and the FBI has established that Sam Giancana was in that city on the same day. And so forth. But even if Anderson's girl sleuth had known of Judy's involvement in this episode and had been able to get Judy to talk about it, she still wouldn't have been able to make her case based on that date alone, because Judy hadn't seen them together either, as I just said. But you can get money down that they did in fact meet and that they used her suite to do so.

She didn't see anything more of Jack down there, though he did call to thank her and reported that the meeting had been what he called useful. He had a speaking engagement that night and afterward was flying back to Washington. As for her, Momo was taking her to the opening night of Sammy Davis Jr.'s run at the Fontainebleau.

It turned out they were a threesome, because Joe Fish came along; this was fine with her, since she was feeling the growing heat from Momo's attentions. But she wasn't at all prepared for what happened when Davis paid a visit to their ringside table before he went on. The two men completely ignored him and went on talking just as if he weren't standing there, smiling, shifting from one foot to the other, waiting to be asked to sit and have a drink. It was incredibly embarrassing, she felt, but what could she do but smile up at Davis and try to let him know she wasn't a part of the silent treatment? Finally he said he had to get ready and left. Momo looked at his retreating back and said to Joe Fish, "Nigger," and then they both had a good laugh. The whole scene shocked her: Momo's use of the word as well as this public humiliation of Davis, who was, after all, a big star, a friend of Sinatra's, and who would in a matter of minutes have to appear before people who had witnessed this.

There was more to come. Davis played the entire show to their table, never taking his eye off Momo and Joe Fish, and after he'd taken his final curtain call he bounded down to ask Momo whether there was anything wrong. She thought he was about beside himself, but the only thing Momo would say to him was not to worry himself about it, because if anything was wrong, he'd hear from them.

As you've heard, she had a background in show business, was on a first-name basis with some of its heaviest hitters. But here was something new. Unless I simply missed it in the diaries Ed had, this might have been the first time Judy had come face-to-face with an ugly fact of show business life in America. I doubt I did miss it in those earlier diaries, because if it was there, way down in the bottom of that Kellogg's box, then she wouldn't have been as shocked and puzzled by this episode as she clearly was. So her schooling begins here, I'd say, and before she dropped out she came to learn that Davis, Dean Martin, Eddie Fisher, the McGuire Sisters, even the great Sinatra himself were owned wholly or in part by Giancana, Joe Fischetti, and their associates in the Mob.

At first she may have reached the easy, comfortable conclusion that these stars' obvious desire to please Momo and the rest was mostly a matter of gratitude. After all, Momo and his friends owned the clubs, the casinos, the resorts and hotels where the stars regularly appeared. What could be more natural than this? Maybe Davis overdid it, but what of it? When you considered the fact that he was a Negro, some sort of practicing Jew, and blind in one eye, maybe these handicaps explained the cringing behavior she'd witnessed. The more exposure she had, though, to Momo and his close associate Johnny Roselli, who specialized in show business, the harder it would have been to keep hold of this comfortable conclusion, and the harder it would have become to avoid knowing that there was a lot more involved here than mere gratitude. But all this lay down the road, and on that first night at the Fontainebleau there was no way she could have understood what was being played out right in front of her. And there's no way she could have understood that she herself had just become part of Momo's world. Accepting *anything* from the Mob, any kind of favor, meant that you were in, that you'd signed on. It's just that simple, and the terrible simplicity of it is what made it work so beautifully for the bosses. Oh, maybe you hadn't signed on just then for the full ride—you know, extortion, the protection racket, strong-arm stuff, cement shoes, and so forth. Still, all that was closer than you could imagine in the moment of your acceptance, just as it had been for Sinatra when Joe Fischetti—if it really was him—had offered to help him with Dorsey (who, by the way, really was squeezing Frank's prunes). So here, by accepting Momo's invitation to the show, by occupying a ringside seat next to him, and by being a silent witness to the humiliation of Davis, she had become a part of the Mob. A very marginal, small part, kind of like a mascot at this point. But still a part.

Now, what I want to know from you is this: would *you* have understood this if it had happened to you just the way I said it happened to her? If you're getting ready to say yes, I think this makes you one awfully smart cookie: to see that your acceptance of an invitation to a nightclub performance from a man who intrigued you a little meant that you were now connected to the Mob; that you would be identified that way by them and by those who were controlled by them; and that soon enough you'd be identified that way by certain departments of law enforcement. And this membership wasn't any simple thing, like you'd get a badge, a ring, a passkey, or a card to stick in your wallet. It was a debt: you accepted my favor, you *owe* me. Maybe a long time goes by and I don't collect, but I still have your marker in my pocket. Pretty soon you find yourself in deep with guys who play for keeps and who keep pretty good books, too—up here, in their heads.

Here's a little item that will give you an insight, a secret one at that, into the way the boys played the game with the stars they controlled.

Back in '61 the FBI installed a bug in the wall of Momo's booth at the Armory, the same one Judy had sat in the spring before. Totally illegal, of course, but the bureau got a lot of information from the device they nicknamed Mo, including talk about certain entertainers between Giancana and two other guys the bureau never identified. One guy says to Momo, "You know, I'm beginning to think we're gonna have to crack Frank, but good." Momo kind of grunts at that, and then there's some discussion about how badly things are going out at Frank's Cal Neva Resort at Lake Tahoe, where Momo is a silent partner. Evidently this is the source of the unhappiness with Frank, and Momo is heard saying that he owns most of the resort and gets all the bills. Then the third guy chimes in, saying they need to crack Dean as well, because he's getting very arrogant and brushing off orders. Momo says, "Right, break his jaw for him." And the third guy laughs at that and adds, "Then he can't sing no more." They all have a chuckle before the first guy comes in again and says, "And while we're at it, we ought to put the other eye out on that nigger." Then the subject changes to local stuff. My point is that even though they're laughing here, they aren't kidding around.

That kind of juice and the willingness to use it, that kind of control—like iron—explains why Davis was turning himself inside out for Momo and Joe Fish and why Sinatra had been so aghast when Judy made her defiant comeback to Momo about costume jewelry. When you try to understand her story from here on, you want to keep the existence of this kind of power always on your mind. And at the same time you need to bear in mind the even more awesome power of the federal government, its ability to reach into the most private parts of your daily life and mess with them. And here's this girl, moving back and forth as a cutout between these two outfits, either one of which could easily reach out and just *crush* someone when they felt they needed to do that.

• • •

Spring turned to summer, and Jack kept on winning—Maryland, Indiana, Oregon, building that head of steam he needed to convince the bosses. Meanwhile, he was as good as his word with Judy: he saw her whenever he could. They met at the Navarro in Manhattan. They met at the Mayflower in Washington and again at the N Street house in Georgetown. They met twice in Chicago, and on one of these occasions she set up a meet for him with Momo in her suite at the Ambassador East. This time, though, when she asked him if he wanted her to make herself scarce, he said no, he wanted her to stay in the suite: there were too many people along with him these days, and he didn't want someone seeing her come out of a room he'd just gone into. How they managed to get Giancana in there she didn't say. No doubt he had his own tried-and-true methods, which were probably more intricate than Jack's. So she waited there with Jack for Momo's phone call and then for his knock. When it came, Momo walked right in, went up to Kennedy with a smile, and stuck out his hand. "Hello, Jack," he said, and Jack called him Sam, and then they sat down to talk. She went into the bedroom and read through some magazines until Jack came for her. He told her again how grateful he was for her help, and that made her feel terrific, like she really was part of that Kennedy team she'd first heard about when Pat Lawford had described its workings for Sinatra. Exactly how these meetings were helping the campaign, she didn't know. The main thing was to get Jack elected, something she now strongly believed the country needed.

Before the convention in July she moved out of the Navarro and back to L.A. Jack had asked her to find him a secluded place that he could rent as a second command post and that they could use for their get-togethers after hours. One afternoon she was out apartment hunting and found herself in the West Hollywood area, trying to find a penthouse apartment that sounded promising in an ad. When she asked directions from a muscular young man watering a lawn, he pointed directly across the street from the apartment complex he managed. The neighborhood was quiet, the man named

Max told her, and not that heavily trafficked despite its location. She rented the apartment the next day, and during the convention Max served her and Jack as a kind of lookout and confidant, in one instance steering away some reporters by telling them that if JFK really was staying hereabouts, he'd have noticed and asked him for an autograph. When it was all over she gave him a hundred bucks. Jack didn't give him anything. It wasn't that he was stingy, she said, only that he rarely carried any cash.

When they got together on the night of July ninth, Jack said he judged he was in a solid position to get the nomination. They were sitting up in bed—or rather, she was sitting up. Jack was stretched out with pillows piled beneath his head and shoulders, easing his back. Their lovemaking hadn't gone very well, and so he was glad to shift the subject to politics, though she thought he might not be so much talking to her as thinking out loud. Johnson had just announced that he was in, and Jack was reflecting on all the backbreaking work Johnson had spared himself by sitting out sixteen primaries. But what Jack couldn't have known then and wouldn't learn for some weeks—well after he'd offered Lyndon the second spot on the ticket—was that the day before Johnson had come out to L.A., he and his mentor, Sam Rayburn, had gone to see Ike at the White House to tell him that Kennedy was likely to get the nomination, and that if he did, it would be a national calamity. They told me the goddamnedest stories, Ike later said to a reporter, about all his girlfriends, how bad his health was, how he hadn't really written *Profiles in Courage*. Ike said they begged him to come out publicly against Kennedy and tell the country Kennedy was a dangerous mediocrity whose only real distinction was having a rich father. But Ike refused to do anything of the sort and told them that if Kennedy did get the nomination, he'd have to run against Nixon, and Nixon would beat him.

Even though Jack didn't know anything of this business yet, Judy said his language got "pretty salty" as he discussed Johnson and Truman, and when he got going on Stevenson it was as if his back problems disappeared. He sat up in bed and began sawing the air with his hand, calling Adlai a "limp dick." She noticed, too, that there wasn't any talk now about that retreat to a desert island if he failed to get the nomination. He was out there to *win*, and his determination was like heat coming off him as she sat there next to him. The longer he talked, the hotter he got, throwing the blanket aside and then the top sheet, too, and when he looked over at her he seemed to forget about politics for a while—or maybe politics and sex were the same thing for him in some way he understood but would never explain.

Maybe he wasn't so sure about that win the next night at the hall, because what happened there was a spontaneous, authentic outpouring of affection and admiration for Adlai, the twice trounced. Suddenly they were out in full force with their signs bobbing above all those jostling heads—WE WANT STEVENSON. Anyone who was there like I was or who was watching on TV will never forget it, with that chant building and then being picked up in every part of the hall, all the way back to the last reaches, where the alternate delegates from Anadarko and Ashtabula were standing around in their too-tight suits, waiting for something to happen, and here it came, like a big, roaring wave—WE WANT STEVENSON! And for just those few minutes, that instant, really, you thought, By Christ! they're gonna do it, *again!* They're gonna go with sentiment, with loyalty, with something that has nothing to do with sixteen primaries or two crushing defeats or electability or telegenics, and so forth. And on that roaring wave Adlai was carried to the podium. It was a hell of a thing.

Well, what happened was that Adlai himself got carried away and began to believe he had a shot. So he went to Daley, exactly as old Joe had predicted, and asked him to hold the delegation for him as a favorite son. Meanwhile, of course, Kennedy's people were wearing the phones out, trying to keep Daley and the others in line. But they didn't really have to worry—not about Daley, anyway. He had no use for Adlai, as I've said. So right off he told Adlai to get lost, that he had no support in the delegation. And even though Adlai's name was eventually placed in nomination along with Johnson's and Kennedy's, all he really had to show for the convention was that one great whistles-and-bottle-rockets moment. For an average Joe like me, that would have been plenty: you could live a long time on that memory, I think, seeing that huge hall just light up for you. But for guys who've gone for the whole bundle and come close enough to it, this probably would have tasted a bit like ashes on the rocks.

Well, as you know, Jack won on the first ballot, which had always been a centerpiece of his strategy. If it didn't break that way, he figured, then the convention would blow up into a floor fight, in which case his hard-won image of inevitability would be shattered and his chances would only be about what Johnson's were, maybe a little less. But they held David Lawrence of Pennsylvania, and they held New York, and Daley held Illinois for him, and when the balloting reached Wyoming—which gave him all its votes—they had it. The place erupted, and old Joe was seen for the first time, wearing a big Irish grin, probably made bigger by the fact that on his way to L.A. he'd stopped off in Vegas to place a huge bet on Jack to win on the first.

None of this is in the diaries I saw. And so here's another of these funny things about history that make it so interesting to me. Historians love their firsthand sources, and I told you how flattened I felt when Ed snatched mine from me and I thought I was done. But my sense is that often enough diaries and the like don't tell you that much about the big events of the time, that is, unless the writer himself or herself took a personal part in them—and even then not always. The reasons why memoirs or diaries are begun in the first place usually have nothing to do with the big picture, only with the picture in the mirror—you. This is what keeps the writer at it year after year, volume after volume. When I asked Keneally if he thought this impression was accurate, he said that basically it was okay—he'd never give you a full endorsement. Then he told me about a shoemaker who witnessed the *Hindenburg* go down over Lakehurst. I think he said the guy rescued somebody, but in any case, he was a source for historians of that event. But after his death, when relatives discovered his diaries and wanted to sell them, they found there wasn't a single line in there about the *Hindenburg*. Lots about shoe leather and lasts and problems with immigrant employees, but no *Hindenburg*. No sale, either. So it really isn't surprising to find Judy in the first days of July 1960 writing along about other matters than what was happening at the convention. She wrote about getting things set up at the Rossmore apartment, about shopping for a new outfit she thought Jack would find attractive, about her mother meeting Jack and being absolutely smitten, about how utterly exhausted Jack looked when he could afford to show it. Nothing about his first-ballot win, only about what happened after it.

She'd taken a cab to the penthouse that afternoon and had spent time there arranging things for a small party. She'd hired Max to do the shopping and help her with the setups. After midnight Jack arrived with Kenny O'Donnell, Dave Powers, Peter and Pat Lawford, and three or four young women who'd worked on the campaign. He looked "radiant" to her as he bounded into the apartment, giving her a quick hug and whispering that this wouldn't take long and wouldn't she please be patient because he was counting on being with her.

He was right about the time thing. Everybody dived into the snacks and drinks, and there was a lot of hilarity and toasts and backslapping. But like champagne, it was over quick, you know? Once you pop that cork, the bubbles fade fast. The party broke up, and then Jack gave Judy one of his famous megawatt smiles, took her hand, and led her upstairs, leaving Kenny O'Donnell below to clean up. When they got to the bedroom, though, there was one of the women workers standing at the doors to the terrace, and when they came in she turned and gave Judy a mysterious little smile and disappeared into the bathroom.

Instantly Judy felt a flash of dread, like the return of a nightmare where with the first image you already know everything that's coming. She turned to ask Jack what was going on, and there he was, grinning at her and unbuttoning his shirt. He stopped that and put his arms around her and tried to kiss her. When she struggled, he quit that, too. Then he took a step back and nodded toward the closed bathroom door, explaining with a grin that the girl was going to join them in bed. "It'll be fun," he went on. "Different." But the look on her face made him change tack. "Wait here a second," he said, moving quickly to the bathroom door and knocking. He obviously knew he'd have to do a sales job on Judy, and that might take some time. But already she was on her way out of the room.

He caught up with her at the top of the stairs, and they had it out right there, the brand-new presidential candidate and his furious girlfriend. If they could hear O'Donnell down below in the kitchen—which they could—he could surely have heard them as well, and yet when they went down into the kitchen at last, there was O'Donnell, straightening up and behaving as if nothing at all was out of the ordinary. And so while Jack continued to try to cajole her, O'Donnell kept on emptying ashtrays and putting plates and glasses in the sink. Finally Jack saw that it was hopeless, that she was far too upset for fun, and told O'Donnell to drive her to her apartment. Then he gave her a peck on the cheek and asked her to call him when she was safely home.

All the way over there through the deserted streets O'Donnell kept asking her friendly questions about herself, her family, her interests, and so on. She was hardly in a conversational mood but did her best to be polite until they got to her building, where he pulled over and shut off the motor.

She didn't see it coming, being busy fishing in her purse for her keys. But then he was on her, one hand hard on her breast and his other arm wrapping itself around her shoulders, pulling her into him. She wasn't even shocked, she said, or if she was, she was over it fast and into a rage that was still bubbling down there inside her from the scene at the penthouse. She gave him a tremendous shove with everything she had, sending him back against the door. He said something she didn't catch about only trying to be friendly, but she didn't stop to listen, just flung open her door and ran up the walk to the building. The last she saw of him he was sitting there with the overhead light on and the passenger door still open. You'd like to know, wouldn't you, what the expression was on his face? Judy didn't say.

An audacious move on O'Donnell's part, you think, making a play for Jack Kennedy's girl? Not really, and here's why: Kennedy knew how to keep things separate and in what seemed to him their proper places. He would never get mad at Kenny O'Donnell for a bit of late-night foolishness, because O'Donnell was much too valuable in the daytime. Kennedy had a mind like a bank of file cabinets in some archive, and he knew what was in every folder in every drawer. A lot of crap, mostly right-wing, I think, has been written about his mind: how shallow it really was; how shamelessly he traded on Jackie's intellectual background, inviting Pablo Casals to the White House when he had no idea who the hell Casals was and had to be prompted when to clap. Don't buy most of this, maybe any of it. This crap comes out of the same place that wants to persuade us that Reagan was every bit as profound as Jefferson. Kennedy was brilliant, period. He mastered subjects the way a power mower goes through grass. Somewhere Sorensen was quoted as saying about this campaign that they not only had the best candidate, they had the best campaign manager, too—Jack Kennedy. He knew about everybody of any real importance in every state holding a primary, Sorensen said, and he knew how to use them. This ability to categorize, if that's the word, was maybe Kennedy's most characteristic mental trait: everybody had a place, a slot, if you like (except the old man, who was everywhere). He valued you for this, me for that. He liked to be around certain men who had no terrific skills but who made him feel good, who liked to drink a bit and laugh and chase tail. He valued Salinger because Salinger was a kind of target, hard to miss with his roly-poly build and cigar and ready laugh. But Salinger was a hell of a good manager of the press, and Kennedy understood the high value of such a skill. He valued Sorensen for being able to impersonate him, so to say, knowing not only his philosophy but even the goddamned *cadences* he'd want it expressed in. And he valued Kenny O'Donnell because he was a great field general with a field general's cold head—like the inside of a Good Humor truck on a hot summer's day.

Judy knew it would have been foolish to complain to Jack about what had happened, that he would simply file the incident under some heading that fit and go on relying on O'Donnell and loving Judy in his own style. Because love, too, had its place, its slot, and not long after the convention she made it clear that she understood this. I wish we had a fixed date for this entry, but it has to be sometime between mid-July and the end of September. She had been talking to Jack late at night on the phone, and he'd told her twice that he loved her. "When he tells me that," she said,

> I hear it and I think he means it as much as he can. But Billy told me that and Travis [?] and some others as well and it hasn't worked out that way. So when I hear these words from him I just kind of put them over to one side where I think he keeps them too. I know just where I've put them but I'm not about to go to bed and put my head on them like a pillow. I'm not going to get up in the A.M. and put them on like a bathrobe.

They saw each other when they could during the run for the White House, but now Jack traveled in the full glare of the spotlight every day and night, and he wasn't sure how much he could get away with. That he got away with as much as he did has got to seem amazing to us living in the times we do. You really have to feel for the men and women who decide to run these days, because the spotlight is so pitiless. It wasn't then.

Back then the press corps practiced a kind of code. I don't know if I'd call it exactly a code of honor, though maybe it deserves that word when you stack it up against the practices of today's media types, who will paw through a public figure's trash to find out if his wife is having her period—that really happened to Kissinger. In those days the press had an unspoken agreement that the candidates' private lives were just that. They all knew Jack was getting around on Jackie, but they never said anything that would even hint at that. Oh, here and there some gossip guy might do that, but never mainstream guys, who looked down on the gossipmongers as the outlaws of the profession. Maybe you're thinking here that I was that type myself, considering the kind of work I told you I did for the Katzen brothers. But the dirt I dished—if it really should be called that—wasn't ever *personal.* I might tell you who to see to get a ringside table at the Pump Room so you could overhear Irv Kupcinet interviewing his famous guests. But I never told you who Irv was banging. As a matter of fact, I don't know that Irv was banging anybody. I think he and his wife had a pretty solid relationship for a long, long time, so I use this only by way of illustration.

Anyway, the press corps was an almost exclusively male club that had that clubhouse ethic: you know, What you hear here stays here. And they *loved* Jack Kennedy. He was handsome, witty, accessible, and excellent copy, especially in contrast to Nixon, who was just not very likable and who seemed to go out of his way to make their jobs a little tougher than necessary. So they weren't going to rat Jack out. They envied him—most of them, I'd guess—for all the tail he was getting, and a lot of them were getting what they could, too, on the trail with Jack. So that part of the campaign—and JFK's presidency, for that matter—never got reported until much later. And even then it wasn't reported very well, almost as if, having failed to write—or is it refrained from writing?—that part of the story at the time, they felt they had to make up for it by reporting *everything,* whether it was true or not. So what I just told you about what went down at the Rossmore penthouse after the big win looks pretty different in Teddy White's book on the campaign. He tells us that Jack went back to the apartment so beat that Dave Powers just fixed him a couple of eggs and a glass of milk, and then Jack fell into bed. Now, I'm not here to knock Teddy White: he broke new ground with that book. And it's very likely that his source for this version was either Powers or O'Donnell or possibly Ben Bradlee, a colleague, friend, and for a long time a member of Kennedy's inner circle, who always claimed he knew absolutely *nothing* of Jack's extracurricular activities, not even when Jack was heavily involved with Bradlee's own sister-in-law. (More on that matter in a while.) But White—and here's my point—had to know what was up with Jack, had to know that the story he was given about that night might very well not be true. He simply chose not to pursue it.

Whether White knew about Judy is another of those unanswered questions. I wonder what was known about her at that particular stage among the members of the press corps. To the best of my knowledge there wasn't a single stray reference to her anywhere in print during the campaign. As far as the historical record is concerned, in other words, she didn't even exist, when in fact she played a major role in Jack's getting the nomination. Which brings to mind whoever it was who said, "It ain't what you don't know that hurts you as much as the things you know that ain't so." Following Teddy White and the others, we thought we knew pretty much the full story of that celebrated campaign. Turns out that ain't so.

They saw each other twice in Malibu, where she went after the convention. They got together twice at the Plaza, and he saw her in Chicago. The infrequency of their meetings makes it odds-on that Jack was making it with other women, and I guess you have to allow for the possibility that she might have had a turn or two herself in Malibu. From her account, that was a wild-ass time, with lots of drinking and bed-hopping. She was escaping, and she knew it. Now that Jack had the nomination she was completely convinced he would be president, and that cast their relationship in a whole new light. It was one thing to be seeing a senator who had big ambitions, but to be the secret lover of the president of the United States was something quite different, and it frankly scared hell out of her.

Her entries from this time are almost all pretty sketchy: "Wow what a night. Wow what a head this A.M." "Dick fell in the pool wearing a pig mask pretty funny xcept he almost drowned." That sort of thing. Their sketchiness probably tells you as much as fuller descriptions might. How many ways can you spell *drunk*, you know? But there was also a snapshot clipped to the back of one of the pages that gives you the flavor of it all. It shows her in a Hawaiian-type sarong with a huge glass of something in hand and wearing as well what I guess you'd have to call a really big grin. And right next to her is a guy naked to the waist and wearing a lei, with his arm tight around her. He has a big bomber of a drink too and that same really big grin. Scrawled on the back of the photo is the caption "Luau at Dick's." Dick's a common enough name, of course, but it makes you wonder if this was the same Dick who almost drowned wearing the pig mask. Hell of a way to go.

So she was almost glad that the days kind of flowed together like they will when you're on a sea of sauce. The crowd she hung with was drinking so hard they spent much of the daytimes chasing the dog with bloody marys or mimosas or daiquiris. Then by late afternoon it was time for her to begin her elaborate preparations for the evening blast. She had dabbled at painting and sketching since her teen years and had taken a portable aluminum easel up there, but the routine she was into was hardly set up for that kind of concentration. Actually, it wasn't set up for anything except escape. She gained weight because she wasn't exercising, something she hadn't had trouble with before. In her diary she noted that extra poundage and tried to shrug it off. "I'm a big girl," she said, "and I can carry it better than most." Still, it bothered her, and at one of their meetings at the Plaza she asked Jack if he minded. He told her he didn't, though he himself was incredibly weight-conscious, she said, and a gain of a couple of pounds was enough to send him into a black mood until he'd worked them off.

There are two diaries that take us through the rest of that summer and fall, up through the election. To me, they are crucial in trying to penetrate the murk, the mysteries, the historical blanks of this story. Together, they give me a glimpse—just a fleeting one—of what the relationship between Jack and Judy was really about and what it tells us about her life.

You know, when I was reading around for background on this project, there'd be times when I'd find myself stopping in my tracks and wondering where in this particular book that fleeting glimpse into the heart of the matter was—if it was anywhere. I mean, after all the stats, the voting patterns, the leverage this guy had over that one, the backdoor deals, secret meetings, quid pro quo arrangements, double crosses, and so forth, where is that glimpse of the strange, mysterious phosphorescence of life itself, the *real* thing? Maybe I was goofy looking for that in these history books. Maybe that just isn't what the historians are trying to catch. Maybe they hand this over to the poets or the fiction writers. And maybe that's why so often I felt kind of shortchanged reading around in those books—because it wasn't there. But what the hell is history if it doesn't reach toward that? I hear myself talking to you this way, and I guess I must sound goofy, especially coming from a guy whose life ambition wasn't nearly so high-flown as this but was only to land a steady newspaper gig, and then, later, to get this scoop of the century and tell all about Judy and Jack and lordy, how they did love. Well, as I've said, I came to feel a lot differently about this story, that I wanted way more out of it than that kind of scoop. I wanted more out of you, too.

These two diaries, then. They make a kind of platform, so to say, one you can climb up on and look around and ask some basic questions. What was this thing between Judy and Jack really about? What was in it for Jack? What was in it for her? And then, where does Momo Giancana fit into the picture?

It might seem simple enough to supply the answers for Jack. For starters, of course, Judy was stunning, as I've said. Eddie Fisher said she was right up there with his wife, who at the time was Liz Taylor. This comparison sticks with me for more than the obvious reason—Liz Taylor was *the* big league—because it was echoed in an unlikely place: one of Hoover's agents who was doing his best to make Judy's life a nightmare said she was as good-looking as Taylor. So there was that. And then there was the fact that she was a terrific lover for Jack. She had this big beautiful build and was very athletic, which Jack enjoyed on several counts, not least of which was that he was often so crippled up he couldn't do that much in the sack. Or didn't want to. Finally, she'd done his campaign a signal service by agreeing to be his liaison with Giancana, and I have no doubt that Jack already had further missions in mind for her. As Keneally pointed out, she was perfect for the job, because at that point nobody knew who she was. All this would have been enough and more for any man, even one as hell-bent as Jack Kennedy was to wring as much out of life as humanly possible.

Still, I think there was more to it than these things. But in order to discuss what else there was, we have to approach the relationship through her, because as far as I know Jack Kennedy left no record of how he felt about her—or any other woman he saw from '60 to Dallas. So here's why these two diaries look so important, because in them she talks about her feelings for him, and she talks about what she thinks his feelings for her were. Also, she begins to talk about Momo, who emerges as something more than merely a shady guy who did something for Jack.

In a way, she set the ground rules for this stage of the relationship. Jack was one of those guys who was ready to wrestle the second he got through the door. We know the type, right? Wham, bam, thank you, ma'am. That style, if you could call it that, had been a problem from their first get-together at the Plaza, but after the convention it became an issue, as we say now, and when they were back at the Plaza that summer she decided she had to bring it up. Look, Jack, she said to him, I want to be with you, too, but I just can't do it like this. I'm not built like a light switch. He laughed at that and said it was just as well for both of them that she wasn't because he'd really flipped over the way she was built. She found that funny, and then they shared a laugh, which kind of defused the thing enough for them to have a discussion. The result was that they always talked before they went to bed, and if it was only conversational foreplay for him, it's interesting that he was willing to go along with it.

For her it was a necessity. She was "slow to ignite"—her words once again—and for that to happen she needed time, and it couldn't be spent watching Buffalo Bob on TV. It had to be spent talking about the things in life that mattered most, things that weren't so obvious. She was convinced there was a lot more to the show than what you got on the surface, and Jack Kennedy was both a symbol of the problem of surface versus substance and a living, breathing confirmation of her belief in the existence and greater importance of the latter.

The problem with him was that the surface was dazzling. Tens of millions in the country and abroad, too, were falling for that dazzling surface even while Kennedy was trying to sell them the platform he was running on. You could make a hell of a good case that many of these millions—maybe even most of them—didn't really hear much, if anything, that Jack Kennedy said during that campaign, even when he repeated these things over and over and over. They heard what they saw. Still, there was a real message there beneath the surface, one that, now that we can look back on it—especially now, I guess—appealed to what's best and truest about America. Whereas Nixon's program, while it appealed to "mainstream" American values, sounded oddly stingy and empty of idealism.

Judy Campbell heard Jack's message, the best of it, the heart of it. She caught that idealism, that call to higher things, that whisper of possibility. And the reason she did was that it jibed so perfectly with the kind of person she aspired to be, which wasn't at all the person she felt she'd been trapped into being. All along she had men, famous and obscure, friends and total strangers, falling all over themselves for her surface and not for what was beneath. But how could she be seen truly when to see her was to fall for what you saw? The same thing as with Jack. What she found she wanted from Jack, once she'd gotten over being dazzled herself, was that when he was with her he quit being the John F. Kennedy who was dazzling the country and was the man whose call to higher things she'd heard so clearly.

He was, of course, more sophisticated, more worldly, more intellectual than she was, but there was one thing she thought they could share, and that was Art with a cap A. If they could talk about that, it could lead them on to a deeper layer together. She'd been interested in it since her teen years, as I've mentioned, and even during that Malibu summer she kept that easel set up, though you have to guess her liver got more of a workout than the easel did. Still, the thing was up there, you see, as a symbol of aspiration, and she did do a piece of work there that shows determination. On one of Jack's visits out there she presented him with a pencil portrait she'd done of him. It might have been based on a photo taken either by Joe O'Donnell or that guy Lowe: both of them had quite a bit of access to Kennedy and the family. Interestingly, the portrait isn't of Kennedy as a public figure. Instead, it's Jack in some private moment, chin in hand, looking like some philosopher-king, with his eyes dark and brooding, like he'd been up all night, thinking about the USSR or Castro.

He was flattered by it, telling her she'd caught something no one else had. I've seen a reproduction of it, and I have to say I think it's pretty damned good, but then, I'm no expert on this sort of thing. So I asked Lucy her opinion; she'd taken some art history classes at Illinois' Circle Campus and knew her stuff. She said it showed some talent, but that was all she would say. But by that time she'd lost a certain amount of enthusiasm for Judy's story and my involvement with it. Maybe the talent level of the portrait isn't that important; the intention would be.

The portrait didn't do what she wanted it to, though. It didn't lead them to that deeper level she felt was there for them, and after a few more tries she became convinced that this particular road was blocked because Art was Jackie's territory. Jack had ceded it to her and wasn't eager to discuss it with another woman. To judge from the one exchange she got down in any detail, Jack's MO here was to entertain the subject—but only for a while. Then he would begin to display signs of restlessness, and they would have to move on.

They were at the Plaza again, and she'd spent the middle part of the day at the Metropolitan Museum, where they had an exhibit on Mary Cassatt, the American painter who hung out with the impressionists in Paris. At the museum shop Judy'd bought some Cassatt prints for her new apartment in L.A., and she was showing them to Jack, still full of enthusiasm from the show. He knew Cassatt's work, all right, as she was certain he would, and made a couple of comments about it that included mention of Degas, Cassatt's friend and colleague. But then he kind of pushed the prints aside with the remark that there weren't any men in Cassatt's paintings, only women and children, and he found that boring after a while, accomplished though the works were. He grinned over at her with that brilliant, toothy Irish grin that had just the slightest hint of mischief in it somewhere—you couldn't say just where—and said, "*Vive la différence!*" And so there you had it: his sophistication, his broad knowledge of the world, his wit, even his appetites. I don't know what her response to this was; she didn't say. She would have had to admire the wit and so forth. At the same time, though, you have to think she would've been disappointed at some private level, considering what her motivation was. Sure, it was funny, and yes, *Vive la différence*. Why else were they up in this room if not to act on that difference, take pleasure in it? Still, he'd slipped the punch, so to say, and she'd failed to engage him in the way she wanted—and I don't know, either, what happened then, if that's what you want to ask.

I think basically they were at cross-purposes here. Art may have been Jackie's territory, all right, but the problem wasn't just the subject matter. It was more generally a matter of what he wanted out of their get-togethers. He wanted *release*. Release from the unrelenting pressures of being the man who was supposed to have all the answers, everything from missile gaps to agricultural subsidies to civil rights to how many scientists we were turning out each year versus the Soviet Union. You can hardly blame him. I mean, this is a *crushing* load to have to lug around, day after day, month after month, wouldn't you say? And wouldn't you, if you were in his shoes, once in a while want to just shuck your shoes and coat and sink into the arms of a gorgeous girl and talk about *nothing?* I know I would. Maybe that's why nobody ever thought of me as presidential timber. But my point is serious. Here they were in a posh love nest in a rare moment of privacy, one of them lusting for depth and meaning and the other just lusting. I don't know if this qualifies for tragedy like you have it in Shakespeare, but in terms of ordinary men and women, living their daily lives, I'd say a situation of this kind, where even with the best of wills the man and the woman don't really connect—they just miss—this will do as a species of everyday tragedy.

There isn't a single passage in these two diaries that tells me this flat out. There isn't a sentence that says she's disappointed in their exchanges. But as I told you, I'm a guy who juggles the marbles he's handed, feeling for heft, and I *feel* her disappointment, partly because she never says, "Wow! What a great discussion I had with Jack!" Never, at least not in anything I had a look at. And when I think about it, the way things turned out between them, the choices she went on to make, I have to feel this was major.

Finally she'd had enough of the boozy, drifting Malibu scene. This was in late summer. Maybe her body told her, Enough, and maybe, too, it was the fact that the redecorating of her apartment on North Flores was finally done and so there wasn't that excuse to stay on. She moved in the first week of September. But she'd only been in it a few days when she decided to go to Chicago to hang out with Momo Giancana over a long weekend. They'd been talking on and off all through the summer, with him urging her to come out, and for whatever reasons, she went and took a room at the Ambassador East.

He met her at O'Hare, and they drove into the city in one of his ratty cars to drop her bags at the hotel. When she got up to her room she found it was almost overflowing with bouquets of yellow roses. The smell was nearly suffocating, like that of a funeral parlor. Nevertheless, when she got back down to Sam in the lobby she gave him a smile, and he tipped his hat. They had martinis and lunch somewhere on Rush Street, not out at the Armory, and when they'd finished he asked her if she'd like to come out and see his house. After the flight, the martinis, and lunch, where Sam had made her laugh several times, she was feeling very relaxed and pleased to be in the company of this man who never asked anything of her—except that he be allowed to please her in his own tough-guy way. So she said sure, and they drove west to the border of Forest Park and River Forest.

Quiet neighborhood tucked behind the hustle of Harlem Avenue. Two- and three-story middle-class bungalows with little front lawns: typical street for the western suburbs. And nothing in the least unusual about the two-story red brick at the corner of Wenonah and Jackson, either. Maybe it was a little nicer, with its green-tiled roof and long hedge, maybe a little bigger than its neighbors, but not by much. After getting a load of Momo's taste in cars and restaurants, she didn't know what to expect of his home and was pleasantly surprised. When they'd parked in the one-car garage behind, he pushed two buttons on a full panel, one of which pulled down the garage door and the other of which alerted the house. At the back steps they were met by a squat, broad-shouldered guy wearing suspenders over his T-shirt, smiling broadly at both of them. "Sam introduced me to his cousin," she said. "I couldn't get his name. He spoke only Italian but was very polite and welcoming."

Momo showed her through the house, which was laid out in long rectangular rooms with all the heavy curtains drawn. The living room furniture was covered in thick plastic wraps that crackled loudly when you sat down, and it was obvious it was seldom used. There were two glass-doored cabinets in there that he insisted she inspect carefully; they were filled with tiny Chinese figurines. She made a show of interest, picking up several and turning them about in her hands, meanwhile thinking that they weren't her thing at all. Painting, yes; miniature figurines, no. The master bedroom above was brimming with another sort of collection, this one of religious items: rosaries, crucifixes, portraits of Jesus, and a painting of a heart on a purple cushion with a crucifix in the background. On the bureau was a little altar: a medium-sized photo of a woman in soft focus flanked by two flickering votive candles and a smaller photo of what appeared to be the same woman, here shown with Sam, squinting into the sun on a beach somewhere. He told her she was his wife, who had died some years back. "He didn't make a big deal out of it," she said, "didn't carry on about her and somehow it was more touching to hear him just state the facts."

Coming down the back staircase to the kitchen, she heard voices and found the cousin with two women about his age and two gradeschoolers. Sam introduced her around, laughing and clearly proud to show her off. They were all talking Italian and seemed very animated and friendly. They were relatives of his, he told her, and lived in the house, taking care of it when he was away on business trips. "All except the kids," he said laughingly, nodding at the gradeschoolers. "They don't have to do nothing but ride the gravy train and keep their noses clean. Don't seem like a whole lot to ask, but these days I guess it's hard." He laughed again at his own joke. She couldn't tell if the relatives understood what he was telling her, but the kids did, because they smiled and looked down at the floor. Nor could she figure out where they could all be bunking, because when he'd showed her around, there hadn't been a sign of the presence of another soul, and except for the master bedroom the place seemed deserted. That had made the house feel gloomy to her, what with its drawn curtains and the heavy-duty religious items, and she was thinking it would be a relief to get back to the city, where she knew Sam had made a dinner reservation for them. But now she heard Sam talking with one of the women and gesturing toward the refrigerator, and then the woman went to it, looked at what they had on hand, and said something to him that made him light up.

He turned to Judy and smiled in such a genuine way that she found herself grinning back, though she had no idea at what. "She's gonna make us a chicken dish, Italian style, that's out of this world," he told her. "You can't get chicken like this anywhere in the city—nowhere!" The women were even happier about this than he was. You'd have thought the king himself had just dropped by to say he wouldn't mind having a bite.

While the women were putting that together, Sam said he had a couple of things to do in the neighborhood and asked her to ride along with him. When he was wheeling them around the city, weaving in and out of traffic, making risky lane changes, and so forth, Momo kept up a steady stream of chatter, making wisecracks, teasing her a little, laughing when she flinched at some maneuver of his. Now, though, he was quiet, and she was beginning to imagine they were on their way to some big-time meet. Instead, it turned out to be Mount Carmel Cemetery and the grave of his wife. He came out here two or three times a week when he was in town, he said, to pay his respects to Angeline, who'd been a good wife to him and a wonderful mother to their three daughters. When he said this they were standing at the grave itself, with its big gray-white marble slab and the names of family members chiseled into it, and she thought she heard a hard edge come into his voice and glanced quickly over at him, but she resisted the temptation to ask about those daughters. A few minutes later she got the answer to her unasked question, when they were driving toward the gates and Momo said that Annette had broken her mother's heart. "Bonnie and Francine, they're doing okay," he told her, "but that Annette, she's a fucking *mess*—pardon my French. You name it, she's done it—alcohol, drugs, abortions—*abortions!* That there killed Angie." He rolled down the window and spat as if clearing the bum daughter from his system—for the moment, anyway.

That was all he said, and since she couldn't think of anything to say in reply, they rolled on in silence into the parking lot of what he told her was his family's church, Saint Bernadine's. Inside he wanted to show her the marble communion rail and the six stained glass windows he'd donated to "kind of spruce things up a little." She told him she'd been raised Catholic herself but had very mixed feelings about what she called her "indoctrination" and hadn't been to mass or confession in a long time. When he heard this, he looked at her steadily a long moment, then cocked his head the way he had when she'd come back at him at the Fontainebleau. It was his way of saying something like "That's no way to talk—but okay." Then he turned in a half-circle, taking in much of the interior, and said, "I don't come in here that regular myself. Only I like to come in here like now, when there's nobody around. That way I get to appreciate the place without being bothered. Lots of beautiful things to look at." He smiled slightly and nodded to the side door and they went out. Suddenly it smelled like fall to her, cool and with somebody nearby burning leaves.

"You're gonna love M.A.'s *pollo*," he told her, repeating that "nobody in this city does it as good." Later she wrote down that Sam hadn't oversold M.A.'s cooking. It was the best Italian-style chicken dish she'd ever tasted.

Whether there was something about her new place she was having trouble adjusting to or whether it was because her relationship with Jack made her feel her life was like a balloon in the wind—or both—she couldn't sit still on North Flores. When she got back from Chicago, right away she went up to Carmel with some of the Malibu crowd to watch a golf tournament at Pebble Beach. And when she got back from that she got a call from Jack, asking her to come to Chicago before the first debate with Nixon. Would she do this for him? It would be wonderful to be in her company, and he thought she might find the event more interesting than the usual campaign routine, since it was to be the first of its kind ever. She said she'd be there, and booked a room at the Ambassador East again, where Jack and his people would also be staying.

Late on September twenty-fifth he slipped his entourage of writers and coaches and paid her a visit. It was a thrill, she had to admit, that he wanted to be with her on the eve of this historic occasion, and she found him especially tender and patient. Afterward, they "cuddled" while she told him about her new apartment and filled him in on some of that Hollywood gossip he could never get enough of. She didn't tell him she'd just been here, hanging with Momo. And for his part, he volunteered almost nothing about the campaign, only observing that his father seemed to be getting more of a boot out of it all than he himself was: hardly surprising, of course, when you remember the old man's driving desire to have a son in the White House, plus the fact that Jack had been at it eight months now, and it had become just a daily grind. He said he'd grown to hate being touched all the time by complete strangers and had to steel himself not to flinch noticeably when the hands came toward him.

They went on talking this way and finally dozed off, so it was after three in the morning when he said he'd better go back upstairs before everybody got worried and called the house dick or the cops or that other dick, Daley. "He thinks he won this," Jack told her. "Bullshit. *I* won it." If she was in the mood, he went on, stepping into his trousers and talking to her over his shoulder, he'd like to come back late in the afternoon, before he and his people went over to the CBS studios to check out the lighting, the backdrop, and the positioning of the chairs and podiums.

It was close to four when he came down that afternoon after a long session with his coaches. Up in his suite he'd laid there in bed, propped by pillows, his hands full of note cards on the various topics likely to come up. When he was satisfied with his answers to the questions his coaches threw at him, he flipped the cards one by one to the floor. He'd also completely rewritten the opening eight-minute statement they'd prepared for him. When he walked into Judy's room he was dressed in khaki slacks, a white V-neck T-shirt, and loafers with no socks. She'd never seen him casually dressed in person, though of course there'd been plenty of photos in the press of him sailing, playing touch football, and the like, but seeing him like this made him suddenly more real to her, more "available," as she put it. She told him he looked fabulous, and maybe this was why for a change she took the lead in their lovemaking, though Jack was quick to follow. "I never feel good about romance that's over and done with as quick as possible," she said. "To me that kind of thing just misses the whole point. Billy was always that way. If you're just there to get to the finish line as fast as possible there are ways to do that that don't involve other people. But this was really sweet short as it was. Something special that I'll remember."

Jack left at the last possible moment, and standing at the doorway, he told her he planned to take the Republican platform apart, plank by plank, but he wasn't going to go after Nixon himself. "I'll let him do that," he said with a sort of grim smile. And that's what he did, too, and brilliantly.

Having told you a while back about what Teddy White didn't have in his account of Jack's night after winning the nomination, I think it's only fair to tell you now that his description of that first debate is still the best I know of, the most thorough and astute: he had everything in there, from the technical details of TV broadcasting at that time to JFK's rhetorical strategy, clothing choices, and body language, which combined to make Nixon look weak and ineffectual. In fact, Nixon really was sick. He'd been in the hospital for an infected cut on his knee and had lost a lot of weight. Then, coming into the WBBM studios, damn if he didn't bang that knee again. He was a clumsy guy, and later they said he used to give himself skull knots all the time getting in and out of presidential limos. Anyway, in contrast to Kennedy he just looked awful on camera. When they dollied in on him for the first time, staring up at Kennedy, who was at the podium, he looked haggard, unshaven, and what's more, he looked positively *jealous* of JFK. It was kind of shocking to see that emotion so obviously there on a face that looked so beaten up. Somebody later on reported that when Daley saw that first close-up, he roared to all the others watching with him, "My God! They embalmed him before he was even dead!" Maybe not the most charitable thing you could have said, but then Hizzoner played for keeps, always.

Then you got your first up-close look at JFK, and as I say, the contrast was just amazing. Maybe the best description of it wasn't any of the ones you've already heard but the one Judy wrote down in her hotel room, where just hours before he'd been in bed with her. "Jack looked like he'd been chipped out of an iceberg," she said. "I've never seen him that cold and hard. I almost felt sorry for Nixon. He looked like it had just dawned on him that he wasn't going to get to be president after all."

For the most part, as you might remember, Kennedy stayed with the strategy he'd announced to her as he left her room. He didn't go after Nixon as Nixon. His approach was as if he didn't consider Nixon the candidate really all that relevant; he was merely the latest in a long line of GOP candidates who had opposed every piece of progressive legislation since before the Great Depression, everything from decent wages for the working man to expanded public school facilities to the TVA and other beneficial uses of America's natural resources. This might not have been entirely fair, but it was effective, because it forced Nixon to answer for a lot. In other words, it put him on the defensive for the first time in the campaign.

Still, when it was over and the pundits and pollsters began their assessments, whereas you saw a clear Kennedy victory, it seemed like you *heard* a Nixon win. I watched it, and my buddies and I whooped and hollered because we thought Kennedy had just trounced Nixon, all of us crowded around a set about the size of one of those portholes you look through to see how your clothes are doing at the laundromat. But as I say, we hadn't been listening as much as we'd been looking at Nixon with his Lazy Shave makeup running in streaks through the sweat on his face, while JFK was completely cool and composed, with dozens of facts and statistics at his fingertips and rolling them off like an assembly line of stinging criticisms of the Grand Old Party.

Regardless of whether you watched or listened on the radio, though, I think it's pretty much agreed that the first debate changed the general perception of the race. After Chicago, Nixon was one of two candidates for the same job and with no more juice or credibility than the other guy. His running mate, Lodge, might not have been right when he said after the first debate, "That sonofabitch just lost the election." But it was clear Nixon would have to duke it out with Kennedy on an equal basis—as equal as these things get, anyway.

Was it stolen? People have been trying to find the answer to that for years, ever since the polls closed, in fact. And still it seems to depend on who you ask and even the way you ask it, because there just isn't that smoking gun. In an odd way, it's like asking, later on, who killed the official winner.

If you want to go strictly by the arithmetic of the thing, then Illinois turns out not to be more crucial than Michigan, which seems to have been fair enough, or Texas, where the results were also disputed. The turnout was huge—something like 63 percent—which these days doesn't look huge so much as it looks impossible. And with that volume, the largest in our history to that time, still it finally came down to a baby's handful of states.

What Phil Keneally said to me was that if using your money to bribe some voters and to make certain that others turned out in force—if this means it was stolen, it was. But if these are your criteria, then what election wasn't? We were having this conversation (you understand I use the term loosely) at a diner on West Fullerton a couple of blocks from his apartment. The night before I'd slept badly, and I was bushed as hell. At the time I was fighting just to stay awake instead of battling to get beneath Judy's straight-ahead style to what I thought must be there. He saw this—or at least part of it—from the command post of his lounger.

"You need a boot up your ass and a cup of joe," he barked, "but I don't have time for both. Let's go over to Dimo's."

This was one of the few times we did anything that could remotely be called social, a mostly silent walk up to West Fullerton, which wouldn't easily be mistaken for an extension of the Miracle Mile. There was this sweaty little diner he went to, and when we were seated at a table and had given our order, I'd asked him that question. Clearly he'd been asked it a hundred times before. He heaved those massive, line-busting shoulders and glanced at the window, which was runny with steam.

"These days," he began, rummaging for his smokes, "it's all open and aboveboard but amounts to the same thing. The fucking guys line up with their checkbooks hanging out like their cocks at a short-arm inspection. True, they don't have to skin 'em back for the orderly to have a look, like in the service, but you almost expect some political suit to take the checkbook and look at the balance to make sure the guy's worth their time. Nobody thinks a thing of it. Just the way democracy works now. If the amount they give is big enough, they get a photo with the president, or they might even get to sleep in Honest Abe's bed. But the bottom line is they've brought their particular need to executive attention, and they know they'll get some sort of return on their investment—maybe not the whole hog, but something. And this happens all the way down to the local-local level, where maybe the checks aren't so big but other things of a horse-trading nature are tossed into the bargain." He flapped his hand as if brushing away a fly. "You know all this, everybody knows it. And that's the real point—*everybody* knows it. What went down in 'sixty wasn't new. Maybe the scale of the thing was different, and maybe the Kennedys had the machine retooled and a couple of extra cylinders put in, but that's all.

"I told you what I saw in Tuohy's chambers, and then, later, we know what Daley said on the phone to Hyannis Port on election night. And we know what your girlfriend said Giancana used to throw in her face all the time, right?" When he delivered this last he hunched forward, and he loomed so huge at that table that it felt like our noses were touching. He was peering at me with a kind of feral intensity, wanting to make sure I was alert enough now to merit his time, the things he knew. I tried my best to look bright and eager and to come back at him in a snappy fashion to avoid one of his foul-mouthed assaults, there being customers scattered about a place that wasn't very big. So I said, Yeah, sure, I knew the references. I did, too, though I don't know if I could have rattled them off just then if he'd asked me to. I knew he could have.

I can now, though. When the polls had closed in Illinois and the state looked like it was still up for grabs, the Kennedy people were barraging Daley with calls, asking him minute by minute how it was looking. So finally, maybe in part to get rid of them so he could get some sleep, Daley gets on with Jack himself and says, Look, stop sweating this: with the help of some good friends of yours, you're going to carry Illinois.

Now, when you're looking for proof the thing was rigged and you have this remark in your hands, you see what a clever bit of wording it was. Daley didn't say, We're gonna steal it for you. He didn't say, We're stuffing the boxes up here in Cook County; get some sleep. He didn't say, We're gonna count the other guy out. If somebody at the time had a tap on that line or if somebody later on got hold of this remark, all they would have in their hands might very well be Daley merely saying, Relax, Jack, your friends out here, the good people of Illinois, are going to carry the day. You ain't gonna hang anybody on that. At the same time, though, if the fix really was in, this could just as easily be Daley reminding the Kennedys that he had their marker and in good time would call it in. Damned clever guy, there.

The other reference, the Giancana one, doesn't have a lot of cleverness to it, but like almost everything else, it seems, there's more than one way to look at it. Well after the election was over and Jack was in the White House, Giancana said to Judy, who might have been gushing on about Jack this and Jack that, "Listen, honey, if it hadn't been for me, your boyfriend wouldn't even be in the White House." Maybe this was bragging, motivated by stud rivalry.

After all, let's not forget that from that first meeting at the Fontainebleau, Momo had made it clear he wanted Judy for his own. But even when you make a large mental allowance for this, I think developments over the next three years tell you that there was a hell of a lot more to this than just a brag, that Giancana really believed it. He believed that his efforts had been a major factor in putting Illinois in the Kennedy column, and that in doing what he did he'd held up his end of the bargain he'd made with the old man back in February. This is the only way you can account for his attitude toward the Kennedys up to the assassination and beyond, too: Hey, I came through for you. Where are you guys?

Now, whether he was actually right about this might be another matter, as well as one we'll never have a definite answer for, because we can't know how many votes Momo actually delivered or how these figured in the final tally. We don't know what the final tally was, either, because when the Republicans hollered foul, Daley was able to quash a full recount in Cook County, and so what we're left with is an "official" tally vigorously disputed by the losers. And all this is without even considering Michigan and LBJ's Texas. Still, the thing to keep in mind is what Momo believed.

Judy didn't know anything about this inside stuff. We can be sure of that. Jack would never have told her, pillow talk and all. And as far as I can tell from what she said about Giancana, he didn't tell her either—about his deal with the old man. All he ever did was to drop that veiled hint about his help, and this, as I say, was well after the fact. No, as far as she was concerned, this was a straight up-and-down deal, though she never said anything specific about the big win, not even if she voted: no exulting comments about Jack and how proud of him she was; no spilled milk entries either, like, There goes our island paradise, and so forth. The first entry of any interest as far as she and Jack were concerned was about ten days after the election, when she said Jack had called her to say he wanted to see her as soon as he could and that when he could figure out how to arrange that, she'd hear from him. Nothing, he told her, had changed between them. But that, as it turned out, wasn't really accurate. She found that out on November twentieth.

On that afternoon she'd been out shopping, one of her favorite sports. When she got back to her apartment and walked through her living room with her arms full, she caught a glimpse of an unfinished portrait on her easel and had a sudden inspiration about what to do with it. It was of a solemn, huge-eyed child, symbolic of all the orphans and war victims around the world. She'd been working at it, not very consistently, it seems, but now she felt she wanted to plunge right back into it. She dropped her purchases on the kitchen table, poured herself a glass of white wine, and put a Rachmaninoff record on the hi-fi.

She was absorbed in it when the doorbell rang, startling her, not only because she was so absorbed, but also because her building had an entry-level buzzer system that screened callers. When she asked who it was, a man's voice answered that it was the FBI. They wanted to talk to her. She was so scared by that that she opened the door and let two guys in without even asking for ID. But they held out their badges while she just looked at them with her jaw dropped: fedoras, dark suits, white shirts, narrow ties—standard-issue Hoover types. That's an easy observation from here, though, whereas if it had been you or me standing there, it would have been plenty scary. Whatever image it may have now in the public mind, back then the FBI was like God's own arm in law enforcement, and your immediate instinct was to buy everything its agents said and to cooperate as quickly as you could.

Just inside the door, they started in on her, one of them focusing on her face, staring into her eyes, while the other guy began roaming around the living room, not touching anything, just casing the joint and managing to be both obnoxious and menacing at the same time. Her instant feeling was that she somehow didn't have the right to be here, that this was a "crime scene," as she put it. Agent One, in front of her, seemed to be in charge and was asking her questions such as, This your place? Who pays your rent?

How long have you lived here? Who else lives with you? Then he got right down to it: "Do you know a Sam 'Momo' Giancana?" he asked. She was so shaken that when she asked in response, "Do I know who?" she could see in the man's face that he knew she wasn't fencing with him, that for the moment she hadn't any idea who Giancana was. Being that rattled up will do this to you, so that if you were asked just your name, you might not be able to come up with it right off. But on top of this Agent Two, standing behind her, asked her if she knew a Mr. Flood. While she was trying to field that one, Agent One pointed at the big brooch she was wearing. Ordinarily, she said, she'd have put a smock on when she was painting, but on this occasion she had been so hot to get right to work on the portrait that she hadn't.

"Is that the kind of present Sam Giancana buys you, young lady?" he asked, gesturing with his forefinger.

(Considering the history of this particular item, here was an unconsciously ironic question, since it was the same brooch Momo had instantly spotted as a fake, whereas the FBI guy took it for the real thing. I'm not sure exactly what this tells you; maybe only that Momo dealt in all sorts of fakes, forgeries, bogus bills, and the like and therefore knew when someone was trying to pass something. But you know, I've thought back more than a few times to that first encounter at the Fontainebleau, and I think now that in its crude way his remark was really a tribute to her, to the way she looked, to the way he thought she ought to look.)

By this point her legs were shaking so hard she didn't think they'd hold her up, and so she flopped down into a chair. They sat down opposite her on the couch, side by side. They still had their hats on, like those detectives on the old *Dragnet* show, and there might have been something almost comic about it all, except they kept on relentlessly with their questions, asking her if she knew a John Roselli, a Charles Fischetti, and any number of other names she didn't remember. No wonder.

Finally Agent One let up a little, changing his tone and seeming to want to give her some friendly advice. He said something like, Listen, young lady, we know you know Sam Giancana or Mr. Flood or whatever other names he uses around you. But what you may not know is that your generous friend is a highly dangerous hoodlum with an arrest record longer than both your arms. If he's buying you presents like that—nodding at the brooch—you can be dead certain of one thing: sooner or later he's going to collect. He's going to ask you for something that will be triple the value of all the presents you ever got from him.

This accidentally turned the trick: it made Judy mad instead of scared. "I wouldn't have told them a single solitary thing about Sam after that," she said, "not if my life depended on it. He's been nothing but nice to me a real friend and when I make a real friend I keep him. I feel happy and relaxed around him which is a lot more than I can say for these strangers who barged in on me and gave me the 3rd degree. I told them I had absolutely *nothing* to say about any of the individuals they'd asked me about and that I wanted them to leave immediately."

Agent One said it would be a lot safer for her if she cooperated with them now, that she seemed to be a nice girl, and that it would be a shame if she allowed herself to be dragged into the gutter by scum like Sam Giancana. He thought she probably wasn't too deeply involved yet for them to help her out, but she'd have to help them in return. Very soon it would be too late for them to be of any help. He told her to think it over and handed her a card with his name and a phone number where he could be reached, day or night. Then they left.

She couldn't remember—or maybe the better word would be *reconstruct*—how long she sat in the chair, but gradually it came to her that she'd been staring at her unfinished portrait and that the huge eyes that she'd hoped would express the pathos of unmerited suffering now appeared to be accusing her of something, as if the thing that she'd started to work on had somehow been taken over by the FBI. She staggered up and turned it to the wall. While she was over there she glanced at the silent hi-fi and saw her half-filled glass. She took it into the kitchen and poured the wine down the drain; then, without rinsing it, she filled it full of green chartreuse and slugged it down. She said she didn't really know what she was doing, and at that moment maybe she really didn't. I've heard of something called a daytime nightmare, but I don't know if the sufferer can recollect what he or she was doing while in that state. I don't know, either, when it was she got these details down, because they seem to me pretty sharp. She also remembered that her first "practical" thought was to call Jack. After all, he was the new president; he'd know what to do.

He'd given her a number in Hyannis Port, one that only he ever answered. She thought she called it but later wasn't sure whether she did or had only dreamed it. "I doubt I got much more than an hour's real sleep that night," she said. "The whole thing was like a revolving nightmare, where the same things kept coming around again and again. And I kept thinking, what in God's name is this thing I've gotten myself into."

4

KILLING MISTAHCASTRO

DAYS LATER, WHEN SHE finally reached Jack and told him what she'd been through, he was surprised, or said he was. Right off, he wanted to hear what the agents' questions had been, whether there'd been a theme to the inquiry. He didn't ask whether his name had come up, but then he wouldn't have had to: she would have told him that. He was quiet for a few moments, and she could almost hear him on the other end, whipping through the possibilities. When he went on, it was to say that as far as he knew Hoover wasn't vigorously investigating Giancana or any of what Jack called his "associates," but for years it had been the director's public position that organized crime was largely a myth. There were only criminals, and he, J. Edgar, was their sworn enemy. Jack told her to sit tight with this—maybe it was a fluke, some kind of aberration, or something like that. He was sorry about it, sorry it had been so upsetting. Then he switched to his own problems.

So far he'd found that being elected was "pretty much a pain in the ass." This guy wanted this from him, that one wanted that, and another fellow said he was owed such-and-such a consideration. There was no way he could possibly satisfy all these people, and the process was going to continue on for a good while yet. It was tiring and tiresome both, but there was no way he could figure out how to delegate it, much less escape it. Then there was the problem of putting together his cabinet and his team of advisers, something he hadn't given much thought to. He'd been so busy trying to get elected that now it was hard to change gears immediately and find the right people to help him run the goddamned country. In Palm Beach, when he'd gone to his father to complain about all the petitioners and the sudden difficulty of putting a team together, he hadn't gotten any sympathy from the old man. Far from it. Joe Kennedy had been a demanding father to his children, particularly his sons, and just because Jack was now the president-elect, that didn't change. According to what Jack told her, old Joe said that if he didn't want the job, "they were still counting ballots out in Cook County." How about that for the purest piece of cynicism you ever heard? She didn't know what was meant by that, except that Illinois had been very close. And she had to confess to herself that she hadn't thought about what sort of a team he'd assemble either. The best she could come up with was to say she was sure he'd choose the best possible men for the job. When they'd finally hung up, she found herself feeling more alone with her FBI problem than ever, instead of being reassured by her lover, who now occupied the highest place in the land. If Jack couldn't offer more than to tell her to sit tight, who could?

When they spoke again, he never mentioned the matter at all. What he wanted her to know was that he'd taken a suite at the Mayflower that he'd be using on and off until he moved into the White House, and he wanted to see her there as soon as possible. What about the week after Thanksgiving? Something about the call bothered her enough for her to say only that she'd see what she could work out, hearing herself saying this to the newly elected president and having at the same instant a vivid picture of his handsome face and body, of their times together. What other girl in her right mind, she wondered, would stall Jack Kennedy—which was just what she was doing? Was she in her right mind these days? She slept badly on it, and when he called the next day she said she could do it, and she did.

How that rendezvous went I have no idea, because the only thing she said about it was that he'd pressed her hard to come to the inauguration, and she'd responded that she'd feel terribly awkward around Jackie and the children. He seemed puzzled by this: the whole show would be great fun, and he'd given her friend Frank a big role in organizing the entertainment. With all the receptions and balls and so on, even a beauty like her might well be lost in the crowd, but *he* would know she was there, and that would mean a lot to him. As for Jackie, she wouldn't be around that much. She hated crowds, lights, hoopla, and was still recovering from the difficult birth of their son John. Besides, when she'd posed for the photographer Richard Avedon at the White House, she'd already worn the gown Oleg Cassini had designed for her, so that thrill was over. What she would probably do, he said, was make a couple of brief appearances and then retire for the night. It wasn't every day, he said, laughing, that Judy would have the chance to see a "mackerel-snapper get crowned king of America" and know that the king was in love with her. So how about it?

The man's personal charm was immense, especially up close, which is where you'd have to guess they were having this conversation. She told him she'd think it over but not to count on it. That, he came back, "is exactly what I'm going to do."

Afterward, outbound at the airport, she suddenly found herself painfully conscious of being merely a stranger there, passing through and surrounded by other strangers on errands that probably meant something to them but that might well turn out to be completely pointless. When she was in Jack's company she couldn't feel any other way than completely special. True, they knew each other pretty well by now, and so that primitive—if I can use that word to mean something like first or original—thrill was gone from their encounters. Still, there were those amazing moments when Jack turned it all on, making her believe she was the only girl on the planet and that each movement of hers, each word and expression, was of a singular and unrepeatable importance to him. If some of this was an act, it was a damned convincing one, and she felt it couldn't be *all* act, that he really felt that way about her much of the time. She'd known enough men to be able to tell the difference between a rock and a rhinestone. Now, though, waiting for her plane, she didn't feel special in any way—except for the fact that among all these passing strangers she was most likely the only one who was being investigated by the FBI. For what she said was the first time in her life she felt physically uneasy about what was behind her, a feeling that was "like an itch but cold at the same time between my shoulders." She would have been ashamed to whirl around to find out what was back there, but what she did do was pick out a seat where her back was to the wall. Having done that, she looked up to find two beefy business types leering at her. Such was her state of mind, though, that for a moment she wondered whether they might be agents, then instantly dismissed it: they were too "civilian." But in the following instant she decided definitely she wouldn't be coming back here for Jack's coronation; even though it was true the agents had found her in her home, she still felt more exposed here.

She told him that as soon as she was back in L.A., but added that her mother would love to attend if he could see to that. He said that he'd immediately add Katherine Immoor's name to the list, if it wasn't already there, and that he was having an invitation sent to her as well. "You'll change your mind," he predicted breezily. "This will be something you won't want to miss."

If he didn't seem to get why she continued to say no, she herself didn't seem to get why it was so important to him that she be there. After all, they certainly weren't going to have any private time together. Later on, she had some things to say about coming to understand how reckless he could be, but at this point she didn't put together all the instances of it that she'd already been a part of, beginning with that poolside incident in Vegas when he'd interrupted a press conference to announce that he'd be right with her. I mean, even considering how the press operated back then, that's right out there. And then later, of course, there would be the daytime visits to the White House, where they were in full view of everybody, from servants to staff.

Since his death, of course, there's been a fair amount of ink shed on this aspect of his character. To many who knew him, he seemed to imagine that even if he might well be fated to die young, in some way or for some reason he was immune to scandal and discovery. Now, whether he thought this was immunity purchased by his family's vast fortune and power is a question. That can buy you a hell of a lot, though as the lives of other Kennedy family members have shown through the intervening years, it can't buy you true immunity by any means: the increasing technological power and reach of the media have drawn even, so to say, with money and position, so that these days *nobody* gets a pass anymore. Maybe, too, seeing what his father got away with sort of rubbed off on Jack, making him think, Well, hell, the old man did this and that, and so why can't I? Lots of beautiful women out there on the loose. Might be natural enough, especially if privately he considered himself more sexually appealing than Joe. But I don't get the impression that Joe got an actual *high* out of living dangerously. Sure, he wanted to bed Gloria Swanson and Dietrich, but he wasn't going to risk everything he'd worked so hard to get to do that. Jack, on the other hand, was willing to take that kind of risk—looked forward to it, in fact. There was something deeply attractive about doing things when the chances of discovery were great, like swimming naked in the White House pool with Fiddle and Faddle or getting Jackie to hire one of his girlfriends, Pam Turnure, as her personal secretary. I use the word *attractive* here because it's been said that there's a kind of sexual component to the high he evidently got from living so close to the edge. I'm no Freud or Kinsey, so I can't tell you how this kind of thing might work, but we're both familiar with the scene where the husband who's started up with the girl from the office then goes out of his way to bring her to the attention of his wife. Tell me where that impulse begins and what its goal is, and I'll tell you that you have a great new career ahead of you. Here, with this inauguration deal, my thought is that Jack was hot to see Judy, this unknown beauty, mixing with the high and mighty while he stood off there, smiling and knowing things about her that none of them could possibly imagine. It didn't happen, though. She stuck by her original decision. Her mother went, but Judy stayed home, watching the TV coverage at her parents' place.

It really was a tremendous occasion all around—Jack was right about that. I wonder if we've had an equal to it since or ever will. Kennedy had Marian Anderson there to sing the national anthem; that was a masterstroke of historical theater, because, if you recall, Eleanor had had Anderson perform at the Lincoln Memorial after the DAR shut her out of Constitution Hall. And he had Frost read a poem, but the winter sun was so bright the old boy couldn't see the page, and so he recited it from memory—which was even better. Judy said she cried at that, it was so touching, and she probably had plenty of company there. Then Jack's speech was spellbindingly brilliant, and he delivered it with an equal brilliance, chopping the air with his right hand as Judy had so often seen him do in the privacy of their bed, and making all the right emphases and dramatic pauses. Right-wingers will tell you the speech was Ted Sorensen's from first word to last, and there's no doubt his hand is on it, all right. But as I've already said, Sorensen knew Kennedy's mind and philosophy so well he could impersonate them, and so what you had there was really JFK, and anyway, the thing went through numerous drafts, with Jack adding more and more stuff as it came to him. For whatever it's worth, I had a downstate lawyer once tell me that Lincoln lifted some phrases from Seward for the Gettysburg Address.

Kennedy apparently told someone he wanted the speech to be as good as Jefferson's—quite an aspiration. Afterward, he confided to Jackie that he knew he'd fallen short of that mark. But whether he had or not, the speech he gave was right down Main Street in its

American idealism, the true stuff, us at our best. After it was over, Judy wrote that "this is the man I love and the country does too." Whatever her full feelings were at that moment in all their complexity, there's no doubt in my mind that she did love this man just then and that she was probably right that America too must have loved the man they saw and heard in that sharp, sunlit moment. It was blazingly cold that day, and Jack sat through the entire parade, hatless and clearly enjoying every band, every float, every twirl of the baton and clop of horses' hooves. When a PT boat labeled 109 was hauled by on a flatbed, he stood up and clapped and followed it with his eyes until he couldn't see it anymore.

I don't remember now how much TV coverage there was of the balls and receptions that night or even whether there was any. But there were a lot of memorable stills: Jack and the radiant Jackie stepping out of the White House for the evening; the couple arriving; Jack sitting with Sinatra at a table, chatting; Jack standing in a balcony box high above a crowded ballroom floor, pointing up at something or someone while Jackie gazes at him with what looks like genuine admiration. We remember these as just the right images for a Stars-and-Stripes, feel-good occasion. But here I have to tell you I remember something else about it as well.

A few of us were sitting around at a bar a couple of days later, gassing about the event, and I distinctly recall that the general mood was good: the thing had made even cynical guys on the beat feel that way, at least for a little while. But then Jack Mabley had to sail in and spoil it with a story he'd picked up about inauguration night. Mabley was a hardass news hawk with a sharp beak for gossip, and he told us that JFK had been able to give Jackie the slip and had gone off to frolic with Angie Dickinson, Janet Leigh, and Kim Novak, a Chicago girl. I was disgusted with Mabley for spoiling our mood and told him so. But at the same time, I'll have to admit that I remembered what he'd said and thought about it, as you will about stories like that. They stick to you like pitch—even after all these years.

• • •

But here's a story that's established fact. Two days after the inauguration, Kennedy called a meeting with Rusk, McNamara, Bobby, Allen Dulles, Bundy, and a few others to talk about getting rid of Fidel Castro. *Two days.*

And here are these guys, maybe still feeling the chill and the sunshine and the bright, brave words of the speech that had welcomed the world to the New Frontier—these torchbearers, as Kennedy had called them—sitting around a table to talk about killing Castro and installing a regime they could do business with. Maybe they never used the word *assassinate*, but there was no doubt that this was precisely what was intended, as it was thought to be the only way to get rid of a dangerously left-leaning dictatorship ninety miles off America's shores. And I wonder whether it's possible to exaggerate the contrast between the high idealism of two days before and the deep darkness—the *darkness*—of the plans discussed at this meeting. I wonder also whether it's possible to exaggerate the fateful consequences of this discussion for Jack Kennedy, and for Judy, too. Well, by the time we come to the end of this story, maybe you'll be in a position to make up your own mind about that.

Throughout the campaign Jack had talked about "Cuber" and "Mistahcastro," tacking on that *r* to the final vowel in the country's name, like they do in New England, and running the name and title of its brand-new leader together when he brought him up in stump speeches. The longer the campaign went on, the tougher and more insistent he became on the subject. But then he found out two amazing secrets, and after some hesitation he decided he could use these as dynamite illustrations of the stagnation America was suffering under the GOP. He couldn't publicly disclose what he'd found out; it was top-secret. But he could still make use of the information. In fact, it might turn out to be much more effective this way.

What he'd found out was that the Eisenhower administration had plans in the works to launch an invasion of Cuba using Cuban exiles, and that at the moment the insurgents hit the beach Castro would be assassinated. By itself, this would be a hell of a thing to have learned, but maybe even more valuable as potential ammunition was the fact that so far the administration hadn't found a way to get the hit done. All that spring and on into the summer, while the exiles trained in Guatemala, up in Washington they were tensely awaiting word that the hit had been lined up. And still that word didn't come. So in desperation they'd turned to the Mob and asked them to do it. Mob guys, for a variety of reasons, were well known to be superpatriots: even after they deported him, Lucky Luciano was eager to help the government invade Mussolini's Italy. Then, too, the Mob had suffered severely at Castro's hands, because he'd closed them up—the casinos, the bars, the girls, drugs, everything. So, hell yes, they'd whack the Commie bastard. They had to figure a way, but it definitely could be done. Santos Trafficante of Miami and Carlos Marcello of New Orleans had been the hardest hit, and it was they who were supposed to be taking care of this part of the operation. Who in the administration told Kennedy about this? The best guess I've seen is Allen Dulles, and his reward for doing so was Kennedy's promise that he would make Dulles's reappointment at the CIA his first order of business.

I seriously doubt, though, that Eisenhower himself knew many specifics of this, though he had been told by a former FBI man recently living in Cuba that there was no other way to put a more friendly government in there. But if Ike knew the operation's code name—Pluto—he might have wondered about that a bit, Pluto being the boss of all bosses of the Roman underworld. But then the name of the operation was changed, and before it shambled and stumbled to a halt after the Cuban missile crisis, it wore more names than many a Mob figure: ZR/RIFLE, Ortsac, Task Force W, Mongoose. If it hadn't had such grave and costly consequences, the whole thing would have been madly comic.

Well, at first when Kennedy gets hold of this he doesn't quite know what to do with it, as I said. It was that hot. Already some of his advisers had been on him for talking so much about Cuba, telling him he was painting himself into a corner he might find pretty tight once he was in the White House. But at the same time, having made Cuba such a big campaign issue, he could hardly just drop it: that would leave him open to the charge that he was too green and impetuous to be the steady, seasoned hand the nation needed.

As the campaign went along, Nixon the candidate was going batshit about the delays in launching Pluto because Kennedy had been beating him up on this, and Nixon couldn't possibly disclose what was in the works. He simply had to take his lumps. Every day, practically, he tried to find out what Trafficante and Marcello were doing about the hit, but he got nowhere: the channels were hardly open to him, so he had to rely on second- and thirdhand information—hard for a guy who wouldn't rely on anybody but himself if he could help it. All he could find out was that the Mob had supposedly explored a number of options: poison pills that were supposed to work in either hot or cold food but didn't work in either; shoe polish that as Fidel gradually warmed up his combat boots one morning would emit a poison paralyzing his heart and lungs; a cigar packed with lethal explosives. At that time, no gunman had been found who was willing to whack the target in the old-time way. Castro, the word came back, had the whole island sewed together so tight that to try for him this way was certain suicide for the gunman. This, you need to remember, was way back when suicide bombers weren't a feature of everyday life. Back then, people hoped to go on living after doing their job, even assassins.

By late summer the situation was looking desperate, with word of the exiles in Guatemala starting to percolate northward. If the plan should become known before it happened, it would give Kennedy and the Democrats a nail-studded baseball bat to slug Nixon with. But by the same token, if the plan could somehow succeed at this late hour, this would show the nation that America wasn't standing still, as the candidate from Massachusetts was tirelessly claiming. Instead, it would provide a spectacular demonstration of what it really meant to "get America moving again"—but doing so in a responsible way and in cooperation with our neighbors in the Organization of American States, which was to be the cover for the whole operation.

So in their desperation the planners turned to another Mob guy, this one on the West Coast and said to be a man who knew how to get such things done and pronto. A CIA cutout was sent out there for a meeting with Johnny Roselli, outlining the administration's time problem and asking him if he could possibly be of help. Wouldn't you love to have a wiretap transcript of that conversation? Think of all the grammatical hoops they'd have had to jump through to get their business done—"It is thought that if," and so forth. Anyway, Roselli gives it the big think and apparently says that possibly something could be lined up, for an accommodation, but that he'd have to talk with somebody in Chicago. I already told you Roselli didn't do anything important without clearing it with Momo, and so now—*boom!*—Momo's in.

That much we know. How Jack found out about this new twist is still a mystery. He clearly couldn't have found out from Judy; Sam would never have told her anything like that, I don't care how many martinis they'd had or how hot he was to get into her pants. And there would be no reason why Momo would have told Jack. That isn't the way those guys operate. To me, that leaves Dulles again. He had Jack's promise in his pocket and must have thought his best bet was to keep Jack current. On the other hand, he had nothing from Nixon, and if Momo succeeded where Trafficante and Marcello hadn't, Nixon would very likely win the election. Who knew what decisions he'd make then about his new team? No, I think Dulles *has* to tell Jack that Momo's now on board, because it's his best shot at keeping his job, whether the operation happens in time or doesn't.

This is where that late-summer meet at the Ambassador East comes in, the one Judy set up for Jack with Momo, where he told her he'd rather she stay in the room than risk being seen leaving it. Because now Jack saw that he had a chance to really swing this whole thing in his favor simply by getting it delayed until after the election. So I think what he said to Momo was something like, Look, I know the administration's come to you on this. And we want it done, too, just as much as they do: Castro's a Commie, and we can't have that in our own backyard. But the thing is, it'll be best for all concerned if it doesn't happen until *after* the election. If it happens before, it gives Nixon a big boost, and this thing's turning out to be a lot closer than we figured. These are my words, of course, not fact. But they aren't wild-ass speculation, either.

Momo was now the key guy for both candidates, but he had to figure it would be a hell of a lot better for him to play ball with Jack than to hope for some reward from Nixon and his people. After all, Momo had already done business with the Kennedys and the machine in Chicago; he knew the Kennedys understood how one hand could wash the other. Besides, what did he know of Nixon, except that Nixon presented himself as a tough-as-nails anticrime guy? Remember, he really owed his position at the top of the ticket to his detective work on the Hiss case; that was the basis of his public image. Granted, Giancana and his outfit would have had no use for Hiss, a Commie traitor who got his, but they wouldn't have seen any advantage in hitching themselves to a politician who would leave no pumpkin right side up if he thought there were votes under it. There was no way to know where he'd stop, whereas the Kennedys seemed to know how to look the other way once in a while, and he already had their marker in his pocket. So my money says that Momo would have assured Jack that nothing would happen to Castro until after the election, and that in the meantime he and his people would continue to work on the project with a very deliberate speed.

If I'm on the right track here, it would help explain a few things. It would help explain that despite heavy pressure from way up the chain, the hit didn't happen in the time frame Nixon needed. (The fact that it *never* happened is quite beside this point.) This same scenario explains why, after a brief pause, Jack went back on the attack on the Cuban situation, ignoring the advice of Schlesinger, Galbraith, and others. Finally, what I've sketched here would further explain why later on Momo felt so badly used by the Kennedys, because this would make favor number three they'd asked, and in his own mind he was convinced he'd come through for them in West Virginia and again in Cook County in November.

Okay. This would be the background—part of it, anyway—for that meeting on day two of the New Frontier. But it wouldn't explain—not really—why, now that he was in the White House, Jack felt so compelled to go ahead with a plan hatched by the old administration. He could have just dropped it, called it off. Here was a plan that, optimally considered, up to that moment had shown no promise whatever. The freedom fighters down in Guatemala were not looking good at all, and their presence there was well on the way to becoming an open secret. It was going to be a real stretch to pass them off as part of an OAS operation instead of what it obviously was. The cover wasn't thin here; it was transparent. And as an American operation it violated all those high ideals JFK had just so ringingly expressed. Also, you'd have to think that Castro's assassination would have inflamed anti-Yankee feelings throughout the entire region, a place where Kennedy had repeatedly said he wanted to lead an alliance for progress in emulation of FDR's Good Neighbor policy. It's worth remembering how much of that anti-Yankee feeling there already was: when Ike sent Nixon down there on a goodwill tour, crowds rocked his car and spat at him. Castro might have made some Latin Americans nervous, but after all, ethnically speaking, he was one of theirs, and a lot of have-nots liked the way he stood up to Uncle Sam.

But most of all, ZR/RIFLE had the potential to increase the already high-level tensions of the cold war, whereas in his speech Kennedy had said that for the survival of the human race it would be best if both sides backed away and took a deep breath. There'd been the U-2 incident that wrecked the Ike-Khrushchev summit, and even more recently we'd broken diplomatic ties with Cuba.

There's no doubt, of course, that the Soviets saw an opportunity there, just as there's no doubt America felt a real vulnerability they hadn't with Batista. Still, why go ahead with this half-assed plan? To say it was better than nothing hardly seems like a good rationale for something with such high stakes.

Remember what Phil Keneally had to say about the folks in West Virginia and how they were so swept along by the rip tide of the Kennedy machine they deserted the Hump? Well, the general analogy fits here, too, only this was a rip tide that was far bigger, far stronger than that one, and far deeper. It was the rip tide of history. Not the writing of it now, which I've already said a lot about, but the living out of it. This rip tide was the cold war, the declaration of which, I guess, you could trace back to Churchill's speech in '46 at that school outside St. Louis, where he said that an iron curtain had clanged down over all of Eastern Europe. But the tide began to run even earlier than that, and I remember, training and then waiting to ship out in Oakland, that after V-E Day Patton said something like, Let's keep on rolling, all the way to Moscow—it's gonna come to that sooner or later, so we might as well do it now, while we're fully mobilized and over here.

The thing was, Jack Kennedy knew all this, knew his history. And yet he was caught in that huge rip tide anyway. They all were, on both sides, and they kept making these desperate, floundering decisions like drowning men, until they'd brought the whole world to the deepest waters, the big drop-off, in October of '62.

All this, you might be thinking, is Monday morning quarterbacking, which I guess is what historians do for a living. But the facts we now have tell us that none of the leaders of that time seemed to have what it took to swim out of that tide into safer waters. Kennedy would seem to have had everything you could possibly want to do just this and lead the world by his example. He had brains; he had that Ivy League training; he'd seen personally what war could do; and he'd surrounded himself with the best and the brightest, as they say. When he was shot in Dallas, some people, including one or two who were very close to him then, said he was already moving away from being a classic cold warrior and making the transition to becoming a visionary for peaceful coexistence with the Soviets. They said he'd learned some hard lessons from Cuba and was determined not to make the same mistakes in Southeast Asia. You could argue this endlessly from either position.

We'll never know, which just might be the most poignant part of that awful event, not to know—*never* to know—and in that not-knowing to think about all those things that might have been avoided. Like the forty thousand and more American boys lost in Vietnam, and I don't even have an estimate in my head of the wounded, the maimed, the nutso guys who never adjusted and ended up homeless or who one morning just wiped out their wives and kids and then themselves. We didn't keep count of the killed and crippled on the other side. But they count nevertheless.

Whatever you think about Dallas, you have to factor Cuba in, one way or another. And it starts right here, at the opening of the New Frontier, when Kennedy had a choice to make and made it in calling this meeting. Hell of a thing when you think of it this way. And she's a part of it, too, Judy. An unwitting part to begin with and still unwitting until it was too late to change anything for her. But she was a player, helping in her own way to wreck the dreams so brilliantly articulated on that January day in 1961.

Four days after that she was at the Mayflower, waiting for Jack's call and not that happy about finding herself in this situation. She felt she'd done the right thing by staying away from the inauguration, but then she had to endure her mother's rapturous, lengthy description of something she'd decided she would have to live without. Those feelings carried over into this visit. She'd said she'd come, and she had. She said she'd meet him at the White House, and she was there in her room, waiting for the call. And that was just it: she now felt like she was a servant, "waiting to be summoned by the king who was going to have one of his palace people bang a big gong or something and then I was supposed to just jump and run out the door as fast as I could." But there was no call that afternoon, and she said she'd be damned if she'd go down to the very public, very opulent dining room to eat dinner alone when everybody else in there would have a partner and wonder why she didn't. So she ordered from room service and had what she described as a perfectly miserable meal, during which she drank most of a bottle of Chablis and then ordered up some chartreuse, by which time she must have been pretty well loaded. She went to bed angry and had a lousy night's sleep.

She woke up the next morning determined to fly back home and was about to call the airline when the king finally sent his summons. "The *president* will see you at eleven-thirty," Evelyn Lincoln told her; a car would pick her up at quarter after. She looked at her watch and found it was already close to ten. Her temperature went up some more, this girl who took hours to fix herself just so. Still, she heard herself telling Evelyn Lincoln she'd be ready and waiting in the lobby.

She could have waited outside, on Connecticut: the cold weather had moved on, and it was almost balmy. But she felt she'd been waiting quite enough already, and the driver could just double-park if he had to and come into the lobby for her. Her little protest was probably lost on him, though. He came in, looked right at her, and out they went. On the way he said almost nothing except things like, We're going to take a left here if I can ever get this cop's attention. Rolling the few blocks to the White House, he explained that they'd be met at the west gate, ushered through, and that once she was inside an officer at a desk would announce her arrival. The use of that word was another bell-ringer for her. Her first reaction to it was resentment—more of the royalty bit, she thought, remembering Jack's joke about being crowned king of America and wondering if he'd been half serious. But at the same time, she said, her reaction made her aware of what a bad mood she was in, and this put the situation into a useful perspective: here she was, on the way to the

White House for lunch with the president of the United States, and just spoiling for a fight with him. "This was really silly," she thought. "I said to myself there's zero point in this whole thing if I was going into it feeling like that. I gave myself a talking-to and by the time we were waved through the gate I felt like I'd gotten little Judy pretty well in hand."

At the desk inside she was indeed announced. The officer dialed some numbers and told Mr. Powers that a Miss Judith Campbell was here for an appointment with the president, and that was all there was to it. A simpler time, sure, but not necessarily a more innocent one.

Mr. Powers, of course, would have been Dave Powers, one of the so-called Irish Mafia from Jack's earliest days in politics. In the post-Camelot era of allegedly hardass reassessments, Powers got tagged as Jack Kennedy's pimp—a bit unfair, but there's no doubt one of his functions was to line up women for his boss. He always denied it, said there were never any women secretly meeting up with the president on the road and certainly never in the White House. The White House logs, he said, bore him out. Where, for instance, was there a single mention of any Judith Campbell in them? All this was pure crap, scandal-mongering. Some of it was just that. And Powers was right, apparently, in saying the logs don't contain a mention of Judy. I've never looked at them, but others have, and there's no Judith Campbell in them. What they do show, however, are numerous entries that read simply, blankly, "Powers Plus One" or "Powers Plus Two." That can pretty much cover the waterfront. What the hell could you prove with entries like these for your evidence?

At any rate, here was Powers to greet her, a jolly-looking, round-faced guy, as she described him, with tiny dark eyes. He took her down a long corridor to a couch, where he left her, telling her the president would be with her shortly. And so he was, Powers alongside. She looked at Jack closely, as if she might find something there that would tell her he'd changed—or been changed—by actually taking office. But what she recorded was just his famously disarming grin. He gave her a quick hug and a peck and said, "What about a swim before lunch—very relaxing and good for the appetite. Dave, find Judy a suit and cap, will you?" The idea slightly horrified her, and she quickly told Powers not to bother, that she hadn't put herself together just to have to do it all over again.

"You're looking at some effort here, Mr. President," she told him, with something of a smile, though not as big as the one he'd had when greeting her.

Powers looked at Jack, his mouth slightly open, and she had a flashback to that moment in the lobby of the Fontainebleau when she'd come back at Sam and then he'd chuckled. Jack didn't do that, only smiled coolly and explained that his doctor had prescribed as much swimming as his schedule allowed. His back and all . . . He thanked her for being understanding, as if they were only good acquaintances and he was reminding her of a condition she might have forgotten about. He said he wouldn't be long. Powers showed her to a sitting room and then hesitated, wondering whether he should keep her company, but she saw his look and said that with as many books and magazines as there were in there, she could easily entertain herself. He still looked doubtful, she said, as if he thought she might get him in trouble with his boss, but she didn't feel like reassuring him further and just plunked herself down and began thumbing through the first magazine she picked up. When she looked up again he was gone.

But a few minutes later he was back, smiling and red-faced, to ask if she'd like a drink on the second floor while she was waiting for the president. That, she said, was the first sensible suggestion she'd heard all day, and he looked a little confused again by that but took her in an elevator to the second floor, where she had a daiquiri. She must have still been nervous enough about everything that she downed it pretty fast, because when Powers looked in on her again he did a little double take and asked if she was ready for another. She actually felt like another, too, but she had the presence to say no.

Jack wasn't long in the pool, and when he came into the room she thought it was like he burst into it, his hair still a bit damp around the edges. He stopped short of the couch and looked at her a long moment, and the longer he looked, the bigger the grin on his face became, until he'd made her self-conscious enough to ask, "*What?*" He'd forgotten, he said, just how gorgeous she really was, and on that they went in to lunch, which they had with Powers: soup, hamburgers, and daiquiris for them but not for Powers. Not very interesting food, she noted, watching Jack smother his burger with ketchup.

He was using a light, bantering tone with her, trying to pump her for Hollywood gossip, but she fenced with him a bit, saying that from what she'd been able to gather about the inauguration, he'd been spending more time with Hollywood types than she had, and was it really true that Frank would get a cabinet post, or was it an ambassadorship? She saw that Powers was getting a charge out of hearing her mix it up with the president. "I don't think you're going to get what you're fishing for with this lady, Mr. President," he said, chuckling. "As your social adviser, my advice to you would be to quit while you're still even."

Powers excused himself, and he wasn't quite out of the room when Jack reached across and squeezed her hand. "Let's see the rest of the layout," he said. "I'm still finding my way around, so don't get mad at me if I get lost here and there." Here were the same furnishings, the same paintings and vases she remembered from the N Street house, and she began to brace for that same feeling to come back to her, the one where she felt like a bad Catholic girl intruding in another woman's home. It didn't happen, though, mostly because Jack was so breezy and kind of detached about it all. He might have been a guide to the place instead of the man who now lived there. If anything, he was more relaxed than she'd seen him in those long months when he'd been running so hard to get there.

When they passed along the hall by the bedroom he shared with Jackie—twin beds, she noted—he put his arm around her waist and steered her into a large guest bedroom. "Now," he said, turning her toward him, "I've finally got you just where I want you." He moved his hands slowly up her, reaching her shoulders and undoing the top button of the light sweater she was wearing over her dress. He was taking his time, which she found very exciting. Getting the tour, she'd wondered how she was going to feel once they arrived at their destination, as she knew they eventually would. Despite his tour-guide behavior, she knew she wasn't there to admire the Lincoln Bedroom or the nursery. But now Jack's approach was so easy and so natural she knew right away she was in the same mood he was, and when he had trouble with a button, he laughed and said he must be out of practice and wouldn't she help him, and she did just that.

Before she left the White House, she and Jack had a serious conversation that went on so long it was early evening when she got into the car for the ride back to the Mayflower. They had the habit, you might remember, of lying in bed afterward, often enough sitting up with drinks; a lot of that, I suppose, would have been pillow talk. This wasn't. This was strictly business, and so here again I think of Jack's emotional makeup, his ability to turn romance on and off like a faucet. And she, I think, had a bit of that compartmentalizing ability herself. I'm not sure just what I think of this trait. When I talked about it with Lucy one evening, she said men were a lot better at it than women, and I came back to say we all might be better off if we kept emotions out of areas where they didn't belong. The Nazis, she retorted, were great at that, filling out requisition forms for boxcars and Zyklon B gas and then going home to dandle their children on their knee and toss sticks for their German shepherds.

However, there they were, with Jack telling Judy he had some "delicate" matters he still had to work on with Sam Giancana. Some had to do with the election, and some were of a different nature, and these in his judgment would be going on for some months, maybe as long as a year. It was hard to say. These ongoing matters were in fact so delicate he didn't want to use the usual channels, even those top-secret ones now available to him. As soon as he mentioned Sam she knew where this conversation would end up, what he wanted from her, and instantly she thought with real horror of the FBI's invasion on North Flores. How totally different she now felt, she thought as Jack went on, from the Judy who had been so hot to make his election team that he'd practically had to force her to look inside that attaché case to see the cargo she was delivering to Chicago.

She didn't want to know now, either, what the materials were that she'd be carrying, and he obviously didn't want to tell her, skirting around this in his adroit fashion. But now her aversion was so strong she thought that if he did start to tell her, she'd stop her ears, put her hand over his mouth, or run into the bathroom—anything to keep from learning what was so delicate that not even top-secret would do. Writing this down, she crossed out the word *delicate* with a single strong stroke of her blue pen and put in *dangerous* instead, then crossed that out, too, so that the sentence lacks a critical, characterizing word. The irony of this grew on me, I can tell you here, the deeper I read in her diaries, like your own shadow when you're walking a long road in summer and suddenly find that your body has grown longer and your legs have begun to look like a giraffe's: you've either set yourself a serious hike here or else you're lost. So before he'd finished talking about the operation, its delicacy, and how critical she could be to its success, she stopped him, laying her hand on his arm.

"Jack," she said, "please just stop." He looked at her sharply, and she rushed on, hearing herself rushing, trying to be calm but at the same time trying to get through to him about her fears. "Look, you know I want to do this for you. I want to do it for the country, if you think it's that important—you *know* that. But I just couldn't take it if I knew I'd have those goons tailing me, breaking into my home—all that. That would just kill me—that or I'd kill myself."

"You didn't tell me they broke in. You let them in, I thought."

"Okay, I did. But it's the same thing—*they broke in on me*. I can't tell you how that felt, how it still feels." She stopped, wanting some sign from him that he had heard her, had finally gotten the message. He seemed hesitant in the face of her urgency, and there was a silence.

She ended it, saying that what she wanted from him was a promise. "You can say to Hoover not to bother me, to let me alone. You can do that, can't you? I mean, he does work for you, doesn't he?"

"He does," Jack said quietly, nodding his head while looking at her in a way she couldn't read. "But really," he told her, "he works for Bobby, and to tell you the truth, he and Bobby aren't exactly buddy-buddy. Bobby's too young for Edgar, even if he does like boys." He grinned at this. "Maybe if Bobby would get a haircut now and then and buy a comb, things might go better. Harmony in the Justice Department makes for greater efficiency." But he saw this blarney wasn't going to make a sale he thought he really needed, so he changed tack and tone and said he'd have a talk with Bobby first thing in the morning and get her the protection she felt she had to have. If he couldn't, he went on, he'd try to figure out some other way to work with Sam that wouldn't involve her. However, since she already knew Sam so well, knew the routines of this sort of thing, she was the perfect person for the "mission," and he really didn't want to involve another person or persons in this if he didn't absolutely have to. He felt sure she could understand this.

That was the way they left it. He had her yes, and she had . . . what? His conditional promise of protection against the FBI. What does this sound like to you? To me it sounds like the kind of deal old Joe had worked out with Momo when this whole thing began.

The car came for her at the same time the day after, and again it was the jolly-seeming Powers who met her, but this time there weren't any preliminaries: he took her straight up to the second floor, where Jack was waiting, and then left them alone for lunch. While they ate she could see that Jack was making an effort to concentrate on her, but it obviously was an effort, and she thought she would have felt sorry for him if she hadn't had so much on the line herself—her peace of mind; her mental safety, as she put it—and as the lunch ground on she felt the tension thickening. Then Bobby came in carrying a manila packet, and the atmosphere positively crackled. He brought it in with the packet, she felt.

She'd never met him, and her first thought was that he was shorter than he looked on TV or in news photos. He was also quite rumpled and tousled, whereas his brother was always perfectly elegant. When he smiled briefly she saw that his teeth were crooked, as if by the time he'd come along the family had too much on its mind to see to such details. Jack made the casual introductions without getting up, as if there was nothing at all out of the ordinary about introducing his girlfriend to the nation's chief law enforcement officer here in the family quarters of the White House. How many times in American history, you wonder, had this happened before? Here was a new frontier, all right—but then, who really knows?

As soon as he sat down Bobby took over, Jack leaning back in his chair with his fingers bridged and hardly saying anything. Bobby talked all around the packet he held in his hands, explaining how sometimes the federal government had to go outside conventional channels to accomplish things that were in the national interest. He explained that this wasn't always the prettiest way to get these things done, and that if people found out what unconventional ways government officers had to use sometimes, it could do a lot of damage. Judy told him she understood that and certainly had no intention of telling anybody about delivering *that* to the right party, pointing to what he had in his hands. Bobby gave Jack a look, and then there was a silence until Jack broke it to tell Bobby that Judy here had been very helpful during the campaign and was completely reliable. His tone of voice, she felt, was "just as matter-of-fact as though he'd been talking about some campaign helper to a man who did something or other for him instead of talking about me—in front of me—to his own brother. It made me feel strange like someone who'd gotten lost and wandered into the wrong room."

Bobby pushed his hair off his forehead and asked if she had a handbag or some other piece of luggage large enough to carry the packet aboard a plane; it wouldn't be a good idea, he thought, to let it out of her possession until she'd given it to the right person. He never once used Giancana's name, she noticed, and neither did Jack. Her answer was classic Judy: she said she'd had her eye on a largish black alligator bag she'd seen in a shop window near the Mayflower but had been wondering whether it was really a bit too big to be practical. But, she went on, this was about as good an excuse as a girl was likely to get to buy something she wanted anyway. Jack had to laugh at that: Jackie was a legendary shopper and spendthrift. Bobby paid no attention to Jack's laughter, just looked across at her with those hooded, intense eyes as if this were a slightly irritating interruption. Then he asked her if she could leave in the morning and return the packet by evening. She didn't know the airlines' schedules, of course, but it turned out he did, and he pulled an envelope from his jacket pocket and silently slid it across to her: they had her on a seven A.M. flight out and returning to Washington at seven the same evening. Whatever this business with Sam really was, she now knew, it was not only delicate, it was deadly urgent, and the presence of Bobby made it feel even more so. And still she hadn't heard a word about what the government—the men in this room—could do to protect her, only what she could do to help them out. So now she turned to Jack, who was regarding her thoughtfully with his fingertips together and held near his lips, and they exchanged a long, charged look. He got her message, all right.

"Ah, Bobby, ah, Judy here would, ah, like very much to, ah, feel that if she's going to help us out on this, that she, ah, won't be pestered by Hoover's men."

"My brother told me about that," Bobby said. He had the packet flat on the table now, with his hands spread on it. "I can't very well order the director to do anything with regard to you. If we did that, then we, ah, couldn't very well ask you to carry these for us." He looked down at his hands, and she looked at them, too. They were square and stubby, she said, with coarse red hair on their backs, whereas Jack's were shapely and virtually hairless. "The less the director knows about you—the less you come to his attention—the better off you are." She started to say that she'd already come to his attention, but he went right ahead, telling her he didn't know what that "call" had been about at her "house." Obviously, it had happened before he'd taken over at Justice. Still skirting any mention of Giancana's name, he said that as far as he knew, Hoover had nothing special going on at the moment in Chicago except an investigation involving the Teamsters. He added a few more things about the relationship between his office and Hoover's, that they were still in the process of getting to know each other, and that, as she must know, the director was practically a "national institution."

On this short winter afternoon it was growing dusky in the dining room, and she remembered looking out at the lights that were on in the hallway and wondering why somebody didn't turn them on in here; was this maybe another service you had performed for you when you became president? Then Bobby came to his offer at last, telling her that if she had problems while she was doing this favor for them, she shouldn't hesitate to tell his brother, who would pass it along. What he, Bobby, would do about it then would depend on the nature of the problem. "I can't very well anticipate what might come up," he said, "and, as I've explained, I can't go to the director and tell him to lay off a Miss Campbell."

Signaling that this was a take-it-or-leave-it declaration, he rose, telling Jack he had to get back to Virginia; Ethel had a big dinner party planned. He left the packet squared up on the table, and Jack walked him out and down the hall to the elevator; she could hear their voices but not what they were saying. She sat there alone, holding the tickets in her hand and staring across at that packet in its heavy sleeve. She couldn't help wondering, even if only fleetingly, what was inside, but then Jack saved her from that by coming back in, scooping up the packet with his casual grace, and carrying it around to her.

"If you want to get that handbag, I'll get you a car right away," he said. "I know you don't ever let me pay for anything, but this is different, don't you think?" He reached for his wallet. "How much do you think it'll run?" While he walked her to the elevator, she made a guess. "Shit," he said, "I don't have that much. I'll pay you back. Just remind me."

At the elevator he said Hoover was an "old fruitcake" who had way too many things on his mind to bother her. "He isn't going to mess with you." The elevator doors opened, and the operator stood within, one gloved hand on the button, the other on the door. Jack nodded at him and turned his brilliant smile on her. "But I am." He handed her the packet. "Call me from the airport when you get back, and we'll have dinner or something."

The next evening she made the time for a quick shower and a change at the Mayflower before delivering the packet to Jack. But walking into her room, she was struck immediately by the feeling that it wasn't the same room and that she didn't belong in it. She actually went into the closet and looked at the clothes—hers, all right. She thought it might be the long day she'd already put in and ordered a martini from room service, meanwhile assembling an outfit for the evening. It had to match the "precious handbag," which she'd had in her grip ever since she'd left the hotel when it was still dark. Fortunately, she said, she'd brought along a suit with a small houndstooth pattern in black and white with a scatter of russet flecks. Also a scoop-neck black blouse and black pumps. I have to admit to you I kind of had fun here, imagining what it looked like and even more what she looked like in it.

It was when she was dressing and sipping her martini that she wondered how she could have forgotten a certain handkerchief that would have nicely picked up the russet. But then she found herself thinking, Mr. President, I'm not going to show up looking like some bow-wow, no matter how tired I am or whether I'm missing some damn hanky.

But when Powers Plus One stepped from the elevator onto the second floor and she found herself staring Kenny O'Donnell in the face, suddenly she felt the full weight of her day dropping on her shoulders and imagined she looked "very dowdy." She hadn't seen him since the convention and was trying to figure out what to say and not coming up with much. But he made it easy, giving her a smile and a cheery "Hi there" and stepping past her with a big notebook tucked under his arm. Powers saw Jack striding toward them and told the elevator guy to hold it, and then he ducked into the elevator, joining O'Donnell.

Jack looked fabulous, she said, and she kept thinking she must look tired and drawn by contrast. But she had that handbag as a sort of shield she could hide behind, and when he came toward her she whipped the envelope out and held it there and he took it. There was a servant standing there to take her coat, so all Jack did was take it and say thanks and guide her down the hall for cocktails. You wonder, don't you, how much different it would have been if they'd been alone when she handed off. Maybe he'd have kissed her, but the expression of thanks might have been just as perfunctory. Separate categories again for him—the errand and the errand person.

I don't know how many details about her trip she went into with him. What she wrote about it was that after her meeting with Jack and Bobby she'd reached Sam, who said he'd been waiting for her call. So when you add these things up—Bobby with the packet and the plane tickets, Sam expecting her call—it's clear the brothers had been counting on her participation and had built a plan around it. I wonder if Jack even had a fallback plan in case she said no. Anyway, Sam knew how tight her schedule was and told her that he'd have come out to O'Hare, where they could have done business, but now he didn't want to go anywhere they'd been seen together—not the Ambassador East, not Rush Street or the Armory or even his house. They met instead at the Palmer House, where she delivered the packet in the dimly lit cocktail lounge and said she was going window-shopping along State. He told her forty-five minutes might be about right. She bought a scarf and gloves at Field's, and when she got back Sam had the packet resealed with Scotch tape and two martinis on the table. When they finished those he stayed behind and she got a cab back to O'Hare.

As I say, I don't know how much of this she went into with Jack. I don't know either if she would have told him about the constant anxiety that had been her close traveling companion all the way out, all the way back. The only time she hadn't had it was when she'd gone shopping at Field's, and this was because Sam had had the packet back there at the Palmer House and she'd felt blessedly free for a moment. But then, of course, she had to go back for it and go back to the anxiety, too. Words like that—*anxiety*—strike me as funny, tricky: you use them and they stand in for states that are common enough but still not easy to describe. And that's just it: they only stand in for these states; they can't really do justice to them. And so maybe what gets us closer to what she'd been through was what she'd felt when she'd taken that first long belt of the Jack Daniel's Jack got her, and it seemed to plunge right down through the center of her like a stream of lava or something, falling through dark space until it splashed at the very bottom. Experiencing this, she knew how keyed up she'd been since dawn. Jack must have been feeling at least a bit of this himself, because after he took the packet somewhere and returned empty-handed he seemed instantly lighter in his mood: funny, and increasingly romantically attentive. They had dinner then, she in her smart outfit but admitting to herself that she'd thought again of the missing handkerchief. Maybe this is standard behavior for a clotheshorse; I wouldn't know. But I do remember coming across other lines of hers like this in earlier entries and thinking they were a little wiggy, you know? But here, by this point, I was used to them and actually found them kind of amusing, like you will when you get on the inside track with someone you've come to really like. Right after she made this admission she went on to say that evidently Jack didn't think there was a thing wrong with the way she was turned out and said he couldn't believe she'd just been to Chicago and back. "Christ!" he said then, flinging his napkin aside before they'd finished their main course. "Let's get the hell out of here!"

He reached across for her hand and pulled her up with him. Actually, she thought, she was really hungry and hadn't had much more than a snack on the hop back to Washington, but she was carried along by his excitement and began to feel it as well, Jack's hand around hers, both smooth and strong, pulling her gently but firmly past the children's room and on toward the guest bedroom, which had some ceremonial name, I'm sure. Then they were inside, and Jack shut the door quickly behind them.

You know, I can remember now in minute detail almost everything about coming to the next pages in that particular diary. I can even remember the diary itself, as a physical object, I mean, whereas I'd have a hell of a time recalling the looks of most of the others, except that first fat, padded one I pulled at random out of the box in Ed's rec room. But this one was a thick spiral number, the spirals themselves white and the cover canary yellow, with a clear protective plastic cover over that. Very stylish, even sexy in a way, and the only one like it I ever saw. I was enough interested in it to look inside the back cover to see who'd made it: a Swedish outfit. No surprise there, because around that time if you saw something that was sleek, sexy, and stylish, chances were it was Swedish: models, movie actresses, furniture, women's clothes, dishware. We seemed to be having a love affair with Sweden, and I'm sure they loved it, too, with all those American dollars rolling in.

And I remember, too, that not being one of Phil Keneally's better days. When I arrived up on Washtenaw, I had to wait so long out on the stoop of his building that I rang again, though I couldn't imagine he'd forgotten our appointment. He was a juicer, sure, but there was a consistency to him that was almost military. If he agreed to meet with you, by God, you could book it. This was a sharp late-fall morning I'm talking about here, and my jacket wasn't quite a match for it, and so when he didn't answer the buzzer right off, I punched it again. When he buzzed back and I got to the door of his flat, I could tell right away something was up. The door was wide open, but he was nowhere in sight. I called out a couple of times and then went in, but very hesitantly. I didn't want him to mistake me for an intruder, huge and wounded as he was. Plus, given his army background and Mob associations, I had to assume he had a gun in there somewhere and knew how to use it, too.

Then I heard him, coming out of the can and into the little hallway and slamming the phone back in its cradle. When I saw him—and *smelled* him—you didn't have to be Dick Tracy to figure out what kind of night it had been. Ellery Queen, Tracer of Missing Persons, might have been the better man for the job. I saw almost nothing of him that day, though occasionally I heard him, going back and forth to the can. And once the phone rang and rang and rang until finally he picked it up and said, "Guinea bitch!" and hung up hard. And I stayed quite late that day, too, feverishly copying down the very stuff I'd hoped to find: the juicy, intimate details about Judy in the sack with Jack Kennedy.

No—those aren't the right words, goddamn it. Even *right*, which I just used, isn't the right word, the *true* word. *Hoped* isn't either. The right words, the true ones, cut deeper. I hadn't *hoped* to find this stuff. I had *lusted* for it—*lusted*. I thought if it was there, if I could find it, I'd get a fat book contract and then maybe a movie. Finally I'd get to see my name in lights, like old Jersey Joe when he floored Louis. I know I told you all this right at the outset, but it occurs to me now that you yourself might have been lusting in a way for just these details—and felt let down because I haven't delivered the truly steamy stuff. One reason for that is that up to this point in her diaries—January 29, 1961, I make it—I simply hadn't found it. Doesn't mean it wasn't there in the ones Ed had. It only means that I hadn't found it until that day in Phil Keneally's apartment, with him spending his time shuffling back and forth between bedroom and can.

As it turned out, I found myself glad he was in that condition and staying out of the front room. Not that I wished any more misery on the man, he having had so much already. Despite his bad temper and worse mouth, I couldn't help liking him, even admiring him in his struggles. But what I mean here is that when I came across Judy's account of what went on in that guest bedroom at the White House, I was glad to be by myself, though maybe not quite for the reason you might imagine: I wasn't going to get off reading it, far from it. Instead, my reaction was more complex than that, and at the time the dominant note, so to say, was an odd sort of embarrassment. Not so much for her, though there was some of that. But it was really more for me, reading it. For whatever reasons, by the time I finally hit pay dirt I suddenly felt . . . well, *soiled*, I guess, like I was there in the bedroom closet with the door cracked and breathing hard with a sort of excitement that didn't feel sexual. The cliché about being careful what you wish for came to mind just then, and I drew back from it because it had come so easily. But then, right after that, I did grab for it, because it served a crude purpose, as clichés will: it fit the situation. Later on, I thought, I'll try to work out the deeper stuff, the complexities. But right now my job was to get this down, and I distinctly remember actually mumbling under my breath, "Okay, pal, you asked for this, now get it down."

And what I got down was Judy coming out of the bathroom in her altogether, which must have been a dynamite visual event, and finding Jack in bed, on his back, with his hands propped behind his head, waiting. "Stop right where you are," he said.

> He wanted me to stop right where I was just as I was. I wasn't nearly to the bed and I didn't have a stitch on and I'm not that kind of girl. When I'm getting myself together to go out on the town I'll take a look at myself in the mirror before I put my clothes on and I'll turn sideways and look at myself from that angle and think not too shabby girl. But to just stand there naked in front of a man and have him watch you—NO!!

But she did it, this time, anyway. Later on she wondered why, whether in fact she'd been intimidated by the situation—being given an order by the president of the United States, the commander in chief, speaking from the White House. That's quite a bit of leverage to bring to bear on a girl. But when she wondered about this some pages further on in that sexy Swedish notebook, I think her wonderings probably were influenced by what happened next, and I guess I'd better get to that right now. They used to say in the theater that if you roll a cannon out onstage, you'd better fire it.

Well, as I said, when she came out of the bathroom Jack was already in bed, on his back and obviously ready for love. And she not only stopped at his command but even stood there, tall, broad-shouldered, long-legged (you see I'm remembering that film footage), and then she spread her arms wide like wings. At that moment she must have looked like a goddamned Greek statue come to life. She held that pose for a moment, and then she went to him, in bed. He was ready, all right, and didn't change his position, though you hope to Christ he at least welcomed her with his arms, pulling them out from behind his head and putting them around her. You hope that. But what he wanted, what he expected from her, was perfectly plain.

There were times during the campaign, she said, when his back was so bad he really couldn't do anything except this, and she understood that and was "glad to do that for him." Actually, she went on, there were things about that act that she liked.

This stuff—as you're hearing—I'm finding hard to talk about, even now, long afterward, without getting that peeping Tom feeling all over again. So . . .

So I've had a lot to say to you about history: the accidents of it; the accidents of the writing of it, and not just the written records, but the pictorial ones and the recorded ones. I could go off here about Robert Capa's shots of D-day and what happened to them—hell of an interesting example of accident and record.

But that isn't what you want here, and it isn't what I need to tell you here. It sure as hell isn't what she wrote about, and I think *that* may be what I owe her, finally—to tell what she told, straight as I can.

Okay.

There were things about that act that she liked. She liked, she said, its "special intimacy." There was a level of trust involved there, she thought, that there wasn't in any other position.

> What other thing can be done between a man and a woman that is so intimate and involves this much trust? After all what you're doing is putting your mouth which is where you speak where you talk about love and all the most tender things a woman can say to a man at the place where a man really feels your love or ought to. What can be equal to this?

Well, what can, when you put it like that? And yet, as we know, the act has a stigma attached to it: "You *suck!*" And it's put there by men, in locker-room situations, or maybe up at a cabin in Wisconsin or Michigan when the boys have been out deer hunting and then they start on the beer and the shots, and then it won't be long before they start talking a certain way, and when they do you get to the blow-job jokes pretty quick. Who hasn't told a blow-job joke—what man, I mean? I heard quite a few when I was doing the legwork on that ice-fishing story I mentioned a while back in connection with the Wisconsin primary. And to be as candid as I can, I probably chipped in with a few of my own. You want to blend in in those situations, you know.

That last bit was pretty obviously ironical, and irony is always a kind of setup, right? You maneuver your audience into a certain position so that you can sucker-punch them to make a point. It's kind of like inviting a guy to have a drink, a guy you think has it coming to him, and while you're talking and drinking along you say something in a very low voice so that he has to lean forward to hear you, and when you've got him in that exposed position, you sucker-punch him. Same thing here: I set you up with that chin music about blow-job stories, getting you comfortable, so to say, and then I sucker-punch you, I betray you, because I'm not letting myself off with that remark about wanting to blend in with the boys. And I'm not letting *you* off either, because I'm taking the girl's part here—Judy's—when I say that the real betrayal here is ours—men's—in making those easy jokes about something that is, or ought to be, just what she said it was: an act of special intimacy and trust. I tried to tell you at the beginning where my sympathies lay, and I don't believe you can get this story the way I want you to unless you make the effort to see things from her point of view, not JFK's, not Phil Keneally's, and certainly not from the point of view of the mass media.

Now if this had been all that was involved in this episode, this entry, it would have been plenty. But it wasn't. Because she went on to talk about how she felt about that experience, the questions it raised for her about the relationship. This wasn't always the case with her entries, as you've heard: they tend to be a good deal longer on the what than the why. This is terrific for historians of a certain sort; if they can get the what, then they can work out the why. Not so great for a guy who's just as interested in the diary keeper as he is in the big picture, if not more so.

Well, there she was, just back from an errand that Jack didn't want to entrust to anybody but her. But what happened in the bedroom made her feel like *she was still on the errand,* that this was really only the last part of it, instead of what should have happened after it was done and love or romance took over. It was the first time that she'd felt she'd been required to service Jack, that this was precisely what he expected of her and maybe had had it in mind from the moment he saw her walking toward him with the packet held out before her. He might have had it in mind even before that—like when he told her at the elevator the night before to call him when she got back.

Remember what I told you about that very first entry I'd copied down, just to have something—anything—in my grubby little notepad about the notorious Judy Campbell who'd been the mistress of JFK? This was the bit about "doing it" a couple of times with her husband, Billy, in between snaps of a televised football game. Then the next day I'd looked at those scribbles and thought they were most likely worthless. Much later on, I came to change my mind about the lines and to regard them as a piece of dumb luck, and the thing that changed my mind was this January episode in the guest bedroom. Back then, she'd been servicing Billy, all right, going to bed with him at his convenience, or maybe they went at it on the couch or even the floor so that he wouldn't miss a play. This sort of thing wouldn't have been that uncommon in those days, when sex was regarded as the wife's duty, women's lib hardly having been so much as a stray, irritable thought in the empty contentment of America in those years. Certainly some things had changed by '61, but not many. And certainly not on this particular night in the White House. And she was bothered by this, maybe even to the point of wondering what the difference was between Billy and Jack when it came to this. And if I'm right about her character, she must have wondered once again and in this intensely intimate setting whether this was really all there was to the show, which would have made for a pretty bleak experience out of what ought to have been a splendid one.

Sometime before she left for L.A. the following day she made some quick jottings, one of the few such entries I'd come across by that point, though later on this became very common. Here they are:

no? what was wanted

bells now for Jack

Jackie??

She never expanded on these. The following pages are about her mother and sister and a lunch they had in Beverly Hills. But I think these jottings are easily enough decoded. First, there was, in her mind, no question of what Jack wanted that night. Then the bells business looks to me like a reprise of her misgivings about the trappings of royalty that now pervaded Jack's life. Remember here that the world press was already writing about Jack and Jackie as "America's royal couple," and this view kept on growing until it was merged with the Camelot business. I'm not entirely sure why it bothered her so much, unless it could simply be that deep strain of antimonarchy, anti-aristocracy there is in this country. Finally, the two question marks after the mention of Jackie: I can't *know* this for a fact, of course, but the context makes me think that what she was wondering about was whether Jackie, the wife and first lady, was also required to give this sort of service to Jack, or whether it was only his mistress, his shady girlfriend, who had to perform this special act. As I say, she never expanded on these jottings, at least not directly. I never saw, for instance, a single complete, fully thought-through reference to what Jackie might or might not have done for Jack. But there are several further references, some of them bitter, about what I guess you'd have to call the lack of mutuality in the Judy-Jack sexual relationship, how more and more often Jack assumed that same expectant position, and how at the same time she more and more often felt as if their times in bed were really the completion of her missions to Momo. Whether Jack actually saw it this way will, I'm sure, remain a mystery, one of the many he carried with him out to Arlington.

From the way I've set this up for you, it's obvious I think that what she was carrying to Momo and Roselli was plans for killing Castro. But it wouldn't be accurate to say, I don't think, that these were how-to kits. Momo was the expert in that business, not Jack, not Bobby or the rest of that sober-suited, striped-tie gang they had working on the project. More likely the packet contained what the Kennedy brain trust thought Momo needed in order to get the job done.

First, of course, cash—what he said he'd need, which would have included his overhead. Then what he needed to know about the administration's end of the operation, up to the minute: names and telephone numbers of some of the important players in what would shortly become Operation Mongoose; fallback names and numbers; lawyers to contact if things went wrong. Also what the administration's intelligence had been able to put together on Castro's habits, movements, closest associates, and so forth. But here I need to tell you, in order for you to get some sort of grasp of the whole situation and Judy's part in it, that American intelligence on Castro—both that inherited from the Eisenhower administration and that subsequently developed—was in such sad-ass shape that *intelligence* has to be used in a way that makes the most savage irony look cheap. We knew almost nothing useful about Castro and his Cuba, and apparently we didn't *want* to know anything useful. Because to know something useful was to know that Ike's plans had been doomed and Kennedy's double doomed: they were all wishful, fateful, fabricated bullshit. To give you just an idea: Right before the election the administration was told that our fears about Castro's regime were about to be removed without Washington's having to lift a finger; the Bearded One, it was soberly said, was in the last stages of syphilis and had already lost his mind. All we needed to do now was sit back and let nature take its course. I doubt, though, that what Bobby handed Judy to take out to the Palmer House contained that "intelligence." What would be the point of getting Momo's cooperation if the threat was about to go away? But whatever she carried out had to be absolutely riddled with false, misleading data, and maybe Momo was savvy enough to spot this. Probably was.

What she carried back I have no idea. My guess, though, is that she carried nothing back except what she'd delivered, minus the cash, of course. That's not to say, though, that all Momo and Roselli did was to pocket the cash and reseal the packet. There were documents of some sort in there, and what they probably did was read through these and make check marks or some other kind of notation or initials indicating they'd received it and looked at it. Also, if these packets contained names and numbers, as I say, they'd have copied those down for future use.

I count twelve trips she made from D.C. to Chicago, L.A., Las Vegas, or Tahoe. Not once did she say she ever saw anything of what was in those packets, nor did she ever see Roselli or Momo reading them or marking them. As she did that first time at the Palmer

House, she made herself scarce for a while, and when she showed up again the packets had been resealed. Near the end of her life she talked with the gossipmonger Dottie Dunne and allegedly told her that what she brought back felt exactly the same in weight and bulk as what she delivered. If you want to try to run this part of the thing down, you could try talking with Dunne. I tried and got nowhere; I don't know that there's anywhere to get.

But from my point of view, trying to get at the truth of her story and tell it, the question that just leaps out at me is, What if she'd known what she was carrying? Would she have done it anyway? I'm dead certain of this much: if she had known what the consequences would be for her personally, she never would have touched that first packet. That I'd make book on. But then, when you think of the question in the abstract, maybe this really isn't saying that much. I mean, how many decisions in our own lives would we want to undo if only at the time we could have looked down the street and around the corner to see where that decision was going to lead us? But maybe you have to ask the question a little differently and leave the personal consequences out of it. What if, in other words, she was certain she herself wouldn't suffer for her actions as a courier to the Mob but that America itself certainly would? That, to me, is the more interesting question here.

From the moment of their meeting in Las Vegas, something deep within her leapt toward Jack Kennedy, and I don't think it's enough to say it was simply animal magnetism—though surely a good amount of that was involved. But not fundamentally. She fell for his message and his delivery of it. As has been said countless times before I said it to you, Kennedy tapped into the vast aquifer of American idealism that's like that big underground lake somewhere out there on the plains. That aquifer is always there, under the surface, waiting for the person who is smart enough, articulate enough, in touch with our realities enough, to draw from it—to draw from it in a way that reminds us of what the heart of the country is, or anyway, what we believe the heart of the country is. That's really what I had in mind when I told you that Judy was Jack's ideal audience—it wasn't just the Catholic issue. She believed in that America he talked about, and may not even have known how deeply she did until she heard him talking up on Sinatra's terrace. And in telling her what he hoped to do for America, he reminded her of her own best dreams for herself, the dreams that had been covered over by glamour, glitz, and bales of money so that after a while she'd kind of let go of them and accepted instead a set of counterfeit substitutes. And what better place to have such a conversation than Las Vegas?

If this were just a regular story, and by that I mean a personal story, it would still have its own kind of pathos. You know: gorgeous girl with lots of promise makes bad choices and ends up lost. And it is that kind of story, too. But the fact is that it isn't *only* that. The more I came to think about it, to brood over it, maybe, as Lucy began to feel, the more it started to have a strange *national* quality to it. Don't ask me to justify that. I wasn't able to with Lucy, and I might not do a whole lot better with you. But I kept on feeling, the deeper into this I got, that there was more to this life than where she went, who she went to bed with, and how she ended up. But I wasn't able to say to myself just what this something more was. In that way, I suppose you could say that she—Judy—and I were more alike than I could ever have imagined when I started out looking for a big-time scoop. She, too, thought there was some meaning hidden in the trash heap.

I think I told you that some months before this phase of the project, while I was commuting up to Keneally's, Lucy began to develop a pretty dim view of Judy. But not of Jack, even when I told her one night some of the stuff I was digging up about him. She went quiet for a bit but then said with a defiance that was kind of muted, "I *still* miss him." The reason for that, the reason she had so much company, is that so many people heard something in his words; or maybe it was the cadence of his talk; or maybe it was what they saw in this handsome guy who was so quick, so articulate he was almost glib at times. Probably all of these things. And that something was nothing less than Possibility with a capital *P*—the possibilities this country was supposed to allow you to realize in your own life.

Have you ever crossed one of the bridges over the Mississippi in the Midwest, on your way from somewhere in the East? It's a thrill. It's a thrill because in some places—let's say at Dubuque, where Illinois and Wisconsin and Iowa join up—the bridge swings high above the river, and you can't miss that this is some kind of marker or dividing line. Then you're down on the far side, and you're in the Great West, where *anything* could happen and probably has, where you think even now, even for just a moment, that you might possibly become rich or famous or meet the girl of your dreams or learn something about life that will change your own. The thing to feel then, if you're not asleep at the wheel when you cross that bridge—though the way I'm trying to talk here means it couldn't really be that actual, *physical* bridge—is that one morning, maybe tomorrow's morning, you'll swing your legs out of the sack and stand up and realize who you were always meant to be: you at your highest height, you at your farthest reach, you at your brightest moment, when everything clicks into place like the tumblers in a huge combination lock and the door swings wide for you. That's the sense of possibility JFK tapped into. Beyond the sappy Sinatra heist of "High Hopes," which became the Kennedy campaign anthem, this was the American anthem that he spoke, and Judy heard every note of it. Given what I've already told you about her life and loves and affairs and so on, and given what awful, dark stuff lay just ahead for her, I guess I couldn't blame you for laughing if I were to tell you that it's occurred to me that in a strange way she just might be a kind of symbol of America: beautiful, full of promise, flawed, fated. That wouldn't make her a tarnished version of the Bert Parks pinup with cocked hip and dazzling smile, but something more somber, more grave, and therefore achingly beautiful, not just pretty. Something you see and want to run after with your arms outstretched, because you can see what darkness lies ahead, down that path.

Which is to say to you finally that I believe that if she'd known that she was carrying death kits from the White House to Chicago and elsewhere, plans for killing the head of another state, she would have been both horrified and crushed. I think she'd have thrown that first packet down on the table and run from the White House to take the first flight home. Jack Kennedy, her Jack, didn't plot assassinations. Sure, America fought its enemies, but always on the battlefield, in the open.

Naive, yes. But I'll bet you the great majority of Americans still believed this in 1961, including guys like myself who'd served in the war and thought they knew what the enemy looked like and what it took to defeat him. So it wasn't naive only; it was also *native,* in the blood. It was surely in her blood, and for my proof I go back again to her instant grasp of Jack Kennedy's message as he ran it down for her in Vegas. Remember, now, this was a totally apolitical girl who immediately wanted to be a Kennedy drumbeater. And this is why I don't think she could knowingly have become a courier carrying death in her black handbag. Maybe that makes *me* naive. I leave that to you. But I'm comfortable living with this part of the story, anyway.

So she didn't know what she was doing for the brothers. That's about as bluntly as I can put it. She didn't know what was in those packets, and she didn't know what Roselli and Momo were doing with what she handed them. Nor, of course, could she have had any idea what happened to them once she'd taken them back to the White House, almost always, as near as I can figure it, on the same day she made the deliveries. Sometimes it took monster days to complete those missions.

I don't know that this makes her a fool. High-level messengers are often in the dark about what they're carrying, which makes the old custom of killing them when the news is bad look especially cruel. But at least *we* know now what Giancana and company were doing with what she gave them. They took out the cash, of course, when cash was included, which couldn't have been every time, you'd think. But other than that and making some marks on the margins of the papers, they didn't do anything with them. That's nothing, zippo, about arranging the hit. We know this because of that illegal bug, Mo, the FBI planted in Momo's booth at the Armory.

At the end of that February, Mo picked up Giancana talking with Roselli about Bobby Kennedy's plans for a new war on organized crime. This was hardly the quo they had been led to expect for the quid they'd ventured in West Virginia and Cook County. In this "heavily redacted" transcription—as they always say in these matters—Momo says the Kennedys have absolutely no loyalty, none. Okay, so these Mob guys were past masters in the arts of backstabbing and double crossing, in setups and knockoffs. But in their own view of things, they only used these tactics when they judged they were called for by the behavior of others or by changes in circumstances. They had their own code, whereas the Kennedys didn't seem to have one at all. How could you do business with such people? So here we have Momo bitching and Roselli grunting along—"Right, right, yeah, yeah" and so forth. Then Roselli tells Momo he's been working some other channels, back channels of some sort, trying to get through to Bobby and remind him that Giancana wasn't supposed to be a *target*, for Christ's sake; he was supposed to be a *valued friend*. That was the understanding that went into West Virginia and Cook County. But so far Roselli hasn't had any success with these efforts, and hardly a day goes by without some more ominous rumblings out of Justice. Then Momo's heard saying that if he could do it, he'd take over the communications himself, only with "Giovanni" now president, he can't talk to him man to man, so that direct avenue is blocked.

Roselli asks, "Well, what about Frank [Sinatra]? Can we use him?" Frank knew the history here, or part of it, and maybe he could talk to someone in the family, get through to Bobby. Momo tells Roselli to get on the phone with Frank right away and report back. So something like two weeks later Mo picks up Roselli, Momo, and a third party, whose identity isn't established. They're back at the Armory, and Roselli's news isn't good.

Frank had done what he'd been told. He'd called old Joe, twice in Hyannis Port and a third time in Palm Beach. On the first two calls, Roselli reported, Joe said he'd have a word with his headstrong son Bobby and see what could be done to straighten this matter out.

But, he told Frank, it was difficult just now to get the proper attention in Washington, what with the new administration just up and running. And anyway, Joe told Frank, a lot of things had to be said for public consumption that would never become actual policy. But it was the third call, the one to Palm Beach, that really ignited Momo, because on this one the old man told Sinatra he'd done what he could: he'd talked to Bobby about their "mutual friend in Chicago," reminding him that certain favors had been done during the campaign. But that was as far as he was willing to go, and did Frank want to come to Florida and play some golf?

Well, like I say, this set Momo off. Here he is on Mo: "What the fuck is that? What fuckin' kind of answer is that?" And then Roselli again: "Well, Frank says it's the best he can do right now. He can't keep calling him [Joe Kennedy]. He'd like wear out his welcome. Maybe if he goes down there he can talk to him, more casual, friendly—"

Momo:

> Friendly, my rosy red ass! Who the fuck do these people think they're dealin' with here—the fuckin' milkman? Are we supposed to be fuckin' *marks*, walkin' around with our thumbs up our ass?
>
> This is supposed to be *business*. If I give a guy my money to do something, I want something back, you know? They understand that—the old man. We talked—it was a year ago—he understood the rules—shit, he practically wrote 'em, the dried-up old piece of shit, him!
>
> You tell Frank to get his ass down there and talk sense to him, and I want an answer—I don't want none of these 'Well, gee, guys, my hands are tied'—that bullshit! Those fuckin' brothers, both of them are scared shitless of the old man. He *ran* that whole fuckin' thing [the campaign?]—wasn't a thing went down he didn't pass on.

Now, there are a couple of things we need to factor in here, and for starters you have to wonder how much of an effort old Joe actually made with Bobby—if he made any. Well before the election Joe told Jack, Bobby's your AG. He's worked his ass off for you, and you owe him. So that was that. The folklore of that time and since had it that Joe had a tighter grip on Jack than he did on Bobby, that Bobby was in some ways a good deal more like the old man and therefore harder for him to control. Maybe there's something to this. Just because you know a guy's moves doesn't necessarily mean you'll be able to thwart them. Remember Chrissie Evert and Martina on the tennis court? Also, things between Joe and Bobby had changed since Bobby was simply his boy; now that he was the AG, Joe might not be too eager to get into an explanation with him of a deal he'd done with a Mafia don in Chicago. Then there's the matter of the old man's character. He was a wily sonofabitch by all accounts, with layers and layers to him. So I think it's quite possible he only *told* Sinatra he'd spoken with Bobby, when he hadn't done any such thing. He might easily have figured, Well, they did do us some favors, and we gave them the money to do them. And then simply washed his hands of the whole thing. That, though, would look to Momo and his people like a kind of hand job—only one hand washing itself.

Meanwhile, things were hardly at a standstill. They were hurtling toward catastrophe. The exiles were still stomping around down in Guatemala, and increasingly broad hints were dropped here and there in the papers that something really big was about to happen in Cuba. The administration continued to finalize its invasion plans, beginning with an air strike that was supposed to knock out Castro's air force. Judy continued to take those packets to Chicago and Los Angeles and Vegas and bring them back. But also Giancana had made up his mind that since the Kennedys had apparently double-crossed him by making him a target, he would run a triple cross: there'd be no hit on Castro, at least not one he and his people had anything to do with. And he called Marcello and Trafficante to tell them he thought they all ought to sit on their hands, so to say, and wait to see just what the brothers were up to.

He had never been keen on the hit anyway, for the reason I mentioned earlier. His intelligence on conditions over there was a hell of a lot better than Washington's. Castro was a national hero, not the bearded bum Washington thought, and he'd very quickly consolidated his total control of the island. Offing him would be suicide for somebody. So Momo just sat there, looking over the stuff Judy handed him but doing nothing about any of it. Here's what Mo picked up on April eleventh:

Momo:

> They think they're so fuckin' smart. Get my help, then, FUCK HIM! Well, now, let's just wait and see how fuckin' smart they are when they do their thing over there [in Cuba]. We'll give them a fuckin' they'll never forget. Him [JFK] and that little snot [Robert Kennedy?]—they'll have such sore assholes they'll have to grab a steam pipe to take a shit. Fuck with us that way . . .

And that's pretty much the way it turned out four days later: the first air strike accomplished nothing, unless you wanted to count the fact that it blew our OAS cover. Then the exiles got pinned down on the beaches at the Bay of Pigs, and when JFK learned that Castro was very much alive and totally in charge, he sacrificed them by calling off a second air strike. It was a terrific snafu, complete and total, and JFK had to stand up there at the podium before the world and take full blame for it. You might remember that press conference. You know, the "Victory has a hundred fathers but defeat is an orphan" speech. Well, it wasn't really a speech; it was as short a talk as he could possibly make it. When I was trying to put this project together I got hold of a video of it, and what you saw there was a guy who looked in total control, just icy, arctic. Underneath that, though, he was *boiling*.

Judy had gotten used to his sailor's vocabulary, but not like this. It was so constant, so violent, that it made what few meetings they had that spring "pretty unpleasant. About all Jack does is swear and ask himself how he could have been so stupid and believe his intelligence people and the military men. He says he'll never trust them again." On June seventh she was back at the Mayflower and was supposed to go to the White House for dinner with Jack but begged off, telling him she'd come down with a stomach bug and wasn't feeling at all well. He said something like "Well, okay" and hung up. It wasn't strictly true, but she was sick of the routine where she'd do nothing but sit there and listen to him rant and then go down the hall and make love to him. It marked the first time she'd ever told Jack something that wasn't true. So instead of seeing Jack in his sour mood, she reached Sam in Chicago and took a flight out there the next morning without speaking to Jack again before she left.

Momo couldn't have been in too great a mood himself, considering the Cuban mess and Bobby's threatening remarks about organized crime. But as things turned out, whatever his underlying feelings were, he couldn't have been more high-spirited and gentlemanly. *Larky* was the word she used to describe his behavior, and for three days they did touristy things like going to the Brookfield Zoo and out to Hawthorne Park to see the trotters, where she let Sam bet for her and came away with $342 of the track's money. Sam told her he had business to do in L.A. and that if she wanted to extend her visit by a couple of days, they could fly out together. She was having such a relaxed time that this was an easy decision to make: here she was, not on a secret mission but instead in the company of a man who was turning himself inside out to give her a good time. Back in Washington, by contrast, was an enraged man who hardly paid her any attention, even when they were in bed together, because he was consumed by the desire to find scapegoats and punish them. Which would you choose, if only for the short run?

On that last night Sam took her out to the house on South Wenonah for another home-cooked meal, and his family couldn't have been more welcoming. While dinner was cooking they had a lot of laughs in the kitchen, with Sam pouring what he called dago red with a pretty heavy hand. Then it was just the two of them in the dining room. He told her this was the first time he'd eaten in there since his wife's funeral, and that made her feel special, and she said so. Up to that moment he hadn't so much as mentioned the Kennedys, which must have been a relief. But now he told her he hated to see such a beautiful girl get "messed over" by a bunch that obviously thought they were better than everybody else. They had no loyalty except to each other, he told her, and you couldn't trust people like that, because when the tough times came for you, as they must, you wouldn't be able to find them anywhere. At this, she was beginning to be afraid he was going to go off on a rant of his own, an anti-Kennedy one. But he didn't. Instead he kind of took a hitch in his belt, like a guy will do in the midst of a street discussion that's building steam, and simply looked at her in silence. Just as she was starting to feel uncomfortable he smiled his sad smile and shrugged and said she shouldn't forget who her real friends were. Nothing more was said about it, and after dinner he drove her back to the city. They sat together the next day on the flight to L.A., and at one point he reached over and took her hand. She let him keep it.

She hadn't been back in her apartment more than a few hours when there was Jack on the phone, wanting to know where the hell she'd been. So she told him, flat-out, motivated by his high tone.

"Well," he said, "did you have to spend so long there?"

I don't know how she answered that, but the exchange might tell you part of the reason they didn't meet again for well over a month: they were beginning to pick at each other. Only part of the reason, though. In the foreground was Berlin, where a major crisis had been brewing since early June that had Kennedy and his team preoccupied.

This was the context when they finally did meet in Washington the first week in August. He'd asked her to come at the end of July, but she'd stalled him, telling him she was trying to work hard at her painting and also had some things to do for her mother, who hadn't been feeling that well. Maybe all this was true. Her diaries aren't often day-to-day, and she doesn't say what she was actually doing during this time.

She called him from the Mayflower on the sixth to learn that Jackie had switched her plans at the last minute and wouldn't be taking the children to Hyannis Port until the morning of the eighth. Could they have lunch that day? She was peeved, knowing she shouldn't be, that in a situation like hers unforeseeable inconveniences were bound to arise; the wonder really was that there hadn't been more of them. Still, she heard herself saying she'd try to make it, though her schedule was crowding up.

"Why are you being like this?" he asked. "I can't very well yank the world around to suit Judy."

She said he shouldn't bother trying; there were many more important things for him to be spending his time on.

Not the best start, you'd have to say. But of course she showed up on the eighth, on time and wearing a clinging canary yellow dress. The weather was sultry like it can be there at that time of year, but she must have been a match for it. When she caught her first glimpse of him, he looked drawn and was moving stiffly, but he managed a small, ironic smile.

"That's a nice quiet thing to wear to the White House," he quipped, glancing at her dress. "Anybody notice you coming in?" She came right back, saying that if he felt that way about it, there were some other places she could take it. There was a show at the Phillips Collection she was eager to see. He'd only been kidding, he assured her—something he wouldn't have had to explain only a few months before. Actually, he went on, she looked lovely, and on that slightly better note they went in to lunch: hamburgers again, with a wedge of iceberg lettuce with Thousand Island dressing. That happens to fill the bill for my idea of a great lunch, but not hers. To her, it was kind of like what the boys might have in the locker room after a sweaty round of golf while they were on their way to getting drunk and swapping dirty jokes.

She thought it would be just the two of them, but then Powers came in, and she found herself glad, because she thought he might provide a useful distraction. That wasn't the way it turned out, but not because she didn't try: she put herself forward to Powers for the first time, asking him questions about his background, his family, his summer, the Washington weather, and so forth. Really turning it on for him, sitting there in that eye-catching dress and only picking at her plate. But Powers was a canny guy. He wasn't JFK's all-purpose man just because he was jolly and socially adept. He answered her questions, all right, but no more than politely, so he must have known his boss had something he wanted to get off his chest, and when finally the exchanges with Judy dwindled into silence, he glanced in Jack's direction.

Jack took it from there. He'd been curious about something, he said deliberately, a story that had come back to him. She thought this would be a question about some piece of Hollywood gossip, most probably about his favorite subject, Sinatra. Not so. "I was wondering, did you ever tell somebody that I once tried to get you in bed with me and another woman?"

She was just then taking a sip of her daiquiri and was so shocked, so blindsided, that she took it in a huge belt and choked on it. While she coughed and coughed, Powers looked at Jack, wondering wordlessly whether he should do something, and then on his own he scurried around the table to pat her firmly on the back. You wonder what he might have been thinking while he was at it, but whatever it was, as soon as she got over her fit, she lit into Jack in a way that had to be unique in Powers's experience, demanding to know how he could possibly imagine she'd do such a thing and then bring it up in front of another person. The way he'd asked it, she said later, strongly implied that the story itself was nothing but a piece of vicious gossip, and yet with Powers there she could hardly say to Jack that he should have been the first to know it was far from that, that it was indeed true. She burned to say just this, and she wanted to bring Powers in as well by telling him he must know it was no gossip because Kenny O'Donnell would have told him about it. But she didn't, concentrating her full fire instead on Jack, as if Powers weren't there, and getting hotter by the minute. Later, thinking it over, she admitted that part of her rage was actually embarrassment, because the thrust of Jack's question—not the story itself—happened to be true: in the days following the convention she had discussed the attempted troika with several of her L.A. friends. Later, in private, she tried to recall exactly how many people she'd told and came up with four names, but she had to allow that there might have been one or two more. She tried to justify this to herself, saying she'd been so upset and disappointed that she couldn't keep it to herself. Maybe for her that was all the explanation necessary. What other motive could she have had?

She certainly wouldn't have needed this particular episode to substantiate any claims she might have been making that she was in fact JFK's girlfriend. In the first place, she was a very private girl in almost every respect, the last thing from a tattletale or a self-promoter—which would've made her unusual out there. And in any case, her close friends would have known for some time that she was seeing Jack. So, apparently, did others not so close: she noted that on at least two occasions, people she didn't know that well had come up to her at parties to ask her if it was really true she was seeing John Kennedy. To which she'd replied, "Why don't you ask him?" And then there's the nature of the story itself. I mean, it doesn't exactly bathe either of them in a golden light. So I have trouble imagining she'd have been retailing it for its glamour value. What does that leave us with, then? Maybe only what she claimed: that she'd been too upset to keep the thing to herself.

But if we move from motive to consequence, here we come to something more substantial, more verifiable, because here we have another example—a glaring one—of bad judgment. Bad judgment based on a lack of concern for the high-powered league she was playing in. These guys—Joe Kennedy, Jack, Bobby, Hoover, Giancana, Roselli and the Mob in Vegas—played for keeps, for all the marbles, for the whole ball of wax. You can pile on all the relevant terms here, because you can't emphasize the point too strongly. Sure, these same guys made their own mistakes in judgment; we're not talking about perfection here. Sometimes even these sluggers can seem to the rest of us amazingly reckless, taking foolish chances, like Joe Kennedy figuring he needed to go out to Chicago to have a talk with Momo in a federal courthouse, or J. Edgar running around a hotel corridor in a dress, chasing his old buddy, Clyde Tolson. But one mistake they didn't make was to ignore power. They understood juice, respected what it could do. It made everything run, and it could fry you if you fooled with it. I don't think she really got this, ever. There was a kind of innocence here, a strange, eternal virginality, to use that word again; and by my using it yet again in connection with her, you might be wondering by this point if I'm more than a little off my rocker to still see this quality in her. All I can tell you is that after brooding on this story and trying to understand why things turned out the way they did, this is finally what I'm left with. When I try to mentally leave all the other stuff off to one side—her beauty, her body, her athletic abilities, her artistic aspirations, her best dreams—this is what I'm left with, this strange innocence, this impermeability. Looked at one way, it could easily enough be taken as stupidity. Sinatra had taken it that way and had told her so. And it wouldn't surprise me if Kennedy and Momo thought of her as curiously naive for someone in her position. That isn't what I see—though I cringed for her when I saw her making the same mistake with these big hitters over and over. You want to reach in there and stop her, you know? Not very professional of me, I guess, but there you have it. I never claimed to be a pro historian.

Have you ever gotten up close to big-time juice so that you got a real good sense of what it can do? I'm not talking here about people who are just rich, who can boss others around at an office or a restaurant, or somebody who's temporarily in the limelight and can breeze past a block-long line at some big-deal event. I've seen that kind of thing, and you probably have yourself. No, what I'm talking about is something different. I'm talking about being in the presence of someone who wields *immense*, continuous, day-and-night power, the kind that makes things run or shuts them down; who can say about someone or something, thumbs up or down; who can make life-and-death decisions. I never had that kind of exposure. But I once had a conversation with someone who did.

His name was Walter Trohan, and he wrote a column for Colonel McCormick at the *Trib* for many years and shared most of the old boy's prejudices—the way you kept that job. He and I were hardly buddies. I think he looked down on me as a journalistic serf. And despite the fact that we'd bump into each other often enough around town, the way you will, he never bothered to learn my name. However. There came a time when I was almost accidentally in a position to do him a pretty good favor, and I did it—doesn't make any difference now what it was. But the upshot was that old Trohan invited me to dinner—not lunch, which is the payoff on a lesser debt. We had a couple of bombers beforehand, and he got to talking about Kissinger, whom he'd spent some time around. I'll never forget what he had to say about being in the presence of that kind of power. It was actually kind of scary, he said, which surprised me, coming from him. Not that Kissinger was blustery. He wasn't. But there was something coming off him that you could feel, something you could smell, like you were standing next to a megavoltage transformer.

Well, Jack Kennedy, of course, would've had this in spades, and so in his underworld way would Momo. Yet here was Judy, moving between these powerhouses and not getting it, not understanding her amazingly unique, amazingly dangerous situation. She just went along acting as if they were *just men*, you know? If she'd really thought about JFK as one of the two most powerful people on the planet—the other being Khrushchev—I don't see how she could have blabbed about his troika bid to her friends. But she did, because there she was speaking as a woman whose lover had betrayed her most intimate confidence, as if the identity of that lover were beside the point. *He was her lover*—that was what was important to her. And now, more than a year later, a stretch of time during which she'd done many things for him, including trying to forget the incident, here he was, bringing it up again and in front of the pudding-faced Powers, who was acting just like Kenny O'Donnell had at the pad on Rossmore: as if this were just another garden-variety lovers' spat. All of which in her view compounded the offense.

And even this wasn't the end of it. Because when she'd run out of steam and taken a deep breath, Jack asked her to come with him and led her down the hall to the bedroom, where he propositioned her. Now, that takes a real set of solid brass balls, I don't care what your position is or how much juice you have. She told him she couldn't possibly do what he had in mind, and so back they went to Powers in the dining room, where Jack said he was going to take a swim, and in the meantime why didn't Powers give Judy a tour of the White House while everybody cooled off?

You won't have any trouble imagining, I know, how it went over when Powers tried to tell her he'd give her a view of the place no tourist would ever get, and no state visitor either. She cut him off quick, telling him he could save his breath by simply calling her a car, or if one wasn't available, a cab would do fine. Back at the Mayflower, she packed and caught an early-evening flight back home.

Of course, you'd like to know what route that troika story took getting back to Jack. I visualize here a spaghetti bowl with all these noodles wrapped around each other: people in L.A., Las Vegas, Washington—politicians, entertainers, media types, restaurant owners, Mob figures, influence peddlers, fixers, business execs. In such a mix any number of possibilities come to mind, so many that if you were looking into that bowl and just decided, Well, I'll pull this strand, you still wouldn't be able to see all the other strands it touched while you were pulling it out. This is only a way of saying, Who knows how it got back? But the point of my crude illustration is that it was *bound* to get back, and either she didn't think carefully about that or, more likely, she didn't care. But these two trains arrive at the same station. She'd offended power, and there would be consequences.

• • •

The immediate consequence was that Jack shifted the relationship off high heat to the back burner, and although there were moments over the following months when they were hot and heavy—occasionally gloriously so, it seems—they were just that, moments, and I doubt he ever thought of her the same way again. I don't think she ever felt the same way about him either.

When she was back in L.A. she wasn't there much longer than it would have taken her to unpack, send some things out to the cleaners, and reorganize her wardrobe for another trip. This time she went up to Carmel and Pebble Beach and hung out with that crowd. She played a few rounds at Pebble Beach but didn't say what she shot. Eddie Fisher was there and was all "busted up" about his marriage with Liz Taylor. One day he'd say it was doomed; the next he'd be joyous because she'd called. This was where he made that comment about Judy's being in the same league as Liz—one night at Casanova's in Carmel he leaned across the table and boozily breathed that at her. But she could tell that he was carrying such a big torch for Liz he couldn't possibly see anything, let alone what another girl really looked like. Anyway, Eddie wasn't her type, or so she thought at the time.

When she left Carmel to go back to L.A. it was with the idea of getting back into her painting, particularly another child's portrait she'd been wanting to finish for some time. But she couldn't find a way back into it now, and so she dropped her brushes and went with her sister Jackie and some of Jackie's movie friends up to Malibu. What I get out of all this is simply drift, like she was waiting to see what would happen with Jack but not really expecting much and not even sure she wanted anything more to happen.

Meanwhile, Berlin boiled over, with Khrushchev deciding to challenge Kennedy there after having bullied the hell out of him in Vienna. Here again I think of that rip tide that was pulling both sides, both leaders, out into more and more dangerous waters, and even though Kennedy saw where things were heading, he didn't seem able to swim out of that force. Well before the Wall went up he supposedly told one of his inner circle—might have been McNamara—that the way East Berlin was hemorrhaging population to the West, it was clear Khrushchev had to do something. So when the Wall went up on August 13, he wasn't surprised, and even though the hawks were screaming, "*Do* something!" he privately said that while this was an ugly development, still a wall was better than a war. But this was a private observation, and in that climate it couldn't possibly become public policy. There had to be another kind of response, some muscle-flexing that stopped short of force. He'd suffered that real shit-kicking over the Bay of Pigs and another one in Vienna, where he wasn't prepared for what a tough old bastard Khrushchev turned out to be. In this new crisis, he told his people, he simply couldn't afford to look weak and indecisive. And so while the Wall went higher, layer by layer, he ordered more troops into West Berlin and sent reinforcements to other bases in Europe, signaling resolve. Then he sent Johnson to the city itself to tell the world America wouldn't be intimidated by the Soviets, there or anywhere else. Apparently Johnson wasn't wild about the assignment: the situation was so tense he thought he had a chance of getting caught in the shooting.

Then, after he'd done all this, Jack called Judy and asked her to come to Washington. It was now the first week in October. She went, all right, but the measure of what was happening in the relationship was that she went to Tahoe first, to stay with Sam. I say "to stay with Sam" because those are her words, not "to visit Sam," and as far as I know this was the first time she stayed in the same place he did. Doesn't necessarily mean they shared a room, a suite, a bed. All the entry says is "Stayed with Sam." And the next entry you find is "Mayflower pretty weird."

That evening the car dropped her, at the east gate this time, where Powers met her, frankly ran his beady eyes over her, and then escorted her to the second floor. When she saw Jack at the end of the hall, she thought he looked puffy, a sign, she'd learned, that he'd been on an unusually heavy dose of his many medications. Still, he seemed handsome and graceful as he came toward her, holding one hand behind his back and smiling a mischievous Irish smile. He too ran his eyes over her, and when they met he gave her a quick peck, still keeping that hand hidden. When they were alone in the dining room, he finally produced what he'd been concealing, a small black box, and put it in front of her.

"Oh," she said, looking at it but not snatching it up. "Big chief has beads and mirrors for little squaw girl." It was a good line for her in that situation, and he laughed hard. At the same time, though, there was a bite to it he wouldn't have missed, and he didn't.

"Jesus, you're tough on a guy, Judy."

Once in Malibu, when they were still getting to know each other, he'd asked what her favorite stone was, but she'd played it coy and hadn't said. But what woman—or man, for that matter—could ultimately resist Jack Kennedy when he decided to turn on all the voltage? Not her, not then, and so finally she'd admitted how much she loved brown diamonds. Now here they were, a necklace of small ones, well spaced by delicate gold links, and while her first impulse was to repeat what she said to offers of jewelry, furs, plane tickets, hotel rooms, trips—"I pay my own way"—the sight of these dark beauties was more than she had the will to refuse. So instead she said what she felt at that instant—"Oh, Jack, you should have."

That was the start of what turned out to be a "splendid evening," which was as surprising to her as it was splendid, because on the flight from Tahoe she hadn't been able to feel any of the old-time excitement she always had on her way to meet him. In its place there was only a kind of emptiness and at the center of it a small knot of irritability she didn't bother to inspect—at least not enough to write about it. But that feeling was gone now, given the necklace, which she immediately put on, and Jack's behavior. He told her that he'd missed her and that it had been a very rough time around there, with pressures coming from every possible direction. There'd been moments, he went on, when he found himself seriously wondering whether there was a single man working for him he could absolutely rely on, except for Bobby. Everybody else seemed to want to advance some personal, partial view, whereas he alone had somehow to find one that was internationally comprehensive at the same time it was domestically acceptable. When you think of the presidency this way, you see suddenly why the job's a killer—and you wonder why so many would do just about anything to get it. "I've been feeling lately like I'm not really in the Oval Office," he told her with a tired smile, "but in a goddamned duck press."

But the longer dinner went on, the lighter his mood became. "It was like clouds lifting off water," she said, and it made her feel wonderful to see that she still could do that for him. It restored—for the moment, anyway—something she'd thought was gone after those first days when they'd been discovering each other and each meeting was like a stretch of new, beautiful country. And so when he took her by the hand and led her down the hall she felt as eager as he did, though wondering whether the lovemaking would again take that routine form she'd come reluctantly to expect.

It didn't.

> Jack was as active and attentive as I can remember. Where this came from given what he's been going through I don't know but he was tender patient and passionate all at the same time and then we lay there talking until the wee hours. When he took me down in the elevator to the man waiting with the car I felt sorry for that poor guy but not too much.

Now here's something that surprised me when I came across it. It happened the next day, when she was back at the White House for lunch. Nothing surprising in that, of course. They'd had a wonderful night, as you've heard, and also, as you've heard, Jack's appetite for action was legendary even then, at least among a few insiders. No, what's surprising is that Bobby showed up, and he had a packet for her. Even more so was the fact that she was willing to accept it.

Who knows what went into that willingness, what portion of it was the result, the residue of what had happened between them the night before and what portion was the expression of her trust that whatever Jack was doing was the right thing for the country? Sure, they'd had their disappointments, and in retrospect we can see where the relationship was headed. But you could have said the same things about the relationship between Jack and the country, too. I don't know how it might have looked at that time to foreigners, but I wouldn't be surprised if they weren't puzzled by public reaction here to the Bay of Pigs, Vienna, and now the crisis in Berlin. Because in the aftermath of every one of these setbacks JFK's popularity rocketed upward, whereas maybe Europeans might have expected it to plummet. Is this national naiveté? Super-patriotism? Or is it evidence that after all the country has a big and trusting heart? Maybe it's all of these things but more the last one of them. So I'd have to say that Judy's willingness to take the packet from Bobby—whom she didn't like—makes her part of the larger pattern.

But this isn't all. Because what's also involved here is Momo's willingness to stay another hand. In view of what Mo had picked up, he had obviously developed a very low opinion of the Kennedys, and yet the presence of the packet in Bobby's hands had to mean there'd been some back-channel, alleyway communications between Justice and Chicago. That's to say, you might send your messenger off without her knowing what she was carrying, but you'd be working some pretty strange game if you sent her to a powerhouse who was going to spit on the message and grind it under his heel without even opening it, right? What would you be accomplishing there? So there had to have been some sort of preparation for this new development, because Bobby and Jack were sure as hell determined to accomplish what they'd set out to do in Cuba. They were more determined than ever to kill Castro. They were *obsessed* by the need for this, as if Castro at the Bay of Pigs had flung a handful of shit on the family flag. Various guys at Justice, State, Defense, and the CIA have gone on record about this in recent years, saying that nobody at that time really understood what this Cuba thing was about, but that after the Bay of Pigs it came more and more to look like a family vendetta dressed up to resemble sober statecraft. It was anything but statecraft. In fact, now that Bobby was running it, it was goofier than ever.

He'd canned a lot of those who'd been in on it up to the Bay of Pigs and had put Edward Lansdale in charge of the daily operations of what was now supposed to be a stealth-type operation. They were going to build an infrastructure of guerrillas, then begin a campaign of sabotage and antigovernment propaganda. Meanwhile they'd be playing a bunch of dirty tricks. I don't know how many of these were dreamed up by Lansdale, but they were just *wild:* getting a depilatory into Castro's food so that his famous beard would fall out, exposing his weak chin; slipping LSD into his water jug so that as he sipped from it during one of his three-hour harangues he'd sound more and more like a lunatic; staging a fantastically elaborate offshore show that was supposed to convince Cubans that the Second Coming was upon them and that Castro was the Antichrist. Finally, when the stage was set, Castro was going to be kidnapped, held at a secret location, and then murdered. You have to wonder how much—if any—of this crap was outlined in those packets Judy carried for the next six months or so. But there must have been some type of assurances in them that the Mob could go back into business with our government's tacit blessing once Castro was out of the way, and maybe Momo, Roselli, and the others figured they had little to lose and everything to gain by playing ball and arranging the kidnapping.

If the whole shebang strikes you as wildly implausible and laughable in its details, we can see now that it was a deadly, deadly business. Because it ultimately had a lot to do with the Cuban missile crisis: it ratcheted up the stakes in the cold war; it helped make Cuba a tempting target for Soviet expansion into this hemisphere; and it turned a local hero into an international figure, which solidified his standing with his own people.

Look at it another way. What if, instead of continuing to poke at Castro, the Kennedys had more or less ignored him and focused their energies on the far greater problem of what to do about the USSR? Would Khrushchev have been tempted to try to arm Castro with missiles? This was a tremendously risky gambit made by a very shrewd customer, and you have to wonder whether in a more stable climate he'd have thought it was worthwhile. You have to wonder, too, whether Fidel would have welcomed it, knowing what he would be exposing himself to. The anti-Castro right had been hollering all along that Cuba was only ninety miles from American shores. Well, America was the same ninety miles from Cuba and could easily have reduced the island to an oil slick. And finally there's Dallas. I'm not going to get into that, except to remind you that there are still people around—fewer now, it's true—who are eager to explain to you that Castro got JFK before JFK could get him.

All this is speculation, a chain of what-ifs, which I'm man enough to admit, and it strikes me as highly improbable that any of them could be proved. Unless, of course, the Kennedy brothers' papers might sometime in the future yield up a mother lode on this whole subject. Stranger things have happened. The Nazis recorded almost everything they did—amazing when you come to think about it. Stalin said it wasn't a good idea to write down too much, and still it's remarkable what they keep digging up from those old NKVD archives. You almost think there must be some inner drive, compulsion, that makes powerful people record their doings, no matter how ghastly, just to leave a record of their power: paper-and-ink versions of the pyramids. So maybe it'll happen with the Kennedys and Cuba, and some poor, exploited prof from East Jesus Tech who's almost forgotten what his original mission was will stumble into layers of Bobby's papers and wonder what in hell he's got here—names and numbers and some Cuban rancho in the middle of nowhere. And maybe he'll think to ask if these particular pages have ever been subjected to fingerprint analysis, but he probably won't. Her prints, Judy's, won't be on them, that's for sure. She'll be invisible. But she sure had her hands on history here.

The last such mission she went on was in late February or early March 1962. She was at the White House again, and something she did or said or some way she looked made Bobby vary his routine just a bit. In that situation, she said, he could never muster up anything more than a chilly politeness. By now it had gotten to the point where if she knew he was going to be there, she dreaded going. He had the coldest eyes, she thought. "I've seen Jack's get that way once or twice," she said, "and you think there isn't anything this man wouldn't do to someone standing in his way."

Despite my job, I was never much of a grammarian. I could get my subjects and my verbs hooked up, sure, but I couldn't have diagrammed a sentence for you if you stuck a revolver in my ear. So I have some trouble with this sentence. She's talking about Bobby and his eyes, but who is "this man"? Is it still Bobby, or is it Jack—or could it be both of them? Anyway, she must have done something that showed Bobby how she was feeling, some flicker or flinch when he shoved that packet across the table at her and stood up to leave. But then he didn't leave. He just stood there, looking at her, then down at the packet. And then he came around the table, walking behind Jack, to her chair. "He put his hand on my shoulder," she said. "I think it might have been the first time he'd ever touched me. Then he asked if I was o.k. with this and I said yes." It's interesting to find here that it was Bobby, not Jack, who picked up on something in her that flashed him a warning signal, making him think he had to make some sort of check on the pony they were still using. True, what he actually did wasn't a lot more than check to see if the cinch was still tight, just staying with the metaphor. How much he knew at that point about his brother and Judy and the state of the relationship, I don't know. My guess is that he knew enough to think that she might be coming close to the end of her usefulness. But he must have been thinking that she still had another trip left in her. In any case, what he did—the walk around the desk, the hand laid on the shoulder, the empty kind of question—was more than Jack did; Jack hadn't registered anything and was way off somewhere.

She sure as hell wasn't at all okay with it by that point. Much later—years, in fact—there was a comment in a diary to the effect that if Jack or Bobby had ever asked her again after this to be their courier, she'd have said no. The whole situation had become intolerable, and it wasn't just Bobby. It was Jack, too.

After that September evening when he was once again his old self, he'd fallen back into patterns she'd come to find unattractive. He was more and more moody, less and less there for her. Once in a while there'd be a flash of the old Jack, the one she'd fallen for: a witty remark, a great smile with all those Irish teeth. But then the ceiling would come down again, and he'd be off in his world and its concerns. "I understand this or at least I think I do," she said sometime after New Year's, "but I'm beginning to wonder why he even wants to see me if this is all it's going to be like." So one evening she asked him that.

This was spring, early March I make it, and they'd finished dinner and were taking the walk down to the bedroom, and it suddenly seemed so pointless and routine that she said, "Jack, why don't I just go back to the hotel, because you're not really here with me. You're off somewhere else where I can't reach you, so what's the point?" He stopped there in the hall and ran a hand across his forehead and then smoothed his hair with his palm. He wasn't even looking at her, only staring off down the hall. But then he did turn to her, with an expression she thought was true sadness.

"There are just so goddamned many things to think about in this job," he said, as if he weren't talking to her but was only thinking out loud. "I never imagined how complicated this would be. Never. Nobody could have."

Then he took her arm and they turned back. The black man who'd waited on them was there in the dining room, clearing, and Jack asked him to get her coat. When it was brought, he helped her on with it and saw her to the elevator, and that was that.

Not right then and there, you understand. But in her mind that was the turning point. Like most turning points, though, it didn't just happen out of nothing and nowhere: they got to it, they arrived at it, step by step. A significant number of those steps were the ones he'd asked her to take, out to Chicago and Vegas and elsewhere, to see Sam.

Maybe I can guess what you're thinking here, and if I can, I would hardly blame you. What girl in her right mind would trade in handsome Jack Kennedy, president of the United States, for a coarse-featured thug who ruled an underworld empire of crime and corruption? That's pretty starkly put, but basically this is what was happening during the winter and spring of '61 and '62. And maybe while you're trying to come to terms with this thing, as I did, your mind has slipped back to that film footage I told you about where Momo rips down the swimsuit straps of the unsuspecting Judy. I make this suggestion because mine did, too, wondering what kind of male friend pulls a stunt like that except a low-life hood like Momo Giancana. The film, though, probably needs to be put into context, one I didn't have when I saw it. It's representative of some things but not of others.

There were plenty of really ugly things about Momo the man. But as I said a while back, I think on balance he treated Judy well up until the very end of their relationship. Even after it was over and he was keeping steady company with Phyllis McGuire, he still must have had a kind of respect for her, even if it was only a respectful memory of the girl she'd been. I say this because, as Phil Keneally said, he never opened that package of her diaries, and he had to know they contained stuff about him. I'd say that alone more than cancels out his gross poolside behavior. But there were other things to add in here as well.

To the extent that she let him, he showered her with presents and took a showy pride in being seen with her in the clubs and restaurants and resorts his kind frequented and often stealthily owned portions of. He opened doors for her, stood up when she came into a room or returned to the table. He must have cleaned out a lot of florist shops with all those bouquets he was always sending. Then, when it was over between her and Jack and he could see where she was heading, he asked her to marry him, even though they both knew it was a gesture neither one of them could possibly have acted on. Still, it was a *gallant* gesture, and I think she must have taken it that way. "You know," he said to her one afternoon at the Armory, where they'd been having some martinis, and then he stopped, looking down into his drink. "You know, you deserve to be asked this—would you want to marry me?" It came out of nowhere, and that's just where it went, too—nowhere. She looked over at him and smiled a little but said nothing. "Okay, okay," he said then, cocking his head and chuckling briefly. "Just don't forget I asked."

"I won't, Sam," she told him.

There aren't many summarizing statements that I came across in her diaries, but there's one she made around the time it became public knowledge that she'd known both JFK and Giancana: "Sam was almost always a real gentleman when he was around me." Could she have said more than this about Jack Kennedy?

Still, of course, there is that glaring, that staggering contrast between the two men, and there isn't an easy explanation for her turn from one to the other.

Momo was a killer. His hands were bloody with the deaths of who knows how many men; some he was said to have killed, but more were hits he ordered. He had a mouth on him that could be way fouler than JFK's, as those FBI tapes tell you. He was a hard drinker who loved his martinis, though I don't think you could call him a drunk when he and Judy were keeping company. (Later, though, I think his drinking contributed to behavior the Mob found dangerous.) In fact, thinking back yet again to that poolside episode caught on film, I wouldn't be at all surprised if that wasn't inspired—if I can use that word here—by a gang of martinis he'd had. Have you ever had a couple of what we used to call "see-throughs" and then gone back to the office and tried to function? Well, there's a funny sort of white haze you're looking through while you're trying to think, and *that's* the really hard work you're doing, not the work you're being paid for.

But here's the thing: Judy found him *steady*, reliable. There was a set of what I have to say were values that he outlined for her that first time he showed her around the neighborhood, the cemetery, the church, and his home. All the while he's doing that he's telling her, This is the kind of guy I am, take it or leave it. Now, it's obvious there're other things mixed in there with family, good times around the kitchen stove, love of your wife and kids, and chicken cacciatore that aren't so damned appetizing. But still, they're values, things you live by. Once I had an Italian friend, pretty good writer, try to explain part of this to me.

A. J. Cannizzaro was from somewhere in the Boston area and worked for the old *Traveler* before he passed through here, where he wrote for the *Daily News*, which is how our paths crossed. A.J. was a hard-working, hard-partying guy, and in the short time he spent here he cut a pretty good social swath—big guy, handsome in a tough sort of way, and he clearly had something to him women went for. One day after work we're up at the Berghoff on Adams; it's totally different now, but for a long time it was a good hang. Anyway, there I was, drinking their dark beer, kidding him about Italian stuff, making stupid dago jokes, which he had the generosity to chuckle at, though no doubt he'd heard them hundreds of times already. But then, half seriously, I asked him about Mafia families, about how that strong family ethic fit together with murder and extortion. After all, I said, the other guy's got family, too, right? He said sure to that but went on to tell me that all of it—the crime, Christmas, and chicken cacciatore—was part of a particular complex that couldn't be pulled apart and separated out.

"You're cooking chicken cacciatore," he said, "and maybe you don't go for tomato sauce or maybe it's the wine. You pull that out, what have you got? Well, you haven't got chicken cacciatore—you've got something else. Same thing here with the Mafiosi. The guys that came over here and then got into protection and bootlegging and the rest, they probably learned the ropes over here, what it took to get along. But they brought these other things over with them from their villages and then figured out how to reconcile them with the Church and with supporting their families here and getting along in the neighborhood. Pretty soon, what you have is like a recipe, and they simply don't see the contradictions you might. *This is how it's done among us.* The wives, they learned not to ask questions about certain matters. And as long as the house is decent and the bills get paid and the sons are kept in line and the man doesn't throw the girlfriend in her face—well, this is life, and it's okay.

"There's an Italian word that comes to mind here—*campanilismo.* Kind of hard to give you a direct translation, but it means something like a real strong allegiance, one you don't question, to your local community and its way of life. Very *local,* very strong. That's the best I can do for you. Might not be that satisfying to you, but you show me a theory that explains all the wacko ways humans behave, and I'll poke some holes in it fairly quickly."

Well, I thought back on this when I was trying to account for Judy and Momo Giancana as a couple, and it made a kind of left-handed sense to me when I compared them to Judy and Jack.

I don't have any reason to believe she ever changed her view of Jack Kennedy's idealism, his voicing of what was best and truest about America. So it wasn't that. But I also think that while she clung to those ideals, she became disenchanted with the man. And really, when you think about it a bit, you don't wonder why this happened; you wonder instead how it could turn out any other way. Journalists like me glibly toss off that phrase "the burdens of office." It only takes up a little of your allotted word count, and at the same time it has a definite function in your sentence and your piece: everybody understands it means the weight of responsibility that comes down on the shoulders of someone in the highest authority—where the buck stops, and so forth. But that same useful phrase actually prevents us from thinking about what's truly involved here: the *awful* weight that descends on the shoulders of the president, like a safe falling on him out of a tenth-story window—the *crushing* nature of the thing. Who wouldn't change, staggering along under that? And so Jack changed—had to—and she tried to understand but finally couldn't. I don't know that anybody could. That's what came to me when I read that passage of hers where he says, thinking out loud, that he couldn't have imagined how many things there were to think about when you were in the White House. That's a confession, a stripped, naked confession that takes you beneath the "burdens of office" cliché and gets you right up next to the man himself in his lonesome, isolating situation. In that hallway I think she felt his loneliness, his isolation, but I don't think she could figure out a way to reach through it. It seems to me that part of this had to do finally with what went on between them in bed—and what didn't anymore.

The relentless sameness of the sexual routine—Jack on his back, waiting for her to bring him—really began to get to her, because over time it robbed the act of that intimacy she liked and made it over into something a lot closer to that locker-room/hunting-lodge joke. Put another way, the way she put it herself, the act was where the special closeness between lovers could most be felt; now it was where she most felt his remoteness, while at the same time she felt how much she'd become just another faceless person who saw to his needs. Here's a one-line entry of hers from the day after Valentine's, 1962:

Dinner with Jack then room service.

That's it, all of it, and it's a lot. Especially when you think back on how they began, when his great attraction for her as a man, when it was just the two of them, was that he made her feel he understood her best aspirations and wanted to know everything about her, including what she had for breakfast.

On the other end of the high wire she was working there was Sam. There were the hoody guys he surrounded himself with, the ratty cars he drove, the plywood and Formica decor of his Armory headquarters. There were also those longish stretches of time when he'd disappear on business, the nature of which she had to know was criminal. There was his temper, his tongue, his other women, mostly Phyllis McGuire, and if you don't know the name, she was a very beautiful and talented singer.

And yet. And yet, when Sam was there, he was totally present for her. There was never any moody preoccupation with business, no talk of problems with some flunky who was chronically short on his tally, and so forth. He was right there, with all his energies and attention trained on her. In other words, he treated her the way Jack had before being elected. Then, too, the extended family at his house included her in a way the staff at the White House simply couldn't. There's probably an Italian word for this kind of total embrace; I just don't know what it is, and A.J.'s been gone from here a long time, so I can't ask him. But the point, of course, wouldn't be the right Italian word. It would be the level of comfort she'd come to feel in Sam's company and no longer did in Jack's. With a woman, especially one who was constitutionally always an outsider, that can even things up between guys who on the surface could look as wildly mismatched as Jack versus Momo. On the surface, that's no contest.

When did the emotional scales tilt toward Momo? I don't know; it isn't down in her words. But I do know this much: the lunch Jack had on March 22 with Hoover wasn't the turning point some have been so eager to make it out to be. There's no doubt it did nothing to help the relationship, but there had been developments in this direction for months before.

Well, the lunch. Hoover had asked Jack if he could spare the time for a confidential chat. There were some matters he thought the president might want to know about. So Jack asked him to lunch on the twenty-second. It's easy enough to imagine the glee the old blackmailer was trying to conceal when he was ushered into the Oval Office, because he was carrying enough ammo on Kennedy to blow him and a flotilla of PT boats clear out of the water. Of course, Jack had known for months that Hoover's men had paid a call on Judy, but it seems he'd concluded that this was in connection with Giancana, not him. Whether he was completely satisfied on the score, I couldn't say. The fact that he continued to use her as a courier would indicate he thought the director wasn't on to him. But then, when you're trying to assess JFK's behavior, you have to make due allowance for his broad streak of recklessness, which is like the joker in the pack of cards he otherwise played with great shrewdness.

But whatever he might have been thinking, he couldn't have been prepared for what Hoover dropped on his plate once they were at the table, because it was then that Hoover told him that in tapping Miss Campbell's phone to find out if she might be materially involved in organized crime, his bureau had discovered that she had what he coyly described as a "telephone relationship" with the president's personal secretary, Evelyn Lincoln. When Jack heard that, he instantly understood that Hoover knew everything worth knowing: he would have known about Jack and Judy; he would have known that Judy was a courier between the White House and Giancana; and he would almost certainly have known that his superior, the attorney general, was also involved. And it was this last piece of information that might have pleased Hoover most and prompted his visit.

Hoover's whole life was involved in subterfuge, both professional and personal, and his remark about Evelyn Lincoln was made merely to give Jack a peek at what else he had in his hand. When you think about it a minute, you see a malice there that's almost beautiful, because he's toying with Jack, toying with the president of the United States, suggesting on the surface only that the president ought to be aware that his secretary has drifted into some sort of unsavory relationship and that he, Hoover, loyal servant that he is, has, as always, the president's best interests at heart. But both men would have known in that instant what Hoover really wanted: he wanted the president to put his brother back in his playpen and keep him there, permanently. If this didn't happen, there would be consequences of catastrophic dimensions.

How much Jack knew about Bobby's relationship with Hoover I don't know, but he knew enough, because the two brothers had laughed about Hoover, made jokes about his famous crotchets, his rumored homosexuality, and so forth. I don't know that Jack knew that Bobby thought nothing of walking unannounced into the director's office and demanding to speak with him. No AG in living memory had dared such an insult. I'm certain Jack didn't know about a foolish stunt his brother had played for the amusement of an old law school buddy who'd dropped by one day to say hello. Well, they got to horsing around about Hoover, and Bobby says, "You want me to get him in here for you?" and he presses a desk buzzer. And by God, in five minutes J. Edgar's in there, with his face as red as a fire truck. So Bobby was the target here, but as I say, beyond him Hoover was letting the president know that the director had information that could bring down the entire administration.

The connecting link in all this was Judy, which explains why, after Kennedy said goodbye to his potential political assassin, he called her and told her to go immediately to her mother's house and wait for his call. When it came, she got an earful. He was in a rage. She'd never heard him this way, she said. He wasn't actually yelling, but his voice had that hard, strident quality it sometimes got when he was making tough points in front of large audiences, where his words, punctuated by sharp gestures, were like his finger stabbing you in the chest.

"How dare he," Jack said, "how *dare* he come into this office and threaten me? That fairy shit-packer!" And while he went on with that sort of invective and what Hoover had on them all, she was waiting there on the other end for some words that would tell her where she stood in all of this, whether she'd broken some law she could be arrested for, and, most of all, whether she now had to brace herself for more visits from Hoover's blackshoes. It didn't come, and so at the end of the harangue she had to ask. Where did she stand and what was he going to do to protect her?

"He told me you're going to have to learn to live with this," she wrote. "We both are. He said my phone had a tap on it and I should have the phone co. take it out and another one installed. He said it might not be a bad idea if I thought about moving in with my parents for a while while I looked for another place to live. Swell."

I doubt she included that sardonic word in what she said to him—it would have been useless or worse. But what else could she have said in the circumstances? That she wanted the president of the United States to get on the ass of the director of the FBI, who just happens to know that the president's girlfriend is also his courier to the Mob? When you line it up like that, you see why she said very little more to him and why they hung up without any expressions of endearment and why they made no further plans to meet. "I was so rattled my whole body was just shaking and shaking and I couldn't make it stop," she said.

> So I just sat there in my old bedroom wishing I had some magic potion that could turn me into a little girl again or anyway into whatever I was before I got into all this. I thought I had to take something to stop this shaking before I broke a bone or something so I went downstairs to the butler's pantry and poured myself a double chartreuse and went back to my bedroom and drank it. Then I called Sam.

She tried him in Chicago and finally got through to him in Vegas and asked him if she could come out there. He told her he'd have to call her back on that. Meanwhile she should stay right where she was while he tried to figure out a couple of things that needed his attention. In something just over an hour he called back.

"Meet me tomorrow in Tahoe," he said. "I have some stuff to do there, but there'll be a lot of time when I'll be all yours, baby."

"I don't think," she later wrote, "I have ever gotten a call that was more welcome than that one."

5

SHADOWS

SHE DROVE IT, setting off near midnight after spending part of the day trying to pack for every conceivable occasion. But while she was pulling clothes off hangers and out of drawers her mind was skipping about everywhere else—which gives you an insight into how shaken she was, this big-league clotheshorse who was so conscious of her appearance at all times. She was thinking about Jack, about their times at the White House and how all that was so definitely in the past. About Hoover, "that busybody meat-head." And about Bobby, who couldn't protect her—or wouldn't, and what difference did it make which? And then she thought about Sam, waiting for her up there in Tahoe. "I'm wondering," she wrote later, "what in hell I'm getting myself into coming up here to be with him and the truth is I don't really care. Right now the only thing I care about is feeling safe TODAY. Right now. And right now I'm looking out over the pines and can see the lake and Sam's off somewhere—meet probably—and I feel as long as I'm here he'll take care of me."

She'd driven straight through the night to get to this postcard view, stopping for gas when she had to. Once, north of Bakersfield, there'd been a car on her tail for miles, and though she was afraid her Pontiac might run dry, she risked it, and at Visalia made a diversionary detour eastward a few miles and was lucky enough to find an all-night truck stop. By then the other car had dropped away. Gas, the toilet, a cup of coffee, and then on again, her foot down hard on the pedal. At a diner outside Stockton she had something to eat but didn't say what it was. Maybe she didn't remember. She was so wired—a word she wouldn't have known—that she didn't feel tired at all and just kept going until she got to Tahoe City and called Sam.

The house was a big two-story redwood with a deck running around the upper level so you could see through the pines down to the lake. It sat on a narrow back road on the Nevada side between a development still going up and the Cal Neva. There were a few trailers along the road and a couple of nice homes, too, and she wasn't particular about the neighborhood as long as she was secluded, so she didn't have to handle the feeling that there was something behind her. And there wasn't—only the pines and the slope that rose to the road high above. You couldn't see the house from up there, she said, unless you got out of your car and walked over to the edge, and that was critical. Probably had been for Momo when he picked out the site.

When she arrived she paced around like a caged tigress and couldn't sit down. Sam watched this for a while, then made up a pitcher of martinis, and they went through that pretty quickly. Then suddenly, with a glass still half full, she felt the huge drag of her night, her day, her life, and went over to a couch to crash. But he insisted she get into a sure-enough bed and helped her to do that. When she woke up the next morning he was gone.

She'd seen the Cal Neva at a distance but never up close because the road curved and the trees were thick. If you wanted to walk there from the house, it might have been a couple hundred yards, give or take, and she was thinking of taking a stroll over there after she'd finally gotten herself together and had fully unpacked. But then Sam returned from wherever he'd been, and after a few minutes, when she casually said she'd like to see the club, he told her that for reasons he didn't feel like going into just then it wouldn't be a good idea for either of them to be seen over there. In any case, he said, the nightlife would come to them here at the house. Saying this, he winked at her and gave her one of his mysterious little smiles. If they got bored, he went on, they could always go around the lake to a cozy spot in Tahoe City. About an hour thereafter she found out what he'd meant with his crack about the club's nightlife when the doorbell rang. It was Eddie Fisher, who was just beginning a ten-day run at the club.

Fisher did his best to act like this was a casual social call, but clearly it wasn't: it was a command performance, and he got zero help from Momo, who sat back behind his shades and watched while Fisher did all the conversational lifting. As soon as she saw how things were going to go, Judy pitched in, but she knew she had to be careful: she, too, was Momo's guest and was there under his wing as much as Fisher was. She could only do so much—and that didn't include getting Fisher a refill when Sam let him sit there and squirm with an empty glass. He was still drinking hard, as he had been down in Carmel, trying to get over Liz Taylor. Judy thought he looked awful, his face bloated and the color of putty. Still, to her there was something appealing about him, like a kid who'd been punished and was trying to be a man about it all; but she was glad when he finally left and took all that tension with him. Another time, she thought, she'd have called Sam on his less-than-welcoming behavior. Not now.

He asked what she'd like to do about dinner, have it sent over from the club or take a spin over to that Tahoe City place where they had pretty decent Italian food? She thought she'd just as soon stay put, but after another drink she changed her mind and said maybe it might be fun to take that drive around the west shore to Tahoe City. When they were in Sam's car and pulling out of the underground garage, he braked next to the Pontiac, a metallic blue convertible with a tan top. "That's definitely got to go," he said, nodding at it. She didn't catch his meaning. "You got the heebie-jeebies? Seeing cops in your sleep? Right?" He nodded at the convertible again. "Right there is part of your problem. Cop bait, we call it. Draws 'em like sharks. Why do you think I drive rigs like this?" he asked, tapping the wheel of another of his dull black units with black walls and almost no chrome. "Don't you think I'd like to be rolling along in a classy rig like that? Well, maybe not exactly like that." But he couldn't afford to, he said, because he had to do what he could to avoid attention. "You're gonna have to learn to fly a little lower now, baby," he said. "No more ragtops or any of that jazz, not for a while, until they get off your sweet ass." He told her she'd have to sell it and get into something a lot less conspicuous, that he had a friend up in Reno who'd take it off her hands and give her a good deal on a Ford.

She started to protest. "I *love* that car," she told him, aghast at the idea of selling what had been a birthday present from her father. "It's really a smooth ride and has lots of pep. I couldn't even think of selling it."

He got very stern very quickly. He wasn't having a *discussion* about this, he told her; he was *telling* her what had to happen if she was going to hang out up here with him. "I can't have that thing seen anywhere near here and have those bastards parked just down the road, waiting for us to use it. It's bad enough as it is, where I can't even go into my own club because every other guy pretending to work the slots is a fuckin' agent. Place is crawling with them, night and day. My fuckin' place, but all I get out of it is the bills!" He ended the exchange by declaring flatly that tomorrow he'd get one of his men to drive the convertible up to Reno and bring back something she could use while she was here.

"You want to see cops in your rearview mirror every time you go out, do it down in L.A. on your own time. Up here with me, this is how it's got to be, baby."

The next day she handed over the keys and papers, and when they came back from lunch and a drive, the Pontiac was gone. She missed it terribly. It made her angrier than ever that the government could do such a thing to her.

• • •

They slid easily enough into a kind of routine. When she got up in the mornings he was gone, but there was a pot of coffee ready for her on the range. He might come back near noon, sometimes bringing lunch from the club. They rarely went out at night, except to the restaurant over in Tahoe City, and when they did that they went early and ate quickly—no lingering over martinis now. She mentioned two occasions when he took her up to Reno and they ate at a casino among friends. Several times he held meets at the house, using a first-floor den whose doors she'd never seen opened.

After a week or so of this she was more or less settled and knew what to expect out of a day. Then she thought she'd like to pick up some art supplies, and he made a few calls to Reno to find the right place and drove her up there, where she bought another portable easel, oils, brushes, and drawing materials. He was so eager to pay for these that she yielded quickly. He seemed both curious about everything in the shop—fingering the array of brushes, examining pencils, tablets, pastels—and clearly proud to be in there with a real artist, especially one who looked like this one. He asked the young clerk so many questions about this material versus another that "you'd have thought he was about to go off to art school," she said, "instead of being who he was." Afterward, driving to a Basque restaurant that sat behind one of the casinos, he broke a brief silence to tell her that Italians were great artists, or had been years back. "That and stonemasons, carvers." But that had been in the old country, and when they'd come over here they'd had to do whatever work came to hand, so that "the man who made carvings, art, became the guy who chiseled tombstones for a living.

"So here I am," he said, laughing and slapping the wheel, "a wheel man. I ain't ashamed. The thing is, be good at what your work turns out to be. This here's mine, and I've done okay. They can't take that away from me."

Romance with Sam, she said, wasn't nearly as exciting as it had been with Jack. For one thing, she wasn't in love with him and never had been.

He knows that and I don't think he's really in love with me either. We don't talk that way ever. We just go along day by day and that's fine with me. I feel I'm safe enough here. I think he'd do whatever he had to to protect me and after what I've been through that means more to me than love which I don't know what that means anyway. Jack used to tell me that all the time and I'd say the same thing back to him. But Jack couldn't protect me and after all he should have done something—don't know what but then I'm not the president. Sam would do whatever he could no matter what. So what does it all add up to?

When you see it put like this, it kind of brings you up, you know? Puts the Jack-versus-Momo contest in a different perspective: what's more important to a woman than knowing that her man will protect her? Wouldn't you think this must be the basic condition for relations between men and women, going all the way back to the Stone Age, before all the hearts and flowers? If he can't do that—or won't—what's his love really amount to?

Anyway, that's how she was feeling during those days as spring was coming on. And there were other compensations, if you like. So Sam wasn't as exciting or dashing as Jack. He was, though, generally pretty respectful and undemanding. That must have struck her as a welcome change after the way things had turned out with Jack—the routine of their times in bed, I mean. There was something "restful" and "relaxing" about her times with Sam, she said. Now, I don't know if these are exactly *accolades* if you're the man involved. In bed, you like to think you've kind of lit your woman up, rather than relieved her tension or her chronic lower back pain or whatever. But here again, I have to wonder what men really know about this most intimate of situations. I mean *really:* what are women actually thinking about while you're imagining that you're *sending* them? The man who can figure that out—well, I have to wonder if he could perform in light of this inside knowledge, so to say. What if she's thinking, This is making me feel pretty relaxed, and maybe when he's done I'll have me a nice nap? Are you going to be up to the job with this in your mind? Maybe men are better off just imagining. Here, I think it might have been just as well for Judy and Sam to have steered clear of any romantic talk. It was evidently good enough for her and good enough for him. She knew about Phyllis, and he would have known that she knew, and it's possible that for him that's where the real romance was. Even so, this relationship had its own virtues, Phyllis or no Phyllis.

As far as I can make out, there's only a single mention of her in this diary or the one that comes after it. That doesn't mean her name never came up, but I have the feeling it didn't. That one occasion came when they were getting ready to turn in one night and the phone rang. He answered, as always, and told the caller to call back in five minutes. He took that one down in the den, and the next day he was gone until late in the evening. She thought it must have been Phyllis and that he'd run up to Reno to spend the day with her. She didn't ask.

But as I said before, when Momo was there, he was there. She found she liked the routine of spending the night with "her man," as she put it, instead of always having to go home alone, as had been the case with Jack: they'd never spent a single night together, and that Shangri-La island retreat he'd dangled in front of her at one time had been only an idle dream. By now she was convinced that he'd never been serious about leaving Jackie for her. True, when she awakened these mornings Sam was always gone, but he'd been there through the night, next to her, and if she wanted reassurance, she had only to roll over and look at him, sleeping peacefully on his right side. She also found she liked the basic regularity of their days, even if she never knew when he would show up or how long he'd stay. After all the fast living and wildly irregular hours and unpredictable comings and goings, she felt a reassurance now. One evening she even tried to surprise him by cooking lasagna, but it was a "bust," she said, and while they were trying to get through it he looked over at her with a broad smile, and then they both burst into laughter and ended up over in Tahoe City, eating hamburgers and closing up the place.

She spent some time at her new easel, working on a portrait of another of her starving-eyed children, but more often she sketched, out on the deck usually, if the weather was good. If it wasn't, she worked out arrangements in the living room, still lifes. A couple of times Sam had flowers delivered from the club, and she worked these into her sketches.

Twice Eddie Fisher came over, both times in midafternoon when Sam was out and both times after phoning to ask if it was okay. The visits were fun for her, she said. They discovered that they genuinely liked each other and felt perfectly comfortable letting their hair down. But both visits ended the same way, with Fisher beginning to show signs of nervousness, as if he didn't want to be found there when Sam returned. On the second occasion, when he'd left somewhat apologetically, she went out on the deck and watched him walking away toward the club. He looked small and lonely from up there, big star though he was.

All this time she'd had no contact with Jack. She didn't want him or anybody else in Washington to know where she was. The only mention of him I could find in these entries was of a midday press conference she happened to see on TV. He made her laugh a couple of times with his spontaneous witticisms and clearly still had the reporters eating out of his hand.

Sometime near the end of April the routine changed, when Sam announced one evening that the next day he'd be going back to Chicago and didn't know just when he'd be back. He didn't ask her to go with him, and she didn't think she would have wanted to, either: the FBI knew everything about his whereabouts, his hangs, his friends. Still, she was afraid to go back to L.A. and told him so. Stay here, then, he said: he'd have someone from the club look in on her regularly. Frank would be playing there after the first of the month, and he'd be sure to get in touch. She said he needn't bother, that she wasn't particularly interested in seeing Frank. Momo looked a little funny at that, but then after a short silence he changed the subject, and they went on with their evening.

After he'd been gone a few days the house seemed to draw close around her. He called twice at prearranged times, but otherwise it was quiet. She had some records she'd put on while she sketched, but said that despite an ideal situation her concentration wasn't there and the sketches were all "botches." Maybe it was a combination of the weather—high spring—and plain old cabin fever. Whatever it was, she found herself taking longer and longer drives down the Nevada side of the lake in the dark blue Ford Sam had gotten her. She missed her car and felt in the Ford as if she ought to be making sales calls.

The stop she began making regularly was at the marina at Stateline. There was a restaurant-bar there, Sam's-by-the-Shore, that had been a local hangout forever and in summer got the tourist trade. At this season it was still quiet at midday, and she could sit by a back window and look out on the boats, many of them still in their winter wraps. She had a glass, maybe two, of Chablis, and then a seafood salad. The bartender was a lanky young guy with streaked blond hair who answered to Bud and worked winters at Squaw Valley, and you can imagine how a thing like this might go: beautiful girl all by herself, day after day at the window, and a young ski-bum type bringing her drinks in a place that hadn't begun to pick up yet. So they struck up a casual friendship that was fun for both of them, maybe in different ways, who knows? Bud didn't seem to have any particular direction or goal in life and was drifting with the weather, and she found that carefree style very attractive. It was kind of like looking from a dark street into a lighted window and getting a glimpse of "normal" life without all the murky tangles and subterfuges of a world she had come to know way too much about.

I don't have any idea what Bud was thinking about, if he was thinking anything, but one day when she walked in it was obvious something was up with him. He brought her a Chablis but had no chitchat, didn't linger, and quickly went back to the bar, where he busied himself with polishing glassware and talking with one of the marina personnel about a fast-pitch softball league he was going to play in come summer. When she'd finished her Chablis she couldn't get his attention, and she wasn't about to raise her hand. Whatever his problem was, it wasn't worth this, and so she simply put a bill on the table and left. Unlocking the Ford out in the lot, she heard her name and turned around. It was Bud. He was standing just outside the door, towel still in hand. Then he came a few hesitant steps toward her.

"Look," he said. "Look, I'm sorry about all this"—making a gesture with his hands and shoulders that seemed to take in the restaurant, the lot, the marina, as if he were apologizing for the whole setup, everything. And maybe that's just what he was trying to do, apologize for something that was far too big for a guy like him to get into. She didn't know, couldn't follow him. She just stood there with the car door open, looking at him through her big wraparound shades. He tried to smile, but to her it looked more like a nervous tic. "I just don't want any trouble," he said at last, and then she could follow him all right and knew what the trouble was he didn't want. She thought about taking her shades off, as a kind of courtesy, or maybe even a kind of tribute, if you see what I mean here: to something, some unrealizable possibility out there ahead of them that both had sensed through their casual exchanges. But she didn't. She only nodded, so he'd know he didn't have to say anything else, and then got into the Ford and turned on the ignition. Looking in the rearview mirror, she saw the sun on the gray-white gravel of the lot, the dark red of the log cabin restaurant, but no Bud. Bud had gone back inside, where there wasn't any trouble, where a kind of safety lay, leaving her out here with her trouble and with the protection of a feared name that walled her away from all the Buds of the world.

She became a kind of day wanderer, if I can put it like that. Sam's-by-the-Sea was out now, but there were other places, and she found them, staying out later and later, until even with the lengthening days she was returning at dusk. Then she'd put on some records, have her Chablis and her chartreuse, and maybe watch a little TV. Then she went to bed with a book or some magazines, beginning to skip even snacks at the dinner hour, maybe at first without quite noticing it. Food had become a kind of afterthought, until one morning when she was dressing for the day and put on an outfit she hadn't worn since coming up here. Both the slacks and the blazer hung loosely on her, and she stood there in the bathroom, looking at herself in the mirror with surprise. I knew I'd lost some weight, she said to herself, but until now I hadn't really noticed how much. Oh well, I'll gain it back.

She drove around the lake's California shore and then as far west as Placerville, which she liked the feel of, and began frequenting a spot called Kayo's Mine Shaft. It was about as dim as a mineshaft, too, and very quiet after the noon rush. She sat at a booth in back, sipping wine. A couple of times she remembered to order lunch, and on one of those occasions she ordered a hamburger, which reminded her of Jack and his curiously ordinary tastes in food. That was also the day she noticed a man at the bar who kept glancing at her over his shoulder. You'd think that after all these years of being stared at she'd have developed plenty of ways of dealing with that, but this time it bothered her enough to write it down. When she went back the next afternoon, later than usual, there he was in the same spot. She turned around, got back in the Ford, and never went to Kayo's again.

But there were still other places, lonely ones like the desert stretches above Reno, where there was absolutely nothing but miles and miles of alkali flats with here and there some black rocks scattered about like they'd been dropped out of a plane. I've never been out that way myself, but one night over at Lucy's I had a look at the area in her atlas, and by Jesus, it does look pretty grim—no towns, just names like Smoke Creek Desert and Black Rock Desert sprawled across it with plenty of open spaces between the letters. You wonder what her motivation would have been to keep seeking out such godforsaken stretches, what she would have been thinking about as she drove the Ford over rough dirt roads, or whether she was thinking anything more than that this place was so remote not even Hoover's gumshoes could track her there.

One evening when she'd rolled into the drive and parked in front of the garage, she had a sudden urge to see what was in that room Momo used for his meets and God knows what else. An inside staircase led up to it from the garage, and she climbed it with the key ring in hand. It was locked, as she knew it would be, and she stood there looking at the thick, dark double doors before she began to try the keys, one after the other. Somehow, she said, she knew before trying it when she'd come to the right one, the one that slid so smoothly through the grooves. And at that exact instant, with her thumb and forefinger still on the key, a phone began to ring inside. It felt like the key was electrified, she thought, "and I couldn't let go of it and that goddamned phone just kept on ringing and I was stuck there until it quit." (I think, by the way, that except for the occasional *hell*, this was the first time I'd come across any profanity in her diaries.)

Somehow she managed to get herself upstairs to the kitchen and was about to pour herself a stiff drink when the wall phone by the fridge began to ring. Her immediate impulse was to run back down the stairs to the car and drive somewhere. Then she thought about the Cal Neva, about just going over there for the lights and noise and the anonymous bodies at the tables and slots. But she did neither of these things. Instead, she forced herself to pick up the phone. It was Sam, from Chicago, and at the sound of his voice she was dead certain he knew she'd just tried the lock.

He was in his all-business mode, with none of his teasing or bantering. There were some people, he told her, who needed to use the house. "You ain't using it anyway," he said. "If you still want to stay away from L.A., you can always come out here."

She felt he was trying to be considerate of her situation, her fears, but overriding that was her sense that she was being shadowed not only by the FBI but by Sam and his people as well. How else could he know she was out of the house all day every day? Trying to keep her voice steady, she told him she'd have to think things over but would call him back first thing in the morning. There was no hurry, he said, but she'd been around him long enough to know that her time here was up and that he wanted the house for some other purpose.

She had that drink then, not thinking over Sam's offer of a place in Chicago but instead of that creepy moment when the key had slid home and bells had gone off in the den and for all she knew over at the Cal Neva and in Chicago and Washington. "This isn't a small world like we say," she said. "It's a *tiny* world, and once you make the mistake of finding out just how tiny it is, you can never get back into the regular world—it's too late for you."

I'm not sure I understand this comment, at least not altogether. When I first came across it, I thought it might be just boozy, you know? The sort of thing you'd think was pretty smart after a couple of drinks. And it's quite possible that she did write it down after having a couple of bracers in the kitchen. Then I thought of it as an example of paranoid thinking, where you become convinced that "they" are out to get you. It might be that, too. But beyond these obvious possibilities I think there's a weird sort of wisdom at work here, the insight of someone who unintentionally had become part of a secret world—of two secret worlds, actually—and wished she hadn't. But as she said, once inside that world, there wasn't any way for you to find your way back to the wider world, the one that looking back you were bound to imagine was so wonderfully innocent. She knew too much now for that.

She spent the better part of that night packing, had a bit of troubled sleep, then returned to the packing, watching the clock out of the corner of one eye to see what time it was in Chicago. When she'd finally finished, she took a cup of yesterday's coffee out on the deck, where everything was a dark silver and gray. Then she called Chicago. It was seven-thirty there.

"What the hell are *you* doing up?" he growled. This was the girl, remember, who was still fast asleep when he'd leave the Tahoe house for wherever his business took him. Early as it was there, she could tell she hadn't awakened him; he might be the don of Chicago, but he still had plenty of that immigrant work ethic left in him. What she told him was that she was about to leave for L.A. but would be there only long enough to get some clothes cleaned and visit with her parents. Then she'd be coming to Chicago, as he'd suggested; when she had a schedule, she'd let him know. While they were talking, she was inwardly aching to ask him if he was sure he wanted her out there, but her stubborn pride wouldn't let her. Besides, she said to herself, what would I do if he said no? There wasn't any other place where she felt safe. Not that Chicago was safe anymore, but it was the best of what she had left.

He didn't say no to any part of her plan, just told her that he couldn't meet her at the airport and that whenever she arrived, she should call the Armory. Then he told her where to take the keys. "There's a guy at the club, Stew. Used to be a big-deal football star. Now he works for me. They'll know who you mean. Don't leave 'em with anybody else."

When they'd hung up, she snapped her suitcases shut and ran a sponge around the sink. There was nothing in the fridge except a half-empty bottle of Chablis and a six-pack of Coke, and she left those. She hauled her bags down to the Ford, and that was when she had a flash of fear, a realization that she hadn't any idea where the house keys were.

When you get that flash about some missing item—keys or a wallet especially—you know how it goes: you kind of lie to yourself and say, Hell, they're probably where I always keep them, knowing with some part of your brain that they goddamn well aren't, but you check anyway. In her case the place to check was her handbag, the big black number she'd bought in Washington, back in what felt to her like a story she'd heard once that had happened to somebody else long, long ago. Looking at the bag, she knew better but checked it anyway, her fingers fumbling quickly down through sunglasses, cosmetics, her own keys, and at last scraping the seams along the bottom.

There had to be a simple explanation; she couldn't have gotten into the house without them. Climbing the stairs from the garage to the first floor, she had it: they were still in the den door lock, and they were. She stood looking at them a long moment, the ring worn bright with use and the right one plunged into the lock. What if, when she pulled it out, bells would jangle all over America? She whipped through some alternatives and came to Stew over at the Cal Neva. What if she told him she'd misplaced them somewhere in the house? But then she put that one aside for the obvious reason that Stew's job depended on his complete loyalty to Sam, and when he found the keys he'd have to report the whole thing. Was there a way around this? she wondered.

I leave it to you to make what you want out of what she wrote down once she was back in L.A. To me, it's a symptom of how desperate she was really feeling—and had been all along during these apparently placid days by the lake.

> I thought of some other stuff too. Now that I'm back here I can see how sick this was. But at the time I thought about Stew and what I could do to get him to go over there and pull the keys out himself and keep his mouth shut. But I didn't do anything like that—just went upstairs looked around had a glass of chartreuse and then went back down and yanked the keys out myself. Found Stew—no problem there—gave him the keys and the best smile I could and then drove home.

On her last day in L.A. they went shopping in Beverly Hills, mother and daughter. The summer fashions had taken the place of the spring ones in the shop windows, but neither of them came across anything they even halfway liked. They had lunch at the Belvedere, an old favorite of Katherine Immoor's, where they talked about the wild popularity of the "Jackie look," which was everywhere. Leaving the restaurant, Judy got that cold, itchy feeling between her shoulder blades, the one that told her she was being tailed. As quickly as she could she pulled her mother into a Brighton Way jewelry shop and pretended that a bracelet had caught her eye. Her mother was a bit puzzled at first, but then the old instinct took over and she began to inspect the displays, her daughter shooting glances over her shoulder to see if she could spot anybody suspicious. Finally they left.

But in the parking lot it happened again—or she thought it had: a man in a hat and driving a black Chevy swung quickly in behind them as they came up to the booth. She tried to tell herself that he was simply in a hurry and was being rude, but when he followed them onto Camden and then onto Santa Monica Boulevard, she was sure she was right. She was at the wheel of her mother's Cadillac, and now she floored it and began switching lanes, with the Chevy hanging back five or six cars behind but staying with her. When Katherine asked what on earth was going on, all Judy could grimly say was that she didn't have time to explain it right now but when they got out to Santa Monica she'd try.

It got very quiet in the Cadillac then, Judy's mother trying not to make things worse by asking questions or making conversation. When they got to Santa Monica and Ocean Avenue, Judy made a quick left, and the Chevy went right.

They walked down to the beach, took off their shoes, and strolled along slowly, her mother waiting for her to explain. But Judy couldn't think of a way to begin. Where the hell would you begin to talk about this tightly snarled ball? Finally she said that some government people had mistaken her for somebody else who had information they wanted and that she'd tried hard to straighten them out but they wouldn't believe her. By the time they'd made the turn back toward the old pier, the cafés and shops on Ocean, Katherine had learned that the government people were most likely FBI and that they believed Judy had some papers that needed to be turned over to them, that it could be dangerous for a private citizen to be carrying them around. "Well, why don't you just give them what they want?" Katherine asked. "Or, if you don't have it, we'll call our congressman and tell him about the problem." So then Judy had to go on to tell her

> that I had once carried some documents to Chicago for Jack but I didn't have them anymore—that I delivered them to the person who was supposed to get them. I was just like the mailman I said. The mailman doesn't read your mail or he isn't supposed to and he doesn't keep it. I didn't want Mom to know I'd carried packages to Sam but said I'd done this for Jack because he asked me to and that whatever was in those packages Jack said it was important for the good of the country that nobody know anything about it.

Well, you can see how this kind of thing was bound to go, with one explanation just provoking another question, and even though Katherine was a huge Kennedy fan, it seemed clear to her that he'd exposed her daughter to a pretty awful mix-up: an honest citizen being followed about like a criminal, and why couldn't the president do the decent thing and just pick up the telephone and order Mr. Hoover to quit this foolishness immediately? Well, it was a bit more complicated than that, Judy answered lamely. It involved inside politics and bureaucratic infighting that she didn't fully understand. "I told her that I trusted Jack to do the right thing eventually," she said, "even though about the last thing I really felt like was defending him just then."

Climbing up from the beach toward the Cadillac, Judy was still worried about the man in the Chevy and suggested they have an iced tea and cool off before they drove back into the city. It was just warm enough to make this plausible, and Katherine was worn down by the excitement and the walk, so they went into a hotel for their iced tea, though what her daughter really wanted was a drink. They sat there in the lounge, trying to keep the chitchat going, about Judy's brother, Allen, who was between jobs again and about her sister Jackie, who'd landed a new movie part. But it wasn't easy for Judy, thinking that the agent might very well be there in the same room with them, watching and waiting. If only, she thought, things could be as simple—or even as simply set right—as her mother had suggested. Instead they were desperately tangled, and she had long ago given up the idea that she could expect any sort of help from either Jack or Bobby. Certainly neither brother could afford to say anything to Hoover.

I have to think that here she must have cast a thought back to the hideaway Sam had provided in Tahoe. Maybe if she'd been content to stay in it instead of running all around in the Ford, he'd have let her stay there until the heat was off. If she did have such a thought, I don't think it was that realistic: that place was probably a Mob safe house that members moved into and out of as they needed to. Plus it was no doubt from time to time a love nest for Momo and Phyllis.

They'd finished their drinks, and so there was nothing left to do except leave and hope for the best. But first Judy had one more tactic to try. Excusing herself to go to the ladies', she tipped a bellhop a tenner, asking him to look around for a lone man in a hat and then to check outside for a black Chevy. When she emerged, he told her the coast was clear, and she and her mother left.

Finally back on North Flores, Judy told her mother that when she returned from Chicago she wanted to move. Katherine thought that was a good idea, considering everything, and said she'd make contact with her realtor friends in the meantime. They sat there in front of the building, talking about what sort of place Judy had in mind. When Judy got out, Katherine slid over into the driver's seat and noticed the Ford parked just ahead.

"That looks just like a government car," she said. "Now you've got me doing it, too—goodness!"

"That's why I drive it," Judy said. "It's mine."

On the flight to Chicago she wondered how it was going to feel at the airport without the one-man band of Sam's welcome, and she was still wondering about that when she came into the terminal, not looking for him now with his usual huge bouquet but instead for agent types. She didn't spot any but nevertheless spent a few minutes in the ladies' and then went to a newsstand, where she bought a paper. Down at the bag claim she paid a skycap to watch her mountain of luggage and then went upstairs again and had a martini at the bar, pretending to read the paper. She might have had another, except there was this college lout in a baseball cap who kept asking her dumb, probing questions and finally got around to inviting her to a baseball game that night. Another time it might have been funny.

Finally she called the Armory and got Ruthie Idella, who immediately handed her off to her husband, who told her a suite had been reserved for her at the Oak Park Arms. She didn't know where that was, but he said the cabbie would.

The suite turned out to be perfectly pleasant, though she missed the high-rise glamour and swish of the Ambassador East, and instead of a view of the lakefront from an upper-floor room there, here she looked down on a narrow bit of park fenced with wire and waist-high hedges. On the way she'd asked the cabbie to stop at a liquor store for a bottle of chartreuse. He'd been nice enough to go in and get it for her, and now she stood at her windows with a glass of it, looking down into the park with its kids and parents, swings and a tin slide that looked dull and tired to her under the gray of the sky. She thought about children, how exposed they were to life—all of it—no matter how privileged, thinking that you couldn't really protect even your own, to say nothing of the children of the world, those hollow-eyed kids she obsessively painted. Just now she was feeling like an orphan herself.

The light was going when Sam rang to tell her he was on his way and why didn't they settle for a quiet dinner there in Oak Park? There was a place he liked on Lake Street that he hadn't been to in a while. It was okay with her, she thought. Actually, anything was okay with her—the way you feel when nothing is.

When Sam came through the door of the suite, something immediately felt very different: from their first glance it was clear to them both that everything intimate between them was finished. Have you ever had that? The first time it happened to me I remember just about every detail of it—a pretty weird experience, and right up there with the great mysteries of what we call "chemistry," though I don't know if it really deserves that word. Anyway, I don't think I've ever come across a better run at describing it than hers. It wasn't, she said, that there was exactly a coolness between them so much as it was the absence of heat. "There's a way a man looks at you when you know each other well in a special way so that your expectations are the same," she said.

> . . . something in his eyes that's almost fierce but mostly tender—Not now—Sam's eyes when he came in and took off his dark glasses were totally clear—don't know if I ever knew till now what color they really were—light almond—and hard and completely clear.

If she was looking at him as if for the first time, he must have been looking at her in a similar way. He'd seen her as close up as a man can see a woman; seen her, too, in flight, when she practically vaulted into the house in Tahoe. Now, I wonder whether she was reminding him of the stunning girl Sinatra had introduced him to at the Fontainebleau who'd come right back at him for his crack about her jewelry: that girl had felt very much on her own at that moment, and this one must have as well, tensed, almost coiled, and trying to figure what options she had left. I'm no judge of pure intellect, if there even is such a thing, and I don't know how Momo would have scored on one of those academic aptitude tests—what could he have known of Plato or plane geometry? But a man doesn't get where he'd gotten without being a pretty shrewd judge of character and emotional disguises. It's true, he'd misread the Kennedys, but that would hardly put him in the dumbbells' club. So I doubt he could have missed what he was looking at now: someone who'd had her eyes peeled for her and had few illusions left about who and what she could count on. And it's possible that the way she looked in that hotel room with the hard, gray light coming in on her and her clothes not quite fitting her the way they once had would have provided some added clues.

Well, they had that quiet dinner at the Lake Street place, and that was when he told her why she was staying in Oak Park and why he hadn't met her at the airport. The FBI was all over him, he said, even on the golf course, where they were either the foursome ahead or the one behind. His lawyer had petitioned for a restraining order, which would force the agents to keep a certain distance, but so far they hadn't gotten a ruling, and he wasn't hopeful because the judge was a hardass. (Eventually they did get a favorable ruling, but that was later.) "We can't do like we used to," he said with one of his sad smiles, referring to their fairly conspicuous style around town. But the words could also have served as a kind of blanket comment on their entire relationship, and maybe that's the way he intended them.

The sheer *ferocity* of the FBI's tracking of Momo at this point tells me that Bobby's Mongoose man, Edward Lansdale, had reported to him that as far as the Castro business was concerned, nothing whatever was to be hoped for from the Mob. That's the only way to make sense of this development. If the Mongoose planners held out any hope that Momo might still put something together for them, they sure as hell wouldn't be following him around on the golf course or chasing him through the car wash—which they did one time in Cicero. No, they'd given up on him, and on Trafficante and Marcello, too, and so the gloves had come all the way off.

Obviously, Judy couldn't have been thrilled to hear this. If they were shadowing Sam so closely, they'd find her soon enough. But what were her alternatives? Tahoe was out. L.A. was hot as hell for her now. She must have figured she was as well off in Chicago as she was likely to be anywhere else. At least Sam still had his organization working for him; he was resourceful; and she thought that even though they were finished as a romantic item, he'd do what he could for her if she played by his rules. So she decided that night she'd stay on and play by those rules. She went out to his house on several occasions but always by cab after dark. As far as I can tell, she stayed the night only once. She never saw him in the daytime and never went near the Armory. Once when he was a bit juiced he called her from somewhere on Rush and asked her to join him, but she didn't. And he took her out to a Mob joint, the Villa Venice, to hear Eddie Fisher.

This turned out to be a very mixed deal for her. On the one hand, she and Fisher obviously dug each other. On the other, watching Sam humiliate somebody she'd come to like was a trial, and it happened every time they went out there. She simply had to sit through it in silence, trying to smooth things over however she could. One night between sets, with Fisher at their table lapping up the gin and tonics like they were mother's milk, he got to reminiscing in a rambling way about his beginnings as a singer and the importance of his Jewish roots. "I had no idea of any of that," she said, "especially about how important being Jewish was—guess I never thought about him being Jewish at all—really interesting to me. Then Sam cut in and said shut up kid." Fisher shut up.

On September twenty-fourth Sam asked her out to the house and over dinner told her he'd be leaving the next day on business and would be gone awhile. Nothing unusual there, but something told her his business would eventually take him to Tahoe and Phyllis. That was the one night she stayed over, and the next morning he was gone. As for her, that night she went to the Villa Venice by herself and had a relaxed, funny time with Fisher. Afterward he went back with her to Oak Park, where they drank and watched the sun find its way into the narrow park the next morning. Later in the day, soaking in her tub, she wondered how Fisher did it, keeping these killing hours and then having to get up, rehearse, give interviews, make himself available. She realized how much she would need the rest of the afternoon to put herself back together. But she did it, and that night she was back at the Villa Venice, and again Fisher sat with her between sets. She described him as between friendly and anxious because there were so many of Momo's people in the house. At one point she put her hand on his and whispered to him that he shouldn't worry about those people, that she picked her own friends and he should, too.

You'd never know it from her diary, but while this flirtation with Fisher—if that's what it was—was going on, the rest of the world was teetering on the crater's edge of nuclear incineration, as America and the Russkies faced off in the Caribbean over Cuba. There's no way she could not have known about it, even if she was sleeping away most of her days. If you recall, it was a hell of a scary time then, and when it was finally over Kennedy told a few insiders he had cut Khrushchev's nuts off. I guess he had at that, but it was a fearsome gamble he took to do it.

About the time the crisis passed and the Russian ships turned back, Fisher's run at the Villa Venice ended. He was going back to California, he told Judy, for a bit of R and R, and then he'd be playing the Carlyle in Manhattan. I don't know that it makes much difference who said what to whom, but however it was, they arranged to see each other there. Sam was still away; she had almost zero contact with any of his people, and Oak Park was boring her. What I don't get is her thinking here—extending this thing with Fisher. Or maybe it isn't so much that as it is that I know now what some of the consequences for her were going to be, and none of them were good.

Of course, reading along in the diaries, I didn't know any of that at that time. I'd established what I thought was a rough chronology for the sixteen volumes Keneally had, but I hadn't read through them all. I'd tried to at one point, but it got so confusing I decided simply to make that rough chronology and then to reorder it as the internal evidence required. That happened often enough.

What I'm saying is that when I came to this arrangement she

made with Fisher to meet up in New York, I didn't know exactly what lay ahead, but still I had a real sense of foreboding. I remember saying to myself, "God, girl, *don't do this.*" A writer, whose name I can't recall just now, said something to the effect that if you really wanted to describe the modern world, you had to have the balls to watch a locomotive bearing down on a child on the tracks and not turn your head away. If that's what it takes to be a writer in our time, then I don't have a set of prunes like that. I'm stuck, in other words, with my foreboding, my fear for her, my inward flinching. Because even though, as I've been trying to point out, I didn't know then the specifics of what lay ahead for her, I could see that casting her lot with Eddie Fisher made no sense whatever. Sam might have been so hot at that point that he really couldn't do much to protect her—he might even have told her that before he split. But what could Fisher possibly have provided in Sam's stead? Nothing but trouble. And that's just the way it turned out.

By the twenty-eighth of November, Fisher's run at the Carlyle was over and he asked Judy to meet him and a friend at the Plaza's Persian Room to hear Robert Goulet. He would have picked her up at the Essex House, where she was staying, except he wanted to avoid an entrance with her at the Plaza, which was sure to be noticed and might even make the papers as a photo.

Fisher's friend turned out to be an M.D. named Max Jacobson, who'd built himself a hugely profitable practice treating the problems of the famous with a drug cocktail he claimed was a unique combination of vitamins and enzymes. His clientele read like the Who's Who of America at that time and included Jack and Jackie, Goulet, Fisher himself, and dozens of Hollywood types. We can take a shortcut through the woods here by simply noting that among these people Jacobson was known as Dr. Feelgood and that though his injections probably did contain vitamins and enzymes, what he was really doing was supplying his patients with low doses of speed. He had offices in Manhattan, D.C., Chicago, and Hollywood. Out there his son Tommy was available when Dr. Feelgood himself wasn't. It seems not many ever asked what precisely was in his shots, because they didn't want to know what it was that made them feel terrific almost instantaneously—never felt better in their lives. So why ask? Jack supposedly said he didn't care if the stuff was horse piss so long as it worked, and he occasionally packed Jacobson along on Air Force One, leaving his official doctor, Janet Travell, behind to attend to lesser problems. Jack took the shots for his back. Jackie took them for Jack and for the fishbowl her life had become. Fisher was currently in need because of Liz—and maybe also so he could tolerate the nightly loads of crap he had to take from Momo and his hoodlum friends.

By prearrangement Fisher and Jacobson took a table in the Persian Room, where Judy eventually joined them, and at the end of the night Judy and Fisher went back to the Carlyle. What happened then will never be entirely clear—there are only a few lines from her about it. But over the next three days they drank and talked nonstop, never ate, never got any sleep. On the morning of December first Judy passed out and Fisher couldn't get her to come to, but he eventually reached Jacobson. The doctor went over immediately, brought her around, and gave her an injection. She remembered feeling suddenly faint, and the next thing she remembered was looking up at two shiny objects that were like small moons floating high above her. She felt a weightiness dragging her down but then seemed to be rising very slowly toward the two lights, as if she'd been at the bottom of a swimming pool and now had been released. It seemed to take a long time, but when she finally came to the surface she found that the lights were Max Jacobson's eyeglasses reflecting the light from her hotel room windows. Jacobson was kneeling beside her, and then she turned her head and found an anguished Eddie Fisher, who took her hand in his. Wherever it was she'd been, she thought she'd been gone a long time.

"It's been so long," she finally said to Fisher. "I've been away a long time, haven't I?"

"Yes," he said, and there were tears in his eyes. "But now you're back, and Max has given you something that'll put you right side up."

The next thing she remembered was feeling wonderful and at the same time incredibly hungry. She wanted all of them to pile into a cab and go to the Brasserie for lunch, but Jacobson didn't think that was a good idea. Instead he gave her a couple of numbers where she could reach him, and she made an appointment to see him. Fisher left for California.

She slept sixteen straight hours and almost missed the appointment. Jacobson gave her another injection of the miracle cocktail, and again she had that instantaneous I-can-do-anything sensation. "I just bounced out of there," she said, "and actually felt like running back to the hotel—but didn't."

That was the beginning. While she stayed on at the Essex House she saw Dr. Feelgood twice a week and thought he was doing her a world of good, especially in the hours immediately after the injections. His office was just off Columbus Circle, and when she'd "bounce" out of there—high but not realizing it—she'd cross to Central Park and take what she called "these really *enormous* hikes." It was nothing to walk up to the Metropolitan Museum, tour its collections, then continue on to Grant's Tomb before turning back to the Essex House.

One day when she came out of the park onto Fifth Avenue south of the museum she saw a fleet of motorcycle cops heading toward her and, sandwiched between them, a black Lincoln limo with two small American flags fluttering from the front fenders. She stood there while the parade rolled by in a blue cloud of exhaust. "It was Jack," she said.

> I knew he was in town of course—it was in all the papers—but to see him this way—actually I didn't—I couldn't see in the car—But he might have seen me standing there trying to see him. There actually weren't that many others standing around. It was sunny but windy and cold and I was all bundled up in a long

polo coat with a fox fur collar. What if he did see me—wonder what he would have thought. How quickly everything changed for us—that's what I thought anyway—

The papers the next day ran stories of Jack's visit, and one of them had a photo of him in a tux and flanked by several women, including a willowy blonde who drew Judy's attention because somehow she seemed out of place in that group.

There used to be a Mob joint out on Mannheim Road, not too far from O'Hare. I passed it once in a while but never had a reason to go in: big, low-slung brick thing with several sections to it, like they kept getting bigger and bigger ideas, and maybe that's the way it really went. Then one time I was out that way with Lucy, paying a long-delayed duty call on an old auntie of hers who lived in Mount Prospect, and when we went past the Sahara we saw that much of it had burned down. You see that often enough with Mob joints: something goes sour, and they have the place torched and rig the inspection so they can collect. And Jesus! the Sahara looked worse than a desert, all blackened and broken open in places and with some orange-painted drums chained together out front to discourage vandals. Anyway, in its brief heyday it had booked some big-time acts. When Judy was living there, it was a hot venue for a certain kind of crowd.

This was the winter, early in '63, and she was there courtesy of Momo. It wasn't a good time for her at all. The word that comes to my mind is *bleak*. She was partying hard at night and sleeping through most of her days. It might sound a bit weird to you if I were to try to assign grades, so to say, to certain cliques or circles within the Mob, like you would to different levels of horseraces. To law enforcement people this might seem really wacko: to them you could take the whole bunch and shake them up in a bag. Something like this might also be said for casual, or civilian, observers: Mob guys and their molls are all pretty much the same, though some seem more colorful than others—the Gotti types. But still, I think there are these gradations, and I get the strong impression that the Sahara bunch she was running with now was rougher—flashier, a bit more vulgar, pretty short in the manners department. For one thing, there were a number of enforcer types who were conspicuous regulars, and that'll lend a particular tone to any spot; you want to be careful when drinking around that group. Judy said that one night she watched a pair of heavies get into a beef at the bar, and then one of them reached back and slugged the other in the chops. When he got up he was missing most of his upper teeth. But peacemakers sailed in, and a half-hour later the loser accepted a drink from the other bruiser—but straight up, no ice. So, for example, Murray "The Camel" Humphreys, very high up in the Chicago hierarchy, would never take his wife, Jeanne, out there. Too rough for her. But that was the Sahara for you—rough, flashy, cheap, though it probably cost a bundle to put it together. The partying was hard and it was constant, and Judy went along with it, partly, I'd say, because she felt she didn't have that many attractive alternatives. It was over with Jack, of course; they never even talked by phone anymore. It was over with Eddie Fisher, too, who had apparently been scared off by the specter of Momo. And that man kept his own distance from her. He'd set her up there, as I say, but he had little contact with her, and that was mostly by phone. He wasn't a frequent visitor to the club, at least not while she was there. Part of this might have been her thing with Fisher, which wouldn't have pleased him. But another part of his reason for this probably should be traced back to a conversation an emissary had with one of Bobby Kennedy's people. The emissary had asked whether something couldn't be done—in consideration of past favors—to ease up on the surveillance of Momo's every movement. And reportedly Bobby had responded that Momo's movements were easy enough to track because if he wasn't with Judy, he was with Phyllis. That's a pretty hard-boiled remark from a guy who not so long before had handed her those sealed packets to carry to Chicago, but that was Bobby, at least at that stage of his career. So Momo apparently had decided to steer clear of Judy—but not of Phyllis.

But there was another part to her behavior pattern, which was that she'd become terrified of the dark and would do almost anything to avoid going back to her room before dawn. When this started is a question I can't answer, though I suppose you could argue she'd always had it to some extent, because I ran across a mention of fear of the dark in an early diary Ed had. My recollection is that back then it was connected to the death of an uncle during a nighttime thunderstorm, but I don't have any notes on that. Many of us go through stages of this when we're growing up, and most of us grow out of it. Maybe she never quite did; maybe it was always lurking in the back of her mind, and the business with the FBI, by some odd process of association, brought it forward again. Whatever the case, this wasn't merely a fear she had out at the Sahara; it was a big-time phobia. At first she tried to deal with it by staying out all night, as I said. But then she saw how bad this was for her health as well as her looks and made an arrangement with one of the goons who took care of what we'd now call "security," who'd go to her suite ahead of her and make sure everything was the way it was supposed to be. That worked for a bit, or seemed to, but then she became convinced that what she needed in order to feel completely secure was to be on the club's ground floor in a single room. Sam arranged the switch for her and was pleasant enough about it, though it was clear he didn't at all get why she wanted this so badly.

But then things took a different twist, and for her a more frightening one: she believed there was somebody in the room next door and that they were there to keep watch on her. When she finally forced herself to go to bed and turned out her light, there was a sliver of light under the door that connected to the next room, and she believed she could see shadows moving back and forth in there. This went on into daylight, with her lying there frozen with fear, staring at that crack of light and the shadows moving across it at intervals, like phantoms who were mocking her fear and insomnia.

When dawn began to break, the light went out, and then she could catch some sleep. When you're trying to figure out what's going on here, you think, of course, that this must have been a pretty serious reaction to Dr. Feelgood's injections. Except I didn't find a single reference to him in the diary that covers most of this time. And so then you think it might have been withdrawal. But it went on well over two months, which I'd say is pretty long for that process.

One day after another hellish night she ditched her pride and tried to reach Sam for help, but she couldn't. The next day she found out why, because it was splashed all over the papers: the FBI had hassled Phyllis at O'Hare, and then Sam had arrived on the scene and gotten into a screaming, profane rage at the agents. There was a picture of him in his hat and dark glasses, pointing his finger at an agent, with Phyllis kind of cowering there in the background. Despite this, Judy was desperate enough to keep trying to reach him until she finally did. He checked with the management, he subsequently told her, and learned there hadn't been anybody in that room next door for ten days. When she insisted that that couldn't be true, he said he'd personally rent the room and see that nobody ever entered it, even to clean. That, he said, was the best he could do for her.

Her rescue, such as it was, came not from Sam but from Tony Bennett, who had a lengthy engagement at the club and was staying just down the hall from her. His hours were roughly the same as hers, if for different reasons, but he was putting his days to better use. He slept in, of course, but when he wasn't practicing or rehearsing with the band he was sketching, sometimes in his room, sometimes around the premises, and it was on one such occasion that she came across him. He'd seen her around and knew who she was, and so at first he had the same problem with her that Eddie Fisher had and Bud the bartender at Tahoe: she was strictly off-limits. But she was so obviously in need of companionship that he couldn't help himself, and he invited her to sketch with him in the afternoons, always in public areas like dining rooms and lobbies and the like.

"I was really rusty—embarrassing," she said. "Perspective way off—also control."

But Bennett was a friendly, mannerly sort, which must have been a hell of a relief after the crowd she was running with, and she was able to convince him that his life wasn't endangered by sketching with her and that in any case Sam was otherwise occupied. So he kind of took her under his wing, encouraging her to work back into artistic shape and showing her some of the artistic problems he set for himself. It was all practice, he used to tell her—practice and more practice, just like singing. If you let your chops go, he told her, it really didn't make any difference how much raw talent you might have.

I'd like to know what he thought of her raw talent, but however that was, it was fun for a while, a break from her haunted life. He'd pick out a spot, rearrange a few things, and then they'd work for an hour and more, usually without talking. He was really serious about his art, she noted, so this was no social occasion—no chitchat. If he said anything at all to her, it was about the work they were doing and the problems it involved.

Eventually, though, her life caught up with her again, staying up late with that crowd, being afraid of her room and the one next door, and so when he'd call the next afternoon she'd have to beg off. She was simply exhausted. After a couple of times he quit trying, though when they did encounter each other around the club he was still pleasant and would chat with her a bit. Nights, though, he never went to whatever table she was sitting at. Between sets he'd visit with others sometimes, but never with her.

One spring afternoon she decided she really needed some exercise and was on her way out of the club for a walk. It had been another late one, and she wasn't feeling so hot, and then here came Bennett through a side door. He'd been out running and had a sweatshirt on with a towel tucked in around his neck. He told her that this was his last day—that he'd be going south, to New Orleans, where the weather would be a relief from Chicago's late, grudging spring. He looked at her a long moment while he pulled the towel out of his sweatshirt and wiped his steaming forehead. He seemed to be stalling a bit, as if he were trying to make up his mind about something. Then he smiled broadly, all his white teeth suddenly on display.

"You know," he said slowly, carefully, "this isn't any of my business, and I know that. We all make our choices . . ." He stepped back, almost seeming to be turning to leave, but then he didn't. "Well, here it is, for what it's worth." He smiled again, more tightly this time. "We're friends, right? Okay, then. I'll be on my way south tomorrow, like I said. And I think—I think it might not be a bad idea if you thought about leaving here yourself. Where to, I can't say. But for a girl like you, I don't know if this is really that healthy an environment." He spread his arms slightly away from his body, the towel held loosely in one hand. "I mean, this isn't exactly what you'd think of as a health club, right?" Then he gave her another smile and was gone.

Obviously she must have taken his advice, because the next entry has her back in L.A., and it's the middle of June. She had an apartment now on Fountain Avenue in West Hollywood and was mostly moved in when one morning she came across a line in a Walter Winchell column. Winchell had once run an item in his ratta-tat-tat fashion that contained a fairly obvious reference to her and JFK. If I remember, Kennedy or one of his people subsequently got in touch with Winchell and asked him to lay off that kind of stuff. Here, though, was another one just like it, only the girl was different: "What blond D.C. butterfly lights up the Chief's day when wifey's away?"

Katherine Immoor had found the Fountain Avenue place for Judy, and she and Judy's sister, Jackie, had helped her with the move. I don't know if Katherine had told her husband, Frederick Immoor, why his daughter wanted to move, but Judy did say he had made her cry when she'd gotten back from Chicago and the Sahara by saying to her at a family dinner that she looked terrible, that she was pale and underweight and had big shadows under her eyes. Living for months inside a hoodlums' club and not sleeping much will do that for you. So after she was more or less settled she drove out to Palm Springs and took a suite at the Racquet Club, where for about a week she didn't do much of anything except lie in the sun. She did say she played a few rounds of golf when she'd perked up a bit, though she didn't say who with. The only other note about this transition was simply this: "Dinner at Frank's—lots of the old crowd."

A few days later she and some of the old crowd went in to L.A. to see the Angels play the Yankees. Afterward they went out bar-hopping with a few of the players, and she wound up spending time with one of them, Bo Belinsky. Belinsky was a thug and a pool hustler who also had enough baseball talent to once pitch a no-hitter. At the time her path crossed his, he'd just been dumped by Mamie Van Doren, whose talents as an actress were more modest than Bo's as a pitcher and pool hustler. Judy thought he was high-spirited, funny, and didn't seem to take anything very seriously. Right then she thought that was about the kind of guy she needed to be around, and so when he said maybe he'd drive out to see her on an off day the next week, she didn't discourage him.

When he arrived, he said he wanted to shoot some pool at a club he knew of close by. It sounded like fun, she thought. "I knew zero about pool but Bo said he could teach me the fundamentals so away we went." What happened at the club was anything but fun, because while Bo was giving her a lesson and leaning over her showing her how to hold the stick, here came Sam and Frank together.

Picture this now: a flashy pool hustler with his arms draped around the girl and both of them probably laughing because they'd had a drink. The situation has a kind of built-in comic quality, if you see what I mean—you actually *have* to drape yourself around somebody if you're going to show her how the stick is held, how to draw your shooting hand back, and so on. I've never played that much pool, but I've seen guys teaching others how it's done, and I still remember a kindred kind of experience during a summer I spent as a locker-room kid at a South Side country club and how deeply I envied the tennis pro. Because in order to teach a girl the backhand, you've got to get into that same sort of instructional embrace. There I'd be, trundling a cartload of dirty towels over to the laundry room, and I'd look across to the courts to this tall, handsome pro with his arms across some young thing's chest, teaching her the proper position. And I'd be thinking, Jesus! What a way to spend your summer! So much for the comedy, which instantly vanished with the sudden appearance of Sam and Frank.

What Judy figured out after they had gone and the shock had worn off a bit was that they'd been in a meeting in the office just off the poolroom, and of course with the door closed she and Belinsky could have had no idea of their presence. Sam looked right through her as he passed the table, she said. "It was like I wasn't even there—didn't turn his head no expression nothing." Frank was behind him, and maybe that's why he was able to register something. Anyway, as he passed her and Belinsky, he made this tiny little gesture with his head and the corner of his mouth: "Just a tiny kind of twist—another situation and I wouldn't have seen it. But here I was just staring and so I saw it."

Remember, now, it hadn't been that many days since she'd had dinner with some of the old crowd at Frank's home, and here he comes across her in the arms of a creep only a couple of rungs up from a barfly. I don't know if he recognized Belinsky, but the point here would be that by hanging out in public with him, Judy was breaking all the rules. In that world, the tiny one she knew of, you're in until the big shots say you're not. Her situation with Sam was very ambiguous by that point, sure, and he was keeping conspicuous company with Phyllis, but that didn't make any difference. Judy was still his girl, his property, if you like, until he made some kind of declaration to the contrary, and he hadn't. And here she was, fooling around with a nobody in front of men who knew him and feared and respected him. It was a thoroughly dishonorable situation, and honor is what most defines a don. Also, he wouldn't have forgotten that it had been Frank who'd introduced him to Judy, a fact that couldn't have done much to enhance Sinatra's standing with a man who owned a chunk of him.

That little gesture of Frank's, that twist of the head and mouth, what did it mean? It meant this: *Too bad for you, baby—you blew your break.* I don't know that she knew that then; she might have. But both she and Belinsky knew that something serious had just happened, and even though he tried to shrug it off, she could see that he was rattled and the fun was over. Shortly afterward they left the club, and as far as I could tell she never saw him again.

When you think about it in perspective, by this point she'd used up an awful lot of her available landscape: Washington, Chicago, the Palm Springs area. She'd never been particularly well connected in New York or very comfortable living there for long stretches. Of course, L.A. was hot, with agents seemingly everywhere. And yet where else did she have to go now except back to her new apartment on Fountain?

The second she opened the door, she was sure somebody had been in it. She stood there at the threshold, looking around as if it were the scene of a crime of some sort and she shouldn't touch anything. Slowly and with great effort, she forced herself to look methodically from one area to another, though I have some trouble imagining that she could have been very methodical in her state of mind and with her heart hammering away inside her. Then she began to inspect it, foot by foot, beginning with the living room/dining room area, bending over books and bric-a-brac to see if she could find fingerprints or some other sign that things had been moved. Nothing. Nor in the kitchen, where everything looked just as she remembered; nor in the spare bedroom, where she'd set up her easel. But when she got to her own bedroom she found what she'd been looking for and had feared to find: on the nightstand, a diary. Before she'd fled to Tahoe and Sam, she'd asked Jackie to keep her diaries until she got back. Jackie still had them, but Judy had been using others since then, still filling those pages—more jaggedly and brokenly, it's true—and this was one of those. She *knew*, she said, underlining *knew*, that she would never have left any diary of hers so "exposed."

When I came across this, I wondered briefly whether that particular volume had contained some especially sensitive stuff, and I even began to try to figure out which one it had to be—if it was part of the collection Keneally had. But right away I quit that foolishness. It wouldn't at all have been the contents of the diary, whatever they were. No, it was the *fact of the penetration of her inner space*—her apartment, her life, her heart and head. This was what appalled her.

A while back I said something about what I called virginality and how it seemed to me that it was possible for a woman to keep that inner sanctity even if she happened to get in bed with a man. If she really wanted to keep it, then I think the sheer physical act couldn't take it away from her, in other words. This thing was different, of course, in the sense that the penetration wasn't sexual. It was physical, though, a physical intrusion that to her seemed pointedly personal: to have been careful enough to have left no traces except with this one item, this personally sacred, enclosed, intensely private thing. It was like they *wanted* her to know they'd gotten in, and not only that, but that they'd gotten in all the way.

When Keneally had been talking about what the bureau had done to Judy, he'd drawn a swift parallel between that and what it had done to Jean Seberg. At that time I didn't know enough of the story to think much about it one way or the other. If I thought anything, it was probably only that he'd been speaking somewhat casually, off the cuff, and making an effective, dramatic comparison. Now that remark came back to me full force. Was it really true—literally—that the FBI drove Seberg nuts so that she ended up killing herself? While I was sitting there, thinking about this with my hands on Judy's diary, I looked over at Keneally, thinking I'd ask him if he'd been totally serious about Seberg. I might have, too, except he was asleep, his huge head and jowls kind of canted over on a massive shoulder, one of the very few times he ever did that while I was up there. So I didn't ask him, then or later on. Maybe I should have. Instead I just went on reading about what Judy did after that, with her penmanship and punctuation becoming more desperate and sloppy as she described going out to call Dr. Feelgood's office, because she felt sure the agents would have installed a phone tap while they were in there; and then driving aimlessly and frantically around the city, waiting for Tommy Jacobson to see her late that afternoon. And when she came out of there she called her sister, who had just finished her film part and had taken a cottage up in Carmel with her current boyfriend, a key grip guy from New York. Judy didn't tell Jackie about the break-in, only asked if there was a spare room she could use for a few days. There wasn't, Jackie said, but there was a cute little place three doors down that was available. She wished, she said, she'd known about it for herself and Vic. In fact, she went on, "I think you know the owner, Sid Korshak." The name meant nothing to her, Judy said, but then Jackie reminded her that she'd once introduced Jackie to him: Korshak was a friend of Frank's. Judy still didn't remember the man, but so what? She begged Jackie to call the realtor.

Sid Korshak's place was on Scenic Road, right on the water and snugged in among cypresses and older homes from the days when Carmel must have been a pretty sleepy place, not at all the swank spot it's since become. He'd bought it and other local properties as investments, which probably tells you all you need to know about his shrewdness. He was a lawyer and fixer from Chicago with the specialty of helping unions like the Teamsters with their legal problems. And Jackie had been right about his connections: he was a friend of Sinatra's and also of Johnny Roselli's. I met him once myself and remember him as mannerly, quiet, well-spoken. You'd have taken him for a man who headed an old and reputable La Salle

Street firm instead of what he was. Out in Carmel in the summer of '63 he could have ambled down the main drag at high noon and nobody would have known who he was—or cared, either.

To Judy, his cottage seemed the perfect hideaway she so desperately needed. When she arrived at the tiny Monterey airport she asked Vic, Jackie's friend, to rent a car at the Hertz office in the shack that served the terminal; she didn't want her name on the contract, she explained. Vic was glad to help out. But after that the Hertz man called him up to report that two FBI agents had come out to the airport wanting to see the records of recent rentals and had pulled the copy of Vic's contract and asked about it. The guy didn't know if what they were doing was lawful, he told Vic, but he'd been too scared to ask, and after they'd left, he'd checked with headquarters in San Francisco and been ordered to get the car back. Vic took it back, all right, and Jackie loaned Judy her car, so as far as wheels were concerned this wasn't a tragedy. Still, it made all three of them nervous, especially Judy, and cast a low-hanging cloud over what they'd hoped would be a relaxing time together. Judy began keeping more to herself and going for long drives down the coast, kind of a reprise of what she'd done up in Tahoe.

On July twenty-eighth the three of them arranged to meet at Tarpy's, a local spot, for lunch. It was a tense occasion from the start, and the drinks didn't help. Then Jackie told Judy they'd hardly had a wink of sleep all night because a car kept crawling up and down Scenic and then stopping outside their house with its motor running. Vic had called the cops twice, but both times the car had moved on before they could get there. Hadn't Judy been bothered by the same thing? Judy had already had two glasses of wine by then and blurted out that she hadn't been staying at Korshak's place the last few nights but had been bunking over in Pacific Grove with a friend. Jackie was on edge with fatigue and the way things were turning out with her sister in town and just completely blew up at her, saying she couldn't help the choices her sister had made in her life but as for herself, she didn't intend to suffer those consequences as well.

One thing led to another, and pretty soon Judy slammed her glass down so hard the stem snapped, and Jackie said that she didn't want to be in the same town as Judy and that she wanted nothing to do with those diaries, which she said were "poison." That was basically the end of the Carmel idyll. Judy went back to Pacific Grove and after a few days packed up her things from the Korshak cottage and got Vic to drive her to the airport. Back in L.A., she used her key to Jackie's place and took the diaries to her parents', where her father put them in his basement safe. And that, so far as I can figure, is where they stayed until she retrieved them more than a year later and took them out to Momo in Chicago.

From this point on the diaries get really sketchy, with longer and longer time gaps between entries and the writing itself more and more telegraphic, with lots of dashes instead of periods and abbreviations galore: wld, shd, cld, abt, sd, and so forth. Some of the abbreviations make no sense to me, and I have to wonder whether they would have to her if she'd ever gone back to them later on, which I doubt she did. On the pages there's a kind of breathlessness, as if the bureau had succeeded in crawling inside her and shaping the way she expressed her most private thoughts. Except they weren't most of the time *thoughts* anymore. That's to say, they hadn't been considered, if you get the difference. They were mostly sensations, flash feelings. It's true, here and there are long passages that read more like those of the earlier years, say, '58 to '62. But there aren't many of these, and at last, as I told you, the whole lifetime project just trailed off into a code I couldn't crack and then into the white silence of blank pages. If Phil Keneally hadn't been available to fill me in on things he knew about through his association with Momo, it would have been hard to get even as good a sense of the whole thing as I have, and what I have is by no means the whole of it or consecutive. Anyway, I've more or less come to think that consecutiveness is actually not that at all but only artifice, when somebody is skillful enough to close up the gaps without your noticing.

For example, without Keneally's help, I wouldn't have been able to figure out what she did from the time she went back to L.A. and deposited the diaries with her parents until December, and Keneally got it from Roselli, who in turn got part of it from Korshak. Korshak found out where she was staying in Pasadena and went to see her at the Arroyo Inn. Keneally said Korshak did this because she owed him money for the Scenic rental, but I don't think that can be the only reason he traced her or even the main one. He liked her and was worried about the steep slide her life was taking. Is there anything in this life more . . . what, poignant? than the sight of a beautiful woman who looks like she's headed down the tubes? You see that, and you want to do something, you know? Anything to prevent what feels like a peculiarly terrible waste, like there isn't enough of that species of splendor to go around as it is. I think that's really what made Korshak hunt her up, not the rent due, though it's obvious a guy doesn't get where he did by playing Santa. But here's the thing: when he did find her, he wanted to help her and tried to. She told him she was hiding out there because the FBI had burglarized her apartment and tapped her phone. His response was to tell her about three lots he had in new development going up in Benedict Canyon, west of Studio City; one of them already had a house on it that was about finished. If she could hang on, she could move in and make his mortgage payments. Telling her this, he held her hand and assured her that soon enough this FBI stuff would blow over.

She accepted the offer and promised to tough it out, but it was a struggle on many fronts. She wasn't talking to Jackie, wasn't dating, and hardly ever went out. And she wasn't working at her art, with all her supplies still there at the Fountain Avenue place. She was afraid to go near Dr. Feelgood's office, maybe because there might have been a reference to him in that diary the agents had looked at. How she passed those days I don't think anybody now alive really knows. Until Dallas, there aren't any entries that would tell us.

On that day her mother called in midafternoon. Judy had been asleep and wasn't tracking very well when the phone rang and she answered, which most of the time, apparently, she didn't. And since her mother was sobbing, it was some minutes before she was able to understand what had happened. Here's what she wrote:

Jack's dead—

That's it, all of it.

Then about ten days later Korshak was worried enough about her because she wasn't answering the phone that he got in touch with Roselli, who bribed the hotel management to give him a passkey and got into her room.

"It was a fuckin' mess, and she looked like shit," Phil Keneally said. We'd gone up to Dimo's for coffee, and he wasn't paying any attention to his voice level. He had this big round voice like it was coming at you out of a barrel. I never heard him in the courtroom, though as I said I did hear him lecture that one time, and what with his physical stature, that voice must have been impressive as hell in court. In here, though, what it was was embarrassing, and the savagery of his vocabulary in this particular instance made it that much harder to take. Not the ideal source to give you a version of this part of her life, but who else did I have? And so I just had to sit there and let him fire away, telling me—and those around us—about the "crap she had thrown all over—clothes, bras, bottles. John said it was shocking. He was always a real sharp dresser, kind of an earlier-day John Gotti, and I don't know what he was expecting when he got in the door, but not this shit heap. She must've looked like a bag lady. Anyway, he tried talking with her, but she just sat there on the edge of the bed, saying almost nothing, and what she did say was off the wall. Maybe she was fucked up on something, I don't know. So then he said she needed a change of scene, some fresh air, something, and he was going to take her out for a drive and get a meal in her—she'd lost so much weight her eyes were as big as her whole fuckin' face.

"But he was afraid that if he went somewhere to give her time to get herself together, she'd take a powder on him, so he got a chair from someplace and camped out in the hall outside her room.

Then, just as he was getting anxious that maybe she'd whacked herself in there, he raps on the door, and after a bit she opens it, and by Christ! he said if you didn't look too closely, she looked okay. Not like herself, but you wouldn't have been ashamed to take her out somewhere.

"Of course, she'd been such a looker a few years back, so she had something at least to work with. I mean, think of those dogs who ran with those guys back then, ugly whores like Virginia Hill and Liz Renay—they must've had holes on them you could drive a dump truck through. Besides, I always thought Roselli had the hots for her and would've loved to have fucked her, but that would have been a very unsafe thing to have done at that time.

"Anyhow, what happened was that he took her out, got some food into her, and then he comes back the next day and the day after that, and then he decides the thing to do was to get her the hell out of there altogether and drives her out to Palm Springs. They stayed there awhile, and I don't know whether old John was putting the blocks to her out there or what—I didn't want to know, either. That might depend on what you make of her character or her condition then. I do know this: she was busted up about Dallas. Not that much crying about it, I guess, just a lot of going over and over the same material, like she expected somehow a different outcome if only she could reassess the evidence and find out where things had gone so wrong. There were a lot of people in that same boat, of course—they kept running that goddamned Zapruder film back and back and back like they imagined that if they could've seen every fucking thing that happened in the last seconds, then Kennedy wouldn't have had his head handed to Jackie and the story would have had a happy ending and America would be a better place than it's turned out to be. Bullshit. I've looked at that thing myself a time or two, and it's just not there. That's to say nothing of the existential fucking futility of that whole industry itself: *we were heading for Dallas the day after V-J Day!* You want another dip of this piss?"

He was wagging his head at my coffee cup, and when I didn't respond quick enough for him, he signaled the hard-pressed waitress for refills and then went ahead with the story, telling me that one day while they were out in Palm Springs, Roselli took Judy to the Canyon Country Club for the buffet lunch.

"He was trying to get her back into the habit of eating, and I guess she was doing a little better—but not that day. Because when they walked in the dining room, there were Sinatra and Martin and Bishop, big as life, and they all saw each other immediately. Then those guys turned away like somebody had just come in with dog shit on his shoes. John didn't know what to do, so he just took her over to their own table, but they weren't even seated when it was obvious it was no go, and they just left." He shrugged his shoulders, signing that as far as he was concerned that part of the story was finished. So, soon after that we left as well, walking back to Washtenaw in silence and to the diary I'd been looking through, waiting for me there with its dwindling lines and ever-growing blank spaces.

But that very afternoon, not long after we'd gone back and I was sitting there flipping through those blank pages, wondering what they were trying to tell me, I came across an entry that got me into yet another conversation with Keneally, a bit unusual in that generally we didn't talk that much on a given day and we'd already had that exchange up at Dimo's.

It took place sometime after she'd moved into Korshak's house in Benedict Canyon. She'd been down in Beverly Hills on some errand; it would seem she was beginning to lead a somewhat normal life, and she mentions that she and Jackie had patched things up. Anyway, when she came out of some shop to her car in the parking lot, she spotted an agent at the lot's back end, leaning on a car, smoking and reading a newspaper. Agents goof off once in a while like the rest of us, I guess. "I recognized him right away," she said. "He was one of the first two who rang my buzzer at my old apartment & I opened the door to them w/o thinking. Wonder what wld have happened if I hadn't—" She didn't think he'd seen her yet, and she was about to hop into her car to try for a getaway, but then something stopped her—desperation, maybe, or was it her old spirit of defiance, flaring up once more out of the ashes, so to say? Whatever made her do it, she strode across the lot to confront her old shadow. When she got close, she saw it wasn't the one she'd thought, though in fact he was an agent. He put his paper on the car hood and was about to pull his badge but she told him not to bother.

> I told him I knew very well who he was & what he was doing here—then I sd why don't you just tell me what you want & if I have it I'll give it to you—I swear—
>
> Trying hard to keep calm but felt like slugging him—what he sd was that if I wld come down to his office & go on record about what I knew about Mr. Giancana he wld promise it wld be all over & I'd be able to live my life just like b-4. God if only he'd known how that made me feel—teasing me w that when he knew I cldnt poss do that. So all I sd was I wished he wld turn to shit because that's what he was made of anyway.

I shoved the diary aside and waited for Keneally, who'd gone to the hopper. When he came out I asked him about the entry, whether he thought the offer was genuine, that it was to be a quid pro quo: Sam for freedom from surveillance.

"Let me see that a second," he said, and I pointed out the passage. He read through it, dropped the diary back on the table, and walked over to his battered throne by the window. "Nice talk from your girlfriend," he said, chuckling as he crashed down.

"That's pretty good," he said at last. "They'd brought her to a good point, where that kind of offer might get her to the office and on record. Oh, they wanted that, all right—wanted to get her in there. But I doubt very much that's what they really wanted from her, what she had on Momo.

"Think of it this way: what could she have on him that they didn't? She might have had a few details about going here and meeting that guy there. But she doesn't even have dates for her own comings and goings, and he sure as hell would never have talked business in front of her. Hell, he talked Sicilian to his guys in front of *me*, and I was doing his fucking legal work and helping his tax guy cook the accounts! She wouldn't have been worth all those man-hours for what she had. That's a shitload of hours for a few stray turds."

He tore into a rumpled pack of smokes and lit up, then stood up there by the window with the light making him look even huger in a dusty, smoky silhouette. "Does she have anything there about Momo getting caught with Phyll out at Tahoe?" I looked around a few pages but didn't find that. What was that all about, and what did it have to do with this encounter and its offer? I asked.

"Ahh, Christ," he spat out, pulling a crumb of tobacco off his tongue. "He got so fuckin' careless I couldn't bail his ass out of one scrape before he was into another one. He was running about five blocks behind his dick in those days, just trying to keep up with it, and it was leading him deeper and deeper into trouble, both with the government and with his own people.

"So this time they tracked Phyll to Reno, and then they got hold of the Nevada Gaming guys and told them Giancana was at the Cal Neva and that he had a hidden interest in it. Which the commission fuckin' well already knew but wasn't going to act on as long as Momo stayed away from the club. The last fuckin' thing on earth they wanted was this phone call from the feds, but once they got it, they had to act—had to. And so they swooped in and nailed Momo and Phyll there, and then they yanked Sinatra's license and the whole thing became a huge fuckin' mess I couldn't save him from. That thing right there was the beginning of the end for him. I really think that.

"I always thought this was Bobby's doing, not Hoover's. Sinatra and Momo had both become incredible embarrassments to him, constantly trying to get in touch with him through intermediaries, asking for this, for that. And so here Momo hands Bobby an opportunity on a silver platter to put both of their asses in a sling. And he did it, too. Know what Momo said to me after this deal went down?" I didn't.

Keneally came across to where I was sitting with the diary there on the table, its pages splayed open, my place lost and my original question lost, too.

"He said to me out at the house one day, 'Giovanni was never the problem. It was always that little prick. He shoulda been the one whacked. That's where the problem is.'"

You can imagine what I thought when he said those words to me. *Holy Christ!* What am I being told here? Is this the key to the whole shebang, the *real* magic bullet?

No. You look at that comment Momo made, and it doesn't say *We* should have whacked Bobby instead of Jack. In fact, the more ways I turned that thing around in my head—and believe me, there were a lot—the more it seemed to me to lead me to another kind of conclusion.

First, it says pretty plainly that Jack Kennedy was never the problem the boys thought they had to solve to go on doing business. Sure, he'd proved disappointing, especially when he'd screwed up so royally on the Cuban deal, just when they thought they were going to be able to go back in there. He was a disappointment there, yes, and in other ways as well. You couldn't do business with Giovanni, because he wasn't dependable, didn't keep his word. Nobody knew that better than Momo. But Jack wasn't going to go after them, and he wasn't going to target Momo or Trafficante or Marcello. Bobby was.

You look at the comment, and you think, That's pretty clever, because you can make of it pretty much what you want. There's the missing pronoun, for one thing: *who* should have whacked Bobby instead of his brother? Momo doesn't say, but then, I don't think he needed to, not to Phil Keneally, because Keneally would have been right there in step with his boss's thinking: in taking out Jack, whoever did the hit in Dallas had succeeded in accomplishing the exact *opposite* of getting the Justice Department off the Mob's case, because with Jack out of the way, now there weren't any restraints left on Bobby. He wasn't just a loose cannon, rolling all over the deck; he was a triple-loaded one—loaded with anguish and rage and his Mick need for vengeance. And again, who knew this better than Momo Giancana? Who would have known it well before Dallas better than a guy who was being tailed on golf courses, chased through car washes, tracked down in the woods in Tahoe with his beautiful bimbo singer? I'm not going to sit here and tell you I know who killed Kennedy, because I don't. But I can't put Momo Giancana together with that event, and I don't know if he ever knew who did it either.

And then we have the subsequent confirmation of just what Momo knew would happen. Bobby went on a relentless campaign to prove the Mob had murdered his brother. This took the place of his obsession with Castro, and he worked it personally. He didn't trust anybody else to run this down, and he was completely convinced it had been a Mob hit. He may eventually have given up the personal search for the killers, but I don't think he ever really gave up his belief in who was responsible.

By this point Keneally was pacing back and forth a couple of feet in front of me—a bit disconcerting, because I had to look almost straight up at him. He'd slipped into his old courtroom mode here, pacing, head down, rubbing that dent. I wondered if that mannerism had come to him naturally, so to say, the way you'll find yourself running your tongue over a molar you've broken off or tenderly feeling for a scalp wound you've given yourself. Or whether he'd developed it as a great piece of theater, reminding the jury and judge that he'd given a lot for his country. But now he stopped in midstride and looked at me kind of blankly for a second or so.

"Where was I?"

I told him: what his guess was about the offer the agent had made Judy.

"Right, right. So it couldn't have been that—too much investment already for what they could've expected. So it had to be this: they'd get her down there, ask her if she'd come freely, ask her some questions they knew the answers to already, and then segue from

Momo to Kennedy. That's what they would have wanted out of her—and not just JFK. What Hoover wanted was the brothers, both of them with their nuts in a vise that he could crank anytime he wanted something out of them.

"His first priority was always politics. The way to keep your job, administration after administration, and the way to keep your budget fat, was to keep your eyes on that doughnut, not the hole. Crime itself didn't pay." He brought himself up short with a bark of a laugh and showed those long yellow teeth in a grin that whenever I saw it—which was rare enough—always looked a hell of a lot more menacing than anything else; it certainly didn't invite you to join him in a grin and a laugh, and I didn't then.

"What he would've wanted was to learn from her what the hell she was carrying from the brothers to Momo and Roselli and whoever else was having a look. If he had that, he knew his job would be safe forever. At the point where he started to really put her tit in the wringer he would have figured Jack a cinch for reelection. And Bobby would run in 'sixty-eight. In Washington, that's forever. So he had her hounded, trying to break her, and I guess he must have done a pretty good job. But he didn't get what he wanted—didn't break her all the way. You've got to hand it to her for that, whatever her motives were for keeping quiet. In that respect, she was a regular two-tit wonder."

I thought about telling him that even if she'd wanted to, she couldn't have handed Hoover what he wanted, because she didn't know what she had carried. But I didn't. I didn't because he'd found something admirable about her stubborn silence in the face of that killing, relentless pressure, and as you might have gathered, this wasn't exactly a guy who found much to admire in his fellow mortals. He'd seen too much, was too bitter and cynical for that. But I wanted his admiration—wanted it for her—grudging though it was and profanely put. But at the same time I knew he'd find out the truth when I wrote the book. So what I did then was to instantly improvise a coward's compromise: I would let him go on thinking she'd heroically kept her silence, and then after he'd seen what I'd written, I'd face his scornful reassessment of what was probably the only thing about her that he did find admirable—except her looks.

Why didn't she go to the FBI and at least *try* to give them what they wanted? She never said, not in anything that I had a look at. She might have feared for her life if she'd turned Momo. That's the most obvious possibility. Then you have the fact that if she'd told them she never knew what was in the packets, they wouldn't have believed it and would have gone on hounding her. The problem with that one is that she wouldn't have known that's really what they were after until they'd maneuvered her into position to ask that question. What does that leave us, then? I think it leaves us with her sense of loyalty to her friends—Jack and Sam both—and that deep maverick streak that simply would not kowtow to authority in any shape or guise. It seems like this is kind of native to us, doesn't it? I'm thinking here of the rebels in Boston throwing all that tea overboard—that sort of thing. There it turned out the right way for Paul Revere and Sam Adams. Other times it doesn't, like for Debs or Billy Mitchell or Big Bill Haywood. And it didn't with her either. In the last days of that year she went out of her way to offend power, and it really cost her.

On December twenty-eighth, Roselli took her to Vegas for New Year's at the Desert Inn, where Noel Coward was featured. His act was strictly solo, only Coward onstage in a tux, sitting on a stool with a cup of coffee. A small band sat below in a pit and accompanied him on his songs; between his sets they played for dancing.

Though she really didn't feel that much like it, Judy found that she was supposed to dance with Moe Dalitz, who was seated next to her at this big, boisterous table and who was quickly conquered. At first she tried to get out of it, but Roselli signaled to her that she needed to be friendly with Dalitz, so she danced a few times and hoped that would be enough. Dalitz was a hood, a real tough guy who'd made his bones the hard way—collecting debt and driving cars in Detroit and Cleveland before going to Vegas to make sure the eastern syndicate's concerns were represented. From what you heard, he arrived there a crude head-buster but quickly learned how to wear a suit and knot a silk tie. One of the stories attached to him had him in some sort of beef out there with Sonny Liston in Liston's days as an enforcer. Liston threatened him with one of his huge fists, and Dalitz coolly replied, "Nigger, you better make sure you kill me, because if you don't, I'll make one phone call, and you'll be dead in twenty-four hours." You have to wonder if Dalitz might have made good on his counterthreat later on, because Liston did end up dead, in a case that has never been solved.

Judy didn't know Dalitz from a two-base hit and didn't care, but as the evening wore on he kept asking her to dance and was coming on strong. Johnny was no help at all; Coward had wrapped it up, and still the band played on into the dawn. Finally they all staggered out of there on their way back to the adjoining hotel. The sun was just peeping up and flooding the desert, and Dalitz was putting on a ninth-inning rally with her. When he put his arm around her waist and whispered something in her ear, the next thing anybody knew she hauled off and slugged him in the face.

So there they all were, frozen in place, and the only things moving were the desert grasses. I don't know exactly what happened next, except of course that Dalitz didn't kill her on the spot. Roselli finally got into motion, grabbed her in a bear hug, and half carried her, half pulled her to her room and told her not to come out until he called her on the phone. She hadn't been in bed more than a few minutes when the phone began ringing, and finally she answered, and it was Roselli, saying he was on his way down.

Somehow she got up and let him in. He was still dressed in his tux, minus his tie, his eyes red as fire. He came in, closed the door quickly, and then shouted, "You must be *nuts!* You got to be gone in an hour!" He held up one finger. "One. I'll settle your bill." He told her not to think of going back to bed or she'd never wake up. Then he left, closing the door quietly, and she sat there wondering how she was supposed to leave and where she was supposed to go. She never said.

6

♦

JUDY

SHE MOVED INTO Sid Korshak's place in Benedict Canyon sometime in early spring of 1964. There isn't anything in the diaries telling me the date and hardly anything at all for this stretch except a few stray scratchings—a lonesome word here, part of a shopping list there. If this is the hidden history of her life, here it looks like she's losing her grasp of it. I have no idea how she was spending these days, who she was seeing, whether she was still seeing Dr. Feelgood or his son, or seeing anyone at all. But it'll give you some insight as to her state of mind if I tell you she moved into the house sight unseen—just called the movers, gave them a date, then followed them out to the address. Now that's someone with something major chasing her.

The development turned out to be a work in progress, as they say, the kind of thing developers advertise as having "landscaped hills, terrific views, and a park for the exclusive use of residents." There were hills, all right, raw terraces of dirt and rock with netting to hold the grass seed in place and a road switchbacking up through them. And on top there was a park, or what might be a park someday. It was a flattened area scraped off a hilltop with a circular asphalt drive and nothing in the center except a few big boulders sitting in the mud. The teenagers had found it, following the road up, and were using it to park at night and leave behind them those items they didn't need anymore.

But the house—that was the thing. It turned out to be one of those split-level jobs that were popular back then. Nothing wrong with that, except that there was a lot of glass to it. She hadn't been in it very long before she thought it was *all* glass: even her second-floor bathroom had a narrow ceiling-to-floor window, though it was true that the lower half of it was frosted. The first thing she did after the movers had cleared out was to go shopping with Jackie for drapes, but even after they'd hung them there was still a lot of light. If it had been hers, she would at the least have had some of the windows painted some light shade to let in some light but still shield her, but she couldn't do that. Korshak had been good to her, and she appreciated what he'd done to get her in there.

He'd done it, of course, before the Dalitz deal. You have to wonder whether he would have done it after word of that began to circulate through the tiny world he inhabited. Maybe not. He was kind of insulated to an extent, because he was a lawyer with a specialized practice: the boys needed him, his contacts, his clean record. But his insulation wouldn't have been total by any means, and it couldn't have done him any good if it had gotten around that he was doing Judy favors. To his credit, he never asked her to leave, and my calculation is that she lived at that address more than two years, though she wasn't exactly in it all that time.

In that first summer she was painting again. She set up an area on the ground floor to use as a studio and was working on still lifes, mostly flowers and fruit and tableware arrangements. I know this because she said she went to see Tony Bennett at a Hollywood club, and they had a very friendly reunion afterward, during which she told him what she was working on and how much his example had meant. The exact date of this encounter isn't important. What's important is the context, because on the same page as her last remarks about Bennett and written in the same violet ink are these words: "I think they found me—cars up & down like Carmel."

They had found her, and so then it began all over again, only more intensely. This time they confined their harassment to nights: cars driving slowly past on the way up to the park, where they'd pull to the edge and shine their lights down on her house. Cars coming down and raking the house with their lights as they made the turn above. If there had been any neighbors, no doubt they would have complained, though what that would have gotten them I don't know. But hers was the only house occupied at this point, and so while this hellish thing went on and on she must have had plenty of second thoughts about Korshak's generosity. At one point she called her brother, Allen, to ask him to stay with her a few nights, and he did. He stayed quite a while, it seems, but finally it got to him, too, and he moved out. In a way his reaction was similar to Jackie's up in Carmel: he was sorry, but really, what could he do about it? Maybe she could get a lawyer and see if there wasn't something that could legally be done to put a stop to this. As for him, the nightly routine of the cars and the lights and staying up with her to all hours was driving him nuts. He was job-hunting again and had missed a promising interview, he said, because he was in such terrible shape.

So once again she was on her own in circumstances pretty much like those she'd endured at the Sahara, though the surroundings weren't quite that grim. She was terrified at night and sleeping through the days in a kind of house arrest. You have to hand it to Hoover, I guess: he really knew how to apply the thumbscrews. Makes you almost believe in reincarnation, where in an earlier life he'd advised Torquemada on how to put the fear of God into sinners on their way to hell. Her painting was probably an early casualty of the new harassment, and then her contact with her family became sporadic, partly because she didn't want them to know any more about what was happening to her than they already did. Partly, too, because her father had developed congestive heart failure and was heading downhill fast. She didn't want to carry her own misery into that household, so she began to stay away.

The cars kept coming. One night, cowering in her bedroom, which she'd made as dark and cavelike as she could, she flared up, a flash in that darkness of the old Judy. When a car rolled past on its way to the park around two A.M., she flung on her robe and went downstairs to wait. Later, when she saw lights swinging around the curve above, she ran out to confront them, hollering and waving her arms. The car feinted toward her, then veered away, and she heard a burst of mocking laughter that told her these weren't Hoover's guys, just kids helling around on a summer night. Seeing a hysterical woman in her nightgown, clawing at the dark and screaming, no doubt made their evening.

"I can't stand this shit," she said. "So here I am up to my neck in it." She wrote this in early October, and "here" was D.C., where she had gone on an impulse and taken a room at the Mayflower, desperate to find someone who could help her. The decision probably couldn't be called rational, though when I look at it, I see a kind of desperate—that word again—logic to it: your path through life has somehow taken a wrong turn, so you go back to that place in the woods where you think you began to go wrong and try to figure it out from there. For her, that place had to be Washington, where four years before she'd so willingly signed on for whatever it would be that Jack had in mind for her.

She had made up a list of names to call, and she had most of the numbers, too, and up in her room she began to go down through them, scratching each one out when the operator told her that the number was no longer in service and there was no new listing for the party she was seeking. Late that afternoon she'd gotten down to the last two names, Evelyn Lincoln's and Teddy's. All the others had been crossed out, though "rubbed out" might be more accurate, in the slang sense: her scratchings-out were so thorough I had to use Keneally's magnifying glass to try to see what was underneath. It was like trying to unearth the dead past, Camelot, a name that, if it ever meant anything to her, must have seemed as dead as anything could get.

Evelyn Lincoln. She tried for her, but no dice. Crossed out. Gone. The same Evelyn Lincoln who had formed a "telephone relationship with a Miss Campbell," as Hoover had slyly put it to the president, pushing the blade in deep and giving it a nice twist. The same Evelyn Lincoln who years later was questioned by the Church Committee when it was digging around in that patch of history. Had she, they wondered, ever heard of a Judith Campbell? And she answered that she remembered a campaign worker by that name, but that was all. Maybe this Miss Campbell had been ringing doorbells or handing out fliers or pouring coffee at a rally in Martinsburg. It was hard to remember all those eager young girls . . .

Judy must have been frantic and bewildered both, because less than a year after Dallas, Washington had changed so utterly it was like the Kennedy years had never been. Everybody who'd been close to Jack seemed to have vanished, as if each of them had been hit in the soul or the heart by a fragment of that exploding head and had fled somewhere dark and private to try to wash it off or in some other way get rid of it. And maybe what they found—O'Donnell, Powers, Salinger, Sorensen, Goodwin—was that it wouldn't come off, that it had stuck to them and become a part of who they were. Maybe that could be said of America, too. It certainly could be said of her.

In the days we're speaking of, it was still possible to reach an actual human being by telephone, even if you were calling the office of a United States senator. So she got someone in Teddy's office right away, a woman. But what followed could only have increased her frantic bewilderment, because when she said she wanted to speak to the senator, that she was an old friend, there was a pause on the other end. Then the woman said that the senator wasn't expected back in the office for some time yet; nobody could say just when. Judy thought she was being given the runaround: surely a senator had to show up for work just like everybody else—maybe more faithfully than anybody else. Where was he, anyway? Again there was a pause, and then the woman said she was going to transfer Judy's call. Judy thought she'd be cut off.

"This is Judith Campbell. I knew President Kennedy and Teddy both," she blurted. She couldn't tell whether the woman had heard this or had already switched the call to another line. She sat there on the end of the bed, pressing the receiver so hard against her head she had to pull it away, fearing that in doing so she'd miss something vital. Just as she was about to hang up and call again, a man's voice came on the line, identifying himself by name—which she didn't register. She started in again, giving her name and telling him that it was urgent that she speak with Senator Kennedy, wherever he happened to be. But the man interrupted.

"Miss Campbell, the senator is still in New England Baptist Hospital in Boston, and we don't really know just when he'll get out. He's coming right along, but his injuries were severe, as you probably know."

She didn't know. She'd been so out of touch with the wider world, cowering there in Korshak's Benedict Canyon house, that she'd completely missed the fact that in June Teddy had broken his back in a near-fatal plane crash in western Massachusetts. The man was still talking as she sat there, not listening but only looking down at her rumpled list of potential saviors lying there beside her on the bed, all the names but one crossed out, and even that one, the last one, unavailable to her. Maybe he too would die, she thought, and maybe he was as good as dead now—to her.

She must have repeated her hopeless, helpless remarks about how urgent this was, because she heard the staffer telling her that the senator wasn't taking any outside calls just now, that he was concentrating all his efforts on regaining his health.

"I still want to leave my name and number with you," she said, "so you can pass it along to him. That can't hurt him any." And when she'd done that, she hung up and drew her ballpoint through Teddy's name several times, as if he really were dead.

Having struck out with the living, she took a cab that afternoon out toward Arlington and walked across the bridge to the cemetery. It was a spectacular autumn day—great sun, a few clouds, and warm enough that soon she thought the suit she was wearing was too heavy. Also, she hadn't even gotten through the cemetery gates before her feet in her high heels were beginning to bark at her. Still, she kept going, toward Jack's grave.

Here and there, as you know, I've quoted directly from her diaries, where I felt it was crucial to have her own words on the record. I hope I've gotten these entries down accurately. If Keneally had ever permitted me to take the things out of his apartment and photocopy them, this wouldn't be yet another question, as if there weren't enough already. But he never would, and he made that clear the first day I started to work through them. I'll come back to this peculiarity in a few minutes. Anyway, I've pretty much kept these direct quotes short, partly because Judy wasn't a great writer, as I said at the outset, and in a given entry often enough you have to pluck what's interesting out of a lot of stuff that isn't. But here, when she's in Arlington, I look and look at these lines, and I'm goddamned if I can do them justice in my own language. So I'm not going to try, not even give you a frame, if you like. I'm just going to read them to you as I copied them out, and you'll have to trust me that this is an accurate transcription. In any case, it's a faithful one.

squirrels why are they alive

big planes roaring overhead I almost can see the faces—

sign for Jack's grave gunshots in the distance frightened me so I had to sit down—man asked me if I was sick. M.T.Y.K. Then I realized they were a salute like they had for Jack that went on & on so I cldnt get them out of my head that night & they just kept coming back like that for mos I'd be over there talking w Mother & I cld see her lips going but cldnt hear her words because of the shots big ones cannons wld smile & nod but what she's prob trying to tell me isn't that good because Daddy's dying— But was so frightened abt Jack abt me abt everything abt the shots I cldnt tell her that I'm scared

Maybe 40 @ grave 2 policemen why are they looking @ me cldnt see the grave because they were standing in front. Then more people came behind me & I was trapped in there & nervous because I cldnt see them & look @ the grave @ the same time never wished for 2 heads until now & Jack doesn't have any What did I expect—alone here w him hardly why shd I have thought that I'm alone all the time these days anyway—after a bit the ones in front moved on & I had to move up & there it was. Looked rough. New—cld see where they put new sections of grass down. You cld see the edges where they hadn't grown together yt—A woman next to me got down on her knees & prayed I had a strange desire to put my hand on her head made me feel *bad* but I didn't cry Why Jack wanted to get me involved from the v 1st I think he did alright & I did everything he asked & now he's dead & I'm only walking around & not too well @ that because my ft are killing me & he's down there somewhere in the dirt closed up inside a box thinking abt him all alone in the dark wch he wld have hated absolutely—always needed people around him to reflect how brill he was—they sd he hardly had much head left Sam sd that Anyway they blew a lot of it away & Jackie had to carry the pieces in her hands into the hosp & hand it to the drs but they cldnt put it back in there they never can. But thinking abt him down there wearing a shirt & tie & how they'd do the collar Jack's body didn't always work so well but was beautiful—all the things wrong w him—these are NOT what I shd be thinking here but what am I supposed to be thinking abt—started to worry other people behind me cld tell what I was thinking wch wld be *awful* & when I started to think that way looked up the hill to a mansion w trees around & there THEY were—THEM in their awful suits Weren't fooling me 1 bit Maybe they were right behind me when I came here & that's why I always have this chilly feeling on my back—Dr J—asked him if there was something wrong w me & needed to see a spec Sd he wld look @ me & boy did he ever says there's abs nothing wrong w you & gives me that stuff that picks u up & drops you out of the plane w/o a chute. Knew all that but still sd give it to me Max & I don't remember whether he did or not that it wld matter what he stuck in me by that pt.

There they were those dark bastards—thought abt waving to them but turned right around & tried not hurrying cldn't anyhow my ft hurt too much Back here thinking abt how many

> times I've checked in here Judy Campbell Judy Campbell Judy Campbell & then over @ W.H. Powers wld sign us in Powers + 1 —that's me. This time I signed in Harriet Moore Sam gave me that 1 & we used to laugh because I hated Harriet Never wanted to be anybody else but me & now I want to be NOBODY NOBODY but they know who I am or who they think I am or who they thought I was—what this is is what I'm here for to find out who I am now so I can tell them just once just one of them look I know who you think I am but I'm not

There are no entries for the following two days. I have trouble imagining what she might have done during them, given her state of mind. She might just have stayed in her room, drinking chartreuse and sleeping. Clothes shopping was a sport for her as well as a distraction, but usually she would note what items she bought. Nothing of that, though. If she had done something that connected her to the past—like walking past the White House—you'd think she'd have mentioned it. In any case, the next entry has her sleeping until almost noon and then being disappointed to find that it was still so early. Gradually she got herself together and went to the Phillips Collection, remembering while wandering its rooms that once she'd wanted to take Jack there so they might have a conversation about art. The recollection made her think back on how stupid she'd been about the whole relationship: it would have been just as impossible for them to come here together as it would have been to escape to an island in the Caribbean. But she hadn't seen that then, even while she was drifting toward this disaster that had become her life.

On her way back to the Mayflower she thought she might as well pack up and leave. There was nothing for her here. But leave for where? The Caribbean floated again to mind, but she dismissed it. She didn't have the right clothes, and if she was spotted on an island, she'd be trapped, with no place to go. The thought made her slightly sick, and back at the hotel she stopped in the lobby to tell the concierge to send up a chilled bottle of Chablis.

When the waiter knocked, she was standing by the bed, paralyzed with fright because her message light was blinking. She was trying to imagine who could be calling her here, since she'd told no one where she was going. Now she practically shouted, asking who was at the door, and felt a wild joy when a voice with a foreign accent answered, "Room service." He was an older man, it turned out, who knew his business, and whatever she might have looked like at that moment, he ignored it with his professional blankness. Nowadays, I guess, you might easily get some kid whose widened eyes would register your own distress. Even so, the man would have had to see that the lady in 535, or whatever it was, was in some sort of state, especially when she told him she was going to the powder room—she wasn't feeling well but would only be a moment—and would he please open the wine and then retrieve the telephone message for her. Before he could answer, she went into the bathroom and shut the door firmly behind her.

Inside, she hovered near the closed door, listening to the sounds of the wine being uncorked and the bottle being replaced in the bucket. Then the man's voice on the telephone and then silence. When she heard the room door open and close, she had another stab of panic, thinking maybe he'd left without telling her who the caller was. But when she burst into the empty room, there on the nightstand was a note card with what she saw as "stiff writing didn't look American," and the message: "Mr. Kennedy would be glad to speak to you tomorrow at 11 a.m., Eastern time." Below this was the New England Baptist number and the appropriate extension. She stood there with the card in both hands, watching it wobble and not really caring, and then went for the wine. Much later, she thought she needed to hunt up that waiter and give him a big tip. She never said whether she did this or not.

When you think of the circumstances, it's almost astonishing Teddy was willing to take her call. I mean, here was this guy, the brother of the just-assassinated president, lying in the hospital with a broken back while his wife and staff tried to carry on his reelection campaign. But he did take it. Maybe he had his own reasons for wanting to connect with his past and everything about it that had been so swiftly cut off in Dallas, and Judy was a part of that. And maybe too he was thinking of how she'd looked when they'd gone bar-hopping in Vegas in '60; you know how it is: the girl looks exactly the same now as then.

Judy clearly wasn't in any shape to get down in any detail what they talked about, and you have to think Teddy might not have been up for a long conversation. So she probably got right to it, asking him if he could possibly help with her FBI problem—though how much she could have told him of just how that problem had come about is another question. Even as dangerously rattled as she was, you'd think she'd have had enough presence of mind to know that she couldn't get into these specifics. However she put her request, we don't know anything here except that they talked about Jack, because she wrote that Teddy had said that "Jack v diff last summer—diff friends etc." Then there were three names listed: Charlie Bennett, Erazmo Carreon, and Mary Meyer. These would have been some of Jack's new friends, clearly. Mary Meyer's name was underlined twice, which makes it likely that Teddy had said something about her that got Judy's attention. Maybe she thought Mary Meyer was her last chance at getting help here in Washington, and if this sounds pretty far-fetched to you, it did to me, too, when I came across that page.

There was an M. Meyer in the Georgetown directory, but when she called the number three times that morning, there was no answer. She decided to go to the address in the book and found herself standing at the corner of Thirty-fourth and O Streets that same afternoon. It was warm again, but this time she was prepared for it, wearing a lightweight blazer and a skirt. No high heels, either, but lower-heeled Italian shoes that were "good walkers." Standing there, trying for her bearings, she said she could "smell leaves burning—

not in fires in gutters but burning in the sun." Maybe she could. She walked quickly enough to the house, narrow, painted a pastel blue, and "squeezed in b/w others like they do out here wld make me miserable to live like this."

She rang the bell and waited. When there wasn't an answer she rang again, fighting the temptation to step off the walk and wade through some shrubbery to peek in the front window. But just as she was about to do that, a door opened in the next house, and a youngish woman looked over at her and asked if she was looking for Mary. If she was, the woman went on, she'd missed her: Mary had left on her daily walk, which meant she wouldn't be back for quite a while. This strikes me as a goodly amount of information to offer a stranger, but then I picture Judy standing there, this statuesque woman, smartly dressed and wearing dark glasses, and I figure the neighbor instantly sized her up as belonging in that Georgetown setting.

What to do? She had enough presence of mind to thank the neighbor—but just enough. "Stood there in front—if she was watching must've thought I was a crazy woman like you see on the st. Then thought abt getting out of there—police—finally found a cab." That was the end of that—for that day, anyway. But she was still determined to make contact, and woke up the next morning with that in mind.

She ordered coffee and rolls from room service, trying, apparently, to do a little better about eating. The order came with a folded copy of the *Washington Post*, and on its second page was a story that scared her so badly she leaped up, flung her clothes into her bags, and left for the airport without showering or putting on her makeup. At the airport she found she couldn't get a seat on a flight out until late afternoon. She spent most of the intervening hours cowering in the ladies' room, coming out only once, to swill down a martini.

Here was the story that scared her: on Mary Meyer's daily walk along the old towpath by the Chesapeake and Ohio Canal, she had been murdered, shot twice by a lone gunman. Two auto mechanics, the story said, had been on a bridge above the canal and had heard the first shot. Then they saw a man fire the second shot at close range while Meyer hugged a tree with one hand and tried to fend him off with the other. The mechanics ran across the bridge to their station and called the cops, and not long after that a search of the woods along the canal turned up a suspect closely matching the description of the man the mechanics had seen firing the second, fatal shot. Whether she even got to the end of the story or not, Judy was certain this had been no stickup gone wrong. This was an FBI rubout, and she—Judy—was connected, because she'd tried to make contact with Meyer and had been seen at her house. This I got from Keneally, who had it from Momo.

"She called him from Washington," Keneally told me, "from the airport, and was bat shit—totally out of control. She wanted to fly to Chicago, but he had something or other going on—Phyllis, probably—and stalled her, telling her to go home and he'd call her there in a few days. She called him every day after that until he said, Okay, come on. I remember the incident perfectly well because at that time we were still trying to wind up the Cal Neva mess—the fucking *wreckage* of the Cal Neva, which had never been anything but a disaster for him. There was a guy out there—employee—who knew a lot of the history, and he had some drug problem or other and the feds and the state both had him by the short hairs. We were trying—shit, *I* was trying—to get to him with some kind of a package that would buy his silence. The hellish thing here was that Momo himself didn't seem to appreciate how dangerous this thing could be for him, and so while I'm trying to get him to help me with some of the details of the negotiations—things only he knew—all he really wanted to do was poke Phyllis. If I hadn't known better, I'd have said his brain was rotten with syph, but that wasn't it. He wasn't really taking care of business, not the way he should have in his position, and if you remember, pretty soon he began to get in big-time trouble: on the run, in and out of the country, a year in the slammer. By the time of the Church Committee there were a lot of people who'd come to feel he'd outlived his usefulness and wasn't to be trusted. Then, *whammo!* Seven shots up under the chin there in his own basement, the night before he was to talk with a committee lawyer." He gave one of his sardonic, unmirthful chuckles, kind of like what you imagine a hyena might sound like when it smells putrefaction in the vicinity. "They had him set up with a woman lawyer. I knew her—Nan Belletto, a looker. I think they were figuring she might be able to get inside with him, harden him up to soften him up, if you follow. His reputation as being cunt-struck was big by then. But Belletto never got to him in time. They used the old silencer.

"Anyway, Campbell came out, shitting her drawers and leaving me to work on keeping Stew quiet out in Tahoe. She had some cockamamie story about how the FBI was going to murder her to get hold of her diaries and begged Momo to keep them for her. You know the rest, because I told you at the Bullpen. That was your lucky day, or were you too fucked up to remember?"

I told him I remembered, all right.

Handing Momo her diaries was the next-to-last thing that happened between them. The last thing was, he gave her a pistol. He'd started out giving her great, huge bunches of yellow roses. Now he gave her a gun, because she asked him for it when he was showing her out the back door. At that last goodbye moment, she suddenly turned to him, and he might have thought, Well, here comes a goodbye kiss. And maybe he was thinking, too, that it was also good riddance, because by this point she'd become too hot for him and for everybody around him. Anyway, it wasn't a goodbye kiss, and after she told him what she wanted, he looked at her a hard moment, and then he went into the house and came back with a Chivas Regal bag, one of those fancy velvet-looking bags with a rope around its neck, and handed it to her. The gun was inside.

"It's cold," he told her. "Stony." Then he shook his head at her once and said, "The goose is out, baby." Whatever the hell that meant, the phrase crops up three different times in those pages where she took a stab at code writing, though never exactly the same way. It seemed to mean something to her, if only that these were Momo's last words to her—the last ones I know of, anyway. And after he said them she flew back to L.A., to that darkened house, locked the doors behind her, and waited for the FBI to come for her. Her nerves were completely shot, her father was dying, and she felt utterly abandoned by the world. You could hardly blame her for that. Even Momo's gift of the pistol could easily have been seen as a kiss-off, as if he were saying, I don't really care what you do with this, whether you use it on one of Hoover's guys or on yourself, or both.

Years later, when she gave her listless okay to a crime reporter to ghost her story, she told him that the nighttime cars showed up again but that she was never really sure whether they were FBI or just cruising kids. She was at least half out of her gourd, as I've said, and then she began to feel a kind of creeping paralysis that each day made it harder and harder to move. Finally the day came when she felt it just was too painful to get downstairs and she stayed in her bedroom. She had a small sack of fruit up there and ate her way through that, and she could still drag herself to the bathroom. But that was all. One of my old newspaper cronies who used to write a health column for the *Daily News* put me in touch with one of his former sources, a neurologist at Northwestern Hospital, and I interviewed him about Judy's symptoms. He told me it sounded like it might have been rheumatoid arthritis, which he said could be brought on by acute and prolonged stress. Whatever it was, by the time her family found her, she was practically skeletal, dehydrated, and delusional. She tried to shoot at them when she heard them coming up the stairs, but she fumbled the pistol, and when it hit the floor and went off, the shot just whanged into the wall. She was still in the hospital when her father died, and when she was finally released she went to her mother's, where she stayed awhile, as much being cared for as helping her mother make the transition to widowhood.

Someday somebody is going to file a request for her FBI file under the Freedom of Information Act, and even though it'll probably look a good deal like that notebook page of hers with all those Camelot names and numbers blacked out, one after the other, still there might be enough consecutive words to tell that researcher when and why Hoover called off the dogs. Because he did. He had to know she'd been hospitalized, and he had to know she'd gone from there to her mother's. But there weren't any midnight cruisers at her mother's, and when she moved back into Korshak's glass house, she wasn't bothered there either. True, the developer had installed a gate up at the park so cars couldn't get through, but even so the bureau could have sent agents winding past her house, but it didn't. Maybe J. Edgar figured he'd busted her up as much as he could, and if she hadn't given up the goods on the Kennedys by then, she probably wasn't going to. In a situation like that, I doubt you get any bouquets from the FBI; they probably just figure you're a real hard case, leave the file open, and move on, leaving you and your life behind in rags and fragments.

That's how her life was left in the wake of this long, dark siege. You can come to your own conclusion about just why she didn't go to the feds and tell what she knew, and it might be that you'll end up thinking she would have done just that if she had ever known what they were really after. Me, I mark it down as a big plus in her column. And I trace her silence back to her strong sense of loyalty and that stubborn anti-authoritarian streak she'd always had. She just wasn't going to give up her friends, Jack or Sam, to some "busybody meathead," no matter how much power he had or how much of a wreck he could make of her life. You've got to admire that when you add up the price she paid—I do, anyway.

At the beginning of 1975, if you knew her name, you were damned unusual. Either you'd have to have known her or you knew someone who had. But by the end of that year a lot of people knew the name, the face, and the story that went with these.

As far as being a public figure of even the most minor sort, she'd hardly registered before. As far as I can tell, there'd been only two items in the press before '75. There was that sly reference to her and Jack in Winchell's column, and there was the AP/Wide World photo of her, snapped as she came out into the night from a club or some such. But you'd have to be some kind of hound to have put the Winchell together with the photo and then to have retained these in your mind to know who Judy Campbell was at the beginning of 1975. More than a decade after Dallas, I think even many of the Hollywood and Washington insiders had forgotten her, and she was long gone from those places and Vegas, Chicago, and New York, too. The Mob had turned its back on her. In Washington, if she was anything at all, she was only a very faded name that was hardly even an inconvenience to the liberals who hung on there under the new order. But then the Church Committee dug her up out of the files and brought her back.

The committee was officially called the Senate Select Committee to Study Governmental Operations with Respect to Intelligence Activities, and it was investigating how intelligence was gathered by the CIA and the FBI, whether that gathering had been lawful, and whether the ways the intelligence was used were legitimate and in the country's best interests. If you liked the general idea, you liked the committee and cheered it on—"Get those dirty snoops! This ain't a police state yet!" That sort of thing. If you were in the conservative camp, you thought of it as a costly and stupid boondoggle designed to give its chairman, Frank Church, the sort of national exposure he'd need if he ran for president.

Inevitably the committee stepped in the Cuba/Castro mess, and when it did it came across the FBI material on Judy. But she'd slipped into such obscurity, as I say, that for a while nobody could figure out where she was or even if she was still alive. Both her parents were dead. Her brother, Allen, was supposed to be living in Brazil, but nobody could track him down. Her sister, Jackie, had retired from films but had kept her stage name. And that was how the committee's investigators finally found Judy, because when they showed up at Jackie's doorstep, it was the Carmel nightmare all over again, and she gladly told them that her sister was living in a trailer park in De Leon Springs, Florida, under the name Judith Exner. That's where they found her, living with her husband, Chuck, and her adopted son, Ed.

Chuck Exxner (his spelling) was a racecar driver who was either fourteen or sixteen years her junior, depending on your source. He turned out to be a pretty rough customer, somebody who didn't take too kindly to the suits who showed up with their subpoenas. Later, up in Washington, the guys in the press quickly learned not to ask Chuck Exxner for a quote. Anyway, the suits served Judy Exner with that subpoena to come to Washington and tell the committee what she knew about the Castro business.

It turned out she didn't know a damned thing about it. Not until a young staff lawyer told her what they'd come across in the files. Of course she knew that the FBI had been tailing her for years, but it wasn't until that very moment and the way the young staffer phrased his questions and supplied some jogs to her memory that she tumbled to the fact that some of the packets she'd dutifully—and, as she had imagined, *patriotically*—delivered to Momo and Johnny in Chicago and Vegas and L.A. had contained plans for offing Fidel. Think about *that* for a moment. Think about that sudden, sucking feeling of betrayal, like what you'd get if you were shoved off a canyon cliff. So *this* was what Jack let me in for! Sam, too. What a stupid bitch they must have thought I was, running these murder plans all over the country without ever wondering what I was carrying, thinking it was government business when it was death in a handbag—a nice one, too, even if it was a tad on the large side. Damned clever. No wonder Jack and Bobby weren't going to protect me. Who the hell was dumb little Judy? *They* were the ones who had to be protected, and I was the one who was protecting them with my ignorance, my innocence, my reliability, imagining that I was somehow helping the country. Imagining that I was doing something nobody else could do. Me, red-white-and-blue Judy.

These are my words here, you understand. But what else *could* she have thought in that flashing instant of insight when some stranger broke the seal, so to say, on those packets and lit up all those dark places she'd been living in: the shit-hole of the Sahara out on Mannheim; the crummy second-rate hotels in L.A. where she'd hidden out, where she was hiding under the covers when her mother reached her with the news from Dallas; the deserts outside Reno where she'd burned up the roads, running from the specter of the bureau; the airport cans she'd crouched in, waiting for a flight; the glass house sprayed all night by searchlights?

Early on, when I was trying to give you my assessment of her character, I said there was something mysterious about her, something I didn't get, even after my prolonged experience with her diaries. This in itself wouldn't be that surprising, since there's a mystery of some sort to all of us, I'd say, some thing or things even our friends or lovers or wives might not get either. With her, I had the persistent feeling that there was always something she was holding back, that there was some impregnable reserve. I would love to believe that in this moment of insight, there in some institutional cubicle, her husband having been sent outside because of the extreme sensitivity of the material and the young staffer trying to guide her and coax out her cooperation—I'd love to believe that she could have thought, Well, I didn't give those guys *everything* of me; I saved something of myself. But I doubt it. That isn't the way the mind works in a situation like that. That might come only later—if it ever came.

Well. Who can say what happened next? Once she'd learned what had most likely been in some of those packets, did she then volunteer that she'd been something more than a mere messenger for Jack? For Momo? Did she decide that since she'd been had by both of them, her stubborn, costly silence was no longer worth it—in fact was now pointless? Or did the young staffer politely suggest that circumstantial evidence pointed pretty plainly to something more than strictly business involved here? Maybe he went on to suggest that if she would come clean about the whole business, the committee would work with her to tailor its questions so as to conceal as much as possible about her relationships with JFK and Momo and conceal her identity as well. What they actually wanted, after all, wasn't who did what with whom. It was the connections between the White House, the CIA, the Mob, and the Castro fiasco. They didn't have the "smoking gun," as we now say: they didn't know what had been in those packets, and she couldn't help them there. She couldn't even answer their questions about when she'd made the deliveries, because she no longer had her diaries, and even if she'd still had them, they wouldn't have been that helpful, because she had so rarely dated the entries. In short, she was a stick of dynamite without a fuse, and when they understood that, they made the decision to protect her as best they could in her official testimony. They advised her to give simple yes-and-no answers to their carefully worded questions and not to volunteer anything. You almost wonder why they bothered—and you wish they hadn't. I do, anyway.

This was the best possible deal for her under the circumstances, but it was also best for Senator Church and his committee. Because really the committee was maybe only a little better than most of these fishing expeditions they put together with such fanfare from time to time, like the one they had to find out what happened in Chile with Allende. The Watergate deal was a rarity, and that, as you may recall, turned on an absolute fluke, when they accidentally stumbled on the existence of the secret tapes. What usually happens is that the committee members find out some of the truth about the matter at hand, but what they find out often turns out to be way too hot for public consumption, and so the final report is pretty much a whitewash job—as it was here.

Here's a small sample of how it's done. Judy was asked at one point whether she'd ever delivered messages from either Giancana or Roselli to the White House, and she answered no. Strictly speaking, this probably was the truth. As far as I can tell, all the documents she handled originated with the Kennedys; she was only returning them. But the committee members knew damn well there was more to this business than that simple one-word answer said, even if they didn't know exactly what was in the packets. The question, in other words, was designed to conceal the truth, just as, in a larger way, the committee report was designed to conceal the truth about the Castro business. The report told the public that there had been numerous high-level government discussions about Mr. Castro, including some consideration of the feasibility of assassinating him, and that these discussions dated back to the Eisenhower administration. It was highly unlikely, however, that either Eisenhower or President Kennedy had ever known anything about these, and still less likely that some of these discussions involved negotiations with members of organized crime. There'd been a courier, the report said, who had been involved in these negotiations, but the courier's name and gender weren't specified. That, at least, was one promise our government kept to her.

For a while, anyway, they kept it. But this was hot stuff, too hot for that promise to be kept for good, and soon enough somebody involved with the committee leaked the vital facts: name, sex, whereabouts, the whole bag. It was then that the image of the dark, smoldering beauty was exhumed from the morgue and put on the front page and on the nightly news programs—that image I think Ed might have had in mind when he decided to drop the nickel on me in his kitchen. When she saw it, she must have known right away that she could run but she couldn't hide, that sooner or later she'd have to say something public. It must have felt like one of those recurring nightmares that stalk you, dragging you back and back again to the same terrible place and the problem there you haven't solved. Only this time it wasn't the FBI doing the stalking but the press, which doesn't have any director who can decide to call off the dogs. What it has is the insatiable hunger of the public for sex scandals in the highest places.

Finally, in December in San Diego, she faced the cameras to read a statement I think she wrote herself. In it she said she'd had a relationship with "Jack Kennedy that was of a close, personal nature and did not involve conspiratorial shenanigans of any kind." She also admitted to a "personal relationship" with Sam Giancana and Johnny Roselli but emphasized that these were separate situations and that there'd been no connection whatever between Kennedy and the mobsters.

Nobody in the media bought that. It looked preposterous in light of what the Church report had revealed. Still, the throng of doubters found it hard to come up with anybody who could refute her. The thinned-out ranks of the Camelot crew had nothing to say, as you'd expect. Powers stood by the record of the White House logs, which were empty of a single reference to a Judy Campbell. Kenny O'Donnell had never heard her name. Salinger, in France, had put an ocean between himself and all that. Giancana—who wouldn't have been a source in any case—had been murdered in June in his basement stronghold, where he had Judy's diaries stashed. And Johnny Roselli was lying very low, his career as a Mob big shot well behind him. Within a year he would be lying even lower: in the late summer of '76, parts of him were found stuffed in an oil drum off the Florida coast.

None of this made any difference: she was condemned in the court of public opinion and came out of the episode with that big scarlet A painted across her chest, like in the Hawthorne novel. That, by the way, was the particular invention of a writer for the *Sacramento Bee,* who wrote a front-page piece he called "How Judy Won Her Varsity Letter." Pretty cute, eh? And she wore it, all right, to the end of her days, remembered as the high-priced spread who—and let's say it straight out—"was fucking Jack Kennedy and Sam Giancana at the same time."

The Church Committee thing wrecked the marriage. It's possible Chuck Exxner had gone for her to begin with because she'd told him she'd been in bed with JFK and Sinatra and Sam Giancana—maybe the whole damned Rat Pack, as far as he knew. A guy who races cars for a living could very well be someone who is drawn to fast living and life on the edge, I guess. That might be one thing, but it's another when your wife's name and face go up there in red lights and she's got that varsity letter across her chest. Suddenly that racy roar turns kind of gassy when people start calling her nothing but a whore, as apparently Chuck's own mother did—then it's a different thing you live with, day in and day out; what you go to bed with, yes, but also what you wake up to. Maybe not too sexy as a steady thing. So only a few months after pieces of Johnny Roselli were found in Biscayne Bay, the Exxners separated, and Judy took Ed out to San Diego, where she raised him on her own, grimly determined to give him that strict Catholic upbringing he later on prized so highly. Meanwhile, she tried her best to shield him from the red light her public image shed and took that stab at telling her side of the story. Pretty quickly, though, she saw the complete futility of that, as Ed told me. It was like Hercules being told he had one day to clean out the king's stable and barn when the place was so deep in shit the smell of it permeated all of Greece. Well, somehow Herc did it, but then, that's a myth, and this is history, and she gave up trying to rewrite it.

I have absolutely no doubt that this was the situation that finally killed her. By that I mean I think the accumulated stress of trying to give Ed a normal life under these conditions did her in. And you might be justified by thinking here, Oh, so now he knows what causes cancer, which is what she died of. I don't. But there's plenty of evidence building up that big-time stress is a factor because it hammers your immune system. And since the focus of her life had narrowed to this single task, giving Ed that good start, it had to have been damned tough going for her. Ed went by Immoor, her maiden name, which bought him a certain amount of anonymity. But as involved as she'd made herself in every aspect of his life, she herself couldn't be invisible, and even though she looked nothing like she had when she'd made Sinatra's jaw drop, and Jack Kennedy's, too, she was still a nice-looking woman and a single one. Single moms, let's remember, weren't the common phenomenon then that they are now. Every once in a while someone would wonder about her, who she was and what her story was; and every once in a while they'd find out. Then she'd have to try to calculate what the fall-out might be for Ed and whether it would be worse for him staying where they were, with that knowledge working its way around the neighborhood and eventually into the classroom, the playground, the playing field, and so forth. This versus bouncing him around from school to school like an army brat. Eventually she decided that the best thing she could do for him was to ship him off to boarding school, which she did, sending him here, to Lake Forest. Considering the ferocity of her devotion to him, this must have been a hell of a wrench. Anyway, he came out here, and she moved to La Jolla, trying to hang on to life long enough to see him safely launched.

I don't have the chronology here, so I don't know if she died before he graduated, and at the time I was hanging around him—or maybe I should say, hanging *on* him—I didn't know enough to ask him so pointed a question. Maybe, too, he and I were never on the kind of terms where that was a question I could ever have asked. Anyway, he did get launched. I never knew anything about his history or his personal life, but he was a business success, all right, you couldn't miss that. On the sales floor and in the clubhouse locker room as well he came off as a thoroughly likable guy. So if he was very touchy on the subject of his mother, who could blame him for that? I certainly couldn't, though as I told you, there was a stretch of months where I was feeling very sore at him because he'd taken my scoop away from me. Then Phil Keneally handed it back—a double dip this time—and by the time I'd laid aside Judy's codebook as an unsolvable mystery and faced the task of writing the book with what I had, if I thought about Ed, it was only to wonder once in a while what I'd missed in that Kellogg's box. But then I'd tell myself to get off that and concentrate on what was there in front of me in my stacks of notes: plenty enough, I felt, to tell the story of her affairs with Sinatra and JFK and Momo and her work as a courier and the harrowing consequences of that. Sure, there were things I didn't have—I've said that to you often enough—and maybe they were down there in that box. And maybe they weren't. Whatever the case, if you wait till you've got absolutely everything before you first set your fingers to the keyboard, brother, you ain't gonna write the book. The world might not be that much worse off for all the books that weren't written for this reason, but my newspaper background was still available for me, and I knew I had to barrel ahead with what I had. That's what a reporter does, how he makes his deadline and his living.

Oh, yeah—here's a page I copied out of that codebook. You can keep it.

I don't have any idea how many words of journalism I may have written during my career—probably not as many as there are in *War and Peace*, but still, I imagine it would run to quite a few. But I'd never tackled a book before and spent some time trying to block the whole thing out so I'd have some sense of how it would look and where I was going. That didn't get me anywhere, though, so one morning I just started writing about how Judy met JFK in the winter of '60, and it seemed to go pretty well—better, anyway, than the false starts and head scratchings that were all I had to show thus far. I was working at home by then, having finished my research, so to say, up at Keneally's. He called me once to ask how I was coming along, and when I made the mistake of giving him an honest answer, he told me to quit fumble-fucking around and get to work. I can't tell you that this was an inspiration for me, but it is true that it wasn't long after his call that I just started writing. Then late one afternoon after what had felt like a pretty decent workday I poured myself a Maker's Mark and called him to tell him I was actually writing. I didn't get him and pictured him slumped on a barstool in some local dive, pumping down the sauce. And maybe you know how it is in the writing game, but if not, I'll simply say that as good as you might have felt at your desk on Wednesday, Thursday can be a different ballgame altogether, and that was the way it was for me.

So instead of calling Keneally again I only hoped he wouldn't call me. He didn't. Several days went by, some better than others, and then there came a blustery late-winter morning and my phone rang early. It was Lucy.

We hadn't been seeing much of each other lately. Partly this was because I was trying to get up some momentum on the book, but only partly. Early on she'd taken a dim view of my project, and then the longer it went on, the dimmer it got. When we did see each other, I felt like I had to skirt around it—not easy to do when it was consuming my days and some of my nights, too. One evening I was up at her place and she was cooking dinner and not having a grand time doing it; she was tired from a day of her own work, and then something didn't go right in the kitchen—I don't remember just what—and suddenly she turned to me and said I was going to have to make up my mind whether I was in love with a dead woman or a live one. It just hit me wrong, we had words, and I stormed out of there in a rage and drove like a madman up to the Old Town Ale House on North, blindly bluffing my way through intersections and menacing pedestrians. The Ale House was a newsman's hang, dark enough to suit my mood, and I thought I could easily enough get lost in its inner recesses. I barged in and glared about, daring anybody to recognize me, but no one did, all the journalists having left and the night quiet with only a scattering of neighborhood couples. Hunched over my Maker's Mark, I didn't brood over what had just happened. Instead I continued to rage over the sheer shittiness of her remarks, as I saw them.

The mood hadn't been good from the start. In fact, the mood had been slumping southward for months. When our longtime friendship had turned romantic, we had said to each other that we had fallen in love, and it sure felt like it. But then things didn't progress much, as if we'd climbed to a height and were out of breath—which would be different, I think, from being breathless. To me it didn't feel like anything new or exciting was happening or likely to. It was like we were stuck somewhere instead of moving ahead toward a mutually happy future. It was peculiar, and I think both of us felt it. I know I had felt it again earlier in the evening, when I'd let myself in and found Lucy at the stove, looking tired after the day's work and almost waxen in the stovetop's fluorescent bar of light. Out the windows lay the city's heavy night, which made me feel at that moment like it might never lift, that I was already in my tomb.

The bottle and glasses were already out on the table, and I was a little surprised to see that Lucy had started without me and was halfway through a drink. I sat down and poured myself one and waited for something to happen. When it didn't, I said, "Aren't you gonna ask me how it went today?"

"I don't have to," she said, not turning away from the skillet. "You look like you've been jilted."

The word was odd, one you didn't often hear anymore, and very strictly confined to romance; I wonder whether it even has any other use. "Well," I said after a swallow, "the muse is fickle, I guess, and maybe I'm not courting her right."

"You're courting all right, but your target's pretty cold."

I shrugged at that, my shoulders asking what she meant.

"You're courting a dead woman," she said. "No wonder it's tough going."

At that moment I didn't quite know what the hell she meant, but then, quickly, I did and wished I didn't. "A writer's got to be in love with his subject," I said. "Doesn't make any difference if it's Marilyn Monroe or John Wayne Gacy," a notorious serial killer of boys. "If you want to write effectively about somebody, you've got to love her, for the moment at least." I raised my glass in a theatrical gesture. "The moment, babe, is everything." I was hoping that my crude comedy might rescue the situation, you see, but it didn't. Instead Lucy tossed a saucepan cover into the sink, where it rattled around a good while, and when it finally quit she turned to me with hands on hips and feet defiantly spread.

"Well, I think it's disgusting."

"You mean the writing," I said, not entirely sarcastically, because I myself had too often felt just that way about it. "Well, there's the chance, I guess, it could get better one of these days." I tried to smile, but it was no go; I couldn't get my mouth to turn up the right way, and Lucy didn't meet it anyway.

"No. It isn't the writing. It's the obsessing. You're thinking about that woman all day every day, and from what you tell me you think about her at night—you *dream* about her, for Christ's sake! If that isn't a good working definition of an obsession, there isn't one."

It was true—part of it, anyway. I had told her I'd been dreaming about Judy, but I hardly saw where that made it some unhealthy obsession. Hell, I dreamed once about Rice Lake, Wisconsin, when I was working on that ice-fishing piece. Did that mean I wanted to fuck a fish?

It wouldn't be quite accurate to say that at this point I knew the evening wasn't going to go anywhere. Rather, I felt sure it was headed somewhere I didn't want to go. I stood up, and as I did Lucy swiveled around in my direction, pointing an index finger at me. I noticed it was perfectly steady, not a tremble in it.

"I think it's disgusting," she repeated. "In love with a *dead* woman when I've been right here for you all along. It makes me wonder what you're really thinking about when we're in bed."

Well, that one took it, and it was on that accusation that I stormed out and drove suicidally up to the Ale House. The Maker's Mark that was keeping me company there tasted like battery acid inside me, but I suppose it was more the condition of my innards than the quality of the whisky itself, which had always served me well enough.

I sat there a good while, and after gulping the first drink, I slowed up a bit, so that by the third I was drinking at what I thought was a civilized pace. Still, the thing was this: I couldn't get beyond my rage at Lucy's remarks, which had about them a kind of thought-out quality instead of something said in the heat of the moment. I kept hearing her words, and I kept seeing that steady, accusing digit pointed at my chest. And that was still the way I was feeling when I left there and drove home with what was probably excessive caution.

The following evening I called Lucy to apologize for my part in the episode, but she didn't even meet me halfway. Instead, after I said my piece, she announced that she'd come to the conclusion that we were at a crossroads where I'd have to make up my mind about what was most important to me at this stage in my life. "I'm not telling you," she said, "that you have to give the project up. I would never tell you that." There was a pause where I thought she was choosing her next words. "But what I am saying is that I think you need to change your attitude toward it. You want way too much from it—it's only a book project, for Christ's sake. It's affecting our relationship, and I have a hard time believing it isn't affecting your ability to work on it, too. Why the hell else does it feel like a life-and-death struggle to you?"

There she had me, though I wouldn't give her the satisfaction of saying so. Instead I said something else—I don't remember just what—and then we hung up. We hadn't spoken in about ten days when she called.

"Have you had a look at the paper?" she asked, and I said I hadn't. I'd looked outside when I'd gotten my bathrobe on and had seen how hard it was blowing, with spits of snow rifling westward at a mean slant, and I'd decided to put coffee on and get dressed before retrieving the paper from the sidewalk where the deliveryman had tossed it. "Well, sit down a second," she said.

"What's up?"

"Your friend Keneally's dead. They gave him a big sendoff in the *Tribune*. Big picture and two columns."

I don't know what I said then, probably something eloquent like "Wow!" But I do remember the sensation of being just flooded with thoughts of one sort and another. After I thanked Lucy for the call, I threw on some clothes and shuffled out to get the news.

There it was, all right—his picture, his past, everything. It said he'd been living quietly. He might have been living in the obscure light of old disgrace, but he hadn't been living quietly. There wasn't anything quiet about Phil Keneally, as I'd found out those times we went to Dimo's for coffee. Even his death, I thought, couldn't have been quiet. The obit said he'd been found in his apartment, where he'd collapsed, and that he'd been there several days before he was discovered. He was still alive and had died on the way to the hospital. So I imagined the tremendous, window-rattling noise his collapse would have caused; the heavy sound of his breathing through those days when he'd lain there alone; the screech of the siren when the ambulance had pulled onto Washtenaw; the groans of the paramedics when they'd loaded him onto the gurney; and then at last the obit itself, with its recitation of his colorful, violent past. No, there hadn't been anything at all quiet about his life or his death.

The cause was a burst blood vessel in the brain, and of course I had to imagine it was in that portion of it lying right behind his deep dent. That would make him a war casualty, I thought, though long delayed. I doubted the War Department extended its counts out that far. Didn't make it any less true, however—only an unofficial statistic off in the margins of history, where so many things are.

Among the other thoughts that came flooding in as I sat there with the paper and my first cup of coffee were the selfish ones having to do with our project. I felt I'd gotten what there was to get out of the diaries Keneally had, so in that way his death wasn't the tragedy it might have been if it had happened earlier. I had my stacks of notes, and I'd looked through them several times when I was trying to block out the book, so I knew what I had and I felt confident about it, even if I wasn't feeling all that great about my ability to make the best possible use of it. Still, there was the fact that now he wouldn't be available for advice. By his own admission he wasn't a skilled writer, and he never would have been much help there, but he was a brilliant guy and a shrewd strategist with a flair for the dramatic, and I'd been counting on him to tell me how he thought this or that section might be shaped for maximum punch. Now I was on my own with the whole thing. The thought felt pretty chilling at first, but then as I kind of sat with it a bit, I discovered inside it a kind of pocket or space of freedom: I wouldn't have to answer to him anymore, with his scalding brand of scorn. I wouldn't have to put up with his temper, his famous impatience with minds less brilliant and darting than his own. I certainly wouldn't miss those verbal pistol whippings he used to give me, even though I'd begun to suspect there was a cruel kind of humor to some of them—that he really didn't mean everything he said, only wanted to see how you took it and whether you could take it.

And finally, yes, I now knew that I wouldn't have to go halves with him when we cashed in. Don't ask me when this particular thought came to me in the flood I'm trying to tell you about, because I don't remember. All I can honestly tell you is that it wasn't the first out of the gate, and it probably wasn't the last either.

I went to the funeral, of course. I did so out of respect and a certain odd, friendly feeling I'd developed for him over the months we'd spent in the same room. The way I seem to be put together, a guy has to be a real prick for me to fail to find something I like about him if I hang with him long enough, even if it's only the casual, snappy way he wears his tie a bit off-center. Of course, I knew very well that Keneally was a totally impossible person, which was why he'd died alone. But as I've tried to make clear, he was for me an intensely interesting one, and in his own ruined way even admirable.

But I had ulterior motives here, too. The reporter in me wanted to see how the story ended. I don't see how you can spend so much of your life trying to make stories out of life's random chaos without developing along the way a nose for endings, a sense that every story has to have one and that without it it isn't a story, only a kind of orphaned fragment that wants to be a story and would be one, too, if only you'd had the energy or the insight or the prunes to see it through. So I had to go. I didn't have to see him laid out and in fact kind of wished they'd have the box closed. (I do have to say, though, that when Roger "the Terrible" Tuohy got whacked, I went because

I wanted to see what he looked like, that old relic of the city's gangland days.) No, what I wanted to see were the ceremonial circumstances and who showed up.

The mortuary was on 111th, not far at all from where I was living, and I could tell a block away that there was going to be a good turnout despite the fact that it was bitingly cold and everything was the color of an ancient lead pipe that had been underground forever. Standing around in back and watching others file past the closed casket, I felt like what they say about drowning: you see your whole life passing before your eyes in a flash. I saw newspaper guys I hadn't seen in a while, among them Studs Terkel, and judges and lawyers I hadn't seen in years, including Brian Conley, who'd been Keneally's protégé but who still felt compelled to testify for the prosecution in the jury-tampering case. Judge Tuohy was long gone, but his two sons, both lawyers, were there, and I thought they might have come as their old man's emissaries. There were a good many politicians, too, round-bellied aldermen and ward heelers from the south and west precincts. I didn't see anybody I recognized, though, from City Hall. Off to the side in an enclave of their own were the boys, nine or ten of them, none of them with their wives. Unfortunately from a color standpoint, they weren't particularly garish: no white-on-white shirts and ties, no loud pinstripe suits. They didn't look that different from the pols and the legal fraternity, except some of them had pretty hard faces.

The obit had said nothing about relatives, and somehow I'd always assumed Keneally had no living sons or daughters, but now I found myself wondering if there didn't have to be at least a second or third cousin, to say nothing of surviving brothers and sisters—you know, Irish guy, big family . . . If there were any, they weren't in charge. Annette Giancana was, and when I saw her, I knew she had to be a major part of the story's ending.

She didn't seem to have a constituency of her own and moved in a kind of neutral zone between the legal guys and the hoods. She was smartly gotten-up in funereal black with a big white corsage, and I thought she looked pretty good. Looking at those big, sad eyes on her, I recognized her father. When the service began I wondered whether it was basically her doing, because the young minister laid some emphasis on the fact that although Keneally and Annette had certainly had their differences and difficulties, they'd remained close friends and had even been planning to get remarried in the spring. He represented Keneally just about as Keneally himself might have wished: Notre Dame football player; highly decorated war vet; lawyer specializing in "labor relations." If that was really Annette's choice of term, it had its sardonic merit, I thought, one Keneally would have appreciated.

Keneally had fallen away from the Church, and so somehow it had been arranged for Evergreen Cemetery to take him. On my way out there I decided I'd try to have a word with Annette, ask her if I could call her. If in fact she and Keneally were planning on remarrying—and I had my doubts about that—he must have told her how he'd been spending his days, helping me on our mutual project. What I was hoping to get from her was the diaries. Given what Keneally had said was her attitude toward them, I couldn't imagine what use she'd have for them, whereas I could use them to check against my notes. And then, too, there would be the wonderful irony of having them at my place after all those months when Keneally had bearishly, suspiciously hoarded them, refusing even to let me have them photocopied.

That had always had an almost superstitious air to it, from my point of view. I could understand his deep, pervasive suspicion of his fellow human beings. But when at the very outset I'd asked if I could have them copied, he'd said a flat, profane no. Then I'd said, "You could go with me, Phil, if that's what's got you worried. Or you could take them yourself." But again he'd refused. When I pointed out that if our ultimate goal was to make a bundle and that by going about it in this horse-and-buggy fashion we were prolonging the project unnecessarily, he said something that struck me as a bit off the wall, though even then I had a sort of secondary feeling that it wasn't *only* off the wall.

"An ichthyologist once told his top student to describe a particular species of fish," he said, looking at me with some sort of gleam in his eye I couldn't read. "So the kid rattled off the standard textbook answer. The prof wasn't satisfied, so the kid looked at the fish again, wondering how he could have made a mistake, but he knew damned well it was what he said it was. So he branched out with his next answer, giving the family connections and characteristics and the like—pretty fucking thorough. Still no go. 'You take that thing in the other room with you,' the prof tells the kid, 'and don't come out of there with any of this academic bullshit.' Well, the kid goes in there with the fish, and he sits and he sits, looking at the fish and wondering what the old bastard really wants. He stays in there *hours*, staring at that fucker. When he comes out, he *smells* like the fish—but he *knows* it.

"The old prof knew what he was doing—he was doing the little bastard a favor. I'm doing you one. You sit here with these things, right here. Then you'll find out what's in their fucking guts, the stuff you're supposed to get. In the long run this is a shortcut. Most people don't understand that, and that's okay. You can't expect that. So all you need to know, numb-nuts, is that it's here or it's nowhere. *Sit* with 'em."

Now, I don't know how that strikes you. I thought it was goofy, either some sort of dodge I couldn't figure, something that was supposed to hide what his actual motive might have been for not letting the things leave his crappy flat, or else the sauce was getting to him at last. Or there was some weird insight there that I wasn't smart enough to get. Anyway, I wanted those diaries. I'd sweated over them, sat with them like Keneally made me do, picked them apart so I thought I knew their insides. And I thought Annette probably would be happy to throw them at me, just as she had thrown them at Keneally. Gravesites are famous places for totally inappropriate, often dramatic things to happen, so my vulturelike last-minute swoop at her there wouldn't be utterly out of keeping. All she could do was to tell me to fuck off—which wasn't out of the question, from what Keneally had told me about her character.

As there always is, there'd been a considerable drop-off in attendance between the mortuary and the cemetery. The Tuohy boys had peeled off, and most of the aldermanic types. The hoods were gone, too: after all, Keneally had been Momo's man, and they'd whacked Momo, so . . . Besides, this wasn't sacred ground; it was just a dump. Brian Conley was there, though, at what was in truth the bitter end, the wind like a blade and the grass on the hillside looking like this might just be the year it wouldn't green up, ever. I wondered whether Conley was there for penance or atonement, or just to see the story through to its conclusion, like me. Or maybe it was that after all Phil Keneally still inspired in him some invincible kind of loyalty. But Annette was there, and now I saw a couple of women around her who clearly were her attendants. In their black coats they looked like crows.

They'd hacked at that grave with everything they had. That's the way it seemed to me, anyway. It looked terrifically raw: hacked, as I say, out of earth that was that ancient leaden gray and shaggy with little root fibers like hair. As I stared into it, my thought was that there was no climbing back out of that thing. He'd cheated Old Man Death once before, in the Pacific. But not again.

The young minister said a few more words, and then they levered Phil Keneally down into his place, and that was that. Everybody scattered before the knifing wind. I saw Annette and the crows making for the mortuary limo and hustled on a tangent to cut her off. She'd almost made it when I reached her.

"Miss Giancana," I said, getting right to it, since I could see she wasn't going to linger and would be gone in a minute. She turned to look at me with those huge, sad eyes that looked like they were in permanent mourning and probably had been since the moment she'd popped out of her mother. But even so, even here at this bleak, bereaved moment, she was her old man's daughter still, and there was fire in those eyes and her mouth shrank into a small, tight line like a scar. "Miss Giancana," I began again, "I was working on a book with Phil, working on some diaries he had in his apartment, and I was wondering if I could possibly call you about them. This isn't the right time, I know—"

She cut me off before I had to go on with this shabby, stumbling business. And *Jesus!* I can feel right now what a humiliating thing it was, too. But what the hell, I'd sweated over those things, and I felt that if they belonged to anyone, they belonged to me.

The scar opened. "Yeah, right," she said, looking at me like I was a lump of garbage wrapped in fabric. "You were gonna rob her grave and then pimp her, whore that she was. Well, you're too late, buster—unless you can get 'em back from the Sanitation Department. That's who has 'em, and that's just where they belong. I threw them out days ago." Then she was in the limo, and one of the mortuary guys closed the big gray door behind her, and they swirled away in a gray cloud of exhaust that blew back in my face.

Well, like I said, I didn't really need them, or if I did, it wasn't a practical need, and so I went back to work with what I had, with all that I would ever have. After describing how Judy and Jack met, I wanted to whistle back and sketch in her background, but when I tried to do that, I saw once again how hopeless those fragmentary notes were that I'd scribbled down in Ed's rec room, how full of holes, how basically useless. I didn't know nearly enough about her earlier years to make it convincing, so I skipped them and took her from the moment Sinatra spotted her across the room at Puccini's and fell all over himself trying to get next to her. The only good piece of earlier material I had I didn't use: that business where Judy and her first husband, Billy, have a couple of goes while watching a UCLA football game on TV. I felt that was significant somehow, but damn if I could figure out how to wedge it in. So I didn't.

That spring I caught a break. That is, it seemed like a break at the time, though since then I've had second and third thoughts about it. I got a call from the son of an old colleague from *Daily News* days, asking me if I'd like to do a local-color piece on the Beverly neighborhood for WLS. The kid was producing a once-a-week spot called

Chicagoland: seven-minute segments on various locales—Greek Town, Grant Park, that sort of thing. Well, I did it, and it went over so well they asked me to do another, and before I knew it I was a regular. The money was good, and I needed it then, plus it got me back in circulation, so to say. I'd become something of a hermit with the project, and I didn't realize how much until this gig yanked me out of that. I think one of the reasons I went over well was that I had a lot of unused social energy stored up inside me, and once I was out there interviewing people like in the old days, it just came pouring out. The thing with Lucy had died a quiet, natural death, and now that I was out and about again, I came in contact with some ladies, which was a nice change, though for some reason or other nothing of a serious nature developed.

The new work kind of took me away from the book, though, and probably more than it really needed to. That's to say I could have been working on it more than I found myself doing. Put another way, I was making the TV business almost a full-time job when it didn't have to be that. I remember scolding myself occasionally for this, but the scoldings weren't that harsh and were infrequent at that, and as the summer rolled onward I could see the end of the *Chicagoland* gig looming up and right behind it the book that by then I'd pretty much lost a feel for. When that time came it was a steamy, sultry August, and I rolled up my sleeves, went back over what I'd written, then went back through my notes, making their acquaintance once again. And then I went to work. I mean, I really *hit* it every day, from eight in the morning till four or so in the afternoon. This went on through August and September and into October.

Given what I've just said, you'd think the pages would have been piling up in drifts, right? Well, they did mount up, all right, but not in drifts, and they mounted so slowly. Tough going all the way, never a day where it just flowed—a word you often hear, usually from nonwriters. There were some days when I'd knock off, pour myself a Maker's Mark, and look at what I'd accomplished with a kind of stupid astonishment because it looked so puny. There'd be mornings when I'd look at the previous day's production and wonder whether there was anything salvageable in it. True, I was a rookie at this game, but still, I was a veteran writer, which ought to have counted for something, I thought. But the deeper I got into the book, the more mysterious the whole thing became to me, when it ought to have been becoming clearer and clearer what I was supposed to be doing and where the road was leading me. Instead I found myself thinking that I wasn't *writing* this thing, I was *fighting* it, as though it were a thing, a something that was against me for some obscure reason.

One afternoon when nothing was popping for me I called Studs Terkel. I really didn't know him that well, but he had a reputation for being a generous guy to fellow writers, especially newspaper guys, and so I asked him if I could take him to lunch and talk about problems I seemed to be having with a book project. He didn't ask me what it was, and I was grateful for that, because it kind of lifted the thing out of the particular, if you follow me, and into the general, which was where I hoped my problem, my mystery, lay. He had an errand to run in the Loop the next week, he told me, and could meet with me then. He mentioned Phil Keneally's funeral and said what a shame he thought his life had become. "You have no idea," he said, "what that guy looked like back before the war, shredding the line at Notre Dame. I covered the local college scene, so I saw him. He could have played for Halas, easy. Could have been a star. See you next Thursday."

The place he had in mind was on East Chicago, just in from the Water Tower. I didn't want to whine to him, but what would be the point of taking up his time if I concealed what was bothering me? So I made it as crisp as I could.

"Most newspaper guys don't really know how to write a book," he said. "Most of the things we have to learn in order to become good journalists are the same things that make it hard for us to write good books. I know that was my story, for sure. Damned hard work, retooling yourself in midcareer. And that's what you're fighting with—you're fighting with yourself and all that training. Know what I did when I was slugging it out on *Division Street*? I was having one hell of a time *orchestrating* the whole thing, so one day I was at the end of my rope with the thing. I had it, but then again I didn't, you know? So I booked a flight to Paris and stayed a week. Didn't take a thing with me, not a pen or a notebook. I just walked around the city with my hands in my pockets and looked at people, especially people who seemed to know their jobs, like window washers and waiters. It was like I was irrigating my brain. When I came back, I felt a hell of a lot better. Of course, after a while that wore off, but I was able to finish the book."

Did I have someplace that tempted me as an out-of-the-way or even exotic retreat? I couldn't come up with one but thanked him for his time and advice. But then, about a week later and still fighting the mysterious resistance, I did. It wasn't exotic, and it wasn't really a retreat either, but when I thought about it, I seized upon it almost instantly, as if it were an oar drifting past me in an ocean of doubt.

I'd been looking through my notes on that last, desperate trip Judy had made to D.C., trying to imagine being in that state of mind and wondering how I could write about that without making her seem like a total nut job, as we say now. And here I came across those three names Teddy Kennedy had given her: Mary Meyer, Erazmo Carreon, and Charlie Bennett. Mary Meyer's name made some sense in a way: she'd been keeping company with JFK during the last months of his life (hers, too, as it turned out). Why that would have been of consuming interest to Judy I didn't know, unless, as I've said, she was so lost that *any* connection with the life she'd led could look like a clue of sorts, even if it really wasn't. In a looser way, this also fit the other two names: they, too, were people who'd hung around JFK as part of a new circle of friends and associates. Sitting there at my kitchen table, where most of the writing got done—such as it was—I thought about Washington as a place where I might go and irrigate my brain, which at that moment felt a hell of a lot more like a desert than like a garden where thoughts and sentences could grow. Also, the geography of the city might come in handy when I got to that place in Judy's story. Maybe, I thought, I could walk around the city like Studs had done in Paris but with a little more specific purpose in mind: those names and the layout of the place itself.

I've taken trips on much flimsier pretexts than this, and in a funny way Studs Terkel had given me permission, so to say, to act on impulse. Once, years ago, for instance, when I'd been beside myself with grief and bewilderment over a girl I was hopelessly pursuing, I unfolded a map of the Midwest, laid it on the floor, and threw a steak knife at it. It stuck at Dyersville, Iowa, and that's where I ended up. Don't ask me what I did there, because I don't remember.

If I could have, I'd have put up at the Mayflower, for the flavor of it. But it was too steep for me, and I mentally put it off to the side with those other things I'd do when this book had lined my pockets. I was still having those kinds of thoughts, but at the time I distinctly recall feeling that I wasn't having them as often or as vividly as I had in the days when the book was pretty much synonymous in my mind with the pot of gold at the end of the rainbow. I still wanted to cash in here, you understand. But somehow after all the work, all the energy I'd poured into this thing, the pot of gold didn't quite feel like an adequate motivation anymore. I can't honestly tell you that some nobler motivation had slowly taken money's place, only that I just wasn't daydreaming anymore about cruising northern California in my Jag.

Anyway, as far as the Mayflower was concerned, I could have some of the experience without that much outlay. I walked around the lobby and up and down the long central corridor, poking my nose in the various dining rooms and conference centers. I had a leisurely drink at the bar. Very classy place, for sure, and with a polish to it that felt deeper, more self-assured than anything we had in

Chicago. And yet given the way Judy looked when she was staying here at the beginning of the sixties, she would have been doing the Mayflower a favor when she walked through those doors. I didn't want to think about what she might have looked like that day she'd thrown her clothes into her bag and raced to get out of town before whoever had murdered Mary Meyer murdered her, too.

The last thing I did before leaving the Mayflower was to call Tommy Madigan, an old newspaper buddy from my *Daily News* days. Tommy lived in nearby Virginia, and before coming out here I'd called to ask him if he could run down anything on Teddy Kennedy's three names. He knew the Meyer name right off and said it was a famous case in its day. The Carreon one was vaguely familiar and he'd check it out for me, along with Charlie Bennett. Now he said he had some stuff for me and could deliver it when we had drinks and dinner later in the week. "I didn't realize you were writing a spy novel," he said, chuckling in a way I recognized from our Chicago days. "These names have CIA written all over them. What I want is a finder's fee when you sell this to the movies. Anything in the high fives will be acceptable." Then we made a date for dinner, and I went out to do the legwork on sites associated with my story.

I began with a tour of the White House, moving in the company of my fellow citizen-tourists, some of them in shorts, T-shirts, and flip-flops. Our guide was a cute young thing in a black dress who kept us on the move, walking backward while she kept up a flowing monologue that she interrupted from time to time to say, "We're walking, people, we're walking now . . ." Must have been a fairly demanding job, I thought, keeping that information coming while at the same time keeping her motley crew in line when it was obvious they all wanted to linger, to touch things, to open doors they shouldn't.

I was right with them there. I wanted to linger, too, and not only because it was hot as blazes outside, even if it was November, whereas it felt wonderfully cool in there. I wanted to pause to absorb these sights, because here, I knew, was the heart of my story.

Even if most of its main events had happened off-limits, still, Judy had walked these halls, seen what I was now seeing, even touched some of the furniture we were pretty smartly moving past. While I was walking, walking, I tried to scribble notes to myself in my own kind of code, and all too soon I found myself turned out with the others into the powerhouse sun. I sought the nearest bar, where I could flesh the notes out before they became something as impenetrable as Linear B.

Sitting in that air-conditioned gloom and working over my scribbles, I found myself drifting off into something that couldn't, I guess, be dignified as a meditation on the White House but was rather only a puzzlement, wondering if there were other countries where the president's house was also a national shrine. What was it that kept us coming, year after year, by the busload, to see this place, even after we had found out—like Judy herself—more than we ever wished to know about what it took to get there and what went on once you did? I told myself that I at least had known what I was seeking in those halls, but then after a drink or so I had to admit that the term *research* didn't cover it.

I was still at this the next day when I visited the Lincoln Memorial and the Vietnam Memorial; at both the crowds were substantial, as if there were an endless supply of Americans to come there and try to work out for themselves the relationship between our ideals and our realities. That, apparently, was what Judy had been trying to do at the end of her life, when she was dying of cancer and knew it. And I had to wonder, walking slowly along the polished wall of the Vietnam Memorial, whether there had ever been an American life that had so nakedly, scaldingly exposed someone to the contrast between ideals and realities as hers had. And yet, so close to the end, she'd told Kitty Kelley that after all—after everything he'd let her in for—she still loved Jack. I don't think Kitty Kelley is the most trusted name in journalistic history, but I trust her on this one. I trust her because what she has Judy saying echoes in that single, lonely voice what is so clearly true of the country as a whole: we still love America. Why else would we continue to make these pilgrimages to these shrines, tarnished though they are by the weather of our history?

When I met up with Tommy Madigan at the Cosmos Club, I was in for a surprise. When I knew Tommy back in Chicago, he'd been pretty much like the rest of our ink-stained tribe, except for this: he was incredibly handsome, with a head of blue-black hair he wore center-parted and combed back. So it wasn't too long before he met Alice, a girl from the North Shore whose family had bags of money, married her, and moved to the Washington area. When we heard about the move we smirked and said, Tommy, you aren't moving to Virginia; you're being moved there. And he laughed along, and why not? It was, he told us, a "morganatic" union. We had to look that one up. Then from time to time I'd hear from him, and once in a while he'd send me a piece he'd written, usually high-end travel stuff for *Forbes* or *Gourmet* or *House and Garden*. And they were good, too. Tommy always could write. I used to wonder whether the ease and confidence of his work was based on his looks, which can give you a daily sense of well-being that most of us don't have.

The surprise here was that he'd gotten enormously fat. He must have gone a good 270 anyway, but I have to say he carried it as well as he could: double-breasted loose blue blazer he kept buttoned; wide gray flannel slacks with broad cuffs; starchless shirt that would give to accommodate his neck and chins. He still had that hair, though now it was white, which matched the beard he'd grown. If it hadn't been for the clothes, he could have gone for a Rent-a-Claus at Christmas. But then maybe you have to discount a bit of this description: it was a shock seeing him this way after so many years. He probably had his own sort of shock, seeing me.

What Tommy wanted to impress upon me was the intricate social webbing that made Washington such a tiny place. The Mary Meyer case illustrated this in spades. "If you haven't lived around these folks," Tommy said, "you can't believe it. It's like Skull and

Bones wrapped inside the Masonic Order—hermetical, mysterioso. Pull one string and the whole town feels it.

"Mary Meyer's ex was Company. Her sister, Tony, was married at that time to Ben Bradlee. So when Mary was murdered, Ben and Tony had to ID the body. Then they went to Mary's house, which was only a few steps from theirs. Among other reasons they went there was that Tony knew Mary had been keeping a diary, and she wanted to get her hands on it before anybody else did, because she knew that Mary and Jack Kennedy had a thing going, and she was afraid the diary might fall into the wrong hands.

"So they go there, and Tony gets out her key to the back door, but when she pushes the key in, the door gives—it's open. So they stand there, not knowing what to do. At that point, with Mary hardly cold, you know, and that loser in the clink, you don't know what the deal really is. Maybe they have the right guy, and maybe they don't. Maybe he was just in the wrong place at the wrong time and the right guy is somewhere on the loose. So Ben calls out, you know, like you would. And there's an answer—somebody upstairs—and then they hear him coming down, and here he is: suit, tie, black hair, smooth as silk. Guess who? Your Erazmo.

"Tony wants to know what in hell he's doing in her sister's house. But Erazmo doesn't even look at her. He's looking at Ben, and then he gives him his card, with three numbers on it, and tells Ben to call any of these numbers. Then he's gone. So they go in, and Bradlee right away gets on the horn to the cops and gives them a description of Erazmo, and while they're waiting for the cops to show up they hunt for that diary." Tommy leaned back then and raised his hands. "They didn't find it—at least, that's the story they stick with. Maybe it's even true." He took a sip of his gin and tonic and then dropped the other shoe.

When Ben Bradlee followed up with the cops the day after, asking what they'd found out about Erazmo Carreon and whether they'd been able to question him, he was told that all the phone numbers on his card were Langley numbers. If Bradlee himself wanted to pursue the matter, there was yet another number he should try. The guy at that number, the cops said, had all the pertinent information about Carreon. Whether Bradlee ever did that and what he found out, Tommy didn't know. What he did learn, though, was that the Meyer case and Carreon's involvement in it weren't exactly a popular topic on the cocktail party circuit.

"He was CIA, that I'm virtually certain about," Tommy said. "I never could figure the nature of the connection, but here's what I was able to pull off the Web." He reached inside that tent of a blazer and brought out a few pages of printout, which he handed to me. He signed that I should go ahead and read them, and I did. Most of the information appeared to have been lifted from an *L.A. Times* story about Carreon, who had become an embarrassment to the government because of his involvement with the CIA, the Bay of Pigs, and the crash of a Cubana Airlines flight back in 1976. So he was perhaps both an employee of ours and a terrorist still wanted by the Castro government. Nobody seemed to know what to do with him, and he was being held in Miami while they tried to figure something out. He was said to be in very poor health.

"Some stuff, eh?" Tommy said when I'd finished. "This town's just full of this kind of thing, but you can only go so far with your questions. After that, you're out of order, and they'll let you know about it.

"Oh, people will talk some about the Meyer case, and I guess they talked a lot about it at the time. They talked about the fact that before her death Meyer told friends she knew she was being watched, and once when she'd been out somewhere she was certain someone had been in her home. And they talked about how many suits there were down on the towpath and how hot the police were to wrap things up. There's a certain amount of paranoia that goes with this town—it's like a low-grade fever you learn to tolerate. And so when they didn't get a conviction, well, that fed the talk. They never did solve the case."

He pulled back from the table and heaved himself up, making

the necessary rearrangements of his clothes. Plainly we were going in to dinner. When we were seated again in the dining room, which had the distinct air of a clubhouse, and he'd spread his napkin in his lap, he ran his hand lightly over his hair and cocked his head at me. "Now tell me again just what your interest in all this is. I didn't get it over the phone."

I tried to figure out a way to answer that without boring him. Clearly Washington gossip was his bag now, not my book project. So I mentioned Judy's name, and that was as far as I got.

"Oh," he said, his face cracking into a smile. "Jack Kennedy's lay."

"Yeah," I said, wishing I could have found a way to avoid her name, "that one."

"Sounds like you might have a hit on your hands," he said.

The next day was another scorcher, but I went out into it, following Judy's traces. I went to see the house on N Street where she'd had dinner with Jack and his shadowy, unnamed friend right after the Wisconsin primary and where she'd signed on to back Jack, little realizing what that was going to mean. Standing in a bit of shade across from its narrow red-brick front and dark shutters, I wondered what I was supposed to make—if anything—of what Tommy had told me at the Cosmos Club. He'd been right about one thing, certainly: the stuff was fascinating, complex, and endless. Judy had grasped at Mary Meyer as if the name had been a pinhole of light in the dark subterranean maze she'd stumbled into. But it hadn't come to anything for her—no true enlightenment and no escape either. And Erazmo—there was another tantalizing figure, an anti-Castro warrior of long standing, and if the info Tommy had given me was accurate, maybe he was a terrorist as well. But what could any of that have had to do with Judy? In any case, both of them were out of my reach. No, I told myself again, these aren't your stories; they aren't even parts of your story. Your story is right there, across the street and up the stairs to that spare bedroom where Jack, a candidate for president of the United States, had asked her to do him a favor and without asking what it was she'd eagerly said, Sure. And the next day when she went off on her first errand, carrying the cash that was to subvert the pure practice of democracy, in West Virginia and beyond, Kennedy had her tailed. Soon enough there were two tails on her, Kennedy's and J. Edgar's, and all the while this glowingly gorgeous girl goes about her duties, imagining she's doing the right thing for America. Her reward? Psychological torture by the FBI; abandonment by the Kennedys; ostracism by the Mob; pilloried by the press; social isolation; and at last a lonely death, at which point a conservative hatchet man like Safire is allowed to use her tragedy to attack the heartless liberals who'd set her up for all this. *That* was her story—and mine as well. That was what I was meant to tell, not this detour into cloak-and-dagger stuff, I thought. So instead of walking up to check out where Mary Meyer had lived and then following in her footsteps down to the towpath at the bottom of Thirty-fourth, I caught a cab to Arlington and the cemetery, leaving Meyer and Carreon and the late Charlie Bennett, whoever he was, behind me for others to ponder for their own purposes.

The signs to the grave were plentiful, of course, having grown in number with the passage of time and the passage of JFK from historical figure to mythological one. You couldn't miss the grave, I was thinking, even if you wanted to. But immediately I got distracted by the sight of a squadron of schoolkids, trooping along with their teachers and smiling and laughing in the sun while they passed ranks of tombstones that were settling deeper by the year and in this season were shrouded by the fallen leaves. The kids divided around me and went on, leaving me to wonder whether I'd ever had their illusion of immortality, the belief that in my case a special exception would somehow be made. I know for sure that by the time I was at the Navy Yard in Oakland, waiting to ship out for the Pacific theater, I had no such illusion. I felt naked as hell. I guess we all did.

So in fact I did miss my turn up to the grave. But still I had another chance at it, on Grant Drive, and I took it, climbing slowly, bent with a sudden, strange fatigue that made me feel like I was wearing lead clodhoppers. Well short of the site I actually had to stop and almost collapse on a bench, where I sat looking up at the people at the site, some of them in motion, coming down the steps and walking on to visit Bobby Kennedy's grave, others standing there seemingly lost in thought. Meanwhile more pilgrims were moving past me with their faces set on their goal, like it was some sort of spiritual magnet that was irresistibly pulling them toward it. Eventually I mustered the energy to join them.

The site itself, of course, was much more formal and finished than it had been when she'd visited it. There were those steps up to it I just mentioned, and graceful curving walls embracing it and inscribed with the best lines from JFK's speeches. I had my notebook with me and copied these lines down—you know them:

> With a good conscience our only sure reward, with history as the final judge of our deeds, let us go forth to lead the land that we love, asking His blessing and His help, but knowing that here on earth God's work must truly be our own.

Damned fine, damned fine.

One thing that was the same as back in '64 was the presence of the crowd. There must have been sixty, maybe even seventy there on this muggy late afternoon, so you had to wait your turn, and when mine came I felt again that strange resistance I'd identified as simple fatigue when climbing up here. But now I knew it wasn't that: I just didn't want to move up into the front line and look down at the eternal flame, which was almost invisible in the glare from the swiftly settling sun. I didn't want to see that slick dark slab with the name and the dates. And I especially didn't want to be reminded of her wild, rambling ruminations about what Jack looked like down there in the dark. I wished I hadn't read that passage. I wished she hadn't written it and put it where I would finally have to come across it.

When I'd really gotten into the diaries Keneally had and I'd come to a passage I knew I could use, I felt a sort of strong, controlled satisfaction. It's hard to explain. You aren't exactly *happy*, but there's a somber sort of pleasure there, the way you learn to feel about all your usable material when you're a reporter, whether you're looking at an auto accident, a train wreck, a crooked politician in the dock, or the happy ending to an unpromising sequence of events. By the time, though, that I'd gotten to the diary that had her where I was now standing, that sort of reaction was lost to me. Along the steadily downward and darkening trajectory of her life it had been stolen from me, and the very entries I would once have been hunting for had become the ones I winced to read, because I didn't want the thing to turn out the way I knew it was going to. I was like all those assassination buffs Phil Keneally had savaged, the ones who kept rerunning the Zapruder film back and back again, trying to make it come out differently. Well, you can't, not certain things anyway—neither that exploding head nor her lonely, wasted death. History should always be open to reinterpretation and rewriting, as I've been saying all along. Not all of it, though. You can't bring its figures back from the dead, even though those tabloid rags you thumb through in the checkout line, wishing your turn won't come too quickly, have had a dandy time through the years telling us that JFK isn't really dead at all but is living as a vegetable at some mountaintop retreat in the Swiss Alps. And before that there were the czar's kids, Anastasia and the one who was a hemophiliac—they were supposed to have escaped death at the hands of the Bolshevik firing squad. That imaginary caper was sustained for decades, and for all I know it may still be going on, even though all their bones have been found by now and the DNA has been checked. Before that there was Jesse James, and they actually dug him up on a Missouri farm to find out if he was really down there. Isn't there an ancient German king who still lives under a mountain with his men, waiting for history to summon him again?

It's a good game, and there's a damned good reason why we play it, too, time after time: a deeply human wish to find a way out of the rules of the Big Game, which is human existence, which has its beginning and has its end, the part we want so much to change.

I don't know that when she was standing here, Judy wanted somehow to bring Jack back. I don't find that anywhere in that particular entry, unless you want to go into some minute analysis of her remark about Jack's body, which I don't. But it was while I was standing there that something came to me with a sudden blinding force, like when you don't make the correct calculation in ducking through a low door and so you hit your head on its lintel: there's that sudden *smack*, and then the inside of your head lights up and everything stands perfectly still and you're amazed and hurt and angry all at once. There I was, thinking about JFK, about the thousands, maybe millions of people who've been trying to bring him back, one way or another. And that's when it came to me with that *smack* that this was what I'd been trying to do for Judy—bring her back. It was what had brought me there, staring at the eternal flame, which wasn't that at all, and looking at that dark slab with its chiseled dates.

Not at the beginning, no, and I've admitted that. At the beginning, what I wanted was her story. Whether she was dead or still alive or alive and suffering somewhere wasn't important—or if it was, it was way back there, in a place that in racing you'd call "distanced." What was important to me was what I knew about her life and what more I might learn so that I could get my lifetime scoop. So I was willing to traffic in drugs to learn more. That's putting it pretty bleakly, but it's true enough. I was willing to help Ed get stoned so he'd be off there in Dopeland where he wouldn't see what I was up to, rummaging through that box with my sweaty hands, scribbling in my notebook, then driving back south with my head just *seething* with fantasies of how this would totally change my life, lifting me out of the relentless mediocrity of my hack existence. On those nights when I'd arrive at my turnoff I'd be truly surprised I was already there, because I'd been driving like a man possessed—and I was. Then, at the end of that phase of the thing, I was willing to swear to almost *anything* when Ed confronted me in his kitchen, and I could practically smell his hostility, like you can smell burned gunpowder and feel yourself in a dangerous place. I was in fact in a dangerous place, but I kept telling myself, This is what a reporter does, how he makes his bread. When Ed told me reporters were nothing but goddamned vultures, I thought he just didn't understand journalism's requirements, even if what he said had truth to it.

Miraculously, then, I met Phil Keneally at the Bullpen, and he handed me back my scoop. And I went after it, too—never missed a day's appointment up there on Washtenaw, sitting at his blackened dining room table, which looked like it might have been through the Chicago Fire and hadn't been retouched since, prying into the guts of those books like the student in his fish story. And during those long drives back to the South Side, when it felt like that beautiful girl was right next to me, maybe with her dark-haired head turned slightly away as she silently watched the gray, scabby landscape slip past us, something was happening inside me, and I didn't even know it. Lucy had felt something of it—women are uncanny that way—and finally called me on it, though I still think what she said wasn't right and had a bunch of sour grapes in it.

I don't know that what I'm trying to get across to you deserves the term *evolution*, which is a pretty big concept. I'm not sure, either, that coming down the ladder several rungs and using *progression* instead is much of an improvement. All I can say is that the guy standing there at the grave wasn't the same guy who found a telling reference in a girly-girly diary long ago and suddenly thought he understood what he had on his hands.

But when I say I wanted to bring her back, let's not get off into woo-woo land. I'm not that wacky, despite what Phil Keneally might think if somehow he could zone in on what I'm talking about from wherever he is. What I mean here is that I had come to want to rescue her from the historical fate that was created for her by the gossipmongers and news hawks and keepers of the Kennedy flame—by all those who saw her as a tart, a scarlet woman, a whore. Because I had learned the truth about her through reading her secret history, what really happened and what she thought about it. And I knew what no one else left on earth did, including Ed: the vast difference between the public image of Judy Campbell Exner and the vulnerable, ultimately idealistic girl who lived beneath that dazzling surface. Armed with this knowledge, I could reach down there and bring her back, telling the story the way it was meant to be told.

Or so I'd been thinking. Maybe I'd been thinking it before Keneally's death but hadn't raised it up to the level of a conscious ambition before then. But I do know that not long after that it did become conscious, even if at first it wasn't very distinctly shaped. It was April and a nice, balmy day with none of that sharpness to it that you get so often in spring here. I had the window open in the kitchen, and there was a soft breeze blowing in across the sink and onto my table, and I had to put the sugar bowl and a half-filled coffee mug on my papers to hold them down. I'd been struggling as usual, but when a particularly sweet bit of breeze hit me like the breath of life itself, I stopped and leaned back in my chair and thought about Phil Keneally and what he was missing and how frigid and dark it would have to be down where he was. Of course I'd thought about him since the funeral; every day I sat down at the table I had to think about him. But this was the first time I'd imagined him, dead out there under that poisonous yellow grass. And who can say where such things spring from? But when I thought about that, his aloneness, his cold, confined spot of earth—all that was left to him—and how no one who passed that spot would have the least idea who he'd been, not the groundskeepers seated on their mowers nor mourners on other missions, I wanted to do something for him. And so I drove out there, stopping at one of the florist shops you always find in such neighborhoods, buying a bouquet, and driving into Evergreen. It's a large spread, with lots of manmade hills and roads winding through them, and though I thought I knew the spot, I didn't and had to go back to the office and tell someone whom I was looking for and get a map with an X on it. I found the X, propped the flowers against the headstone I thought Annette must have arranged for, and stood a moment, thinking that however profanely Keneally himself would have disapproved, I'd done something. I'd *intervened,* so to say, in the Big Game, putting a bit of color and life where before there'd only been a nearly anonymous stone of death. That was when the thought came to me that in another way I could do the same for Judy—intervene—and that was the thought that kept me company thereafter. When I put the book pretty much to one side to work on the *Chicagoland* series, I always felt I could come back to it with energy and enthusiasm because I'd rethought it in this way. And I thought the writing would go better, too, more smoothly—if not flowingly—with that goal in mind.

Here's a measure of how deep this altered ambition had gotten with me. One night after I'd been knocking around Pullman all day, looking for color and characters for the TV show, I got into bed, tired but feeling I'd been productive, and instead of reading a bit to put myself to sleep, I turned off the light and lay there with only the lights from the building across the alley finding their way around the edges of my shades. I know now that it was staring at a sliver of light that put me into a kind of trance, but at that time, of course, I didn't know that I was drifting toward that borderland between waking life and full sleep, where you have a foot in both worlds—and in neither. That's where the images get scrambled and crazy, and I know you've tried to describe to someone your own experience with this state and failed because it doesn't come out the way you wanted, the way you saw it. But here, with me, the odd thing wasn't the craziness of the experience; it was the normality of it. The images that made up the scene were all precise and exact, except for two things: I never could see my face, only my back; that and the fact that the scene disappeared totally before I could see what finally happened.

I read a magazine piece a while back about someone who claimed to have developed a technique for going back to old dreams that were incomplete and dreaming them again so he could find out what happened. It didn't always work, he said, but it did often enough so he felt this actually was a technique that could take you back into that closed-off world.

Anyway, the scene I'm trying to tell you about was dimly lit, not quite like sunset but more of an even umber light, without shadows of any sort, and I was walking along a path through a meadow. The grasses were shin-high, and the path through them led steadily downward. I could see where it led, where I had to go. It was dark there, at the edges of a thicket, and darker still at its center, but I knew that's where she was, waiting for me. As I got closer, I could see a glimmer of something white, as if she were wearing a gown and what I was looking at was a part of her sleeve. That's when the screen went totally black. But when I try to reconstruct the experience, I can't seem to recall whether at the time this felt intensely frustrating. It has since.

Well, these were the odd, obscure beginnings of the idea that my job wasn't to hit the jackpot with Judy. Instead it was to rescue her, to bring her out of darkness and dishonor, back up through the meadow to the light, the real woman revealed at last to the world that had so unanimously misunderstood her. And when I had the book on the sidelines while I was doing that work for WLS, I went along happily enough, because while I was glad to get that work, as I say, I knew how superficial it really was, whereas this was the real deal, the thing I'd been meant to do all along, the thing that would eventually . . . what, *validate* me as a writer, as a person even? It was this that would make sense of all those false alarms a reporter has to answer, the utterly meaningless, forgotten, forgettable stories I'd filed down through the years: a case of arson never proved; a municipal swimming pool where the water drained slowly out through the cracks of a corrupt construction contract; the senseless sacrifice of a child caught in a drug war crossfire; a ballplayer's wife who went missing and whose body was found years later, entombed in her car at the bottom of a reservoir. And some of these worthless, fleeting notes on life in all its random chaos, as I called it, weren't even printed. They were chased down and written and filed under the gun of a deadline, and then forgotten. This was different. This was the big leagues.

Except it wasn't. What the head smack at the gravesite had suddenly, blindingly revealed to me was that there was *nothing* I could ever write that would make that rescue good. The way down into the underworld is easy enough—she learned that. It's the way back up that's so perilously hard, and almost none of the would-be rescuers make it with the would-be rescued in hand. Almost none. It was as if I'd made a grab at that bit of white something in the thicket but missed; I hadn't been able to hang on and bring her out of that darkness, up through the meadow, with the color changing from unvarying umber to amber and then to gold, with the light of our world shining on her hair: Here she is . . .

Ed had been right all along, and I just hadn't seen it. You couldn't undo that kind of thing, change an iota of the image caught once and forever in a wink of the lens and stamped deeply into the public mind. I saw that at JFK's gravesite in the red glare of an unseasonable sun. Ed's anger at the bottom of it had been the human urge that wants a way out of the rules of the Big Game and can't find one; that wants to rewind the film and find, miraculously, that there at the very beginning there's a sudden white space, a blank, and then a notice announcing an alternative take. There wasn't going to be one for her, and not for me either. Her destiny was to go down in history wearing her varsity letter and to stay down in history that way. And mine? Well, I'm no hero, that's for sure. But that doesn't make me a bum, only another guy who grabbed at something big and just missed. And it wasn't my background, my training, that had gotten in the way, as Studs Terkel had said, bless his big heart. It was, quite simply, that there are some things that can't be changed.

After I got back home from Washington and dropped my bag in the bedroom, I went into the kitchen and got the manuscript and notes out of the freezer, where I'd stashed them in case of fire. I opened their plastic containers, which were stiff and frosty, of course, and the creaking sound was like prying open a goddamned coffin. It felt that way, too, I can tell you, staring down into that pile of dead hopes. It was only midafternoon, well short of the legitimate cocktail hour, but I poured myself a drink anyway and sat down at the table with the coffins, which had already begun to sweat a little. I don't remember thinking anything particular then. I didn't really continue with the death theme, and I certainly wasn't thinking about what to do with the book, because I'd already seen there wasn't going to be one, not from me, and not from anybody else either. Without the diaries, how could there be? So I was just sitting there, looking at things: the containers with their enlarging beads of moisture; the lamp on the table with its shade that was coming apart around its bottom rim; the sink with its nickel cocks. Everything seemed . . . just itself, a thought I'm sure you'll find strange, though it didn't to me then. My drink hadn't taken effect yet, so I know it wasn't that.

I can't tell you how long I sat there in that neutral sort of state. A while, because I became aware of the light dying in the room. The year was dying, too, in the increments of its briefer afternoons. I reached into one of the containers and pulled out a thin sheaf of papers of what never would be a book and asked myself what difference it might have made if I'd finished it and had it published. What if I'd told of her marvelous singing voice, which went mysteriously silent? Of her artistic ambitions, which she tried to keep alive on portable easels and dozens of sketchbooks in rented rooms all over the country? What if I'd shown that she'd undertaken her courier work for the most patriotic of purposes, however dark and sinister the contents of those packets proved to be? What if, in short, I'd brought out the real Judy, the one she wanted—and didn't want—others to see? Then what?

And so I'll ask you that, since you've heard me out: what difference has it made to you? Or is she still what she was when I first spoke her name and you thought, Ah, yes, Jack Kennedy's lay?